The Gospel According

To Tomàs

Oliver Peers

To Mum and Eddie

Chapter One

My name is Tomàs. Tom, inevitably. Once, *briefly*, Tomek, *my Tomek*... Years and years. Now, in this more distant room, half a life away, I sit so taut – my skin shivers. Muscles freshly gym-trained, upper body upright, though the legs and my red pumps after the legs drag. An alert state. Big, surprised eyes, all of grey-blue-green, squinting a little in this unpleasant room, on a half paracetamol, Spanish-strength, pained by strip-lights, set in a great big, size 8 cru-cut head, which, to look at, wouldn't much notice if you smashed hard a bottle of Grolsch on it. My face is well-boned, and in friendly fashion, an English, Saxon face, though I have never been upper-class, the underlying bone structure very well defined, but generous. I am counted by the poor people I go to serve lunch to *guapo*, lips, cheeks – and my skin is freshly excellent, with its light Spanish tan, and a self-prescribed daily regime of tomato and carrot juice. I make time in the college gym as often as they let me and, in addition to the muscle I've gained, I *feel* skinny. There is a non-padded, non-oily-fatty feel to my skin when touched and scrunched about my lower ribs and abdominals. Touched by air – I seem lacking in padding of any sort. I look exposed.

The Rector said to me: 'Tomàs, I don't know, maybe you have a vocation, but it is like you are the princess and it is the pea, and there are so many layers of the blankets between you.'

1

I cross my legs in a half-lotus position, for the sake of my spine, pre-dawn in the college chapel, during morning meditation – distant though most proximate noise of – whisked cars, flying outriders. The Rector said to me:

'We are not Buddhists! Tomàs, you experiment. And it is in your breathing. This does not come from God. This disposition is foreign to us.'

He really did.

I said: 'You said we all have a vocation.'

The Rector replied to this: 'Well yes, you know, you say these things.'

Words. Only words. When hunger's grip on language overwhelms. And words are solid here. Words are things. Not in synaesthetic sense: I am not tasting verbs or touching-scenting-seeing-feeling… not within the physical register. Words are things.

That was The Room Where Faith Dies, The Rector's office, where I periodically go to account for my life in this seminary. And to cry, for faith and all life's exiguities. And death and loss which press so closely. And – monumental dread and love. The Catholic Church.

The Rector: James Michael Keith. Monsignor. Neither fish nor flesh but of Gibraltan abstraction. There is a little square box of tissues, like your granny has, always near at hand, as in a counsellor's consulting room, though this office, far from being bland, seems lush with treasure – books, an uninitiated game of chess on a crystal board, little polished things, few religious pictures, more in the way of family, little gifts.

We might emerge from The Room Where Faith Dies with a can-do spring in our step – or stunned utterly.

*

Now in class, the Vice Rector, slow and steady Father Richard, slowly begins to conclude his thorough explanation of the lesson he's wanted to do with us. His theme is courage. Though not an old man, and carries in him barely more years than I, yet perhaps Father Richard's years weigh heavier. So, inevitably, I tend to diagnose – bad experience – serotonin issues – .

Father Richard has gone and got himself stuck in an embarrassment of options in classroom-space. Here the board, here a chair and his desk, here students, himself *here*… We, the students, meanwhile bow our heads to time or gaze unseeing. Our once body-language positions have all collapsed. I – disposition being currently equable – entertain a thought of prolonged examination of consciousness.

Father Richard takes his moment – extricates himself from wherever he goes in these times – this conundrum. Father Richard's face clenches, but hanging onto it. Not now gripped with the worst of pain. Father Richard smiles a lurid stuck-on smile, a Greek-grin, if not – *rictus*. As he would have it be at a joke we all share. Then he says:

'If we can think about courage, then. What do we mean by courage *as a human quality*? I've said a few things, asking you to think about courage. So there it is. If we can think about courage as *a human quality*. We'll have a think now. I'll give you a – I'll give you two minutes to have a talk with – your partner. Then we'll.'

It is, admittedly, a little embarrassing. Not to mention in practice awkward. The implicit proposition that, in having to speak with my partner/neighbour first, a, I have anything at all worth saying, and, b, I am somehow incapable of saying it to everyone first off and without such rehearsal.

Plus which, c, Josh's breath is bad – rotten – .

3

I can't remember the point when it started to bother me. Initially it didn't, but now it does.

I have a fondness for Josh. Almost, from a certain perspective, you might call it a *tendresse*... If you blur your eyes – following after him. Gap-jeans cinched about his waist... Josh's bum-size rendering the waist inappropriately commodious. Heavy – work-placement office-shoes – unpolished.

A strange, disjoint composition of boy-man bones in a little-boy-man shape. Josh. There is something antique about it, an evolutionary oxbow-lake, and bones and the CGI-modelling-clay reconstruction. Solid beige. And unusual behaviours inferred from the set of the bones they found.

But it's not like Josh has merely neglected toothpaste, toothbrush, mouthwash. And not like musky-bum... Not like dogs checking each other out – .

As memory serves – like Dad knifing-open a game-bird's gut. Like opened-graves and epitaphs. Mortality and that feast of verbal accoutrements. Death and shit.

(And how do you say that? How do you as *compañeros* deal with that? (*How do you even cope with that?*) With love – hang an anonymized-bag with a bottle of Listerine on Josh's door? To baffle and confuse – to crush and isolate and injure and cause pain – with a polite-note?

I wonder how this might be – for we barely communicate.

Talk to the Vice Rector? Ask Geoff?

''Ere, bruv,' Geoff'd say – and Geoff might fully monopolize – might subdue – overbearingly. 'No talk. Got you this.'

No, no. Nonsense, nonsense. (Don't hurt Josh. Never hurt Josh.)

4

Light breaths through the mouth...)

He's a funny fella – Josh is. On the spectrum – doubtless – all that.
Blissed in sunshine, a huge smile no-one should ever have got at,
obsessed with liturgical detail, falls to pieces when given an essay to cope
with. Big donkey-teeth, probably no need to shave. One might see him –
surpliced, old. One of those men in parishes. His cassock labelled – to
shepherd the boys at the Sunday incense Mass. And hovers at the edge of
the ceremony: a Saturn's moon beyond gravity's well. Nudging.

All in its right place. A stickler. Like how he nudges me, a sharp
quick thump of his little sharp elbow, for he is goofy-small, when I nod
off in class snoring stentorian!

And he likes his Latin! But you keep that to yourself in this place.
No altar-stones, no Roman chasubles, no liturgical east...

We number now, this early March, sixteen. In class, we are sat like
a bad school, like a terrible school. We're guys on the wrong side of
history, but dead-set on winning it. In class: the pain of strip-light
exponentially magnified... A *non-outstanding* school... Though we all,
that first bright day poured into it, and briskly we re-arranged class-space,
re-empowered it, in horse-shoe, conference formation – 'Right, chaps!'
said one Young Catholic Man, no longer with us, organizationally
disposed. Our scraped-together desks standard classroom variety, though
unvandalized, unenscripted, gum-free mottled grey.

That was last September. We are this year's cohort. We are to be
here for one year, and we are the only year. There are no seniors, there
are no juniors. Sixteen souls. (Two did not return, one upon compulsion,
following the Christmas break.)

A long, broad, off-white-painted room, as if an almost-grey

underlies a watery, rubbed top surface. Maybe-last-year-modern. Though in fact merely half-submerged, the room is effectively and in its soul subterranean. There is the low suspended ceiling with the lights embedded. There are high, square, small, frosted windows, each two layers of double-glazed frosted glass, the outer reinforced with metal threads, and never-cleaned, black muck, six of them in a row, which if opened give onto a trench at the pavement's edge, but they don't like you opening the windows.

There was a reason The Rector made-up for it, that people throw things in, though He left it to us to see – used prophylactics, snorted baggies, cigarette butts. He went cagey and put on the voice He does when you're not supposed to listen exactly.

The room, therefore, The Ministry Of Love, lacks ventilation. The priests even like the door shut. Nested – possibly. Cosy – maybe – nice. Lest the wave collapse, they, perhaps, do not enjoy to be *observed*… Recording devices are explicitly prohibited by signed agreement. It is secret. (Don't look!) And into this the student-body-olfactory remorselessly flows… A certain low-stink of imperfect ablutions gathers and sours through the morning hours. And breakfast milk. Cloying. Pushes *inside* conscious senses. As we might have been fourteen, fifteen, sixteen. And not the best and not the brightest.

Not set 1. (Never mind bloody private school. Never mind bloody *public* school.) The smell of a certain intelligence, a certain caste.

So obviously, it had to be me, Tomàs – *moi* – asked if we might open one of the windows to freshen the foul air. At this, the Vice Rector, Father Richard, scrambled beginnings of possible, thrown, broken sentences. Father Richard got visibly distressed. Finally, forced to

6

improvise, gritted-in-tooth-pain: *Noooooooooo…!*

In encumbered phonemes, reached through – waded like a sticky molecule – liquid air. By God, he was what you might call flabbergasted! Four meters' long inertial space, when he wanted only ever to squat in it. Got to the base-point right near the window, which I had already, a wild Liverpudlian, stood on a desk I'd scraped to open, tugging at bunged-up metal.

'*No!*'

Then recovered, flustered, Father Richard got back his grip on what's *good* and *right* and *proper* – these being Father Richard's holy words. He said to put the air-conditioning on instead. Not quite following the mechanics of the issue. Chill the stinking air. Round and round the stinking air must flow.

Around half of us are what you might call young. Adedokun is eighteen and from Barbados. Benedict and Julian are nineteen. Henry, who declares himself post-adolescent, is twenty. Sean would be twenty one / twenty two. Then things become indeterminate, fanning the twenties and thirties. Then there's Michael.

Is Michael the *most* unusual? Geoffrey – 'Geoff' – comes close, with his incontestable gleam and his little crazy eyes. A soupy, beached hulk, stylistically located someway between darts and wrestling, draped ever in black, and he's dripping beads, equally extreme in faith as Geoff confesses his sins have been.

But Geoff is indecipherable – you simply can't tell. (Is he mad, bad, or simply dangerous?) He rises to the moment – God's – the Church's moment. Geoff *knows* God – the Church holds us. He knows that with antediluvian intensity.

7

Unbidden, and certainly unwanted, epic-slut, Geoff throws his arm over me, when he isn't bumping into me, and *squeezes*, in an unwieldy act of technical assault. He somehow *grills* me. For I have experienced affective response to Geoff unusually – confided unusually.

Geoff must blab it all up to the Vice Rector. Blab everything. Those late, incautious revelations. Blab everything. But the littlest piece.

Michael, on the other hand, seems almost credibly benign. He has a real thing with God. He wears it unmindfully: creamy-fawn slacks, socks, sandals, and the digital watch. He looks like soap and he smells clean. He's fathered children, and there are pictures on his Facebook page proving this. They are at Durham and Bristol. His wife is dead. Michael delayed his pursuit of vocation to see them through school. It is pleasant to hear him speak in his native Lancashire.

We are young. We are on our way to our becoming Highly Conscious Human Beings (HCHBs). Priests-to-be in talent-grooming school: The Priest Talent. Tuned to a high frequency. (Certainly that.) We're rising: we're a rising tide… If we are water, then we are not yet water which wants – *desires* to sink back to its own level, its lowest energy state. Nor are we washing-waves which energize – which *locate* your state.

And it must be a great venture. For we are not boys, and our first work, our first industry, must be – surely – to force it all – all that is ourselves, all that is *in* ourselves – up and out – through Herculean effort – act of will. To how it might be if we were most initially young, flowing-fountains, and entered, magically, raced, expanded…

Mostly, we've had jobs, of one sort or another. Most have not been schooled, in the sense of a formative experience. The youngest, particularly, gape wide open. A significant quantity still of fresh clay.

In class, I sense their school years. It seems a history of private, unsatisfied nakedness. It is as if our lives must be *acted against* that fault – which shames and hinders and precludes. That great beach-stone, weird and green and feeding, waves and tidal muck, which is a human soul. And dogs, old men, and families… A cigarette-plod at dawn, in clothes that slip and cling unusually… For boys need teenage rooms. Because boys need their proto-life.

We have not seen it all before. We cradle into some thought that had never been possible. Led by the good life posed by Catholic faith, they chant at evening, pre-supper: 'Who do we love? Jesus! When do we love him? Now!' And run, shrieking, from long concentration of evening prayer, through strange and achingly old institutional corridors – school, hostel, 'home', with the board and its notices – and pale furniture – and it overflows, as in some desperate re-enactment. Their youth must seize the old space, make it their youth's own. Yet they might turn in a moment, and preserve some necessary formal aspect, as we gather for lunch, a class, or Mass, or a spiritual reflection activity. Outward-silence. School-rules: this the chance. Though it seems late to attempt these things. Revenant. A brute-force attack on it – human-age.

We rattle in this great botched-together palace of a space. The buildings sprawl inside… Though built for precious few, who came from England, in the time of Elizabeth I. Martyrs. They trained to be priests knowing that in England they would be captured and executed. We are of their order. Since then, as the power of the Church enters into the modern age, now tweaked and retrofitted…

Though from the street it looks nothing. When we first rolled up in the coach, it appeared on the outside a bland structure. It's not ugly. More

9

as if it just isn't interested, doesn't care, can't be bothered. More cement than brick, the front *wall* – you wouldn't call it a *façade* – it sort of disappears inside itself, bespeaks some – mystery, and at the very door literally glass-hard, bullet-proof, set in the wall. It runs the block's length, mostly, until it forgets and neglects itself in an area of scrubland. It runs out of confidence. Loses steam.

It didn't seem quite right the first time. When we drew up in the coach – my forehead glued like a Post-It note stuck on the near-side window, buzzing-throbbing at the rhythm of some expectation, lolling in a dull thump as ochre-Spain strolled by, its brutal-flaws like no-body ever asked for this. Seeing it, with my lips but silently, to the tinted still-vibrating window – no-one could hear – my lips needed to say it: 'Oh no. Is that it?'

I'd have disguised my mouth to say it, even with a clumsy operation, such as a pretend cough, or an old scratch, or flaky skin, or an insect bothering my face.

Within three seconds, I'd brightened up, and we were going through the motions. Getting our bits and pieces. Such was the exterior of college… It might have been just a dirt street – psychologically speaking. A rock. A brand-necropolis. Fully modern if you analyzed the fact, with the semi-disposed cars and the brutal high-rise. Full now of our spilled baggage. And the huddle over it, manfully hauled from the crated underbelly.

The speed of occasional, widely disbursed cars, as the lights changed, when you hadn't got your city-nouse on it yet. Low-fear in traffic-wind. The brain not in control, the body vulnerable.

Within college, things are a different story. The outer door locks

10

like a vault or a military installation. It can only be locked or unlocked from the inside. You turn the handle, on a wheel – three beams of steel lock into it. This opens into a one-and-a-half-meter by one-and-a-half-meter area, which on the walls features a brief, guide-book account of the college history. Then there is an old door – massive wood and an electronic lock. A PIN: 'In 1492 Columbus sailed the ocean blue.' It goes beep then you swing the thing.

Within college grounds, there are sky-lit cubby-holes, light-wells, precious spaces. A spiritual purpose applies to each, and an obvious ornament, sculpted, niched, with always fresh flowers. You might stumble on women-people, living on air, like old films, water licked from bricks. Like cats. All those women – baying at faith's masculinity... Smudged-ink, scribbled Tip-Ex, hand to face. Her mouth strong, the tongue a trained muscle, big as her heart must be. Sometimes there's holiness – in a long-remembered formula. The way you kneel next to her might tell you something of her thoughts.

It is a rule that we don't wear clericals – priest-clothes. Each day each each wears becomes burned into view. A change of shoes must be remarked. This make-believe... A new idea of self – as real and not, as was, as theoretical.

The Rector said at the start there *are* ~~were~~ cameras everywhere. This was in relation to security and locking our room doors or leaving our room doors unlocked. (There were questions pertaining to trust and brotherhood.)

There are no cameras. (The Rector only said it in His slippy way.) There are no cameras in any of the corridors... So now, in a sense, there are cameras there and not there.

They are long, gaping corridors, Just-For-Men-brown, and slashed

11

and bumped against – Pickfords-van portraiture – no museum would want. What with the cameras there and not there, in this sense from our beginning, from the point we were set to create, the point we were set to believe, one's sense of what's what might be displaced in the corridors, pulled in each insistence fractionally apart, in what's set to be consistent navigational error, only barely indiscernibly gradual in each instance...

*

However. Now. It's time to share. Courage. Our theme is courage. Here we go.

As a general rule, Father Richard doesn't want us to say very much. A little something no-one has to think about greatly pleases him most, while class response and (God forbid) discussion are neither invited, nor encouraged, nor condoned.

There is no knowing what sad histories persist in the slow gravy-depths of Father Richard's being sent here. He presents undiagnosed. Valladolid (B-aye-ad/th-oh-lid/th) doesn't want it. It shows as in morning meditation, prior to prayer, his balled-up, wincing face, screwed against itself, begins to cry – the exhaustion of the sheer act, the sheer role.

Father Richard looks happy in a souvenir-album of pictures a class of little children had given him. An infant/junior school class in a parish he'd had near Doncaster. It *looked* not too long ago – we gathered.

Maybe it could have been ten years or maybe just five. His genuine eyes smile as though bemused in love. And those blue lips, his purple sausages, his conditioning, overwhelmed by love in a perfectly cooked grin, swamped in children – babies. Kiddiwinks crawl – with their elasticated-waists and their Wellington boots on! Father Richard shared with us this album as a piece of his treasure – honest in the offerings he could of himself. They seemed fingerpaint pictures of Christian scenes.

Life, death, judgement, heaven, hell. Little kids scrambling uncritically all over him.

But he doesn't like teenage boys. Father Richard can't put it into words, so does one of his complicated facial impressions he does of them. A clown's – *boufon's* unhappy face. An exaggerated drooping. Because he doesn't have the words.

Father Richard as he might have been, basic mother hen, might have been 'safe'. (Kid A to his mate – and what with the supply teacher – getting restless: 'Nah don't do that; he's safe.') But there is that from beneath, which rubs-off – wubs-off and infiltrates, and won't reason – not without complicated knowledge. (Where does it touch? Where does it hurt? Nowhere particularly.)

This is an absorbent environment. Brain leaches into brain. We all are infected with each other's thoughts.

As we speak our bits and pieces, Father Richard sits on his desk, not unlike a schoolboy granted privilege. He clutches the desk each side – his feet swinging. It is the norm, for each who speaks, Father Richard then for each speaks a hell of a lot more, so that really you forget what a person's said by the time Father Richard's had done with it. Then he gets his bullet-points up on the board.

So now: 'There have been times when I've sat on my own looking out of the window before Mass and I've watched a woman struggling with her children to take them to school and I've thought, my life's not so bad really…'

Father Richard spells each bullet-point right at the far-edge of an otherwise empty whiteboard – the width of the wall. He shields his work with his left arm – whether to protect careful words or to prevent the person next to him copying. They are careful letters. Checks to see it all adds up to a word. At the end, sort of bows to it. Sits back on his desk again. Courage.

Geoff speaks first. Each time – Geoff sits at the start of the horseshoe. It is a powerful position – Geoff must have instinctively chosen it.

What Geoff says, as-often-as-not, confronts the issue of a child's termination in the mother's womb.

And if you wanted an issue in this place – definingly, unifyingly – .

When is a life not a life? (What is human?)

Father Richard's face is lit red. Lips and tongue pulsating slowly. Father Richard's face is glowing coals. Geoff says:

'You need courage to do the right thing. And saying to people what's wrong and all that people say don't make it right. It's an important quality.'

Before Father Richard – all the expanse of the whiteboard lies wide open. Though not originally pure and if not empty – a palimpsest – half-scrubbed. Fearfully hiding the wrong words and yet unclean.

He thinks for a moment. Then he says: 'I'll put: right and wrong.'

Father Richard stands to address the board. Pen poised. The pen is ever-low on ink, and they are pre-faded letters scratched into the board. He considers it further. Spelling-words. Weighs it up. Satisfied:

RIGHT & WRONG

Father Richard returns to his desk and sits on it and makes himself comfy and says all that about choosing right and wrong. It's lonely and sad to listen to. Much that goes on here leaves you lonely and hollowed-

14

out of any good energy. Not afraid exactly but more like it is when your blood-sugar runs low – though without the beauty of a planned-for and spiritual fasting state.

Now he tells us what he might say in an intervention. He's saying *how he might say*: 'Is it right that you're doing what you're doing? Is this the way things ought to be in life? *It's not normal.* Put some proper clothes on. *People can hear you.* You don't seem to want to be a *normal person.* You're saying things that confuse people. Half the time I wonder if you're even there when I'm talking to you. There's something not *right* here. There's something *wrong* here.'

You're turning up late to Mass… You're turning your nose up at things… All the beers have gone from the fridge… You're not seeming to concentrate in lessons…

That's about me, of course.

Then Alex has his turn. Then Paul. Then Jon. Then Trevor. (Trevor features in my dreams, where he is nice, where I reconcile him.)

It gets to being Julian's turn and Julian's ripe and ready. His forehead works – Julian's crushed-to-a-question-mark milky-brow and curl of infant hands on last year's iphone. This too is about sex – which tends to be something of a social hand-grenade in this place. Julian shrimps in his seat, and stripped to the logic of it, way low, little suede moccasined feet thrust forward, all with a washed-look like children's clothes. Fading mint and tangerine. Way down beneath desk-level, flinch-level. Don't touch – don't ever touch.

As with pressing concerns, Julian-targeted – Julian-filtered news breaks through on him. Our Daily Maily time arraigned. Our Daily Maily time discovered grievous-wanting.

Julian-news. A tabloid-form of licensed moral-outrage. And boys

15

in school-skirts, and the acid attack in a venue. Gender-neutral sausage rolls. And being a man.

Julian says for the first time that you need a man to teach you how to be a man.

He wears the silver-ring-thing – to propose his undoubted virginity. When he makes a fist – when not twisted and fiddled with – the whites of his knuckles dig into it. It seems so far from sex – and yet.

Julian's lips never quite will open save in open song. He sings on sort of a planetary trajectory. Julian sings beautifully. Julian *disappears* inside his song– singing beautifully.

Now, his gesture's thought reads: Can this be for real? Does the *so* obvious really need…?

No lusty-touchy thought, no secret garden. Grumbling, fluking vowels:

'It's like… manliness,' says Julian. 'You know: being a man. You've got to be a man. You need to know: that's a man. That's what it is to be a man. That's it. Not like…' Julian sneers: a small, despised universe of half-men and not-men and faggotry. 'It's just… And people don't get that. You need real men to teach you how to be a man.'

Julian crooks, bows and shakes his head. His lips blow *tssssssssss* that it should be even necessary. He says: 'It's just obvious really.'

Who knows how they touch themselves? How at the edge of sleep with the little pebble?

Father Richard:

'I think what Julian's saying is that it can take courage to show manliness. And by that we mean true manliness. Not just manliness, like some people maybe might think they're being manly,' Father Richard harrumphs, 'but they're not really. Not… *true* manliness.'

16

Geoff calls out: 'Catholic manliness, Father.'

It breaks on Father Richard's face: this saving thought.

Quickly recovering, he says: 'Very good, Geoff.'

Then Father Richard gets to the board and there, to the board, he says, as he uncaps his dry-wipe marker: 'I'll put: manliness.'

MANLINESS

And what should I, Tomàs say? Let it drain and run emptily. Internal rhythms – truth – seem reduced to a childhood staccato. Chop-chop.

Think of a boy on a distant shore. With the little fellas playing behind him. A sea full of horses. Tumbling into it – launch, twist, slap – Aaghh! Two-out-of-ten pain as the body embraced sensations.

I flinch from such scrutiny to come – look to the gentlest available spot in my crumpled mind. To place myself, and speak and not offend.

And this is not friendly space. And I know I am being fragile. And each day slides from view.

*

Last spring, we came down into Spain through the high pass above Roncesvalles. I was in a mad panic. Priesthood. Of all things! Priesthood. That was life's 'out', was it? Do I even *believe*? Like *that*, like *they* do? Not *publicly*… Oh I had my intuition of God alright. I was alone in a desperate room – I prayed my books. And that was holy-holy.

Secretly, I hung a Byzantine crucifix on my wall, which, I fancied, glowed gold when I was having the right thoughts. I was at my desk. I was reading. It may have been a trick of the eyes – which relaxed, sought goodness. Knew there was faith to be had. God loves if you are warm. My application was in process. There had been soundings, initial

17

interviews. Begged references. Squared past. We were grieving, me and Mum, shattered by death, and the thinness of the present tense.

We drove west to Santiago de Compostela, shadowing in the new motor-home the pilgrim camino – which is a long walk pilgrims undertake to the sanctuary. In Compostela, we attended the pilgrims' Mass. On a variety of levels, Mum and I seemed tourists, rank impostors, not inside the thing. I performed my Catholic business. I hadn't a Spanish translation on me, so I was only running it through, timing a little askew, and the necessary actions. My correct thoughts missed the beat – so I compensated prayerfully – slowly. The homily was all gabble-gabble – love and journeying. My Spanish has barely improved.

I couldn't help but follow Mum's twitchy-eye tuned to the time o'clock. I wanted her to like it. Mum's hair was thinning gold. There were many young people squatted all over the church floor. They wore those clothes you wear when you've stepped outside of things, clothes you've tramped about with your feet in the shower if that and a scoop of washing powder. A look – valid if you happened to step into that zone. There were thousands of them, spent, knackered, all over the church-floor, pulling their knees up, colour all tending to Gore-Tex, legs strained, spindle quads and hamstrings… Mum's *look* – washed – more – *Okay! Seen this! Box ticked! Can we go now?* A lady – she poked me with the corner of her eyes like a little bird.

We'd left the dog in the van, of course. With the radio on and water – all home-comforts. Mum likes a good Songs of Praise. A child of her time – she pleases herself and otherwise doesn't much do God.

What happens, in the cathedral, comes at the end of Mass – whether or not you are Catholic. The Mass is sent! *Podéis ir en paz.* The great sending-off is a show-stopper, by anyone's standards. To me,

Tomàs, it came as a complete surprise – a real blinder – so much so that it brought wonder and real joy.

What they do is, they lower and swing the great censor, massively, powered by a team of a half-dozen liveried men. Your heart pops out of your eyes reaching up to it, in such wise no barren atheist might refute it. And I thought: it is a roller-coaster universe. Breakneck swooping troughs – giddy highs. (*Look, Mum!* – that's what I thought.) A swing climbing its altitude… Up, up… Stupendous daring. And I thought at the time – for there was plenty of room for thought – God rolling over himself in laughter, splitting his sides so a world flows out – as God is said to rejoice at a sinner returned home.

I dared to look at Mum. She seemed impressed, though yet sated, and in any real sense untouched.

A religious priest told me in England it was meant to clear the stench of the pilgrims.

Such highs, such bathos!

*

We noodled south through Spain. In the north, it was cold, and barely spring-fresh. At leisure, though, and perhaps this too was Mum, time pressed. There was this vague, impending sense throughout of time pressing. But the road was having none of that. If there were a clock networked into the brain, if, moreover, so much in the brain was pure flight, the days, the drive, the roads panned out. You watch the traffic regulations in Spain, like everyone else does. Cruise-control. They'll do you like a shot. Our destination was Aunty Grace's house near Malaga, the family outpost where Aunty Grace in her golden years rocked up.

Valladolid we noted on the way on a signpost. It wasn't technically avoided, though it had been mentioned, and in those days I imagined an

Oxford, a Yale, an LSE, a Brown, and I wished to avoid disappointment – this as much as to keep the whole matter fantastical.

Unreal – so that the movement of too-few letters and emails – all not mine to control – so as to do it unconsciously carried in fantasy… Had Valladolid not been mentioned we should never have known of it… Why would you?

A signpost. It – this – had been mentioned by one of the priests at lunch in Jamie's Italian in Liverpool, where the young Liverpudlian waiter smiled and spoke in an accent from years ago, and I drank a small glass of house red, by way of saying that was normal. It was a Friday so we both had a dish of cod and muscles and other such seafood cooked in a parcel, and it was okay and I understand the restaurant has now closed. Then as now, each next step – life's second half – so much audacity. Too much had turned into memories those last years.

It was a sordid sending off at the crematorium. This was a vile place. Godless with the smoking stack, the waste of wreathes, the *Bye-bye-Grandad* immortelles, propped at the edge and left there. Biffa-bins opposite the door – you wouldn't credit it. Smuts (imagined?) dripped through an empty, vacated air… (There were no birds – birds avoided it.) There were two chapels, two furnaces. Half hour slots. You could book a double. A door you went in and a door you came out. A conveyor belt system. Just so you knew what death meant, as you held up your Mum and the hearse arrived.

Mum was broken. The non-denominational chapel squashed full of baffled love, and blind terror… Ron was 65. They had plans for when he retired. He was diagnosed in January, then they dragged it out for the best part of two years. A plan *had been* to go away in the new motor-home –

and by the sound of it, they pretty much meant for ever.

The death-professional was a man with an academic hood.

But I stole the best lines. In my eulogy, I drew on 1 Corinthians 13 – part faith, part reclamation of the words, part a kind of desperate insistence, part some poke at God. Concluding what I had already said, it goes: *Love is patient and kind; love is not jealous or boastful; it is not arrogant or rude. Love does not insist on its own way; it is not irritable or resentful; it does not rejoice at wrong, but rejoices in the right. Love bears all things, believes all things, hopes all things, endures all things. Love never ends.* Then I said: 'Love never ends. That was Ron.'

I looked up at the end to see just how many were all packed in there. Each one of them squashed in his own clothes too. Old black, that light slides against. Shopping-trolley faces, with the owner's right to buy and the B&Q floor – Ron loved.

Flash! A photograph. A kind of precise exposure. A 'freeze motor functions'. An arrest. They clenched at my hands, after I'd said my piece... Frozen meat-packed panic. Not yet grief. The loss was too extreme. There was not much left of manliness. But there was a whole load in that room of being a man.

Then in travels with Mum all the adult-man left in me shed its small load.

We were at Lourdes before we crossed the Pyrenees. This lies back in the days when I wanted a clean faith, a vertical faith, where I could just be me, and nothing to do with home. Later, I have come to know, and quite to like, that modern Catholicism's splashed all over the blessed place, a more womany religion, and perhaps that is its secret heart. Fundamentally vulgar, squalid, domestic, this, necessarily, was an attempt to share. All manner of things. All manner of stuff and business. Normally, the rule is, Mum and I talk through the dog: *Samson's very happy to see you. Samson was missing you. Oh look, Samson's giving you his paw.* That's how we share most directly. That's how we confer such mutual feeling and human emotion. I *had* wanted to share a lot, but we never did – not directly. Now this delicate matter of Catholic faith… Well, here at least was a respectable institution, a solid thing you could put a name to… A brand you could trust. Which she might 'get' thereby. In order to share – possibly. ('This is my son…') We were close once, when there was no need to say anything.

She always was a bit make-believe. She used to dilute Dad's brandy – so did I – hidden behind Dad's books – a male equivalent of the sort of thing she read. (He gave me his PIN when he wanted more so I'm not saying I didn't do that.) All part of a package. Like prawns and fillet steak and the fucking Range Rover. Back in the days before the music of the eighties became sentimental, and Mum found Ron.

It is hard not to think Mum didn't like adulthood. Or not mine – not *greater* adulthood yet to be uncovered – not an implicit rejection in the will to explore. As for my blundering impressions – *haphazard* impressions – one's bumping one's head against adulthood… Delinquent years – which ran contrary to monetary stability and, *apropos* manliness, natural modes.

Perhaps it was that life floated now. Life pottered – and that was an end to it. Buoyant – light as salt-froth. She seemed an electron-field about a rare and more beautiful element. An end, perhaps, of too much impermissible-evidence, and make-believe, smoothing and quickly recovering and covering under. There, there. Just a little spot of the old DV. I watched her once in the unionized hell of an infant class and what

22

with that on the one hand and the rest of it… Life pottered – the hurtness kissed away. It was always the little things, and they more than adequately soothed life's troubles. We burnt a lot of petrol, and it wasn't like driving, at this speed, on these roads. We cruised. And we had never before been to Auntie Grace's new house down in Malaga.

So at Lourdes, there is the long, somatic thump of the processional; they sing toward a state of religious-incontinence. An hypnoidal state. Mum and I carried our lanterns. We played that game – together. It was a thing to be a part of. A crowd event – a mass rally. A new way of walking the old cliffs – son-and-Mum things.

This was more than an echo of an action – those days in that Jurassic landscape – Dorset. It was not simply to repeat that we were doing this. I, Tomàs, *ached* – and I didn't know and I don't know how to read anything deep into Mum. For that restored connection. So at the end of the day it seems best to take her only on her own terms as a woman. In terms of what simply communicates as a woman.

Mum's van was brand-new. Her 'motor-home' – a transit-van conversion. Because she couldn't drive the old one: it was too wide and in her head she couldn't encompass it. This was just a van – you could drive it hell-for-leather. It wasn't very nice inside – plastic-browns, the loo-closet seeming to dominate, and with no real storage space, though it was custom-built. We slept in bad conditions, known as campsites. The van was too high to get into any city car-parks. We had to park up – so we'd be settled – then get the bus to go anywhere, or walk the long walk – always the dog in mind, who was skittish in those days. And a taxi, a cab, in a wrecked country, costs about the same as a room for a night.

I was drinking far too much, mostly beer, so that wasn't comfortable either. When I had to get up in the middle of the night – get

23

some clobber on – *try and do it as quietly as possible for the sake of the game* – fall over the dog – find the door – navigate a shanty town to get where the bogs were. The motor-home loo was all wrong. A thing of leaky women and personal space declined. And socially-marked words like 'toilet'. And good taste, and refined sensitivities. And adolescent needs and adolescent behaviours. I wasn't generally mucking in with the spirit of things.

I should have taken the tent. My midlife-crisis grunge-pod. And let my hair down and my jeans rot... My happy-traveller! *But why?* (Why the rage? Why *so* obstreperous? Why such *difficultly...?* Why refuse the love?) It required my, Tomàs's, absolute certain destruction while Mum was Sellotape.

Only quite recently, and for life's second half, did I come to know Jesus. I was on my own, living in London, in a house. Newly unemployed – England had crashed – so there weren't any moral brakes. I had the thought and stepped into it, hand half over my eyes.

This was not a complete innovation. For me, the possibility of faith stretches back and back again unto the cusp of childhood and into my teenage years. But I forced the point, became external, and – all despite churning insides, as a kind of deeper gut-morality – I seemed to be getting away with it.

It was nice at Lourdes. I'd been here once before, with the Archdiocese, helping out with the sick people, whom they call *malades*. Dressing them, putting them to bed, mopping up, helping them scream when they should have used a hoist, and wheelchair duties. All replete with middle-class men in white and a troupe of posh boys – these in their teenage years already in the order of – I forget the name. Posh boys in contrast to the state-maintained teenagers also there.

That was the height of summer, though when the weather broke there were hailstones like nothing I'd seen. The sky broke and hammered them. The sun had been dazzling only a moment before. And everyone raced, first battered, now miserably drenched, to cover-up the sick people and race them, having borne no umbrellas, to places of safety. They all scuttled in different directions, like a terrorist-attack, though here was a line of cafés with their awnings out over the road's edge. I can only remember the teenagers scurrying with their wheelchairs while they didn't know what to do and had no compass desperately. Lank and imperfectly accomplished hair dragged. And I can only see the horror on their faces. They were driving them around like cattle – themselves in teenage pain and shielding their faces. In their wheelchairs, they could only endure.

I and my *malade* John watched the scene from the cover of a street-side café. John's was a lime and lemonade, because, and for myself a cold beer. And here's a thing: Trevor was there. It is odd to see him as he was then. Though there is still an unknown mess of outer-London (zone 5 – north-west) all balled up inside… He – Trev could hardly speak. Even undercover, the hailstones ricocheted, and we grew cold and damp.

I wasn't nervous taking Mum there. My heart burst vividly. (I wanted to show.) We'd stopped at a half dozen places on the way down France, and it was really far too early in the year to be doing that. Most sites weren't really open. It was muddy. It was better at Lourdes – with the drainage at the site we found.

I *desired* to show her. She'd like the cheery make-believe. (It passes through the mother's line: otherwise wouldn't be heritable.) The gypsy-gothic might be right up her street. So this *me* is *you*... I suspect there might also have been a measure of: keep my boy safe.

I, then, remembered the mornings on top of the hospital, when John liked to be wheeled up to it, in the lift, to watch the sunrise, and he was happy there, no longer able to smoke, as the light rose so quietly into the air through the Pyrenees. And Mary in the queue for the cold baths, when she was still a 'she' through some human construction. I did that as well, though it seemed off-message to lower your pants, get naked, with these three uniformed – aproned attendants, in the compartment, who dipped you in and hoiked you out. Cold shock therapy. It was a long rusty hut where we all queued waiting for processing – praying. The attendants wrap a cloth about you, then you're meant to say a prayer to a little statue – it was probably supposed to be Mary. They catch you in their arms for the assisted half-plunge. I knew – like magic – Mum would get this sort of thing – not actually *in* the bath-block. Charming, like the candles, it could decorate her narrative. *Look, you see*, it was as if her son said might have said to her; *it's not so bad.*

The site we parked-up in was just up a road into the hills past the sanctuary – on the other side. This turned out to be a good find. The sanctuary was but a brisk stroll below, though there were doubts as to whether the back gate would be open or closed at night. But then, and this was the thing, mere footsteps above, and I consulted the map, pre- either of us owning smart-phones, to insist on its discovery, lay the forest. Well, we had Samson, the new woof, who was about eighteen months by this stage, and about the most nervy Labrador, who had to be kept in a harness rather than on a lead, and we crept up the side of the road, which wound, and sure enough. Here, then, were the dog walks. This, then, the other main offering for two days. Here a place of happiness! Perfect

26

scenes are dog walks.

You could have camped in that forest forever and never been found. Hidden away and had adventures. Judging by the map on the board, at the entrance to the forest from the road, we only walked a tiny, truncated bit of it, a whale's tale in a long infinity-loop, which in itself was a long walk and took an hour. Mum walked steadily though having got to an age where she sort of yomped. (Her only son not happy at all with these shifting powers and hip-replacement possibilities.) It ran for miles – anyway. The dog kept close, always an eye on you.

We wore traveller clothes. It seemed a monumental elevation, as the river churned seemingly so very far beneath, while forest hush was better than silence. The mountains stacked above felt powerful. Once, a car drove by – a little old tinny thing. Mum was pretty much always yelling after the new dog, and I feared for the health implications, in case she gave herself a stroke doing this. It seemed more trouble storing up – it seemed, after Ron, death was everywhere. Granny had knocked herself off her legs, with a stroke, shouting after a dog, pretty much by Mum's age. Samson ignored her, anyway, and wasn't running off. There was no need to bother about him. But, I thought, you can't tell them anything, once they get stuck in a certain behaviour. You can't break the loop – . Stubborn they are – old. A mind clenched.

The rosary procession begins on the cusp of evening. Mum and I bought candles in their spell-bound lantern hoods – scrolled prayers. It's an extraordinary thing to witness. The emotional impact is intense. There is the great lit façade of the gipsy-gothic church and its outreached tendrils, lobster-like, and the runway around which the pilgrims walk, or they are wheeled in carts – rickshaws – which are called *voitures*. Mum

27

and I raised the glowing lanterns at the *Ave, Ave, Ave Maria*... The weirdly forgettable mantra of the verses' bass refrain held the beat of an old rave: *Immaculate Mary! Our hearts are on fire. That title so wondrous / Fills all our desire...* Digging – depth and undertow. Hero-Mary! Courage! Reminiscent of dance, and bodies, in the solar-plexus. Nagging-bass. Compulsive-undertow.

Toward the end, the float goes through the crowd, with the statue of Mary on. Then you kind of look away – distracted by your own emotion, absorbed by the crowd – and the statue re-appears, elevated on the upper level, as an illuminated body. That's like a rave, like one of many revelations, when you've danced the drugs up and the horns blow. For seconds you feel you've made her – the magic, the illuminated body – as that light blows inside. Your way of thinking has compacted with ritual in progress. Especially with the surprise, almost there is nothing outside this act.

What follows is strange. That odd, quiet dispersal, when everyone's had his fill – it worked. A difference is, this experience has been *all* focused on one thought, fixated on the statue. It is positivistic. You're in company but not in an eye-to-eye sense pulling each other up, creating anew a fresh-made moment, from the body-up, whereby the hierarchy only can be said to have constituted technical support.

With Mum, it was pleasant to walk through these satisfied people, and glazed-looks catching faces as they self-congratulated, self-admired, having for a slow and ascending hour climbed the ladder, and then as the party dispersed away from everyone.

Mum and I walked back along the river, away from the town and toward the back gate. The sound of the water had bubbles and pockets in it. We didn't speak. We were even honestly contemplative. It was like a friend playing his fingertips over your face. It sort-of in a way refilled the people we sort-of were. The grass was drenched wet and musky-sweet. It smelled green and woodland smells washed over us. Pine-scent, and the river-contained, and soil, penned-animals waiting the time to be unconstrained, mountain spring.

I went to confession the next day, in the enclosure, to a priest who might have been a Redemptorist, to apologize to God for the way I was treating her.

We stayed that one day extra, then we crossed the Alps.

The sat-nav led along the French side of the Pyrenees. This was flat and agro-industrialized territory, the mountains' backdrop all misted-out on the day we travelled. Mum drove the first stretch – she didn't trust my driving until around midday. She was driving like a maniac these days. Her hold, her brain, her grip on life, was tightening. Mum didn't do emotion, unless she was tragically broken down. Maybe it deflected and came out in other mad forms. Maybe it did that years ago. Maybe it had gone the way of avatar-arrangements by the church-door. And it would kill her in the end – I thought. But there would be some grievous accident and a medical holding together of life.

She drove. I was awoken way too early. Mornings were a thing – they were all agitation and one of those showers in flip-flops. The van was on the road. My body – liver, kidneys – drained of contemplative soul-time – cumbrous vigil every night-before. In the absence of anything civilized such as a very-very hot bath – almost boiling – to reset and to liquidize books and to endure in.

Flop, turn, river. Only a little way down the road. Looming – some mad moment – of weird acceleration and no reverse. As for any third-parties the accident might entail… I saw it terrifyingly. I saw too much: death was everywhere. There was disconnect: some lack of conceptual flow to the whole machine – to her machine.

I dreamt of death and terror. Terrifying machinery, hung from, beyond, a false sky it was impossible to focus on, for the processing power of the dream stretched only so far. Come to burn us. Great burners clamped the space beneath a death-machine too multi-dimensional to know about. And rain-down lethal and utterly annihilating fire on top of our big house. Boy-girls clambered all over the machinery – boy-girls in shapeless boy-clothes. It was as if merely going through the motions of tracking a logged plan, as if the timing alone had been at issue, as with a sinking heart, as with an emptying awareness.

It seemed such a pity. Help! Very small with the prospect of life's cancellation. And in a way, unexpectedly innocent, a soul newly granted the full realization of hell. Tiny – the fluster and bluff knocked out – it was so very sad and such a pity to contemplate. A boy recalled, rebuked. A gulping child.

I must have taken over the driving as we climbed toward the pass. I remember switching the sat-nav personality over from female-French – whose company we had enjoyed the last thousand miles – to male-Spanish – from the bossy and somewhat peremptory Jacqueline, to the occasionally inscrutable Jorge.

The hills gathered, the air changed. The mist cleared. They were stark pale green hills, neat settlements. They cultivated land up here. The odd stone dilapidated cottage fallen down, and seeming tumbling still. But neat. All neat. It was laid out nice in agricultural settlements. Then we passed, on an alp, through a last wooded dip, and so began the climb.

It was wooded all the way now, hereon-in, when the forest began, through a gulp, as we began the climb, winding up and round and round, and now a mountain, in ways they worked out years ago, and which fell down either side and into the forest.

Pretty soon we were behind an articulated lorry that wasn't going any faster up this hill. This was all good. There wasn't a tail – for I did keep checking the mirror. I wouldn't have liked anyone behind to think I was the one creating the hold-up.

Maybe the whole thing was about an hour. We had the Pimsleur Spanish on. (Mum resisted this through France.) We passed pilgrims, with their staffs and the scallop-shell.

It was steep, and gravity hugged us in the new seats. And the lorry in advance of us… All as this should be. Just trundling after. Little in the way of clutch-work. The lorry in front maintained a constant speed. I was concentrating mostly on the Pimsleur Spanish. Even Mum knew in her brain there was no possibility of getting past this. But there were plenty of seconds free for my eyes to turn full-on toward the periphery, and a certain hunger there was satisfied. Adventure! it spoke to me. Into the pine-barbed forestry. Into the trees.

There was a thought of possibilities. Other-life. There was a thought of awakening. Though it was muddied, and not something to consider – or confront too closely or the brain would clench and hurt. Still, with a measure of confidence, there was a living quality outside, so as not to feel *trapped here*, trailing off into the forestry, into the trees.

Mum's Spanish was pretty much non-existent. She spoke French. And my self-taught Spanish came not from childhood classes – this compounded with the fact I'm with Mum now, which piles on extra layers of wilful helplessness. Instance: right on the cusp of Spain, once we had just passed into it, there was a café. Now, I had been in Spain a few times, only not like this. Prior years, when my Pimsleur Spanish covered, albeit cack-handedly, those most immediate essentials. And, perchance, I might venture a nudge beyond... But they, in those places, were easy companions. And I was doing my twenties in my thirties... And I was alone – and in the sun's heat well-oiled. But I was never going to get it exactly right. I'm the spit of my Mum like that: getting things wrong. (And it's because I hate not getting things just-so exactly-right – hence getting things wrong.) Mum's presence full of love – and certain standards there of warmth and difficulty.

So in the café, I couldn't think of the correct inflection to the obvious verb. I corpsed, and I didn't have a go; I pointed. There was a vacant table and Mum and I smiled and Mum pointed to the table as well. She ordered. In an Anglo-French-intonation of one-word Spanish. Then I had a beer – Mum assuring me this was fine – and she drove.

There was a monastery, right on the cusp, but again, what do you do with that? You have a quick look from the outside. You think: Is it even? Because it doesn't look like anything from the outside. A monastery: life's crackling. There was no one there. No prayer – no pilgrims, of which there were a handful, seemed to notice it. No monks – the very weirdest creatures on God's Earth when you first encounter them. (They're at a threshold. They're liminal. They're sublime.) And there seemed to be no front door... Oh well. Rather: look down over it... Spain. It gaped – so flat. So long-haul. Toward Pamplona.

We went down there – Pamplona. In the van, we had a quick gander, at my insistence, and by chance saw *what might have been* the bullring, though it looked like a shopping centre. It looked like Manchester before the bomb. It looked like the Elephant and Castle. It looked like a shitty walk – what with the grilles, and ads declaring something political.

Samson didn't give two hoots just so long as he could curl by the gear stick, such that second and fourth became untenable, and under your clutch foot.

We drove, from the motorway, up, up, into the hills – to see a little Spain. The map said there was a point of beauty – but the sat-nav didn't know about that. It must have been shortly after Pamplona. There we stumbled, through scenery, up a mountain lane, on a sanctuary church, with a saint in it, where it began to snow, great flakes, at the peak of it, marked on the map as a beauty spot, up the windy road, which took the best part of an hour while I said and kept saying: *Let's just see a little…* Wrenching the van, which I had a man-hand on. And cars and a band, out of pure randomness, gathered as a wedding was only about to take place, like Spain showing us, telling us not to be scared, and we were looked at firstly, in the car-park, then within the sanctuary church, as the band set-up and tuned their instruments, askance invited. There were Mum-reasons why we couldn't stay which were to do with Samson. (*Pero… perro…*)

It was a thing to see, getting away from that. It was right up the mountains – I really want to say that it was sublime without cheapening that word. Snowflakes, huge great flakey non-melty ones, coming in from nowhere on a mountain in northern Spain. The potholes in the road – deep pits – Jorge the sat-nav no longer helping the joke, me driving. (In France, I played the sat-nav's estimated-time-remaining game, and we'd had some fun with that down one-track lanes – white-van-man with a loo on board – the aim being to shave at least an hour off – when it's all coming on all French – if you've ever done it.) But one feared for the tires in this place. One feared for recovery. Took things real slow. (Can

33

you imagine if we'd bust a tire?)

It's odd to fear a country. It's odd to be afraid of a continent. Not where it meets the sea – not like the south or the long, slow hike down Cataluña. All beached-bodies and family encampments with their tents and gazebos on. And twinks and sows and pricks and tummy-wobbles. Concession-bars parked on the beach that just aren't friendly. Because this wasn't/isn't Greece… And that one year of comparative youth… And there was no village here, not the little quiet cove, old cafés, clustered-up, and the family arrangements. The ship-a-day, no planes, a mellifluous language… Spain is hard Latin. And skin-prick hot. And they come from a different order of beach-understandings. If you've ever been here.

It's odd to be afraid of anything. This was when – where I learnt for sure that Spain is not a country but a continent. Fear the great mass of it. I'd never been *in it* like here; it didn't wrap up nice. There was an awful lot of it.

The motorways over the hills to Compostela *are* extraordinary. Billions – as we hurtled on – free money – they surmounted the hills' architecture. The bridging structure almost touched the hills condescendingly, as if in fundamental truthfulness we hung from the sky, traced with some whimsical 3-D-print of beauty from a higher plane.

Mum just liked being in the van. She felt if we'd passed-by a sign for a place, we'd seen it. (And after the event: 'We went there.') She chewed gum and she put her feet up. (I worried in case I should disable the passenger-side airbag.) This was *her* van.

After Compostela, just south, in wooded hill and lake country, we stopped in a site so that *my* soul, at least, being male, might catch up with us. Mum agreed – I persuaded her. (And Mum doing all that she could to

34

please.) To pause again, from the drive, where there were very few people. Was it even March yet? The ground was dry, and the sky and air clear. There could be very few objections on Samson grounds. Just a stop – a pause. To get a bit back together. And stop moving. She disguised her anxieties. The site was under-attended – there was hardly anyone there. And it can be very difficult finding walks in Spain, where there is so much barbed-wire about the place.

We found a walk up to the village up the hill. Mum said how relaxed it was, whether that was a good sign. I wangled from her three nights, two complete days. A concession. So I could have my bit of make-believe too, and cook our food, which was delicious, really a reward in itself, and camp-out, and wander about the trees, and recollect different places.

It was nice. Under the trees – which were oaks, but different, being Spanish. There were the usual rough-bits to do with being-Spain but anywhere really. There was that rusty iron fence which is ubiquitous and angry and Spanish. But there was warmth so you could cook and eat outside. The evening long-enough. No then need to brood massively into the dark-night. There was the lake, and its bit of beach. There was a functioning campsite café-bar, and one or two paying-or-otherwise customers, scootered-in friends of the people who ran the place. You could have stayed for your summer hols… Maybe not. But it *was* nice.

But she wasn't where she wanted to be. Not at a still point. We were going to Malaga. (That was the A-to-B: we were going to Malaga.) I *genuinely* wasn't sure she would ever be happy again in the place she was now.

They were one-flesh, she and Ron, and now a missing piece. One-human-being who settled her. A perfect-match. (One cute thing: Mum

35

donates her Shell points into my airmiles, so that I might fly.)

I have photographs of how it was when we set up a kind of camp – opened the sliding door of the van – the motor-home to cook, with chairs, a table, gas, and a clever induction hob, to make my one-pot suppers, and refrigerated fresh ingredients. A vat of slow-caramelized onions I'd made back home. The guy in the camera shop in Chester wrecked the negatives of the entire trip. (Probably having failed to recognize this was a slower film – HP 4 – but of course, in the shop, he stonewalled.) The photographs were shot on a portrait focal length – 130 mm. This is my favourite lens for those of my cameras I preserve. As such, they tended to compress the event of each scene – they put a lot of action in a certain place. But the contrast in the photographs was ruined – it was terrible.

It's a little difficult to remember, but there must have been two full days. This is because there had to have been time for me to strike up the friendship I did with the man who was parked next – perhaps around eight to ten meters away. He had a wife and his dog, a beautiful golden retriever, but the women didn't speak and the dogs didn't speak. The women waved; the dogs just weren't interested. They kept home. It would probably have gone from the first '¡Hola!' Then a bit of Tomàs-Spanish. Then, surely, mild, imperceptible increments. I don't remember how it happened.

He was Ernesto, from Madrid. There was the landscape to consider. It was Ernesto who told me the trees were oak. And he told me – they came here as a regular getaway – about the surrounding paths – which proved more problematic to discover. He told me he came from Madrid – and there was enough magic in that word. On my part, about that being Mum, and that the dog, and the travel plan – and where we'd been and where we were going.

36

It was really casual. It was in three-four minute manageable chunks. We did not, for instance, pull-up together two deck chairs and throw away bottle-tops. Ernesto spoke in a stripped down Spanish so that I might understand. He and his wife had a motorbike, so they were quite comfortably doing their thing. It was safe to meet.

But we communicated. I feel quite moved by this bit: Mum and I were leaving just ahead of them, packing, and Ernesto came across from his now-too packed motor-home, crossing for the first time into our space, with a bottle of wine, a good Duero – one of their holiday treats, he said, and explained it as a precious thing. He said – and he said it in English: 'My friend, I should like you to have this.'

I get emotional about that memory in a good way. It's really nice. It wasn't calculating.

The road south was cold. We did a little zig-zag arrangement. We had a little wander about: Salamanca, Segovia, Toledo, Avila. Almost without fail this was within the siesta hours, such that the impression became of a series of ghost towns. Then we took the plunge. Over the mountains, down toward the sea, through no place logged through the matter of experience. From strange toward known territory – the map itself meant nothing until we got to Seville.

It was a long haul but she didn't mind it. The mere fact of movement. She had her feet up on the dashboard, scoffed when I did suggest I had perhaps better turn off the passenger-side air-bag, fed and sucked her mints and chewed gum. The nest travelled. And indeed she required nothing of the places she passed through. Basic utilities – from out-of-town superstores on motorway-exit roundabouts – the Mercadona, the Super A – a Carrefour! Playing *coche amarillo* – which is 'yellow car' if you don't speak Spanish. Somewhere so Samson could take a shit. Some nominal nod to an instinct to lick things squeaky-clean.

And much lay increasingly muted in my insides, as if we *were* driving further away from it, and that it was calmed by her presence and filtered, saved for later. And she *was* – and she *is* extraordinary.

One night, in the range we had to cross, we booked into a quarry – which was what it was. There was a town of little-note – I forget what it's called – about a million miles away, a bus there we had to sit around and wait for and an expensive cab back – and the money.

Then, when we were coming down, from the sierra, into the sun, after already almost a month's travel, toward Seville, hundreds of miles yet, it seemed the fuel-consumption idled, and life became warm, yellow. You could watch the fuel-efficiency meter signify nothing, drifting, long, sifting, motorway swings.

We were coming home.

Life's a beach. Remember! Along the strand they wolf-whistle – and honk and reach out of their cars – like I'm really something. And little kids chasing after me giving me stones. Their skin browns differently – Mum and the towel and that. A sixteen year old boy performs shoulder-stands turning into hand-stands and back-flips onto his feet, then settles-back legs-spread in the low, slung beach-chair, and he slips his *very* white headphones on. I wear Ray-Bans and a beach-book not turning its pages. And not desire, the observation, but reverence, desire's cancellation. And remote-fact. That beach even now is considerably elsewhere. The family-gazebos encamped overflowing incuriously insular. The sand is burnt and gritted. There's no centre to any of this place – the strip goes on. I am alone and that's fine – that's what's wanted – during the day at least. Life's a beach.

By and by, Mum and I made Malaga province. Down, down, into the sun and the soupy air… The roads weren't exactly as Jorge – the sat-nav – imagined them. (Spain was bust, of course.) And it was not a nice ride in the passenger seat. Lorries crashed by like all that is angry in this world, all pain and fear itself, half your face and an elbow's width away. A tire-and-axel-crippling drop at the road's edge. The little brown roads.

Aunty Grace didn't have an address so much as co-ordinates. And: 'It's second on the left on dirt-track road!'

We met in Coin.

In some ways, Aunty Grace's new home replicated aspects of English life. Maybe it was more literal, less suggestive – less a matter of pointed looks and quiet words. More New York, less San Francisco. Dogs all over yelled like pitted maniacs. Neighbourly, community feeling there was none. (The man to the back was a criminal.) Here the wire fence – and that garden-centre green-webbing stuff, which lines every pathway if they can't afford walls.

English. England. London English. London England. London and the living and the intricacies. But, as it were, in an exposed sense – sort of honestly. The predominant accent, one gathered, *was* London town. But that wasn't very many people. One or two in whom it might have seemed terminal – vitriol-ingrained – released to naked sky. One or two *unhappy* people – yelling on dirt tracks. All grimy and hot – like football-colours translocated… Life a pub transposed? In sleepless heat, perhaps, which brings it all out. But it was more an accumulated sense of things. Really, you hardly met anyone, less even than the extent of an English suburb. It might have been all *no-cold-callers* stickers in their porches' misted windows – failed double-glazing… It turned out it was best not to go for a walk. I tried it once and so came to conclude it wasn't really appropriate. 'Uncle' Jake laughed and told me they'd track me by the dogs barking.

It was scratchy old scrubland. No common land. Jealous protectorates. Walls if it wasn't the fencing and sun-shrunk-lemon groves. Perhaps it was a question of water. There was no sense in going for a walk: it only excluded you. Only you could sit in the dust at the road's edge and try to see different pictures. Beads, jeans, wrecky dust-red-pumps, loose-laced and seemed to smile accordingly.

Aunty Grace's gait about her not-yet-gardens could be mistaken for Mum's back home. We got the tour, which was surreal because none of it had actually happened yet. This was how it was going to be… They'd lost about half a million on this place, after the crash, though, presumably, you'd need to move and find a place into which you could integrate when you could drive no longer. Here (there was to be) Auntie Grace's ornamental pool, her water-feature, here the trellis, with flowers. Here the mystery sheds, and here vegetable gardens –Jake's. There were olive trees, and a couple of lemons. And over there (not yet) an acre of cash-crops. Here – when quite sloshed – the dishy Lithuanian they'd just hired, who puttered in on his motorbike, 50 euros a day.

The two sisters became a unit. They maintained, like transponders, a pitter-patter slow-running-commentary between themselves. Putter-puttered like the dishy Lithuanian's motorbike. Sometimes it was merely a narrative expression of how relaxed they were and what they were doing and what they were about to do in the next ten seconds, like a voice-over on a film for the visually-impaired. Other times, the sisters entered into deep and hermetic analysis, and leant together heads-close-up, while more difficult, darker truths discovered utterance. Ruminant coven-noise… Man-issues, probably. Where life begins and life maintains control. Female noise. Life's actuaries.

I read my book and, at meals, we talked about the food, and we went down into Malaga and drove up into the hills, with Franco's lakes and hydro-projects, and we did all that.

Issues pertaining to Church were off the table. Quite rightly. Out-of-context, zero-real, at lunch, as through those liquid evenings – when we talked. A rival claim to human drama satirically misplaced – existentially *contra-comedia*. Auntie Grace is cool. She is the one who ran away to London to study at the Royal Academy. (The student-squat in Mayfair, the bleached-to-the-eyeballs cigarette-high of the King's Road. I have since learned that Granny suggested London, because she thought Liverpool would be too dangerous.) My memories of my and Mum's trips to London to see Auntie Grace's shows, in the eighties, make the place out as almost pre-Wolfenden, quite loosh, and very sophisticated. It was in her flat once, with her then husband, the music producer, that a very young Tomàs first experienced a (sonic) TV remote-control.

Perhaps religion lends a certain charge. Perhaps they were right at the 'centre', in June, and now, when I cry practically all the time, when, to be fair, they did say I had to have counselling. They told me that seminary – which then was an unknown concept – would certainly destroy me. I told Mum they'd said that, after the 'centre', and she said it was a shame, meaning a shame it should be still inside me – Dad – after all the years. And one rather imagined she rather thought I should have pulled my socks up.

It isn't easy to remember it. There are no difficult memories. I don't mind. There is nothing altogether challenging. Just it's blurred. I

41

was alone when he – . Then there wasn't very much time before he – . Back to Mum, and Ron's death, and now Malaga. (Not meaning to withhold information for a fancy sort-of narrative trick – just, later.) I had gained weight fast since the start of February. It was only May.

But I didn't refuse food. It is a lie as a statement of fact to suggest otherwise. There *was* loads of wine – but alcohol even then took me the wrong way. And the sun was sort-of irritating: it got in your eyes, and bothered the skin's exposure, unrelaxed – shivery.

Maybe it was Jake – 'Uncle' Jake – and the necessary man-talk. We shared late-night brandy on the patio, Jake's confirmatory muse a low, blunt 'mountain' – he said it was – over the valley ahead of us. The voice is maybe Acton Town – and with a history of smoking. Jake could be forceful in terms of what he wanted from human males. Within his glass and now-releasing brow he might seem to unfold and he wanted his own replication – that mountain – with the irritating stripe down the middle of it, which was a fire-break and totally fd with the reverie to my mind. This was Jake's psychological and competent equipment – fixing a plug, installing a new bath, kitchen, and the electrics, carpentry, building this house. (Siring a child he acknowledged in her thirteenth year – in time when the march toward death – angry death – be possession and love again – my niece – my God-daughter.) Jake's a man.

I sort of envy him. Jake's vegetable garden was pretty contemplative. It ran heavy on the diesel in the combi-van, down to the nursery where he got his plugs. There was plenty of grunting and staggering about the place, half in song and prevailing two-thirds man-noise. (He's like Mum in that respect – most people are.) The required posture with Jake was obeisance, occasional mimicry, and – unlike a teacher and not to get him over-excited because he was dyslexic before

42

that was a thing – never your own thoughts.

The house stood and yet stands a little less than a winding, dirt-path kilometre from the Villafranco, which was/is a forced relocation resulting from the now no-longer-functioning hydropower-project in the mountains where the lakes are. It *began* as the howling-dog walk away, then emptied. The village looks scruffy from outside. (I haven't been back.) Then it was white, and one must think Sergio Leone, and no people, but pointing its back-end out on scrubland. And there 're pockets. The central square could look nice given any kind of human activity. There's a bar – you have only to open the door to it. There's tables set outside... Four people turned in their seats there to look at you. And once you've tried your Spanish, and taken your cap off... Life on its own scale, sure, but nonetheless.

On the square: a church with no regular priest. Still, the church was open, that first exploration, and it was clean, loved and well-maintained. Prayerful, you might say. The interior walls new brick. Simple and holy. Two women were making arrangements with the flowers and such like and they looked at me blankly then upon enquiry in Spanish they told me there was to be a Mass on Sunday.

Dogs howling, I went along to that Mass on Sunday, reasonably clean, and wondering what would happen if you let them out, the dogs, assuming I could probably take one with a fist while the other mauled me. A new-ish black-ish T-shirt, and pumps and blue jeans, my favourite rosary threaded through a belt-link and into my jeans pocket. Thinking that in terms of probabilities, they were at something of a fanciful edge of their breeding – in a northern clime. But there were so many people – when you'd expect an old priest and a couple of grannies and me! It

43

turned out it was a First Communion – as I unpacked the scene. A bristling copse of children arranged at the church door – pews ram-packed with family, dressed to the nines, and otherwise admirers, dressed to the nines – while the kids were in sailor-suits, miniature army-wear, braid and epaulettes, little white wedding dresses – for the girls.

All the flashing ipads in the world were there! The priest's thumb and ring-finger pinched the air and gesticulated heavenward. Love, love, love. *Cada uno de vosotros es un pensamiento único en la mente de Dios...* (A fine sentiment.) I, having slotted in toward the rear of the church, snuck a look at them over my shoulder. There was an energy about it. A warmth and a solicitude welled beneath the Andalucian and the prickly specificity – gaudy and unfathomable rhythms of deepest Spain. They waited at the foot of the aisle to parade. I caught one boy's eyes catching mine, as so many of them so often seem to. And smiled – the boy sheepishly, tucked himself in. I smiled – or if not quite that, then I deliberately softened the face that had grown on my old face.

For, at some point along the way, my face hardened, though it seems crazy to think that, with some people, the most casual scrutiny might be perceived as a steely glare. Give, sympathize, protect. (That furtive gaze. The furtive whisper. That – offer. So immediately offered as withdrawn.)

They are funny with it, children, and these yet that. All squishy on the inside, within the tightest-of-tight definitions, ingrained to a ruthless exclusion and little worlds, so urgently pursued on their part. Their outsides in serial-projection of all they get thrown at them.

My instincts, the counsellor explained, are hyper-corrective – predictably symptomatic given the formative experience. Love-instincts healing-to-a-fault. To give, to heal, to throw one's life away. This is the consequence, this the *hamartia*, the predictable model, for there is nothing new under the sun, like the counsellor said it was.

So, then, employ relaxed eyes. Smile like a memory-implant – like a real-unreal synthetic fudging issues. Don't get close. Make like your thoughts are blown like leaves in Christian prayer...

I continue to experience the seeing of a genuinely happy and integrated child as so different – and myself as so deservedly apart. (To speak truth, one basic likelihood is that I am simply jealous.)

They find my eyes. They find my – Tomàs's eyes. *Namaste...* (How I longed when I was thirteen-fourteen, fifteen-sixteen. How I longed...) But there is literally nothing there. *I* was never there – and I have done so much to annihilate everything. They are so small and they are so far away... And it has been such a long time – years, years.

*

It is time. We are in the classroom. I must speak now. Courage! Our theme is courage. Courage as a *human* quality...

It has become the habit for students to preface our thoughts with a moment's material hand-wringing and the words 'I got...'

We might then speak like a meeting or, in Jonathan's case, and to an extent Sean's, as if disturbed at prayer. And so like this:

'I got, that we have to have courage to forget about what we think is right, and to give ourselves totally to Jesus, so that he can do with us only what he thinks is right, and then we'll know we'll always be doing the right thing.'

To the which Father Richard: 'Very good, Niall... Very good, Jon... Very good, Pete... Very good, Jo – Joseph... Very good, Carl... Very good, Harry... Very good, Mark... Very good, Patrick...'

It is hardly here: nothing remains. It is dust always-already.

45

Memory. Now I say:

'I wonder if you recall the events of Diana's death – the Princess of Wales. My apologies: some of you may only be aware of this through subsequent reportage, or the news may have seemed remote and insubstantial. As regards courage, I am thinking of the Queen. It was an extraordinary time. People went a bit crazy. It was an extraordinary surge of mass feeling, as so much became entirely emotional. For some of us, it seemed as if a kind of hysteria overwhelmed rational capacity. It seems true to say also that the emotion fused with so much that Diana expressed to us. There's even a strange sense of history coming into shape around these moments, as in some amazing ways England was on the brink of change. 1997 could be thought of as a watershed year, and indeed at the time registered as such.

'Anyway, the Queen made one or two mistakes, and it so happened, the Queen was denigrated. The flag at Buckingham Palace wasn't flown at half mast. Her Majesty did not immediately return to London. She would be comforting the dead mother's children, one might suppose. The mood of the great unwashed turned black.

'But then this was courage. Also quite exceptional humility. The flowers had piled against the railings of the Palace. The crowd massed. There were thousands upon thousands of people there watching and judging her. People had said terrible things. The Queen walked along the bank of flowers. She was seen to read some of the inscriptions. It was ostensibly no great show, but of course everyone knew what was taking place. She did what she had to do and she turned it around. Perfect humility and courage.'

Ah well. I was down in Kent when the minute's silence was. (I was on my way back from the beach – if memory serves.) I indicated left

46

and pulled-up in my second-hand Astra – in Maidstone. No cars passed.

I have spoken using my hands. My mode of speech has been ten-fingered. Cat's cradle. Good relationships once having been established, they'd get me to sit on my hands – in class, at school – and so attempt to speak and fail – to all-round and good-natured hilarity.

I lay the two hands on the desk yet splayed – my attention, corpsed, blanked, absorbing them.

Once, when young, I got on a transfer-coach from an airport in France to a ski-resort. The seats were very narrow and neither one of us was wearing his ski-jacket. My skin-experience touched a human-being. It sent something creepy and warm inside of me. A package holiday, there was no escaping my left-arm and left-thigh touching – a student-age lad who wasn't risking the beginnings of a conversation. At the time, it seemed that was a thing that school had done to me. Beyond an occasional handshake, I hadn't touched a human in years; the force-field lay about an inch and a half around everyone – meaning boys, meaning men.

Father Richard says: 'I'm not sure all of us will understand what you've been saying there, Tomàs. What are you saying, exactly?.'

He says it in a nice voice – he says it in a kind voice.

I quickly look from my hands to Father Richard. My surprise, which is acute, must be evident. Father Richard says:

'I'll put…'

Father Richard uncaps his chisel-tip dry-wipe marker and addresses the whiteboard. There, bulleted, faint with the failing pen, the litany-of-courage states: RIGHT & WRONG; BEING TRUE; CHASTITY; CHALLENGES; TEMPTATION; CHANGE; MANLINESS. Father Richard holds his uncapped pen toward it, at the force-field distance, an inch and a half. But the words will not be conjured. He says: 'I'll leave it for now.'

He does his little thing to his desk before Adedokun speaks.

A bit like Mum, on her crabbier, negative-thinking days over the phone, when all you want is joyful. All careful advice, precautionary words, as it were there be incaution sensed, or mild peril. Or language, Julian scenes, some new and undisclosed mishap, a diagnosis...

In my conceit I fancy Father Richard's eyes glint faintly, frail-wet, in moss, drooping pools, sunken like a garden pond with the reeds and a frog in it. You might see what's going on in there... Not much. It's shutting down but there's a kind of life struggling to get up on top of there. There isn't much going on in there.

That they only are an admission of emotion. They are honest. Silenced lustre. Sad-ghosts which had never been sacrificed... What does it do – this formation?

I think of me – myself – this skin – and seem un-Photoshopped.

In a way, it suits Father Richard. This it is he wanted. He it craved. If – *this* – black-gravitational-hole of Father Richard's extraordinary existence... If a slow program, split-ends, chewing RAM, Windows 10, all broken registries, background-processes, running on obsolete kit. But you could read things in those eyes – you could probably read yourself alone in his eyes and there'd be no Father Richard.

Chapter Two

My Mum and I returned to England in June. Prior to this event, it was said the southern climate would have been too much for Samson's health, though this was overly precious. We drove the whole leg up from Folkestone in one stretch – barely on speaking terms, we two in one flesh, wasted by time-out-of-solitude, flip-flop showers, no bath, no sweat, the road, the weather… At home, I discovered a letter awaiting me. While not from the diocese, it was to do with the application. It was a nicely worded letter from that 'centre' where I was to go for psychological evaluation. (Of course, they wouldn't email, and no-one would pick up a phone.) The envelope sat in the accumulated pile beneath the letter-box. I had four days.

It was a *fat* questionnaire, medicinally blue-and-white. All dotted lines in GCSE-style boxes. Desiring merely a space alone, I lay sarcophagal two whole days on the sofa in Mum's conservatory. She kept me informed about the washing she was getting through, and the drying, which wasn't quite finishing-off outside… Hands tanned supple with Spanish oil. Each next hour proved impossible. How, I dared to think, did women do it? Maintain core-existence within such wild and such dispersed materiel.

The glass-sky crackled. I crackled. Pigeons landing on the conservatory-roof needed an air-rifle – dark clatter-clatter – appalling noise. As I withdrew from a two months surfeit of Becks and Rioja – dry, drying out – England and blue-grey sky came at me. My brain, rewiring, unmedicated, gripped by vile, psychotic fragments of family drama. *You made me live with that man… So stupidly simple it could have been… Winters could pile-up pretty solid and cold… A fall… There'd be no inquisition… His brandy…* But there was nothing to be done with it. It wasn't going to write itself. She tip-toed theatrically with bundles of towels and bed-sheets. She obsessed about the little place in woman-undies hoovering ants up.

My self-invention faltered – seemed a void. There was nothing left of me. What a shell, what a fragment – I seemed a husk in Mum's wake. I needed dog – hours-and-hours of dog. Marsh-hours. (Out there on the green toward the mud and silt and estuary – child-time when we couldn't get Channel 4 but S4C instead – from Wales.) But there were issues with Samson. (A perfectly healthy dog, so far as I inexcusably imagined him.) I could have mown the lawn. I could have built a house. I could have dragged a sloppy class of eighteen-year-olds through lessons on Milton. But what this questionnaire asked me to fabricate… There seemed a missed quantity of simple self-idolatry during the past months. What had we done but drive? It was a three-hour flight away! We might have lazed like stones and beached and sunned – and self-admired like depilation – stillness and nothing we might have had.

Not even in the trees at the foot of the garden, into which I American-back-hand slammed a slew of posh-new Wimbledon tennis-balls for Samson to eat. And clouds were but alien passers-by, mere spectators, not in-play, which you couldn't make anything of. Despiritualized essences. (Fly on by, you fuckers!) Distinct from plane-trails, utterly remote up there in the grey-blue. (Take me air-side. Take me to Africa.) I spent those two days prone. Sorely I needed a holiday.

50

English sky. Peasant-weather.

The questionnaire ran for thirty-six A4 pages, and required the most basic disclosures. Have you ever…? When did you…? What are memories about…? Describe your… Tell me about your… Only the good things that come to mind.

It was exhausting to contemplate. Mum made cups of tea. Tentatively she broached solid food… Two days dwelling on this and I thought: 'Enough. Enough! Enough right?' A man has his limits. There is so low you go before you turn like a terrorist. Enough was enough already. That was it. I drove up to the Tesco Express and bought a box of Stella.

Right then: God.

I, Tomàs, set to with the questionnaire.

A wiser man might have known there are times when less is more. But, you know, I desired to communicate. I felt the need. Obviously not *everything*. That would never work. But to bring it outside the confessional. As if it mattered. As if, through partial confession, they must be contractually obliged to forgive the lot.

'Sorry about any sins I might not have recalled or found words for.' Then the priest absolves you and the Devil can't touch you. Besides, I sensed missing years glaring me down, and didn't want to be ashamed about this, now, with all my young-life judging me. I was not unaware of what you might term a sense of betrayal.

A new self. An alternative fiction. Such as might seamlessly integrate: a slow hack.

A bold, a new and a truthful relationship. Soiled with closet-drama. Mulched in deep-past.

Organic. Natural.

I filled the form in. I filled it all in – every space. My confessional-prose ran complete to the end of the dotted line. I used no extra sheets, though there was one rather late-night PTO, strictly for the sake of borderline-accuracy, in case they checked. I supplied irrefutable detail. I left no empty room they might peer into, no weakness they might lack… A wiser and more cynical head, on firmer shoulders, might have noted this *plan* harboured certain flaws. Yet I did myself credit. I quite liked this Tomàs I – Tomàs created. And I came to believe in him. (What did they want anyway? Who was I meant to be?) I included significant honesty, along with the obvious lies. All transformative. God's light. Mary-prayers for the miracle to happen. The life I committed to paper seemed not – different, unusual. Wayward: yes. But relatively bland. A rude CV. But not unpleasant – not queer. (Hide Soho. Bury Dolphin Square and the credit-card days and – .) So Mum was… La, la. Dad was… Yes, that. All that.

But there were regular muckings-about in stretched youth. Artistically, I shared with my inquisitors one homo-erotic line, which turned out to be an ill-judged scenario. The women quizzed me on that. I spoke my heart about sexual awakening. Love amorphous. Love – I thought to offer them.

It was important to have him there. He resides in the awakening. His name was Tom 2. I still know him and he didn't like my coming here. The boy I offered, coaxed from ether, was perhaps not true. And what with the mess and my own vulnerabilities at that age... But it felt nice saying it – a romance of friendship – 'He was called Tom too.'

I remember him clowning with an antique-musket rammed in his boxer-shorts in his room which was boxy and where there was nothing to create – no art – where it was easy, happy, by-the-book, and middle-class, and undivorced, and not political. Only – enviably nice.

But of course I had to change all that. My skin's warmth waxed in recollection. 'Nothing happened...' Except this one time... But not like... I smiled and in one of the interviews looked to my lap from their women's-eyes blushing. First love. It seemed a pity we hadn't sinned at the poetic age – which you can always remember with fondness. But that was the way of things. And so much never happened. Laughing in the village on the streets there. I was lucky with our friendship group in my school year – Tom was the year below. What with our fresh powers. Never grow old.

It went threateningly wrong when, in the report they wrote, based on the questionnaire and the days at the centre, they aged Tom. They put the whole grim business in my Oxford years. This, beyond being crass to the point of futility, was a lie, and categorically false to what I'd given them. Tom 2 was fourteen, fifteen, sixteen. He happened at school. Indeed, one piece of sideline-utility in going *away* to university was getting *away* from him. For in the end it had become something of a fraught and destructive relationship.

By the time he was seventeen, Tom had got into drug kicks – no longer pretty addictions – battering 'Tomàs! Tomàs!' at my bedroom window, which you could climb up the ivy and onto the porch-roof to get to. Even at the age of seventeen it lacked pseudo-intelligence. Such relentless charm this *youth* possessed all drowned-at-sea in a kind of degenerative forfeiture. It wasn't even the pop-song curled in the lavatory cubicle. Balked-up cider and heroin. (*'Tomàs... Tomàs...'*) The man in him not having found his beauty – and my construction of his temporary boyhood withering given time and fact. It wasn't easy to read what they put in the report when I'd been so careful about it.

Otherwise, I, Tomàs, had never quite found myself wanting to develop as a person in the context of sexual relationships, and as such I supposed that meant I was a virgin. I didn't smoke, which was true at the time, and had no tattoos or piercings, which was true at the time. I consumed what was then the recommended twenty-eight units per week of red wine or whatever you tell me I get through. Certainly, at university, one was aware of the proximity of substances. But the women didn't think they needed to dwell on that. I conceded the point: they didn't need to dwell on that.

And it was strange how many long, boxed, fruity weekends slid from view. There had been that anxiety which wasn't there now. And sure enough, none of all that showed up in the report they wrote.

I told them in the questionnaire how Mum was supportive of the journey, and how she was always a rock, all through 'the most difficult times'. An incautious phrase, that was. They stuck on it like vultures, and picked me apart on it. Which is to say, Dad was back again, set to loom heavy and large. *Which is to say, Why? Tomàs. Why? Could he not have been a much-loved Dad who died quietly in an accident? What possessed you – what were you hoping to achieve – in bringing* him *up?*

So many lies – so much truth.

I drove up on the sat-nav to the place on the outskirts of Manchester. There was an Asda on the main road in spitting distance. It was only a shop-depth from the main road, which was dirty and grim, to leafy old big houses – treed, hedged. The only thing carrying a sign was a private clinic.

It was to be a three day residency. Rather than call it an assessment, they pulled that meaning back within the way they referred to

54

the whole place as a centre for healing ministry. The centre was called Saint Luke's. You might think of the opening lines of Luke's Gospel. There the Gospel writer declares his intention to construct a more orderly account – one might infer a rather glorious plethora of source-texts – more-or-less inadmissibly garbled junk and treasure. And such is the way of the Christian world – languidly tangled, syncretic, a broad church. They and I were going to edit Tomàs. Okay...

In the blurb, visitors were asked not to ask other people why they were attending the centre. Such Churchmen whose prayer had deserted them. As it happened, there were only the two of us – me and the other guy. And we weren't there for healing. We were there to be checked out.

There were computer psychometrics. Questions included: 'Have you ever felt you were being watched?' 'Have you ever heard voices inside your head telling you to do things?' 'Do you ever experience violent urges?' My baseline scored normally, though the test results implied a tendency to self-present with greater wellness than was accurately the case in response to conflict. Then there were the interviews. Aside from the three women, who conducted the interviews, there was only the one priest, who initially answered the door to me, and who celebrated Mass on the second day.

The chapel was a windowless basement. I occasionally experience difficulties preparing for Mass. Still, it was friendly, a safe space, rules known, no untoward surprises. The Stations Of The Cross ran the breadth of the front wall at eyelevel while you were seated. They were quite good – square, fist-sized, bronze castings – and you could meditate on them, and think about where you might be now in your life and in life more generally and in relation to Jesus.

The other man was a maths teacher from a different diocese who hadn't been to university but went to a polytechnic and was applying to be a permanent deacon – not a priest. He was nice and we spent time together in the garden. It was sunny, even warm, and we did a lot of tea-drinking. Down in the basement, we ate such a lot of food. The bouncy young man-of-colour who spoke like a rave in the kitchen laid such a spread for the two of us. There was a catering-tray full of bacon and another of fried eggs. And the rest – mushrooms, beans, and fried bread. It's true what they say eating staggering quantities of breakfast. Your heart goes BOOM-BOOM!

I then thought it only polite to get through it. I did not realize we were the first sitting and that staff would follow.

I liked that man – the teacher. We sat quietly watching a film one night. He being a mathematician, the film was the one about game-theory. I didn't quite follow it at the time but I have watched it since. The centre had the same problem with the OAP-home furniture as we have at seminary. The diocese paid – I later learned – two thousand pounds for my visit. The letter said to arrive by ten.

Feeling better than I had on the main street, I found the big, old house down the leafy avenue, scoped it then drove around more of the same, for the time's sake, with Radio 2 on. Eventually, I parked-up ten meters down and waited. I took the sat-nav and its holder from the window-screen and hid it beneath the seat. My Asda-bag contained salt-and-vinegar crisps, salted peanuts, lemon-juice, sparkling Volvic, vodka, and two small bottles of unrefrigerated white-wine. At five to ten, I restarted the car and drove into the forecourt of the centre, where I parked in neat alignment with a mottled, secretarial car beneath a sagging beech.

Yawning myopically, that priest wiping slugs off his face as he opened the door – to a smart young man in a business suit – this being me.

'Well,' he said, 'you'd better come in.'

The room he presented was, he said, the better room, seeing as that I was early. Then that was it for the day until supper. Nine hours. (I had been told to arrive at ten.)

It was a plain, milky-white hotel room. I didn't much fancy heading into Manchester, so changed and walked back round to the Asda. And there was the kettle and there were sachets of a range of teas. It was exactly a room you'd go crazy in. The phrase I'd snagged with Mum was that this visit to this centre was to 'stress-test'. This dumb, evasive phrase struck me in my demented lie as clinical, modern, business-can-do, business-optimal. While this room evoked – heavy-lidded skin-thick musty-childhood nuclear-family weekend-getaways to Yorkshire or – whatever – the Lakes or anywhere beige in the 1970s – toast and wallpaper. (I don't remember Dad – I remember Dad/I don't remember Dad – I remember my room in an hotel – horrible narrow little space with a television in it.) A little while, I took my clothes off and sat in the shower. There was no curtain: the air steamed. My crumbly toe-nails half-gone on-and-off these last half-dozen years. There insinuated hesitant explosion of tracery at each inner-heel. I was 40: I am yet. It was one of those days when you're not getting any younger: time pressed.

To get away, I thought. To get away. (Why do men drink? For Mums will insist on reality. For Mums will clatter their dishes and spoons...) For the pressure really did get to be a bit much. I got to know the room, and achieved equanimity. Rooms can be alright just dobbing around with your socks and undies on. Eventually, I settled at the desk and read the first book of Samuel, then kicked back and snoozed to Radio

4.

Interviews took place over the course of the second day. It was in the one about my emotions that I started to cry. And after that, this ensuing year, it's come to seem I can hardly stop. They never asked accurate questions when I had been so precise – had most assiduously filled their form in. I'd completed their sentences: 'I believe…' 'Women…' 'I describe my sexuality as…' 'God…' 'My mother…' 'My father…' 'If…' I had responded with such absence of obvious sarcasm.

Ron was still dead, of course. She sat directly opposite, spooning me tissues. She milked my tears as I confessed. *Sorry sorry sorry…* I made firm use of the tissues while I talked about Dad and Mum. They didn't want to hear about Ron. Maybe because they weren't married. It could have been that. They made me cry and smear my nose. Teenage childhood took on the form of the present tense. Was I then lying, obfuscating, eluding, or did I tell them everything? I no longer know. They seemed themselves to cry where any waters had long dried-up. Those faces might truly have been pictured as crying bar wet-tears. Great sobbing etiolated brushstrokes – blue-grey – as an early Picasso might have painted them – barring the wet-tears.

The report they wrote was hardly even in sentences. Cut-and-paste syntax like it was plagiarized. That really hurt. That shredded me.

*

It is Shrove Tuesday. Pancake Day. We're having pancakes. Mardi Gras.

Elsewhere in the Latin world, this day, Fat Tuesday, marks the culmination of carnival. While Valladolid – B-aye-ad/th-oh-lid/th – proves quiet, our religious sensibility all looking forward to Holy Week, yet one knows that out there human life is getting messy. To an accompaniment of drumbeats. Gross, sweaty, ritual.

To dance and grow and swell – to conjure fertile land. Through sympathetic magic, a law in the religious world also, our seed might swell and grow. Dance as the crops as the wind blows through them. Pray and dance and sway and then – propitiate. Imitative magic. To make the crops grow[1].

Henry and John made the pancakes. They asked me – as one of the known cooks – but I demurred. It is too risky in the kitchen when I try to create.

The pancakes are excellent, served with Demerara sugar and lemon-wedges. Each table's got a pile, and they haven't gone soggy. They might have just come from the pan. Henry presents the gifts with easy grace, suggestive of natural entitlement, and it is awesome to receive, and sit and eat, when there is quite enough 'doing' in this world. I feel thankful to Henry and John for the pancakes. I wonder at Henry – not so much at John. I wonder at the energy at this stage, and experience affection.

It is Lent. Ash Wednesday. In England, a new hope of spring should be settled by now, for this is not an early Easter. 1000 kilometres south, in Valladolid, at 700 metres above sea level, the days hold, as it were in mittened fingers, chill promise of warmth already. Delicate, tiny

---

[1] I feel it incumbent upon myself to say at this point that I have read merely abridged versions of Sir George Fraser's *The Golden Bough*, the more recently published including matters most directly pertaining to Christian faith – ISBN 978-0-19-953882-9.

birds in city trees trill with laughter, expectation, industry. The sky displays a washed blue so instinctively familiar, as if the soul were ill-equipped for less. Life flickers in the streets of Valladolid, and in Campo Grande, the central park.

Silenced air is pricked by lacy birdsong, and the dinosaur wail and hoot of the eerie peacocks. The song instils a further elevation into the pine-scent. Musky bed-smells earth the gravelled regularity of my pumps' tread. I savour time digestive – after lunch. There are benches to linger and channel a life's variety. A lunchtime sandwich on the steps of Saint Paul's. Playing fields. Edge of the wheat-fields. Bracken, briar and brambles.

The word *lent* means spring. It is an English word. It derives from the Germanic *long*, meaning: as the days lengthen. The Spanish for Lent is *la Cuaresma*.

My love, the sun is come again… It might seem an odd time to do penance. Contrary to nature, you might say, a slight on the budding trees.

It is thankfulness.

Ash Wednesday. Well, you can imagine the fun in the Vestry. Henry is one of the Sacristans, and this among the high-end of Churchy stuff Henry loves most. In my room, in the mirror, I am thinking: *Should* I wear purple?

I take off my clothes and stand in the shower a minute and give my face a scrub. Then I consider myself from the ground up. Will anyone else wear purple? Will *everyone* else wear purple? What might my token-purple be? A jumper? A hoodie?

I decide that, on balance, it *does* need something. Each choice will be remarked. It's all choice: there is no non-choice position. The skin you stand up in alone is flesh and choice. What should my clothes *say*?

One thing this seminary does is it wears a man's brains to shreds. That's no ancillary offer; it is core-functionality, minutely crafted to distress and enact psychological injury. Your brain fights back against your own brain... I, any case, am convinced, when you step from your room to the corridors, that if you once let your mind rest, and go with the flow, then that failing agitation and easy-time will be remarked, and they'll have something additional to put on you.

In the mirror, I first of all wear a favourite trinket, which is a wooden lozenge, olive wood from the Holy Land, on a leather strip, depicting the Holy Spirit as a cut-out dove. This went down well in Greater London, with the young black man behind the counter in the Tesco Express. He said: 'Oh that *is* cool.' Rather than, say, an externally necklaced crucifix, worn as a statement by adult males, tubthumping blatant God. (And not the salt-and-vinegar crisps and the can of Strongbow.) A bauble – a pretty gold crucifix best kept for a holiday's different skin.

There is a T-shirt I picked up in Liverpool – same the kids were wearing, long, to mid-thigh. My underpants are merely a high-street brand. The nth incarnation of All-Stars a non-negotiable... There was a look boys had found again. When worn correctly, by beautiful people, this look struck me, that day in Liverpool, as startlingly – double-take, look-away, blush-to-acknowledge-it – sex-free. Boys wore powder-blue. (And yet how highly sexed... How *powerful*...) Towelling-white-socked ankles bounced on shiny hooves – yet somehow *purified*. Even the socks were sufficiently washed to look tangly and nice and not new but rather freshened and nice and unselfconsciously family and washing machine – such as merely to see you could nearly smell a fabric-washing brand.

61

Perhaps it was only that one day – beauty proposed celebration – a new hold on human form. Legs beyond conjecture. And so many of them went to the gym, while their complexion, in this day and age, exceeded Photoshop. As though they had been crystallized from clean air, and youth's commuted selves, and teen-identity-propositions, cruised shopping-malls buoyantly. Often their heels didn't touch the floor.

Adedokun's funny. His jeans were really cool. (Adedokun being both black and a teenager: Adedokun's jeans were really cool.) The jeans stopped before they'd ever even heard of Adedokun's ankles. A good deep colour, old-fashioned denim, a good shape, like the rear-view you get on an album-cover of a hobo-esque Bob Dylan and the slung guitar on a lonesome road in America.

But this term, when they were clamping the screws on things, Father Richard said to Adedokun he, Adedokun, black youth, had to go shopping and buy himself a new pair of store-bought jeans. So he did, and now Adedokun's new jeans look shabby and excess-long, like a white man's in the queue on Jobseekers', and not in the least cool.

So I dress plain in a tight white T-shirt from a packet and spray-on skinny jeans. I have my thick brown leather belt, monk-thick, drilled with the extra hole. Red All-Stars… An old chalk-stripe suit-jacket by Crombie… A purple scarf and loop it… Yeah, that's all on message. Borderline-invisibly-disconcerted – one of the angels as such. Mind on higher things. So I head downstairs.

*

Once, I taught theatre in a little school… Once I got an A in lighting – for the boy – and I continue to dream about lighting rigs. In chapel, they are proper stage-lights. Proper high-watt bulbs. It took a team of blue-overalled men with a snap-up scaffold to focus them that time The Rector felt the need, and the men all stood around, Spanish men engaged in a collective think, which is a sight, not honestly seeing what the issue was, or what the new demands were. In subjunctive.

The lamps are controlled from a panel of switches in a cupboard in the Sacristy – in the jumble of old wood at the back of the reredos – on a brand-new dimmer rack, which *could* power a reasonable theatre. The switches are sticker-taped by The Rector according to occasion. He is particular about it – it is one of those things He gets harsh about.

With the lights off, even on the brightest of days, if you crane your neck, you can just see the panes of glass of the coronet of sky lights, grimed beyond reach of maintenance and regular man's work. It is then ever-dusk below – a dim infiltration of natural light. Our chapel is of Jesuit construction. Octagonal in design, it is said that the Jesuits shaped their churches psychologically, a kind of emotional seduction implied in the openness, and clear lines of sight. The Mass, then, is in a sense plain-talking, a direct conversation with the many believers, though above, the wholeness, grandeur, overarches. Then, in the walls, each recess is a gaudy devotional. Pilgrims, saints and angels. Glaring putti. Implanted with empty reliquaries, glass or a piece of crystal, hollowed, open-mouthed – gaping, empty.

But the furniture is modern. The pews are all straight lines. Solid wood – hard edges, no curves. They look as expensive as you like but aren't much use for sitting in. It's okay in Mass, when you're up and down anyway, but in morning meditation conducive to terrible back pain. No accommodation, you might say, as you can't sit straight and not slip in them.

63

The altar is modern. The Rector asked that we recall it is yet a consecrated altar – it has been baptized. Thick gold paint daubs twin Corinthian columns... My eyes tend to drift to the floor, laid with octagonal marble tiles, in swirling shades of grey, like a cake. They play the eye around the central body of the church, then stop at an edge where square tiles radiate into the sanctuary and side-chapels, stretching the picture. Once you have the trick, you sort of follow it around, angling like op-art, all queasy and alienating. At the chapel's centre, a glass octagonal tile looks down on a circular well of unknown sacramental significance. A uniform pattern of tiles throughout could have been less worrying at floor-level.

I bow my head fractionally, lidding my eyes, to breathe quietly and empty noise from out my head. Preparatory, this might be, to a formality of word and gesture. I look up, around the walls of the octagon, over above the arches, encircling the whole, where wooden lattice grills conceal the galleries, which we call tribunes, a crouch-height recessed space where, once, young martyrs-to-be sat hidden for public Mass, at the time of the college's foundation, so as not to be seen by English spies – in Elizabeth I's time. It is said there were those who never once celebrated Mass in England, that they were caught first, before they had that opportunity. Then hanged and drawn and quartered – as traitors. Their life-expectancy was very low. All that to bring the sacraments to England – to keep the flame alive. They boiled them up after they'd chopped them up. Come time, when they were here, they had to take an oath to say they'd go through with it. A few dropped out. So they made oaths, perhaps at the height of an initial enthusiasm. In a silly sort of way, we, this year's crop of students – we took an echo of that oath, and, in chapel, signed our names in a book to say we'd carry the faith to England, or some such.

Concelebrant priests enter chapel from the Sacristy severally over the course of perhaps ten minutes. There are a fair-few today. All wear the polycotton albs, and a purple stole. The words which are to come during Mass will read as follows from the book of Joel:

Blow the trumpet in Zion, sanctify a fast, call a solemn assembly:

Gather the people, sanctify the congregation, assemble the elders, gather the children, and those that suck the breasts: let the bridegroom go forth of his chamber, and the bride out of her closet.

Let the priests, the ministers of the Lord, weep between the porch and the altar, and let them say, Spare thy people, O Lord, and give not thine heritage to reproach, that the heathen should rule over them: wherefore should they say among the people, Where is their God?

Each priest makes his slow, preparatory tread to the consecrated altar. He bows and kisses the altar, then takes to left or right, to sit in the choir stalls either side the open sanctuary. Each sits and gathers prayer, as it seems through a life's trained conditioning. In moments, he's settled like boulders at the roadside and disappeared. Guest priests visit to teach. Or there might be a conference. Or for a bit of a jolly. They sit as in bath-chairs. Silence gathers. That deep, cultivated space where communion with God lives, and where it solidifies awesomely. They can be pretty good value at lunch, and over coffee in the gardens, when they come fresh with parish life into the blue sky. Though strange and always unexpected in the corridors, where it shines an unpleasant light. *Here we are at our make-believe, here we are on our make-believe shore...* Like lifting lids off houses – weird, domestic ways Mums and Dads have you wouldn't want seen – though poddle-socked ageing pyjamas are all in the mind with the baby-steps. (This is how we are.) By day we merely look institutional.

The word they use for priestly training is *formation*. This derives from the Latin *formare*, meaning *to form, to shape, to fashion*, or more basically *to train*. It isn't all raw and moist, though. Maybe it wasn't in any age – given human material to work with. If it takes a lot of cracking and discipline and pulling apart – maybe had we all been young and fresh it's still not destined to work itself out to the right shape.

The Mass bell sounds.

Adedokun, serving, precedes Father Gerry. (Old Father Gerry, from County Donegal. 'Alright, alright, I'll not be hurried…') Adedokun ever bears immaculate posture and the African knowledge he is right. It is appropriate Father Gerry is doing it.

I compose my thoughts and prayerfully. I have a place which is somewhere around my ribs and in front of my lungs – a reality which is where God can be checked. For such is God's audacity – such the gift. The rush of love can be permitted to flow – the known structure of Mass a pledge of safety. (This now draws to the pit of my lungs.) I confess – to the priests, to the religious sister, Sister Angelina, to the two boys the housekeeper brings to Mass, to the housekeeper, to the computer engineer, to the three handymen, to the gardeners, to a brace of nuns, to three consecrated virgins, to the cleaning staff, their hands carcinogenically raw with mops and chemicals. *And you my brothers… Y a vosotros, hermanos, que intercedais por mi ante Dios nuestro Señor.*

*

It might seem quite an odd thing to have wanted to convert to Catholicism. Given what I wanted and didn't want. Given the history. Given the dry state… I wasn't getting married. I wasn't on the cusp of divorce. I didn't have kids and no money and the local faith school. But it had been on the bucket-list years… When I am asked, which I often am, I might say to my interlocutor it had hovered about me – a more distinct reality – at the upper-left corner of my eyes – as I demonstrate – this by rolling my eyes to my upper-left.

In childhood, for a time, I came to understand, via my parents, that the Catholic Church *is* the Christian Church. Mum and Dad not doing God, I worked it out from such information I had to hand. In the news from Northern Ireland, for instance. That there are Christians on the one side, and there are Protestants on the other. Thusly the child-brain unscrambled it.

'So what are we then?' I once asked. Then, it seems, I recall an unknowing, *complicit* look – as between parents… That was on the canal boat, pre-teen, when clothes weren't a given, and we were all close-up with each other. Though not at the time, but in memory, also the time I first knew I was naked and stiff, because another look passed between them, and I, almost, halted, was getting told off. Until they realized I didn't have a clue what the issue was.

Later, nearing the end, and with an old suit on, Dad was spotted, head-up-high, walking to the Anglican church on Sunday. That was the same church where I was baptized – a C of E church. Mum said he went looking for a rich widow to marry. She can be tacky like that. She's only just now coming to terms with it. Even at that stage it seemed to me a violation of a basic truth about him.

I used to cross myself surreptitiously passing the local church. That was before I was free – and in London, passing the church on my way to and from the tube-station, where it was only a track, down the back of some houses and what-not, and it was quiet. I'd planted something precious and of value in a building like this – the possibly-twice I'd snuck to a Sunday Mass in high-adolescence – fifteen, sixteen. A kind of faith touched base with school trousers, school legs, and (sacramental – mild-adolescent-cigarette-high) Marlboro-light inhalation, dry October air. Though that was back of the Anglican church again, with the view of Wales and mountains. Which I loved – the smell of dung – cow and horse: local accents – green-field-sites-to-come – under-utilized paddocks – the odd horse. Of late, the town accent on kids is, at its finest, a dry and pure velar fricative, though, of late, I've heard in it a reedy staccato, compressed into bite-size machine-notes in order to sound at all – on, now, an eighteen year old. Though he might dress like a kid from Fame and sling his head back – striding, laughing. (*His* Dad – who drinks…) We share a surname… I had a copy of the electoral register… Anyway, childhood scenes, built of sandstone.

If there is a core to childhood, then it is not to be looked on directly, or it would glance off your dead-spot, and then it would disappear. Besides, so much is plain conventional. The photographs look okay. Memories hardly flicker into discontinuities and become set-scenes. The rooms look okay… One aspect chimes with Catholic faith: colourful cartoon picture-books depicting the ancient world. There is an illustrated Ovid – ancient myths retold. And two books I particularly treasured, which the library stocked in the children's section, down the steps, into the round. Life In Ancient Greece. Life In Ancient Rome. *Amavi, amavisti, amavit…* There was a Life In Ancient Egypt also, which lay outside of what I immediately wanted.

I was definitely Perseus. More generically: Roman Emperor God. I was also a slave. Not a real slave. A fantasy slave. A Roman Emperor playing at being a slave.

68

When no-one could see, in pre-pubescence, I dressed in my room in a white bed-sheet. I undressed and pretended I was tied to a chair I liked. The chair was painted white with purple stickers – an elephant, a rhinoceros, a giraffe, a hippopotamus. There were no locks on that door. I was eight. Maybe I was nine. I wasn't ten – the house was different when I was ten. *Like* slavery... Unaware a Roman slave was living-dead, crimes against life being unknowable, I would tie myself up and bend – coil over it. Pure.

It was not sexuality's ascent, though it was a world. The abnegation – to cleanliness. Perhaps then I knew my own baptism – the faintest fleeting heart of the reality in the sacrament – as I lay coiled – my neck and spine and – rear-view – buttocks, no thought of my anus – clean, exposed. Some incipient act of naked... Perhaps it was my own noise, the clatter in my own tongue, from which I sought respite; or the annoyance of their socializing play on the cul-de-sac; or, physiologically, psycho-biologically, ongoing substrate-upgrades clashed with a given code. Or my childhood bothered me, beyond what they stick on you, exogenetically stunned in Mum's womb.

I conceived and laid plans for a city – which I wrote out on graph-paper. And there were temples, the forum, and baths, the palace. And more sybaritic retreats: my Capri, my Villa Tomàs, my Tivoli. My *then* tradesman's – grocers' instincts parcelled out necessary tasks. And, as command-economies go, Tomàsopolis went wonderfully. A vision in marble, terracotta, depilated skin, philosophy and tunics.

It was not until my later teens I first visited Rome. Then in my twenties I got so far as Athens, and had a wander through the archaeological parks, and sunned my fantasy. In those days my vision ran high. I'd been on the islands all summer, and I looked like a bronzed twink, with the linen shorts, and legs. With the adventures of the islands behind me, I didn't need much from Athens. The heat and open-plan-time had by now taken over as the dominant reality. Like television, each day's succession of scenery looked by and large the same. I sat on top of the great hill, the Hill of the Muses, overlooking the Acropolis, and that was probably the one time I stopped and thought about it.

What I thought I might know wasn't much. A papier-mâchéd book-slew of bluff while a hot bath cleansed me. Yet my interest in God was piqued. The cultic world. Eastern Med at the time of Jesus. The obscure near-to-middle east. A few texts. Such scraps gleaned weren't very much. That there was nothing *new* in the Christian story... Attis, Adonis, Tammuz, Osiris... Mystery cult, fertility rite. Bound with death and rebirth. Scourged – there was even that preceding. Whipped they were to purify the offering – man-god – prior to sacrifice... Crucified gods-incarnate. Slaves substituted for three days the priest-king – and I recount this now sparingly. Spiritual life-pulse of the Eastern Med.

Or take *parthenogenesis*, for instance, virgin birth, in those days as mainstream as television... Or take the *parousia*... I read a website about what happens when a cult predicts the end of the world and it doesn't happen. What happens is the faith of the faithful intensifies. So that clears that up. Dissonance. An open space – between the real and the impossibly unreal – where faith lives. Psychology explains it. Ecstasy! Yes, that was all very good to know. I got that.

Once, on one of the islands, I took a quad-bike all over it, with the girlfriend, medically bonkers, I had at the time, whom I had to keep telling to hold on so I knew she was physically still there. We had a moment at one of the shrines, which had been brought within an early

70

rendition of Christian faith. But the thing is, and this is it, I *needed* this…
So the triune God was a neo-Platonic construction? Great! For it was
safer – it was better. *You could believe…* It forestalled the preposterous,
explained the yarn, gave the Christian story legs. It was like you were
believing without being a bit thick. *Yes!* so you might say. *Yes! And I
believe!*

That there once was a man called Jesus, I had no doubt. It seemed
unnecessarily fanciful to claim Jesus was all made up – whether through
honest, devotional piety or parlour-game nonsense. I *believed* an
originary life of Jesus… A prophet… Nazarite – maybe as construed.
(Nazareth didn't exist then – probably – the website said.) Son of God. (*A
son of God?*) Who walked and healed and preached in an abolished space
– erased by Rome in AD 70. Written out of time outside of history. At
which point, you might as well pray and believe. At which point, you
might as well turn it around, within the space inside, and get, logically,
Catholic, God the Son… *Breathe….* Take breath. The least probable
option. There is no disentangling an historical Christ from the Church
that developed him. The Church is true.

*

Three years prior to Valladolid, I, Tomàs, made a beautiful first
confession. The scene is pleasant: a gentlemanly London study. Here is
the armoire, here shelves and sets of books. *The Decline And Fall Of The
Roman Empire* occupies unabridged one full set among them. Here, upon
the fireplace, social invitations, of a kind, I thought, you can read with
your fingertips.

This is my teenage bedroom. The priest said it was a beautiful
confession. And it was quite a draw – love in the Catholic Church.
Permission: love again. I was never going to be a Catholic

fundamentalist. There *were* things which *would* mollify Catholic faith. But at this level, quietly, love forgiven – lapsed, disfigured, shamed – could start anew.

For five years, I lived alone in London. It was a good house, prestigious, and I liked to pretend it was a final arrangement, but I didn't own the place. I'd wander room to room and window-gaze. A quaint disengagement of rooftops rolled into the city lights. The house was cold – even at the height of summer seemed never to catch the sun. It lacked a woman's touch and could feel quite depersonalized. By and large inexpensively furnished, the look remained that of the absent landlord, whose tastes and proclivities thereby framed my own-life. He – the man – had a fondness for wooden toys, and oddly pleasing, tactile objects, such as used cricket-balls, which, with varicoloured bowls, vases, clocks, pebbles, candles, I rearranged on each pine shelving-unit, otherwise given to paperback books, in such wise as from any angle they satisfied natural proportion – logarithmically.

By way of wall-art, the better pictures had been taken away, and space-fillers substituted. No matter their intrinsic merits or otherwise, it was the incorrect sizing – the scale which satisfied least, and pulled the stitching apart, within the overall volume, leaving the walls with a look of neglect, like awkward, grammatical words within the metric of an unloved child's rhyme. (I resolved the problem with a handful of canvasses I painted. These were thrown away shortly afterwards.)

In the downstairs living area, there was a garden bench to sit on, or a futon. Indeed, the bathroom even then was the only involved place for reading, and that fed from a hot water tank and so didn't have enough proper hot water. (You had to use a kettle to top it up on an extension lead.) I did the hoovering most Fridays, and cleaned the cobwebs from the ceiling, but let the shelves with their books and the fetishes be. Little by little, the scope of life shrank. I'd stopped going into London. The windows single-glazed – car-engines rattled. I might count planes' descent into Heathrow when local atmospherics took noise from the miles of sky that way. The clatter of the letter-box alarmed me. The doorbell made me creep. And when the friend I liked got himself a girlfriend, that was that.

I'd liked that friend. I'd found the friendship sympathetic to love. Dave was twenty-one, at first, and quite bright… I'd liked how, when I pulled him, in the pub, he was reading with his little legs crossed – manspread… The way Dave's skater-boy pumps flexed – reminding me… Last of a line – it seems a fair bet that was a tipping point out of an age when you're still tooled-up to instantiate fresh love.

We'd played a lot of chess, smoked weed, and drunk Strongbow together. It didn't take long before I timed my days. The mornings I spent reading up on God – in Whom I had by now developed an interest. In the early afternoon, not minding the weather, I walked to the park, and around the park, the perimeter of which was exactly one mile. I took my tennis racquet down, for the tennis courts, to practise my serve, with PE-skiving solo-youths, and a basketball-gang of more socially edgy delinquents. God wasn't *out there* at the start, but when I had to go on benefits. My budget was five pounds a day. The empty-space, a ghost, came out inside me. The money-construction of human-self wasn't there.

The church was packed on Sunday. It was a diverse congregation, multi-ethnic, London village-sprawl. Big on the Irish too. Not so many Poles as you'd think. A spread of age – a remarkably broad demographic.

The church was of a size as to be not-quite anonymous, and I got involved with the charity fund-raisers, though one rather tall, rather proud, west-African lady barely shook my hand when we were all supposed to love one another. But they were crying out for readers. And once, when I did the necrology, death-day anniversaries and the recently deceased, I mispronounced in hesitant English an Irish name.

But I read beautifully. The microphone gave me back the entire church. I lowered my timbre – down within resonant thinking-ribs. My shoulders, neck, and the top of my head seemed to resonate also. Slowed to and so felt at a sub-morphological level. Though the speakers might sound quaint – somewhat educated, somewhat trained.

It was okay, not having any money. Except the house got a little damp, and I phoned-in the meter-readings. I was always checking the spy-hole before answering the door. I had thermals and a woolly hat. Joints of pork seemed forever on offer, and that took the chill off. I looked merely rugged in clothes that weren't built to wear-out and there was nowhere you had to dress-up for.

On weekdays, Father Guy led morning prayer, then after the nine o'clock Mass, Father Guy knelt before Our Lady to sing to her.

Salve Regina, mater misericordiae;

vita, dulcedo et spes nostra, salve.

Ad te clamamus exsules filii Hevae.

Ad te suspiramus gementes et flentes

in hac lacrimarum valle.

Eia ergo, advocata nostra,

illos tuos misericordes oculos ad nos converte.

Et Iesum, benedictum fructum ventris tui,

nobis post hoc exsilium ostende.

O clemens, o pia, o dulcis Virgo Maria.

It is a world away to think of it. That year – God's year.

Lady, Lady. *Theotokos*. This – this *word* having been (poorly?) translated *god-bearer*, not *mother-of-god*. The terms are not synonymous – though the verb τίκτω is ancient and implies an equivalence. For, dear, sweet Lady, how in this age of the genome can you be God's Mum? Were you there with the Father before all ages? Did you then redeem? Did the Word spring maternally – outside of time before time began?

Pray heaven it might be so. Nonsense thoughts. False categories.

Chapter Three

Father Gerry turned seventy last term. We had a feast, and the photograph we took was the funny. We did the thing with the quivering jazz-hands Father Gerry does when his thoughts reach their here-be-dragons moments. Everyone loves Father Gerry. He's a legend – the word disconcertingly middle-aged – public school – 'Sloaney' – though sounding on Julian's lips.

Legendary. Lege. (They – the youth say that still?)

We all look knackered – in the photograph. Eyes like olive-stones stabbed in an airport-blancmange. He is youthfully-disposed, Father Gerry, a good sport. His seventy years a lark. However, when he speaks about God, he becomes immeasurable. He must have smoked, once, and he likes his Duero. When he speaks about God, he isn't taking the mick, when his voice becomes more deeply profound than you'd have thought a contemporary body could get to. One Friday, when I wasn't in the gym, I got it in mind in a funny way to go and confess to him. I hadn't done so much a lad couldn't run past Grandpa, so waited stretched-out, sat on the bench in the corridor, matchstick-jeans and red-pumps laid-out straight, as though in moody contemplation, a gawky fact of body, slimmed to a cinched belt and a crease at the knees. The Rector passed, at the juncture of corridors, and paused to stare into the quiet space – the stillness in my form perhaps obscuring me, or the chiaroscuro suggested a form more akin to my perspective – to the inside view. A long, long moment, then

The Rector said:

'I couldn't quite see who you were!'

Me: 'Heya!'

The Rector: 'I couldn't quite see who you were!'

Then, once The Rector had passed, and having been seen there waiting, and, really, with nothing to offer confessionally, I thought maybe-not and I didn't want to fake it and I went my way.

It seems about right that it is Father Gerry ashing us. *For know that you are dust, and unto dust you shall return...* It seems consonant. At the ambo, rather than give a big spiel, Father Gerry says:

'There is nothing I can say to you now that you don't already know. I suggest, we have a few moments quietly with Jesus, and we say to Jesus what we need to say to him, and we ask of Jesus what we need to ask of him.'

There follows silence. Silence piled upon silence – until you could stay here – rest within – down-drawn like sleep's paralysis. A lower depth of silence – once we are fully inside of it. As it were then at rock-depth of serious prayer, which I assure you I go to albeit non-communicable, this is all froth-on-top, Father Gerry says:

'Jesus, you are our Lord and Master. Please take from us our difficult thoughts. Help us through the Lenten time ahead. Be our sustenance. Guide us to what is true. Let us be your disciples.'

(Personally, I'd like to think of Jesus as a mate. I don't buy all this kowtow. Like if your mate's your mate – you can say stuff and have a fight when you get pissed. If you can't have a fight with your mate, who can you have a fight with? It's flipping bollocks to say I'm going to kiss his feet afterwards: that was last night.)

77

Duly, we are ashed. Communion follows. Adedokun, serving, puts it all together, takes it all apart. Our thoughts rest, solemn, as we aren't asked to sing our way out of it. It is one of the good times. Quietly, just sitting like that, it's pretty good. Dry. All careful-minded. It seems they must see we are taking it the way it is meant to be – solemnly.

Lady, Lady.

We students leave for lunch, yet minding our tongues in the corridors. The priests have long dispersed… And there she is without us – there she squats. Blessed Virgin Mary: BVM. Her niche recessed in the reredos – over the tabernacle. A gnarled wooden thing, squat, as a latter-day Venus of Willendorf. Served with counter-reformational pomp to the weird faithful.

She is one thing – even the main thing – the college is known for around town. Our Lady Vulnerata. The Wounded One. This instance of BVM – who crops up in so many places. Hacked by English swords in Cadiz, when Raleigh put down the Spanish. She was dragged from her church and desecrated, the Child reduced to dust and bits of hands and feet, Our Lady's arms lopped, her face blunted. Thuggery. They must have had themselves a lovely time – butchering her. England's shame.

We honour her now. She was brought here circa 1600, at the request of college priests and seminarians, who hoped to make reparation for the insults to Our Lady, inflicted by Englishmen whom, with their Queen, they studied to save or betray.

We offer prayers. Each week she receives a rosary. And we recite the litany. Mother inviolate, Mother undefiled. Tower of ivory, House of gold… The fairyland bit of the dream – for the well-fasted. Mother so fragmented. Such apparitions, so many graven images, so much light. Odd to be a mother and pray to her. Queen of Virgins. Not like me.

78

Mother most pure. Touch of guilt, that maybe touches them? It is the cross, though, they clutch when they fetishize – Mary is just beads. Lady of lost time, Lady of history's lacunas. So multi-tasked. Who loved you all the way into this world. Stabat Mater.

Lady, forgive us for squatting you – carving you, painting you. Grandiloquent Lady. Good for when you don't have the words. *Hail, Mary…* Forgive the merely human. And let my cry come unto thee.

*

It is a quarter to three in the afternoon. There is no possibility of going to the gym, lunch having been a rare treat of carbs. And Sean did it for himself as he piled on seconds. The Rector, who endures a restricted diet, could hardly say to stop and to take the plates away. Anyway, He told us about waste – and I've seen all we send back goes straight in the bin. (It was kind of gross to see it and a little bit shocking.)

The Rector arrived late, as is entirely His prerogative, in harried capacity scanned the Refectory, and saw He must sit by Tomàs.

I said: 'Bad luck.'

The Rector didn't acknowledge that.

I placed my spread of fingers on the table's edge.

Eight years The Rector's been here, first as Vice Rector, for five years, before becoming Himself. Still, we all know, He reckons He's served His time. There are dioceses in England going vacant, so it was funny when a visiting Cardinal put Him down, saying: 'In Rome, you can spit out of a window and you'll hit a Monsignor.' That was in front of everyone, leaving the students to interpret the meaning of it afterwards. The career not working out, perhaps. Things not quite fulfilling the long-term plan. For He wants so very much to be a bishop. Often, one suspects He has just got off an unpleasant phone call. The tall Cardinal wrapped his hands about His shoulders – as if He were a little boy – laughing at Him.

I helped serve lunch and the pain in my wrist was manageable. (Braking on a turn when a kid threw a prank at me – head-over-handlebars – that scene.) It was when I returned to my seat that The Rector said:

'You do not look cheerful, Tomàs.'

'What would you have me do?'

'You might smile.'

'Shall I force one?'

'Tomàs, there is a gift of happiness. It is for you to share. Our Lord is Risen.'

'Good. I was worried.'

'What do you mean?'

'I have been thinking. About the darkness. Perhaps we feel ourselves particularly close at times to the spirit of the empty cave. Like a stone.' I clenched my right hand into a fist, and examined it. I opened it suddenly, let an imaginary weight, a ball, drop, then pulled the fingers together again, turning them upwards, clenching and unclenching slowly, then said: 'Perhaps a darkness here [as it were thereby to signify: this pulsating – beating hand] is a path to – .'

'Tomàs, it is not dark here; here it is light.'

I nodded once, to signify demurral, conceding a point, when there was nothing to explain and no point in attempting to. I took a quantity of pasta, which could barely have amounted to 200 calories, and fastidiously twirled a half-forkful. Lunchtime small-talk tends toward the esoterically banal. As a general rule, The Rector doesn't sit with 'us' (at 'our' table) but with the noisier elements – 'the children' – and less-reclaimed animal-properties down at the far end. It is presumably for reasons of contrast He prefers to be there. All bayed masculinities, adolescent gripe, Scouse grouse, mewling estuary. While here, we are pretty sedate – the mere fact of life less volubly quite confounding.

The Rector's special diet is because He is a bit fat. He isn't *that* fat. He's only mid-life fat. A high wind on the brink of exploding inside of Him. Nutrition For Dummies™ fat. No more pies. He could just as easily crash and lose it all in a couple of months or so, though His five foot eight and a half doesn't help matters. But He's decided to be bitter and long about it, addressing His plate of highly processed meat like an epidural, and steamed salad and wilted greens.

Three o'clock. ¡Buenas tardes! A post-prandial stroll seems about right, and could take in the beach. I have a quick wash. I rake what I can of lunch from between my teeth, with floss and an interdental brush, and rinse my mouth with Corsodyl. Perhaps it *is* age-inappropriate clothing… Expired-twink. Moreover, having survived the Propecia years. (So long, ye saggy Kikwear phat pants. Weep no more, ye Harrods-basement casuals.) Besides, it is plain to see I precisely identify mid-life. Witness Father Richard: 'That's a very bright lime-green T-shit you're wearing there, Tomàs.' To the which: 'Yes, it is rather wonderful, isn't it.' Such, so it might be, the proposition: this time in seminary. For one must, in a sense, self-infantilize. Because *it* infantilizes. That's what it asks you to do.

As when my *thirties* struck and I thought I'd better have a go *doing* my twenties, so now I, naked, dress with greater range, from celibate-skin up. I string a rosary through the belt-loop over my pocket. I get my woolly gloves and a woolly hat on. The foreign-exchange rate I'm getting on my Amex is *okay*…

Downstairs, the quad is fresh with bees and the scent of marjoram. Often we come here to pray. It is good to walk the cloister, which delights the eyes, and soothes, and, it seems, suites the trickle of beads through your fingertips, rendering this adopted act of prayer less self-conscious. They are gross, rather fanciful, as it seems quite pagan statues, though ascribed religious names. Willow trees draw a veil over the whole scene. That is like the garden when we had goats – I was nine, ten – and that would be the pond – the drainage – where the goats drank. A scent of rose and cyclamen. Under cover of moss, a fountain memorializes – saints. There is garden furniture as you might find in an English garden. It is overgrown a little and seems to absolve, a little, Spanish light. There are places to sit peacefully and reflect, and clear your head, to no particular goal or outcome, let your thoughts wash and dissipate.

I have on me a little cash for a beer. I can go to the supermarket later. I'll be wanting a walk later. It isn't good to stay in my room before the night has settled.

At the door I meet Henry, whose scarf *is* bright green.

I say: 'Hey.'

Henry stands by the unopened door as if waiting for someone. Henry is all dressed-up. (He is a window display. He's high-street. A notch above Next. Maybe Jaeger. Not Zara. Nor – preppy. He is not Polo Ralph Lauren or Banana Republic. Maybe Henry has his own special category? The *fabrics*, if not cut, look a bit better than your average.) Maybe he's hanging out to see who happens. Home-comforts – Henry looks like. Wholesome-brown.

He wears inexpensive brogues, which he said are 'stained' and look like he's stepped in a puddle. Casual-smart. A fine amount of fabric goes into him… The cable-knit cardigan is *nice*… though *new*… And you'd have to be Henry. It would not cost more than a mother could rightfully afford. And at the same time the throwaway-end of the youth-market wouldn't have suited him. (Henry is *not* Top Man, River Island… *Is he* Marks & Spencer?)

Maybe he wore it for Boxing Day? Mum, Dad, his sisters. Family warmth. More real than ineffable luxuries.

Henry's voice is a fluted arpeggio:

'Hullo! You've got the same idea, have you! Beautiful day for a nice walk! Which way you heading?'

'Well…'

Old chap. The road gleams white outside.

'Head along with you. Full of lunch! Rah. Look at that. Rrrr!'

So saying, Henry's hands splay, his fingers hook, and scrabbling to dig up the water, Henry lifts his shirt, untucking it from his jeans, and he grips and waggles his tummy. Which is porcine, hairless, save around the navel, where long, curling threads become pigmented, puppy-dark wisps. Henry's girth.

I *have* seen it before – at the poolside. He's put on weight since then. It overspills his plaited leather belt. It hasn't been to the gym since then. And there *has* been a lot of food.

Three days we all spent together last September at Country House. The pool wasn't quite long enough to swim true lengths in, so it was only play. Benedict pounding into it tirelessly – mounting the dolphin to kick around – and the sloppy octopus we somehow all took a turn to inflate for the minutes that lasted. It was warm still, the air comfortable after the pool. Sun and clean, fine air must have given us all a lift. September. And together we were peaceful. Our souls, as they say, yet unarrived from

83

England at a camel's pace. Sky-high – they must have trailed sagging after – a blue-sky view of the Bay of Biscay.

Henry's had yet to fill-out and to become a man's body. Great, broad shoulders, no chest, thighs like any stuffing had slid to his carves. An odd thing to look at it. The mass-distribution seemed that of a younger adolescent – if only by two years. But there was no provocation to challenge such under-examined – disappeared years. The scale – the size was wrong – but then *wrong* is wrong. Dysphasic. And hard not to think a little somewhat defused. Inexpert. Pubic. Adolescent. Simply odd. Parodic.

Henry is tucking himself in. 'Top notch!' he says. 'That what you say? Yeah? Course it is. Top notch!'

A great flash of natural affection in a sudden instant… Besides, there is no getting away from it. My smile a moment super-exceeds the 'natural'. And, truly, there is no cost to it. I've never been alone before, socially, with only the one of them.

'I was heading to the beach,' I say. 'I thought via Plaza Mayor. It should be about the right sort of walk.'

'The beach, huh?'

'Yes, I thought I would go there.'

Outside, against the wall, there sits on the pavement a man to whom Jon gives two stubby-beers and a sandwich each day. Henry and I turn, readying smiles, our faces to catch his, as though we are implied in the spirit of Jon's charity. Beyond, they are literally empty streets, as Spain endures siesta. The man sits immobile, knees bunched, his pumps twisted any old how on the pavement. Dirt like blackened oil has dried into his skin and his burst spots. It is uneasy to do nothing seeing him. (One failed, embarrassed instinct to offer a coin.)

84

We aren't saying anything: Henry and I do not have to mention it once we've passed. Subdued, we head down Don Sancho, and I steer Henry to the kerbside to cross. After an interval, Henry says:

'Look at it! Empty! Lazy ol' Spaniards, hey? No wonder their economy's down the pan! Where are we going?'

'The Cathedral is just through here.'

'No it isn't! It's up there, then…'

'Left?'

'Oh yeah!'

He giggles.

We cross and head along what is still a modern and boarded and shop-grilled and bricked-up street. Henry says: 'Funny, isn't it. It turns you around on yourself.'

'Lost in Valladolid.'

It becomes apparent Henry is amenable to silence, and not a bad walker too. We skirt the plaza which features the first of the magnificent buildings. Then in the backstreet it's again grilles and garage doors, paint-sprayed with 'for hire' – *alquilar* – notices, and overhanging concrete and balconies where people live. At the crossing, you can see right down to the Capuchin church, the vast concrete arch of it stamped on the side of a city block. The arch crops otherwise little-square office-block windows. It seems extraordinarily arbitrary design. Iglesia de Nuestra Señora Reina de la Paz. I don't know why I don't now say to Henry: *Look! Look! You can see straight through here!*

I've been to Mass there on Saturday. It strikes me – Henry is right – the topography throws you. But it wouldn't be to Henry's taste. Indeed, that church is exactly the kind of thing – church-wise – Henry loathes outright. You could never have enough lace with Henry. In class, he is forever doodling roodscreens in place of notes. The Rector smiles at this, and with the gentlest of reprimands: 'Put that away now.' The detail in the drawings is extreme and astonishing – they seem at once gorgeous, unfathomable climax, and jejune, ornate.

There's Henry's height as well. Henry is commandingly tall. He has the extra inch. And then, with his shoe heals... Moreover, the big thing about Henry is that Henry has decided that he is going to be posh. That is his cornerstone. That the determinant. That is Henry's fiction. And it is absolute. Whatever *it* – posh – is or might be, Henry's going to be it. To the point Henry exclaims convincingly: 'I'm not posh!'

And – all credit – I said to Henry too along with the rest of them: 'Oh Henry!'

It will be curious to meet him again in a few years, to see how the energy-spent might resolve in pursuance of it. We all in college believe in him – where all ready-fictions are up for grabs. It could be the Church has been discovered as an answer – that within the hierarchy there might be performed the grand swap – via mere social difficulty. Henry's voice, his vowels, his accent, spring remotely, south of the river in London, gain steam through formative years in the nice bit of Kent, and now veer through exploratory trajectories. He's working it out. The hunger to learn is palpable – even, it might be, ruthless. All style... Henry wants to know how to be more posh... All style and surface construct... Henry's Rome shines gold – as Caligula. As resplendent self-transcendence. (Nero might have sung it...) All style and where's the money...? Faith-imperial. As a latter-day Caesar's legatee.

So a modern world burns... *I want what you have* – Henry's most spiritual thoughts might say about posh people. And Henry's not knowing shit about class *must* be an enabler. Henry's not knowing shit about class

86

– the pez, the filth, the money, lebbage – an absolute boon.

He *looks* posh, buttered fresh bread, what with his teapot lips and his button nose. Henry's *skin* looks posh... He, too, is a convert to Rome, and he's retrofitted it. More so than I – it is a glowing capacity for make-believe. Wild-energy up to the hooves. And other fearsome quantities. Often, one discerns a time-delay while Henry adjudicates new thoughts – new information – not in order to distinguish the good from the bad, but the correct from the incorrect. For Henry's *turn* to Rome calls the shots on everything. He gets the Catholic Church. He gets the core-power and the heart of the faith of it. That your belief *be in* the Catholic Church. The mystical body of Jesus Christ: the Catholic Church. Not as administrative arrangement, or general group-hug. He gets that you *cannot* know Christ outside the Catholic Church. And any thought-adjustments he might make in relation to that be forgotten in the action of the instant he's making them.

Valladolid [B-aye-ad/th-oh-lid/th] is triune – Trinitarian – a city of triangles. The vast, extraordinary edifice of the Church seems to tower all over it. I imagine something like an interior view of a massive ossuary, all involuted, niched statuettes. City-lines – street-lines radiate from their pinch points, marked by a church or other significant building. Dry and undisturbed – cobwebs strung on leaves, twigs, branches, witches' fingers. Though more brutal streets stretch long and hard, the map could yet disconcert you through no apparent curves.

As we pass, I glimpse, only in a moment, the cathedral. There is a well-placed café down there, on the corner of the plaza. It gets the sun, and you can watch all the various skateboarding, even as the air is fresh for sitting out in, with a coffee or a beer or a gin and tonic. The cathedral is bullet-pocked, pitted like acne-scars, inside and out, though worn like a kind of choice, like something that needn't have happened. A rump of its initial plan, the cathedral was conceived and construction began at a time when Valladolid [B-aye-ad/th-oh-lid/th] was Spain's capital, then that moved and the money left, mid-construction. Henry and I maintain course for Plaza Mayor. Given time and sentimentality, you'd love the old colonnades, for there is nothing spectacularly awesome to take your breath away, and they might have supported a romance in an old film. It is a dignified town in many respects – the faded terracotta of the low-rise apartments.

At the corner of Plaza Mayor, Henry points across to the far side, and to the passages leading from the square. He says: 'Beautiful tapas, all through there.'

I can hardly imagine Henry exploring Valladolid alone. I have only thought of Henry as a person real to himself in terms of effects worked on other people. And, for a moment, I wonder if the college persona might be self-sufficient. I say: 'Oh *right*.' I think to add: 'Is that your Saturday treat?'

'Sometimes,' says Henry, mysteriously.

We cross the plaza, then into the backstreets, which are unknown territory. The sun is high, though the narrow streets keep the café fronts in shadow, and they are geared to exterior life. Henry's sense of direction holds better than mine. There comes a point the walls close over and there is nothing but paint and brick at street level. Then the sun breaks through again and it could be a city – just that there aren't any people here.

To walk B-aye-ad/th-oh-lid/th, you'd not get its being a university town. There are what must be university *buildings* visible enough. There is an old one shielded in wire and DANGER signs. We were told it is bad luck to count the number of heads (like in stone) on the columns. But there should be twenty thousand of them – students – because I checked Wikipedia. The university professor who visits said they are the most significant contributory factor in buffering Valladolid from The Crisis. Ten percent of the city population. Where are they?

Of those in college, most have not attended a university... Philip went so far as to say: 'I can't think of anything worse than attending a secular university.' All bar one other (remaining) and possibly Geoff. It seems altogether crazy to think about what that might mean for a person. *Not* getting away. Each day – that's it. As for here – they should be lording it round the place. Tote-bags full of books. High on Blackwells! In deep thought... Unremitting expansion. Humans in their prime. Adolescence. What do they do, for instance, for lunch?

Once in a while, by cold, crystal night, one hears warnings of youths. Once in a while, one encounters them. Entz-committee-arranged – on a trawl, sex-segregated, mummery of courtship, one gathers. They howl faint-heartedly, as one assumes to each the other, though I am between streets, unquantifiably proximate. Drifting youths. And some more formal chant they have – which I do not capture. At my window, I cannot distinguish their words, by night, looking out on the scrubbery. Innocent. Whatever they get up to these days... Who knows? Who *knew*? (A play on time (and mood) within the limits of English verb tenses (and mood) is insufferably limited. Spanish is better.) The boy at the bus-stop at Mum's by the Tesco. Last school year. Fifteen? As many as four girls together paid court to the ripening peach, who was smug-as-a-bug with it, this piece-of-luck he inhabited. And it could have been me-adoration Netflix-chill, and they fucked him and he fucked them, and they weren't competitive. Whatever it might have been. 'Thank you,' he said in a pretty voice, when they fell into the road at the car-park exit, at the Sainsbury's, and I good-naturedly slowed to wave them through where they shouldn't have been crossing. *Thank you. You're welcome.* Innocent tongue on him. Spiritual matter at that age? Who knew?

We come out at the main road edging the old town and running alongside the parkland at the edge of the river. We cross the road and enter into the park through a stone gateway. I have never been here. It is pleasant territory, a mix of predominantly deciduous trees, groomed box-hedging, grass that maybe does what it can to sustain itself. Urban fringe. For the old city stops at the river bank. Medium-rise gives way to high-rise tower-apartment blocks – over on the far side separated out like toothy implants. Bald-ugly – which clears the head. Their sparse functionality settles the brain. Flattens it. Modern. Pre-post-modern. Image of God in your mind kept from wandering thoughts too gargantuan.

Along the green river, where no fish could live, we pass the beach. Our accelerated steps become strides. We aren't talking either: it's better than that. We stride in deliberate synchronicity. I fall in with Henry, half my age, and, in turn, Henry is a gifted mimic. A great impressionist. Surely, you have to suspect, at his deepest level, he knows it is make-believe. A fake: Henry is a fake. And, thereby, makes royal fun, tantalizing Tomàs.

On love, twice a week, we students participate in what is called *lectio divina*, which happens upstairs in the Conference Room. With Father Gerry, we read a passage, of considerable length, of Saint Matthew's Gospel, then Father Gerry says:

'Let us lower ourselves into the text…'

And for minutes, we stare at the text real hard. Beyond the limits of textual history. You are not meant to interrogate the text. You are not meant to dig with it someplace beneath its declared bounds. All you are really meant to see is yourself – as God's word acts upon you – in translation.

A long while. When spotless – *Catholic* exegesis is frowned upon. Until Father Gerry brings an end to our suffering. Then the idea is love.

Father Gerry asks us to say what has struck us 'as it were downstairs'.

'Let's see what we bring to the light now. What's touched you? Any little ways in which Our Lord… speaks to us.'

All you have to say is: 'It just makes me realize how much God loves us.' That's all.

Or as Henry parodies priests and bishops with his Vatican II voice: 'Because God loves us. It is about love. We have the – love. And love, our God is love, it is all the love – this love – *this* is God we have…'

So now in *lectio divina* – . As Jesus sits apart with his disciples, and one imagines a tent, with perhaps a little fire, and walnuts and pieces of cheese, and the disciples wish to know why, to the crowds who are gathered outside the tent, begging a crust of him, Jesus teaches obscurely in parables. And Jesus answers the disciples, saying:

'To you it has been given to know the secrets of the kingdom of heaven, but to them it has not been given. The reason I speak to them in parables is that "seeing they do not perceive and hearing they do not listen, nor do they understand". But blessed are your eyes, for they see, and your ears, for they hear.' (Mark 4: 11-12)

For to those who have, more will be given, and they will have an

91

abundance; but from those who have nothing, even what they have will be taken away.

Inside, outside. Secrets. Jesus wants his cult inside. Business of the altar concealed by the roodscreen. Faith *in here*. Cultivated. Exclusion of those *out there*.

Odd to think: there was a cult of Christ before Jesus. There are Christian graffiti on stones that never knew a day-story of Jesus in this life.

Well, now, in class, maybe Kieran, who is from Plymouth, might offer a share of the flavour of his thoughts. The words bubbling out of him, tickled like fish, like a spinner at the end of the line in a mackerel boat:

'It just says to me [pause – and chuckle and pause – four beats:] how much God loves us.'

Lost now in wonder-tones: 'It's just – *how much* God loves us.'

Nice lad. Mid-twenties.

Conversation's end.

Except he hasn't said it enough yet. Must, then, emphatically express: 'It's just – *how much* God loves us.'

The obvious words too much for him. He chuckles again.

It's put the kibosh on anyone with anything to say *maybe more specific.*

Ergo:

'It's like a love so immense,' perhaps now Geoff says, 'that we're just left dazzled by God's love.'

Back to Kieran: 'It's even when we don't understand, God never stops loving us. We are so stupid and God never gives up on us.'

Geoff: 'It's bonkers to think about.'

Kieran: 'And all we can do is offer our love to God in return.'
Kieran laughs: 'It's the best we can do! Can we respond enough? Can we love God enough? If you think of God's love and what we have to offer God back – It doesn't exactly balance!'

Geoff: 'Ah, brother, you give what you can. God knows that. He loves us!'

We walk close by the river. It is pea-green, clogged with basic life. It doesn't seem to flow. Slew of human life emptying into it. Farmland irrigation – most probably. Fertilized bright green patches scorched to dust through summer months. It seems unfeasible complex – eukaryotic life could survive the choked river.

I say to Henry: 'Funny colour.'

'Horrible, isn't it. Shouldn't be allowed.'

'Perhaps isn't. Odd what they see and what they don't see.'

'Yeah. *Beautiful* things. Beautiful. Then: *bluhr*. Monumentally hideous. I mean… Ha! Hideous!'

I make laughter too. Braced by Henry. I know what he means. While such lordly aesthesis as Henry's chimes ever but distantly. Yet. Even so. In thought, perhaps. In its abstract substitutionally. Dry I feel today. Henry's whole face giggles. Life! He slings his head back: Spain's flamboyant tragedy! He is so high… We come to a further recreational facility, a small park, and press on ahead of it. There are geometric shapes arranged, formed from painted metal, random municipal art or a designated area for supervised play, then picnic tables and happenstance trees. The feral thread of greenery lining the path gives out on us.

'I've never been this far.'

'Neither have I!'

'Shall we?'

'Onwards!'

'Vamos!'

'Vamos!'

The city we don't know disperses and fades. Our eyes keep taking photographs, *click, click, click*, through scrubland, wired enclosures, low-intensity modern homes, and those which are more like renovated outhouses. Then, at a dual carriageway, the city stops. Ahead, the river's wooded trench runs through countryside through and toward hills. The scrubland is littered quite heavily. This, then, only confirms me and him in our prejudices.

We are stood at the roadside. We look back and forth. There is a lot of sky, and traffic on the road. Looking back, it's at any town's threadbare margin. If you were lost here, probably you might go the way we'd come. If you had nowhere to go, you'd probably go that way. I say to Henry:

'About turn?'

'It looks as if that is it.'

Not now, but at some point, there is enough in the view to suggest going further. There is nothing in that thought – obviously. Miles and miles. *Upstream* is it? Though at the same time, thought of the river has stopped. Dust-land. Cars and that's that. Roads in all that dusty space because they had to put something there. This is the edge. It could be nice to say something. Or, in college, that spirit could have us both execute a military turn. Peas in a pod – or not so much as we are stood here. *I am – you're not. You are – I'm not.* When we look to one another, we touch eyes at least in glancing fashion, before we head off back.

At five, in college, standing duties are resumed. There is prayer in chapel, then a spiritual conference, a talk, in the oratory. This is led by a visiting Franciscan priest, and concerns the way of poverty. It's good, and each of us finds something personally important to take from it. As so often, it is helpful simply to receive an intuition of a visiting speaker's clarified-pure humanity, and so too his holiness from what perspective he's got to that works for him. It is such time I hoped for. I can see myself imagining myself being that priest. *What if...?*

If... in all the grit and granularity of this place. *If...* in the human-linguistic of this place. *If...* in a – mid-phase-transitional... Within the 21st century logic of this place!

When you might be all happy believing in a half-assed way, and The Rector has to go and say anything, so it goes *snap* like a bird's wing, all bits of reality cracked in pieces. All that was living – the true form. *If... then...* If – spiritualized essence like that priest. And science, and the God of this seminary... Two worlds – when it is hell to connect. Though, in void, as a matter of tentative uncertainty, each world mutually acknowledged in otherness...

(If a Rector falls in the forest, and there is no seminarian to hear, is anything real?)

With supper, we are able to drink quite a lot of wine. (The priests and any consecrated guests dine apart from us.) Wine is important. At this stage of the day, one is apt to thirst considerably for plenty of wine. And initially distributed quantities per table might seem restless, limiting, but you can go and beg more from the kitchen, though the nuns rag you.

Incidentally, Chapter 40 of Saint Benedict's Rule permits each

monk, humanely, his bottle of wine. We are allotted two bottles per table
– iffy white and okay red. This evening, at 'our' table, both are fresh. I
uncork the red while we are standing at the tables prior to grace. With the
cork's pop, I pleasurefully sigh: 'Alleluia.' Then whisper sharply: 'Oh
pants it's Lent.'

Francis sings – *sotto voce* – in ordinary Mass tones: 'Amen.'

I – *sotto voce* – say: 'Glug, glug, glug.'

It is a bog-standard and somewhat metallic Duero. But it's wine.
(On special occasions, they wheel-out for us the produce of the college's
vineyards, which is very superior stuff.) The white is okay with a splash
of the gaseosa, if you really have pushed it with the nuns of late. Geoff
has us all waiting while we all arrive, then it's for Adedokun to say grace,
the job of the server at Mass on a weekday. With that, chairs scrape, and
sixteen borderline-heathen backsides crack their tonnage – full of day –
smack-down on them. As each pent-up day explodes. Our noise... As
when a microwave-oven explodes on its insides. Like Yorkshire-puds and
farting gravy and sausages blowing on a microwave's insides. Like sage-
and-onion stuffing. Like tinned stew... Bizarrely, English lads, English
noises.

This evening, Geoff sits with 'us' at 'our' table. Geoff claims the
seat like this were as natural as anything. As is entirely Geoff's right. As
is entirely Geoff's prerogative. There being no rules about this. Indeed,
technically, the rule runs the other way, meaning we are meant to mix
things up a bit, for the community, and really it's me and Francis and
Alex and Paul and Jon who are the stuck-in-the-muds – staking time with
our senior moments – *out there* – sedated, knackered, spent – as we mull
upon each day's end – in vicarious territory. It is extremely menacing
behaviour on Geoff's part. For such a move disturbs the order of all that

is decent substantially. Some monstrous scheme of cunning, one must suspect, blind-sides us. For it is a hive-environment. To say 'yourself' is merely by extension to gesture toward the collective. And blocked, unrelieved adolescence, which overwhelms, rolling over you.

As often as not, our evening feed is child food. It is the stuff of the multi-hued, poly-chromatic aisles, a great bulging breeding-woman's shopping trolley, such stuff as what gets advertised on TV. England. Not much there. Better off with God. Or it's one of their more full-on bat-shit-Spanish creations. The nuns have way too much time on their hands. And theirs can be a warped sense of humour. You can see the little horrors giggling when you fetch the trolleys in.

Tonight, though, I am off Refectorial duties, and Julian and Philip are on. (I don't mind the job: it presents opportunities to do what I can to endear myself.) Platters of salad drop askew to the clattering tables… *It might be* quite sneeringly dismissive on Philip's part – Julian's just copying. *It seems* the hostile gesture *might* confess deeper matters *than mere* pointed aversion to menial service. But it won't get back to The Rector. Some quality – swollen grudging rage – all mangled, mucked-up and wonky-set. But, if Philip eschews empty ritual, perhaps it's just his way of making us feel 'at home'.

The corporate groan arises: 'White asparagus!' This is mock disgust – it roars like the opposite of any antipathy.

I pour for myself a measure of wine, then Francis receives the bottle, and I say: 'Wait for it, wait for it…' Hand raised concelebratory. Glug, glug. A taste of it. 'Now you may speak.'

Geoff raises his plenished glass toward me, as though it were in silent proposition of good health. I draw deeply on the wine, and when the bottle is returned take a refill. I do what might be done with the salad.

I tear my bread and dip the morsels in olive oil, mashing them slowly, with tongue, with teeth.

I have no particular feelings either way concerning the white asparagus. It is slimy going down, and comes with a *yellowing* aftertaste in its canned vinaigrette. People tend to push their food around at supper and send a lot of it back, whether in the slops buckets or on the metal serving platters unattempted. Either way, it all goes straight to the bin. When you see them doing that, the cleaning staff rather than the nuns, it can be unsettling. No-one is hungry at this hour – the day is spent. Even so, the thought of food curls over and dies some more in your stomach to witness it. The day's rougher edges with wine smooth. Pieces of the day, like ancient hardship, grind around the table like six o'clock pints at a ruminative public bar. But you can't linger at supper: come ten to nine, they'll be getting impatient for the washing up.

Geoff is *useful* at table. Shiny-eyed – a gargantuan slob – Geoff'll wolf it down for you when appetite fails. 'Look Boys!' he'll say. A tape-worm. Wriggle it over his mouth, a prawn, for instance. Then lurch about the tables as the Spirit moves, fishing for scraps and delicacies. Cold, leachy fish and the undercooked belly pork, even those cubes of pure pork fat they boil. Greasy-fingered acquisitions hang delectably suspended – Geoff's broad upturned slavering mandible yawing. It can be odd to think Geoff isn't lavishly pissed *all* the time. He glows each day, and he never looks dry. He shines by night – he glistens. Nor can there be much doubt they'll make him a bishop one day. (LOL – Geoff as Pope!) Part Jabba, part hut, part workman's shed, part vast, misshapen Labrador… He likes to sit exactly in the way, and round you up.

When Geoff says: '*Listen, pal…*' it could be anything. *It might be* a grave religious error he's seen in you. *It might be* he's just won the lottery and here's a million quid. In the evening, and into the night, he pours with sweat. You meet him in the small hours as, slip-shodding his great, flattened feet, he walks an interminable cycle, round and round in the upper corridors, telling his beads.

It is said Geoff's as soft on the inside as ever they might be. Henry said he is easily hurt. When Geoff's repented years, perhaps, draw blood in him. By his own account, Geoff has been to the bad and come back again. By his own account, Geoff has been to the very bad… Brother, Geoff has been a sinner. Geoff has sinned. But what *actually*…? On a scale of…? From, say, little Cormac's first saying sorry to Jesus, to, say, some kid's childhood robbed by the very same priest who said Mass and put the Communion in the morning on the boy's tongue. Probably, Geoff basically means he'd shagged around a few slags, drunk too much, powdered his nose, and skipped the occasional Sunday Mass. There is no reason to suppose it got exotic.

Who is this man hanging onto his rosary as if for life?

Geoff is apt to corner yours truly for a late gin – 'Come and join me, brother!' – Spanish strength, easy on the tonic. Late on a Friday night. Or Sunday, if there's football on. Inevitably, one succumbs. A right royal tedious pain in your unconfessed arse it might be. Still, one wonders, dare not probe, clueless as to what any terms of reference might be. A line in the bogs – all skin and designer clothes. And drank and fought and fucked… Had Geoff been there? Has Geoff transpired that reckoning? Jesus saved Geoff. It was the most over-bearing submission in the entire world.

But then Geoff's world is all animistic. Demons clog the air. Geoff disowns the obvious fraud of less spooky volitional capacities. The priests love Geoff. The Rector *fancies* him. Geoff supplies – the want, the

99

authenticity.

At unusual times, you might catch Geoff bowldlering into the corridor through the Vice Rector's office door. He'll be saying, 'Thank you, Father,' in briskly conclusive administrative fashion. Thank-you in the sense of thank-you for doing that for me. He seems buoyed and unusually emolliated. Geoff being elected student-representative – one of their little talks… Considering the odds of your being there at just the right time in order to catch these moments, Geoff must be doing that a hell of a lot.

Is he spy or is he *agent provocateur*? Has *everything* I've told Geoff, late, gone the way of the Vice Rector? The morality here would be all skewed and messed about. I cannot fully remember exactly the things I've said to Geoff, however it's a fair bet some of it has been true.

Or Geoff'll be corralling people into the common room to watch TV, and always sliding against you, like there never is adequate space. Or he'll call order at supper to preach – to *proselytize* some new prayer – it'll be anti-abortion, or an ex-gay event. I made a mistake and said to The Rector in honesty: 'I know I shall have grown in spirit when I have learned to love Geoff.' And might have added to myself privately: I know I shall have learned to love myself that bit more when I have learned to love Geoff.

I analyse: My antipathy is something *in me*.

The salad is messed to oblivion, and most of the red wine drunk, but no-one on the table next is drinking theirs. Julian and Philip lug plates to the trolleys… And with the main course – a shift in the experience of being occurs. It's different. Entering into a slow world of low-expectation – like hospital trolleys – gurneys – old people stacked in the hospital

100

corridors – . *The food is breakfast…* Bacon and fried egg, black pudding, tinned beans, tomato and hash browns, sausages, mushrooms. Those nuns… Bastards! Boom, boom! Drawn into being as one, the Refectory howls exultant. Wimpled bastards!

There follows time quite simply mouth-breathing – simply beholding it. Then Geoff fills up and starts to cry. Geoff smiles in a sort-of choppy way, then takes hold of a plate and implements, and starts dishing it out.

'Come on, bruv,' he says. 'Pass us that plate.'

Are we, then, a thought insists, bought so biddably? I know I am being unpleasant. My brain is. (Fundamental process – fundamental wiring *is* being unpleasant. Not *me*.) Not wanting. In the manner of a big sulk. (Here is the train and here is the tunnel… 'No, no, no, Mummy!' Little-boy lips in a vast-ledge.)

I decide it is definitely bad for me. I pass my plate.

'What wine goes best with breakfast?' I gaily say.

Brain. Warm fat explodes – exploded.

Decisions which might later seem insane in time seem rational. That we are here for accountancy purposes… I know, I know. That we are maintained for the sake of the seminary's assets, which otherwise revert to the Spanish crown… While bishops of England and Wales take their sweet time trying to think what to do with it… And yet, given such hazing, gaslighting, goal-post-moving, we students diurnally endure, one must believe as, fathomlessly bestial, each human-brain labours to birth its illusion – its consonance.

I don't want to do it – it is *morally* disgusting. But I chomp down on it, slaver the first bites, then keep eating, gorging, fleshy as hell on it, utterly inured to it. My eyes strobe. The blood in my arms quivers. No-

101

one speaks now.

Later, alone in my room, I put Radio 4 on. I check Facebook – I don't post anything. The radio is one hour out, though we are half-an-hour west of London. Spain runs on German time. That's since Franco. The Greenwich meridian passes, give or take, through Barcelona, 576 kilometres east. Today, solar noon was at half past one. Sunrise 07:48. Sunset 19:14. The days imperceptibly lengthening.

I give myself time in the bathroom mirror, to dig with an interdental brush for the bacon-fat painfully. Then I rinse with Spanish mouthwash, and all the bits come out from between my teeth. (It is disgusting to contemplate when it does this after a day not eating anything.) I look into my face and into my own eyes.

This calms me. When everyone reverts and it gets fundamentalist, still sanity-plain is the mirror's eyes, beautifully green, like winter cabbages, looking back at me. Where love's definition of God informs me who that Tomàs is. *Guapo*. I look good for my age. Such fluff and swill on my insides quite suddenly negligible.

I, Tomàs, look good. Which was a teenage discovery. The teenage-mirror, framed in pine, hung over my fireplace, down which the Easter-wind howled, a full complement of teenage condiments – body, face, nails, mouth, hair – pleasingly arranged, as was my teenage-view of towering birch and sycamore foregrounding the Welsh hills, on my teenage mantelpiece, also home to experimental fantasies, oil on canvas, tubes of paint laid out on the hearth as a spectrum, with candles, joss-sticks, pine-cones, ash-trays, driftwood, a vase of lavender, and other such girly bric-a-brac. My wire-thick, lustrous hair was all ringlets in those days. Prolonged mediation with Mum's hair-dryer transgressed

102

natural limits. But it would all boing back like a youth. I look hot in the photographs.

My eyes settle me. Tomàs's eyes make Tomàs unafraid. To look inside – when *they* conspire to addle and confuse me, such that a man might be brought to distrust himself. My eyes tell only honest messages. Each time, I know fundamentally, Tomàs is okay, when I check on how Tomàs is in the mirror.

One thing I do is go out nights. Never for more than an hour, and it's only round the corner, but it is life apart from what we call our community. Weeknights, I am often the bar's only customer. Tonight, I intend to begin a Lenten diary.

I put my laptop to sleep and get my woolly-grey beanie hat and my rucksack on. I have in there my new book, which is to be my diary. The book's paper is unlined, chunky-thick-smooth, parchment-style paper – though acceptant of a school pen – a cream Parker loaded with Waterman brown ink from a bottle – and to the extent of its being almost rough-cut at the edges, for the authenticity.

I sign myself out at the door, on the pad, so I won't get locked out. It's half-past nine. Really only eight o'clock – solar time. (Though politically bad, it breaks no stated rules – technically – going out on your own like this.) The night-weather is cool and in the street it is amber dark. They are early nights still – the clocks have yet to change. It goes dark around a quarter past seven. The pavement is clear – and cold.

Earlier, at sundown, people gather in the little plaza over the road, where there are benches and things for the kids to do. Boys play ball against the shops' metal shutters. But this isn't a place you hang-out nights. Lower down, and everywhere, midweek bars are empty in the

103

sense of zero. This city must have been drained of cash. Though small, it can hardly be said to be lacking in population density. Or they just aren't that sort of people – in which case, why the bars? I have scoped them all – it seems like. Empty of the day-earned money looking for solace – or – is it? – emptied of a social need – trickling out through your room's walls into the midweek streets, bars.

The bar I like, and which I've made my local, was a good find practically the first day last September. First thing you do in a new city: establish base. It is, howsoever unintentionally, strategically positioned: close but in the opposite direction to anywhere anyone in college might walk to. Turn left, you get to it; they turn right. The ant-routes about the place would never allow it. They wouldn't come here. Plus which, it is a dirty, urban, city-road, high-rise fringe and that below. Shop-fronts all sell random things. By mood, you might kid yourself you're in the lower east-side. There is even a cinema, though it looks like the setting for a film, some bleak, French, dystopian near-future, and the films are all foreign films dubbed into Spanish.

The windows of the bar-café are frosted at eye-level. The interior well-past basic and firmly into grotty. In the wall-art, there are off-the-shelf nods to a bar-claim to a brand-identity. Big stencilled polka-dots – black on white. And a fruit machine. A string of old men hold fort around the bar afternoons. Their remains remain. They drop their shit about their feet, like it would have been rude not to, and it sits there, maybe until morning, sprayed about, twisted bits of paper, scratch-cards and cocktail-sticks, all like a car's front-end spattered with pigeons' and seagulls' muck. There *is* food, but catch one glimpse of the cook... A sizeable man, like a sewer, with the welfare bum-crack, there is a lot of him not to have washed, him or the clothes he sags-up in. Fattened and penned – like one of those poor sows you see in animal welfare films, clamped to the floor on their sides so the piglets can feed off them. Illegally unhygienic – it has to be.

Now a regular feature of this hour, I tend to eat the slivered-anchovy expressed on a lozenge of bread they offer me, though if I catch them in time, and express how full I am – hands-to-belly pain, in a sympathetic-gesture toward retrospectively the meal-time scenario – I get let-off with a scooping of some kind of *feed* or pop-corn.

Apropos sacerdotage: I have been nice and polite and put a good spin on things, and they've been fine because I'm mad and foreign. The girl once giggled hilariously and almost gave me a free pint when I pronounced Valladolid as a native might. B-aye-ad/th-oh-lid/th – the weight on the first trochee. Two young people work here, one at a time, a young man and a young woman. The TV is always on, usually with the same game show, always involving Spanish words, daft clues, missing letters, and often *a drop*, when they fall through the stage *and scream hilariously.* And the beer is chilled, comes in frozen, gelid *jaras,* slushed – the glasses being kept in a chest-freezer.

Now we have our little routine:

Tomàs: 'Hola'

The girl: 'Hola'

She has the glass out of the freezer, under the tap, and eyes me cocky as anything. I say:

'¿Que tal?'

'Aci, aci. ¿Tu?'

'Buenos, gracias. Pero cansado. Ha sido un dia muy largo.'

'¿Si?' And then she says… And then she gives her little cock-eyed look, which is full and yet un-round – *shining* on my right, while compressed – *slitted* on my left like a half-fingernail. And she says again, slower: '¿E-stud-i-as mucho?'

'¡Ah!' I so-so – hands. 'Aci, aci. No que mucho que preferiero. Pero…' I shrug, obliged for complicated reasons to express root dishonesty – all the way down to the core – and the want of a true confessor, and of natural language. Hoping she'll accede, but she continues to look at me, sharp about these things.

She says something more to herself, while the beer pours, not expecting interaction at this point. A wise and tolerant teacher. I like how she has a brain. I like how she seems to indicate I have too. Then I take my beer and am duly dismissed. She gets on with her stuff – a puzzle she has in the paper.

I am alone here and sit at the table I like. Maybe in exceptional circumstances, I might have a second beer, after at least an hour. But it isn't like England – it does funny things to my head. For all the squalor, there is a neatness, an order about it. A great, blown, beery, egotistic squall wouldn't fit in here. I like and respect her. I want her good opinion. And one beer is treacly and rich already.

Anyway, I sit at the table I like. In terms of the arrangement of space, the café's blind-spot, and on the cusp of nothing. A natural point, it seems. A clear view of one of the televisions. Hidden from the door by the fruit machine. For natural-sense – the time-alone. One might say, for the artistic disposition. And yet recall such meditative afternoons back home in the light of dust and a pub's carpet – so flavoursome that my dog, who was off the leash so she could socialize, once turned circles in the manner of a dog who is about to poo, and so I leapt up and picked her up and carried her to fall on the marsh, just over the road, where she pooed. It was a near miss and can you imagine the irrecoverable

106

embarrassment? Where on a Friday-night, boys wearing Adidas trackies don't get ID'd.

And I have my new book. I get it out from its plastic. Definitively quite-posh Spain: an El Corte Ingles carrier-bag. Tourist-posh. To protect, and to seal it up, in the jogged-about rucksack. I bought it in the El Corte Ingles. It was on seeing it that the idea came to me: to keep a Lenten diary. I'd had no intention of giving anything up. Well, how stupid. Chocolates, crisps. Meat could have been good, but there was others' inconvenience to think about, and it would have been showy and see-through fake, disregarding the mortification in the eating. The gym, or a day without wine – imagine. The news – over the radio: the BBC news – but I didn't think of that. So I thought I'd give-up thought and time – and more than that – as I'll put it if anyone asks.

A Lenten thing. Self-examination in relation to – all this. Here I am, Lord. Knots and tangles. By way of further justification, it has been put to me that it can be a good thing to journal. The priest who said it to me used it as a main verb: to journal. He wore Roman chasubles, and quoted in Greek, back in January. Own-time. It seems not-bad-advice to cling to. There are other of the visiting-priests who talk about making sense of things. Often, they seem as if they want to confide a piece of knowledge – to just one of us, maybe, and then whatever it might be, it will have been passed on. *Are you sure?* perhaps they want to say. Over drinks, or as the visiting-priests linger, inexpressibly possessed, each-one his spiritual pearl, which re-arises in such context-revisited of seminary. In the quad, or at the edge of the garden, when there isn't any small-talk, and they turn and get an eye-full and drink you in. They perhaps want to say that this rabbit-hole doesn't yield happiness. Ache to give something. But holiness is always alone like that and it doesn't speak. Aches when it

107

means to – kills when it pretends to. Is in fact solitary. Own-time. A betrayal of The Rector – might not go unpunished as such.

In its own tacky way, it is a beautiful volume. The book has an allure to it. Fat, hard, padded. A good Christmas gift for a literary cousin – male. Engrossed in silver, elfin, tracery. Scrolls, leaves, curlicues – all upon a variegated aqua-marine. Oh it is tacky enough! With two magnetized metal clasps, and two ribbons, one gold, the other red. But it is thick, creamy paper, which takes a proper pen.

I open my book to the first page. Smooth paper. I can hardly hold a pen, what with my wrist being all fucked up. Bottling at speed on a hard turn when those kids leapt at me. Pranking. Teenage kids huddled in rain not taking drugs yet. Lolling in the Sainsbury stairwell when it really was pissing-down. Their velar-fricative – how the football game went down to pennoes and that. (Overhearing them.) Distinctly of-that-town local, though with more than a shadow of Liverpool Football Club.

I run my hand over the paper, at ceremony, like a minor-Royal. Accepting the blessing from it. I mean only to write on one side of it. Probably, as I write and as my writing degenerates... Probably, for all best intentions... For it should not become a rough-book. (Everything always is. Once, I saw the most beautiful book in Venice – in a shop. It was leather-bound, and the most-beautiful paper I ever saw.)

Without further ado, I head the page, in brown: 'A Lenten Diary.' Then beneath, justified left: 'Ash Wednesday.' Then stop. I cap my schoolboy Parker pen, and close my eyes. When I open them again, I take a mouthful of beer, and fix my attention straight-up on the slung TV.

*

Once upon a time... There was a young man called Tomàs. Then, once another time, a middle-aged man called Tomàs signed-up to the

Catholic Church. But the story begins a long time ago – humanly speaking.

For faith seemed possible. Once upon a time... Once upon a time... Each day – and what with the age-inappropriate clothing – it seems close. It's true – it stripped me. There was – *nothing*...

Once, then, Tomàs – *I* was fourteen... It was Ry who first drew me there. Ry didn't go to my school; he went to the Catholic grammar up the motorway. But Julia knew him from church. Ry was younger than me, evidently pre-pubescent, one mad day, but we never articulated that. He was taller. And blonder. And he had a big head. Pretty and weird at the same time.

Ry was of an age when his tennis-racquet cover played double, on the one side for lead, on the other for bass. My being – fourteen, fifteen. And while none of this seemed strikingly other-most, it was like being children. Besides, Ry was living-text cute, with no groggy undertow. Kid-A. We first met at Julia's. I first become conscious of Ry in Julia's room. And in the whole downstairs of Julia's house. A modern new-build. There were limited-edition lithographs Julia discussed, and an enormously long sitting room, the depth of the house. A bar – a carbonated soda-squirt on display. Solid, plain furniture, pine or beech, of a kind I have later come to think of as Catholic. I snogged with Julia once, at the end of summer, when we had to go to school next day. There was minimal iconography in the hallway, and a picture of the Pope.

I decided, then and there, Ry and I were going to be best-friends. There were the three of us, mucking around in Julia's room. I watched Ry give her a kiss as she straddled him, pinning him down. *Submit.* He snuck a cheeky kiss – smiling, upwards. I watched that... Razor lips. (How could he do that?) Ry was perfect. Then we went for a walk.

109

We did a lot of that: walking. Around near where we lived, village had rolled into village, a fat, wandering ribbon of flatland squeezed between the joins of marsh and the arterial road and planning-restricted farmers' fields, though it was not so built-up back then. A seventies-eighties suburbia gave out directly on woodland, the farming, boggy spaces, and all the fields you could play in.

The heart of the main villages was pretty rough, while the newness of the newer residential developments seemed clear-headed and optimistic in those days – bright and unconfused. Most of the building has stopped there now, apart from in people's gardens. There are, now, rusty old signs up in fields, one day hoping to be housing, choked with thorns. Other under-utilized land has been wired off and given to cash-crops. Even where the mines were, and the land unstable, they've built to the limit. There are roads left over, though, where it's a small ring of two dozen bungalows forgotten and circled by big, empty fields, and it's like time-travel into a different world.

That was a hot summer. England blazed. Not just in the way that it's memories of childhood. The air itself, each yearlong day, felt hotly supportive of the becomingness of it all. There are memories of pumps tramping black, sticky tarmac. Ry's were mixed-up, pudding-coloured, kiddy-coloured hi-tops. His legs went on forever, and we wore slender Ocean Pacific Bermudas, and in the evenings Pepe jeans, which we rubbed with stones to create the worn spots, and big, loose, white, slogan T-shirts, though a variety of musical forms coexisted. We were brooding to Marillion and waiting for Prince.

Developmentally, it's fogged – a shapeless, catatonic, unreal gloom before this time. Since – twelve? There is a hole within life where – *that* Tomàs didn't do people – friends. There was school – and all that there. But I remember it was summer's approach when I thought – I had better do something about it. In a way, then, Ry comes at a point of sharp focus. In other ways, there seems a fair degree of sifting through people – until it came to pass that a set formed… This through decision and complementarity – not just local habit.

And when you're sixteen, seventeen, everyone comes-out unwrapped. Social structures get their correct shape. But it was then, that summer, for a moment, an individuated human life became sharply distinct. And the form of it, like an idea, finite. A piece of life cut-out from the inter-relational. With Ry, at fourteen, fifteen, there first seemed an exact and a thought-yielding edge to it. Skin of the known and the possible. Ry's skin.

Mostly, to remember, I must have been more or less simply immersed in the flow and drift of it. The rope-swing over the brook at the back of Ry's house. We had crossbows and air-rifles. Bikes. Music. Walking, walking, walking. Walking like they're forever doing in films based on fantasy – books, novels, while we discussed such. Always the level of talk at that level when you're only just getting to know someone. Always in concord of shared belief in a pre-existent – a privately owned world. A commentary on all of it – our worlds – already beating and pre-equipped. Like sharing your heart. Holding your heart in your hands from your chest and holding it out to a person. And, though memory hovered around, at the time, observing all this, it was happy, passively spectated for a period. And any remaindered thought hadn't blinked, didn't feel left out and isolated, didn't grasp.

That came and happened. Slowly, and without any words. The impulse from the chest – from the base of the chest where the lungs quiver. Only, with Ry, about the size of a football. Not swelling up all

111

over – overwhelming him. Not that yet. It was observable. What's this? Subject to enquiry. A taste without flavour. A substance. Meat – that came with no packaging.

The first time I felt it, we were sitting in my room. I sat back on my bed, Ry at my desk, stretched, all legs and pumped feet, and his goofy head at a philosopher's angle introspecting it. I wanted so much to stand and to clench Ry's shoulders. And the thought of doing that wandered at the base of Ry's neck and behind his ears – over his shoulders. And fold my arms about him. Nothing I could think of could justify even a token of that gesture. Instead, there was only a halt, and it was the first time illusion of the flow of it broke, and I got bored and frustrated with him, burdened with drag like my room had plenty of stuff I could be getting on with.

Maybe I dumped Ry. Maybe you'd say I outgrew him. Maybe it just stopped seeming appropriate. Maybe I'd got what I had to get, learned what I had to learn. Maybe some powerful instinct did it for me. When one day, I'd twisted the lock in my teenage room and I'd shut himself in. Protection.

The last real picture is summer. Of the front lawn, from my window. Ry come to call for me. Ry's bike spread on the lawn. Me hiding – peeking at the corner of the window. Ry picks his bike up and walks it to the front gate. I have absolutely no idea what underlay that – what conditions surrounded the scene – why I did that.

There he goes, off between the yew trees, onto the main road. Call after him: Ry! Too late.

Once, I, Tomàs, worked in a little school. Boarding – public school. They used touch upon each other – it was strange to see. Oh, and

112

behind the scenes… 'Nothing a nice middle-class boy like you wants to know about, Sir.' Buggery and coke. A strangely overlapped world – so it seemed it might be. Crawling into each other's beds at night. Whether for comfort or pleasure. Asked how they were and they said it was okay. Whether for youth or love. At food, they stroked each other. Man-spread on the work-top, in the central feeding area, waiting for the toast to do, not minding my non-presence, Sir, in sports shorts. As boy-14-15 with his fingertips stroked the insides of boy-14-15's thighs… evoking in a moment the sleepiest responses, deep, beneath the disappearing mask, as one were hypnotized and triggered, after a day.

Once in a while, still, you see boys playing out. A flock of reckless bicycles… Memories fall apart and are such liars. I can only suppose my middling teen-years conventionally ragged. Boredom, shove-ha'penny. A fair bit of sitting about the place. Twenty wasted minutes at the start of each school day – like drying socks.

Julia said to me I only ever flirted with the idea of becoming a Catholic because I was *like that* with Ry. It was around this time I first knowingly entered a Catholic church.

The scene is washed – a volatile fraction of oil on tired water. Milky tea, and English afternoons, and bedroom windows. The sky reflects the paving – slate-blue – fused at the vanishing point beneath the steel traverse of the railway bridge. A daubed canopy of trees, and post-war housing, sandstone walls, and brick furred a palest speckled grey and purple. There is no temperature whatsoever. Neither hot nor cold. Neutral weather. The forecourt of the church is its own empty space, and I try the door. I'm doing this incredibly *normally*. A working Catholic church: it's open. Entering, I know to dip my finger in the water in the little font. Then inside, toward the altar, I genuflect. It's like television. *Brideshead*

113

Revisited. It's Madonna. Only it's curiously real. I walk a little up the aisle toward the altar, and sit in a pew, and in an unhurried time, simply look at it.

I knew no information regarding the tabernacle. There were no questions I'd ever felt I needed to ask about the wafers – nor knowing consecrated hosts were reserved in the tabernacle. Yet, received with no wise intermediary structure, there seemed a simple meaning, a stillness to what remained alert self-consciousness, a clarity in my own body. Orderly. My soul the exact same shape as my body. Fused in each sensation – every nerve of it. Feeling it move and continually adjust inside of me. River of life.

My gaze wandered up to the apex of the arch that enclosed the sanctuary. It was a small crucifix there. Quite discreet. Not asking to hold your eyes – just there. No contest occurred to me. No human agony – no *agon* drew me awe and suffering. Only the love spoke. All that was in my heart. The love spoke so directly. It seemed that was all that there was in it.

I kept this to myself. Knowing it wouldn't communicate properly at home. It was spiritual. Pure. The stillness, this being, could only be jolted with reference to home, domesticity, Mum, Dad, nagged at, domestically normalized. Crude and unseemly words other than.

By and by, I knocked on the presbytery door, and I met the priest. By and by, Mum had to get involved. There was some background kerfuffle. And wait till you're eighteen. There was a class – of an evening. A half dozen pieces of age. Like carpets, jumbled wool, wet ashtrays, canned soup. Smoke and hair. Odd, cloying smells, like aerosol furniture polish. A close little parlour. It resembled a canal boat's cabin in the local museum.

114

It is difficult to see their faces. They seem withdrawn in hair and shadows. It *was* discomfiting when mere textbook politeness, breezy pleasantries, sounded-back off of it nothing at all. The air's feculence stirred to the extent of a lip's curl, as though it were morbidly damaging. Forget the rest. Slow words, and such apparent struggle, such apparent difficultly. If they churned like cauldrons… As if a piece of grade-school information were entirely obscure.

It might well be a question of subsistence-level – functional literacy. Our world was new, then, and such the milieu: we all were emerging from dark times. Still, in church, there is a tendency to read *the most* synthetic translation – *The Jerusalem Bible* as if it is visceral, sheer, plates of stone.

It seemed it wasn't going to be what I'd wanted. Not so simple and obvious after all. It wasn't light, it was dark, and a perception was missing. Beauty, truth, love. Low IQ. Platonic form and Ry – the bedroom mirror. The 'I' of it. And, then, youth's more decreasingly nebulous discoveries.

I pushed the letter through the priest's door:

'Dear Father, I've thought about this really deeply. I wish I could be a Catholic, but I cannot. I've considered this and I'd be lying if I said that I could. I'm sorry. Yours sincerely, Tomàs.'

I rang the doorbell, though maybe didn't wait too long. But the priest wasn't in, so I stuffed it through the letterbox.

Then it was the same blue-grey weather, so many years later, in London. A similar sort of wash, the church a blue-grey white, like seagulls. For a while, as I half-believe I might have said, I'd been passing this church most days, between the village and the tube station. I'd surreptitiously crossed myself. Sometimes the windows were lit from the inside. There was a primary school, physically attached, full of children, like miniature, trainee human beings, who experienced diverse dramas and clung to the rails to yell. When I crossed myself, I experienced some kind of blessing. It didn't bother me to think of God abstractly, formally, remotely. Trinitarian. It wasn't *myself* entering into the metaphysic which might then have been sickening – hollow, performative – and absurd. That was just their religion – a nod to it.

There are so many fragments. Once, I found a whole floor of an old bookshop, in one of the Medway towns, dedicated to Christian books. I bought, and read, a *King James Version* Bible, and a *Catechism of the Catholic Church*. When I was living out of the boot of an old Astra, clothes hung-up around the windows so I could sleep on the back seat. (And pity the poor. The police woke me in the early hours. *Oh now…? What now…? What is it now…?*) Around the time Princess Diana died. It was wet and cold.

Mass weekdays was the home of the old, the devout-foreign, and the unemployed. I entered the church for the first time intending to be part of it. The days were empty. Once each day, I took my tennis racquet down to the municipal park and municipal tennis-courts to practise my serve… You could say it was a form of poverty, if you can say that when you've got a home. I didn't mind it – I *liked* it. It was a pretty good place to be poor – in the sense of not having any money. I liked the progressive step-change in the reduction. Heat cast by incandescent light-bulbs. Layered thermals. Reading weeks under cover of duvet. Phoning in the readings and that sort of thing. And no alcohol. Only in the moment of

116

the present conditioning. No release.

I became a mere stick of a thing. I went down to 56 kilograms. Faith emerged – as maybe it must in such circumstances. Mum is far away. I start talking to God. I'm not, by any stretch of the imagination, radicalized. Praying, it seems I'm free now. I don't have to pretend.

Personal ways, I thought, to find a truth in Christianity – Catholic. When Ron came to the reception, he couldn't walk far and he couldn't carry much. We sang the psalm we'd sung at Dad's funeral. I played host, and pranced around, offering sandwiches and telling them about the new life. And made a point of getting out of the house each day.

Soon, getting involved, I joined the choir (I can sing) and raised church funds. Pasties, dolmades, and cheesecakes, for the bazaar. Charged cost plus whatever you fancy. Days grew indistinct… I went to Mass each day. Slowly and prayerfully, many times, I read in church the Gospels.

My thermals got to be saggy and loose on me. The house started to smell and the windows turned green. It became unimaginable to go into central. When it got to be icy, and there was a dump of snow, I'd exercise. And I would play at the edge of my blood-sugar. A narrow, gripping panic could become me alone completely, weeping with hunger, just playing with it, until I knew a half-glass of pressed-apple-juice might soften – re-complete my thoughts.

Even in the snow, there were others of us, joggers and striders, along with the kids, and the old Indian man on the municipal exercise machinery. I kept my rosary pocketed. I tried with it dangling once, so it was visible, Hail Mary, but that was false and therefore disempowering, diminished in its inward capacity to institute change. *Gunpowder in my pocket*… Secret love. Secret heresy. *Hail Mary, full of grace, the Lord is with you. Blessed are you among women and blessed is the fruit of your womb, Jesus. Holy Mary, Mother of God, pray for us sinners now and at the hour of our death.*

They mocked the old Archbishop when he talked about Mary... Also, this was to do with other things, which the Arch had begun to articulate. The rock and darkness. Gethsemane, the tomb, and the empty space. His Grace put to us the students the thought of our imitating Mary. He spoke of Mary's *complete* humility when she said *yes* to God. And she relinquished, emptied everything, beyond any ego-concerns for her own protection she might have had. So she became the point life vibrates only to God and to God's Word. To her son, to Jesus. *El Ángel del Señor anunció a María – Y concibió por obra del Espíritu Santo...*

And why should not the angel have visited Mary? Why should Mary not have relinquished so thoroughly? This cloud, submission to God, in a spiritual sense, come on her answering this world's prayers. Was it so contrary to reason? Would time cease to agitate? Would the clocks stop?

Julian is very Blessed Virgin Mary – BVM – Mother of God. He wears the silver ring, he does the silver ring thing, which proposes his undoubted virginity... Blunt as a pig's head, Julian was having none of it, when the Arch asked that we the class consider the quality of Mary's virginity. Julian *noised* contempt. It was an ugly scene to witness. He said: 'Well she hadn't had sex had she.' Duh!

He'd dropped so far in his seat, phone in hand still, landscape, playing a game. Regenerative, putrid fecundity. Puberty. Sex-filth. Mobile phone.

118

That there was once a young man called Tomàs, who, one August, years past, left the house of Mum to travel south, where contractually engaged to work of pedagogy… A little job at a little school. Then things didn't work out quite so well as they might have done. And one thing led to another. A meandering course rode the busses from San Diego to Portland and back again. Then he flew to Morocco, thence did coastal Spain, Cataluña, and into France. And, one day, awoke from the wreck of an incomplete dream, a little way out of Nice, and checked into an hotel, got a fresh change of clothes, looked fine in the mirror, and in a matter of hours was in London.

Entering into west London, from Heathrow, solo-occupancy back of a black cab… It seemed the first treat. Home. Well… London. Price of this already factored into account and already acceded to. A stretch of new time.

And, though it was random, arranged with the first, weirdly-logical call at the baggage reclaim, my host, the old MP, instantly agreed with joy and – on arrival – threw open that same knackered night a new world awaiting the two of us.

Transactionally, *that* Tomàs, nights, gave the old man wings, and made the old man less ridiculous. And in return, there were all these little parties to go to. All charm, and mutually enabling. He never gave me a key.

And I was paying. Some nights, *he'd* get Tomàs wasted, and others he'd ration me. Then, while that carried on, there were semi-crashed-out games of musical-beds and brand-new, too-small sofas. Whoever they were – way beyond the energy at that hour for strenuous moral lapse. For they were fine nights. (Soho was different in those days.) They were banging long-weekends… Not saying I, really, wasn't really wanting to claim from it something that wasn't there… Monday, Heaven again, when it really got partied-up… Youth night. (Popcorn.)

Then, midweek, a more lubricated, café-society affair, the fashion rip-and-slash – again – super-skinny up top, clean armpits, estranged hair, come-and-go Mykonos tans. I devilishly pretty – one child told me I must have been *so* fit when I was young. Drugs that mostly worked. And velvet curtains. And plenty of rope.

By days, the nights refreshed themselves. There'd be cricket on Sky prior to brunch = in Dolphin Square. I got anxious – not anxious but wondering what the fuck use of this time this was supposed to be.

While the old man – the Honourable Member fiddled his mobile for texts from a new and a next 'naughty boy' the old man had it in mind he'd recruited. Days slow-fuelling in cafes in Pimlico. Virgin Marys for the Honourable Member. As for Tomàs – glancing sunshine crept with next year's age, because it was not sustainable, and it could not last very long. Already, I wore my skin borderline gaunt, but my skin refreshed itself those days. In Dolphin Square, I bathed, and often I went out ahead – to meet later in Soho.

I preferred the evening street-scene, which was strictly democratic, no matter the long wait for what happened later. That was the life of it. The flat was merely tired, and texts, texts, texts, interminably. I never wanted, nor did I seek, an appropriate lover. Though, in my heart, I might warm to a short, slightly cheap-looking boy, with his manners about him. And made my friends among young people, with whom, therefore, relationship would never be sexual.

In Soho, then, there were loose affiliations and constant churn. It was a bright little crowd, in our little bright world, in trash VIPs, which sprinkled Soho. There were simple things to love – the brickwork terracotta-rose, an evening sun giving way to the manufactured light upon it. And books in bars – for I could never read back in the flat. And all so many people. That too, though less dependent on wealth, could not last very long.

*

I drain my beer. There is no time for another. I have the thirst – I have the re-creative memory on me. Soho. (So *close…*) Valladolid… There are cans in my room. Alone time. Nightly – 'meetings with yourself' The Rector calls it. Not meaning that in a good way – quite the opposite.

Probably, it might be a good idea to clean my teeth, though there are no rules about it. Minty-fresh lungfuls of air on the street-scene back… I keep a brush and a tube of toothpaste in a pocket of my rucksack. (There is an interdental brush in my wallet.) Maybe more for that braced spirit-of-mind. Though – nothings they'd seize upon, logic-defeated-style – Catholic-style – if they were in the mood. Facts all twisted – any which-way bar straight-up and straight-down. Round and round and side-to-side – such as they fancied them. Faith's journey, Pisgah-view. Lenten meanderings, desert-long. Basking faith – won't survive onshore. Human society fact-checks your grip on insanity, should you get a religious urge. Valladolid disproves God. I wonder how long it will take Geoff to get me. Geoff has the tenacity – and the urge.

It is one of Geoff's redeeming features that he hasn't read the

Bible, though *he be* mad keen to believe every bit of it. Geoff thinks things like Job are *supposed* to be history. He thinks Moses recorded his own death. The very notion of Esther as an historical novel bounces right off Geoff. Geoff's occasionally more inspired outbursts are, as often as not, *purest* heresy… Geoff hasn't read the Bible at the level of words. Geoff's text exceeds text – it is super-voluminous précis! Whatever text Geoff *be* – . Other to any text I swear I've ever been part of or party to. But it is savage how… None of them.

I drain my beer, pack my rucksack, and button my jacket up. We say, 'A lo,' which is short for 'hasta luego', my loosely capping her, she engrossed in her puzzle book, perched on her high stool, feet up on the bar, her back curved against the wall behind. She rarely turns a page. It is a meditation. I've never noticed her hands or the pen move.

The blue, homey street chills my face pleasantly. Nigh-on ten o'clock. Trash-skips, discount-clothes stores, the cinema. One shop where all the vegetables are labelled, one shop where all the meat is labelled, to help you learn Spanish. There is even a knocking shop. Whores come and go, and it isn't pretty. While there are no people, there is an air of unthreatening nostalgia to be here. It could be half-past two in the a.m. Breathe deep. The faintest aroma of city air. Between settled points – the one where you just sat for your beer, the one where you will code the college gate. City air: freedom. 'City air sets you free.' So you pretend – in movement.

I check the pad, on the clipboard strung on the door, and no-one else being out, I cross my name off on the pad, and bolt the outer glass door and the inner wooden door. Meeting no-one in the corridors or on the stairs, I unlock my room door, step within the warm, receiving space,

122

and I lock the door again, leaving the key in the lock.

Indeed, the heat is stifling. Our heating – the chunky, industrial radiator – has a life of its own. Clockwise-lockwise... Though that doesn't seem to work. The system is, ironically, so expensively drained of air you can't hear which way to turn the bloody knob on it. I well-nigh break sweat as I open the shutters and the small window. I give the room a precursory glance-around. There is no sign of disturbance. (The cleaners being committed to shutting the window and turning the heating up.) Everything looks to be in its right place.

I am settling in for the night, and half-undressed, when I notice I am out of water. That, to fill my bottles, means a trip to the common room, beyond the whole length of the corridor. I lock the door again behind me for this. Though public, yet after-hours, and thereby to an extent permissive, in comportance, of dishabille...

I wear scruffy sock-like thigh-length – 'shorts' whatever. Top Man. And I still have the T-shirt on. I am not wearing any socks: I am barefoot.

Geoff's in the common room. And Geoff's been drinking hard. So he is still. Drunk and shining – honest at last. And Sean and Luke are here. Philip sits dozing. Beached seals, wailing walruses. And other less fortunate beasts washed-up on it.

They have the television off, so the only other colour in the room is magnolia walls and cushions and the old people's furniture. It is very much too late to be discussing God. (They are discussing God.) It is a bad time to be joining them. Proof of this, if any such were needed, in the fact I want to join them. A little fellow human company... In other words, I must myself be quite pissed.

Geoff says: 'Pull up a pew, me ol' mucker!'

'Hiya!'

Convivial. Though not really listening, I catch a gist of rare flavours introduced to the body of discussion. I hear what I hear I hear – and know enough of their philosophizing. Most absolute precepts of heavenly worship, doubtless at Sean's instigation, worry modern times. Post-Enlightenment. Devilish chicanery. 'Wisdom' such that ain't worth Pope Saint Pious X's milk-teeth… Cosmology, evolution, relativity, psychology, neurology… Stuff like that. Our 'evolving religious experience' – 'imminence' – which is to Sean a constituent of truthful modality. Doubtless – at heart – though the field lie uncertain… While Geoff's is ring-fenced holy mountain Zion, Sean's, stalwart, yet to reconcile… At the least, come on a place, and to define, limits… *Sicut erat in principio, et nunc, et semper, et in saecular saeculorum.* Lost cause. Missing particle.

Geoff's *zone* of interest – plumed zeal – is really only the obviously crass, the most obviously lustful-material. That *world*, at its most baldly stated, Enemy enough. Antique certitude chews a legitimacy drawing on nothing more… Sean's despised-less dull, intoxicated fat of a common world. The resource, *his* thought, asks its questions more intimately.

One might even sense the people in their homes, wasted of spiritual purpose, and they are desperately famished. Imminence. Christ Child in ashes new – and live-form. Contrary to what you might think to look at them: Sean's within a people's experience, Geoff's without.

Stuff like that. *Compressed* stuff like that. Sean is sober; Geoff is pissed. Which is never going to end happily. I pour myself a gin. Which is a euro no matter the measure. *Ergo*... I can't find a lemon in the fridge, and start dicking around. The tonic's splashing up. As though it's all a joke – being sociable. Like how else might one concede to the norms of their parody. And saying things like:

'So hang on, where are we these days on...'

I'm not really listening to myself. Head stuffed in the liquefied rot of the crisping-drawer. Broad assent to the incontrovertible thrust of it... Blown dogma. All manner of fruit and plastic. *Surely* a lemon... Hidden in plain sight. Blending in.

Sean's belief intuits an originary life of Jesus. As he has said in his own words: 'Something happened.' And to qualify that: 'I believe something happened.' Unusual to say. Such thought preceding stuff like that could not have been owned by anyone – of the others of them. (Odd to say: 'The postman delivered a letter. I believe in the postman.') Doubt not in God but in history. The Church a kind of botched attempt to capture a thought it had first missed. Odd to say – but closer to it. Something happened.

Tall and unfanciably handsome, Sean's voice happy as a mild Brummy. A brain, and he did his degree online, when he could have gone to any university. And, if you wanted to argue with Sean, regarding matters of Catholic faith, you would need to step outside of what Catholicism says to you. And read your own claims and your own understandings as adrift and strangely loose within themselves. And unanchored – seemingly to anything.

Still, though, much of it leaps direct to abortion with Sean – not unlike Geoff. That's the issue – that's everyone's issue – and, no matter the issue in itself, it is liable to hoover-in everything... I reiterate: When is a human not a human? When is a man not a man?

125

Sean wears a gold lapel button of a baby's feet – the size they would be at ten weeks into pregnancy. It is a powerful statement. Gay marriage is, therefore, wrong. It encourages abortion. Contraception is wrong. It encourages abortion. Oh sure, you can argue it. Then again, if you're that's the way inclined, you can argue – whatever – used chewing-gum trodden on the hot strand, with the pricks and the tummy-wobbles, into the base of an upturned flip-flop encourages abortion.

It is beyond my capacities, anyhow, to untwist such complex logic from its insides. I fail to dispute from its insides in creditable fashion. (Once you get to weakening a basic human sanctity of procreative married life, you're basically home. Your mortgage encourages abortion. Your HP on your dumb car encourages abortion. Your food encourages abortion. Waitrose encourages abortion. Tesco encourages abortion. Aldi encourages abortion. Morrison's encourages abortion. Marks & Spencer encourages abortion. Asda encourages abortion.

Encourages abortion. Your beach-holiday encourages abortion. Your connection – . Your vote. Your helpless wilting low-IQ...)

All I have in me when a boy loves a boy and they snog and that encourages abortion is something like: *Yeah but hang on, that's a load of bollocks – that's untrue...* And those aren't words from inside Christian space. Words of that sort don't stand up in church.

This is in a sense a Zeno's paradox.

Even from a distance, to see them, as I do now intermittently, Sean and Geoff are in posture sat with their thoughts about God and their ontologies delicately spaced apart. Marginally-colliding – essentially agreed. As, say, Sean might say:

'Whatever you might say, and however much you might wish to

126

deconstruct it, I believe something happened.'

Geoff might say: 'Oh will you give it a rest. It's true. It's all true.'

Perhaps if you also knew, seeing this, howsoever intermittently, Sean's death-metal-noise through his room door. The walled sound of his inwardness. That degree of emptied, teenage purity discovered in there. Something happened… When earliest Christians prayed and the Spirit moved. Piety. Everyone says stuff, and everyone lies. Fake news. Then so-and-so heard it from such-and-such. Best keep shtum if you happened to be there and you didn't.

I am to be heard indistinctly as, in the fancied manner of a stand-up philosopher, I declaim – to the disposable plastic knife, to the lemon:

'When did that even change? We don't still say the world's three thousand eight hundred and blah-de blah blah blah blah. Though it's barely a century since that was reluctantly conceded. *Do* we? A whole, shining, murderous, human century. Providentially arranged, so it might be, to make out it's longer than you think. And thereby ourselves less ridiculous. We're good on the monkey-front now, right? As in, woo woo, monkey-hands! Checking insofar as we do all have opposable thumbs round here. One or two, I know, dead against it, though powers that be… The Church view – ….'

Fade out. Fade in again:

'Mass extinctions – there's a good one. Just how ineffable would you like your God to be? I mean, one mass extinction you might let pass. Two mass extinctions starts to look like carelessness. But there's been five! Do you reckon we'll do it to ourselves first, or will a massive-great Jesus-shaped asteroid suddenly *appear*…? Parousia! Dear valued customer, we value your call. Please take a moment to complete our

127

survey. Please hang on the line until your call is no longer important to you. How ineffable would you like God to be? For utterly incomprehensible, please press one. For a bit barking, please press two. To speak to God, please hold. To hear these options again...'

I sip my drink. Brimful. It would make more sense on more of an honesty box principle. I split the drink in two and add extra tonic to both glasses. Then I think about it too long and put an extra euro in the tray. There: this is sociable.

I steady the glasses, two not looking good, for the long diagonal, transverse space of the common room. Conversation. (Fianchettoed: a corner-most armchair receives me.) Geoff *draped* centre-stage. So then... Promptless: What would you like *to know*?

We become subdued, and I, embarrassed, nudge one of the glasses, as it would hide behind a leg of the armchair, then wish I hadn't done that. Geoff overflows in his. All dangling arms – the octopus. Geoff's legs spread. Swishing his gin-glass to-and-fro. Plastered-hair like bull's blood – *banderillas* streaming-off of him. A bull – in the confusion of its own tragedy. Watch how it whinnies, womps, turns in its own mire...

'Well,' I say, 'this is cosy.'

Sean says: 'Well, perhaps for another time.'

I think to meet them at the level of seriousness. I think I'd better say something – no matter – and something religious too. It is a thought – and I trace it in the air ahead, speculative. It is really in the manner of Sister Angelina – with my right pinkie. I describe her imitation and the view from my window – calling to it – trees, leaves, branches... So at once I feel secure ground, and I say: 'It can be interesting to consider how some of the more nonsense bits of the Bible are yet to be read as drawing

128

the soul to God.'

Geoff says: 'You shouldn't be here. You have no place in a seminary. Unbelievable. I can't believe you even said that.'

'?'

'You shouldn't be here. You've got no business here. You shouldn't be here. If you are one scrap of a man...'

'Eh? Oh for heaven's sake. Oh for heaven's sake. Fuck's sake – Okay, fine, poor word choice, choose a different word. *Nonsense* was a bad word. Go on, what would your word be instead of *nonsense*?'

With rising, fake ire, I speak the word *nonsense* to try to provoke Geoff more.

Geoff says: 'It's all true!'

Then it seems to dribble all out... Half-baked and lazy Veronicas. Spain, and the low, swinging EU motorways to Andalucia.

When is a human not a human? We cannot even trace our beginnings. Endogenous mass-death. And the ickle pretty humans got better and better and better until they died. For God slow-cooked the Earth... Where will they draw a line and say that was an end?

'We looked at this with Father O'Brien,' I say. 'It was one of the things he wanted us to understand. How do you think it was written? We are allowed to know, by God, that these are made-up stories. That is perfectly reasonable orthodoxy. Yes, so I should not have used a word: nonsense. Howsoever I beg to be permitted the right to keep my left and right brain in a switched-on position even as we are responding to God's call. I don't see that in this age that be not possible.'

No, I do not like the sound of any of that at all. None of that came out in any way well at all.

Geoff says: 'I'm not sitting here and…' He can't stand. Too pissed and tired. His *banderillas* drag. Docile. Steaming. Ripe. Tired.

We sit in self-help attitudes. Obviously, I now have to hang about forever before I can leave.

It'll all get back, and some way around four, I'll wake. Not *nonsense…*

For instance, God does his burning bush, then off goes Moses, Exodus 4, to do what God said – so that God can harden Pharaoh's heart, so that God be justified. And there goes Moses, doing what he's told, when God, in an ineffable moment, meets Moses and He tries to kill him. Exodus 4: 24. But Zipporah, *her* wits about her, takes a flint and cuts off her son's foreskin, and she touches it to Moses' genitals. So then God lets Moses alone to go on to Egypt and carry on his business with Pharaoh. Which all makes perfect sense.

Sean says: 'I don't think any of us knows very much about this.'

It doesn't even occur to me Geoff might be actually hurt.

Geoff says: 'Sorry, bro. I shouldn't have said that.'

'Ah no worries.'

'Ay, it's late.'

No-one wants to move.

It's too comfortable. It is nice not having the telly on. Compañeros. It is good unspeaking in others' proximity to contemplate God's love. I draw, deeply, and replete, upon the first and then the second of the glasses of gin and tonic. Room-warm sticky liquor barely fizzed. I feel blood-sugar curl from the base of my cranium. From the perspective of the corridor, we must look quite dredged-up. Yet, from within, there seem passages. 'Hear, O Israel.' Human bodies, God's faith.

After a little while, it becomes appropriate to break company and to go to our rooms. I lock my door, turning and giving the handle a firm tug to make double certain of this. I have remembered my water, and line the bottles up next to my bed. There is more than enough for tonight's sleep. I wake my computer and get Radio 4 on. Then I get my top and my pumps and my jeans off. I open the first of six remaining stubby-beers.

They aren't cold and froth deliciously. I open a book on my desk to a random page, marked with the stub of a plane ticket. Numbers 22: 23-31: 'And the ass saw the angel of the Lord standing in the road...' Swiss Air Heathrow to Zurich. 2001.

I sit in my office chair and roll it around a little – plastic wheels on the wooden floor. Hello, Father Richard! (He'll have put himself away in his room – below – at this hour.)

Helpless, of course. Afflicted with spastic paralysis. And Father Richard monitors our internet usage – so that's another dumb way to communicate. *Direct thy steps to the perpetual ruins; the enemy has destroyed everything in the sanctuary...* Search. Find me... Presumably, it's not really monitored. Like we can't use a café or phones. Or an encrypted browser. One of those ways they watch – or not – when they're not really watching you. So you might continue to experience the social dimension to privacy. So, at knock-on-wood, at thoughts' edge, you might continually enjoy the impression of real implication in each tired wandering mental twitch...

So I throw in the march of such nonsense as comes to me – search-wise.

It is a comforting security knowing it might be seen.

At the open window, I am standing in order to watch the night beyond. I, as it were, offer custodial care of it. I *look out* for the trees in the back-yard lit like coins, yellow-green, for the half-lit gym, the gym-equipment on the mezzanine, the stacked-containers of the tower-blocks overlooking us. The apartments sell at 40 000 Euros a piece. You can just see the tops of trees, whispering together on the street outside, blue and amber, just over the wall. Thermals from the still-hot radiator rise across my body.

There's nothing till eight tomorrow. I'll be done with this vigil by two o'clock. Up then by five for the hot bath. I crush each can, with my foot, within a towel to muffle it. I must tread softly. My bare feet can't make too much noise. I won't sit in that chair again. Days can be so bothersome. Nights are so peaceful. Air full like liquid. Muted. So much erased, and it all lies ahead of me, rolls from inside of me. Paradise. Back in time. The simple heart of it.

Chapter Four

With the passing of lunch on Friday, it is effectively the weekend. Lunch is easy on Fridays. Through Lent, lunch is penitential. A plain, green, vegetable soup, a taste of lentils. And bread, and silence, while one of the students reads.

Strange to say, the student reading reads from my own bath-worn hard-back copy of Pope Benedict XVI's *Jesus Of Nazareth: Holy Week.* (The book has seen a lot of hot-baths. The pages are intact. The spine has split and crumbled.)

There was a meeting in The Conference Room we had to decide this. It was formal and The Rector asked if we would like to celebrate Lent with lunchtime readings. The Rector told us, students had wanted to do this in previous years… Perhaps it was the kind of suggestion which, if not taken up on the spur, might have gone quietly the way of dispersed responsibility. But I took it up seriously and put the suggestion out.

I was being keen. (I *wanted…*) The motion passed by default.

Those students not frozen-in-context at the meeting reacted. So they – yes as at one of their meetings. They didn't really want to do it. As it comes to pass, four step up to it. Oddly, Geoff doesn't. But Henry does.

The Refectory is designed to function as an auditorium during meals. There is a recessed alcove, like a pulpit, up the steps, and when you lean right back into it, push yourself back up there into the scoop, it projects with extraordinary resonance, all over the gnat-bite clatter of plates and spoons – which you hear while you are trying to concentrate. Your skull vibrates. Eerily magnified – buzzed. A sound-image. Sister Angelina complemented me to my face on my reading. Today, Francis reads, and the Vice Rector, Father Richard, sits by Tomàs.

Quite funny: Father Richard is (unsurprisingly) ill-at-ease with penitential silence. Like Mum so when he wants the bread, *he whispers theatrically… 'Could you pass me the bread, please, Tomàs?'* Prim, dead-proper like, channelling monasteries, I pass the bread. But don't openly smirk as the silly – blessed man whispers: *'Thank you.'*

Our remaining, brief, commitment is evening prayer… Spring. Days lengthen two to three minutes each day. Soon the hour will change. We are leaving chapel after prayers for the Pope, which through Lent is the *De Profundis*, and I so happen to be walking alongside Alex and Alan and Guy and Sean. It occurs to me to ask if they fancy a beer tonight. Tentatively – near with them. (Obviously, this recapitulates *being weird* at school and all.) Casually – ready at once to withdraw if the offer proves bad. I fancy I catch their surprise, and then the momentary readjustment. But, then, they seem delighted. Yes, of course. Even gratefully.

Well, as per previously stated, I've done this before, having translated a small group of school-friends. Once – when a whole summer-holiday loomed vast. And in England – where you really don't want to be alone if you really don't want to be alone. Knowing I was not dispositionally fit for it – though happy to receive the many, many hours listening to records – and going into Liverpool – all that noise of gigs and browsing HMV!

134

That time – when memory begins to communicate. That year – 14, 15 – when other people had become necessary. When it was *shameful…*

We arrange to meet at nine at the front door. We'll go to Downing Street, the Irish bar round the corner at the top of the block, right opposite the back-end of college. #10 on that road – hence the joke.

A complete afternoon… There is the luxury of gym. And pool, and sauna. I can do a full session in the time we have. Probably, at this hour, a lane in the pool I can call my own. I get changed into my gym kit in my room, my custom being to walk the moral high-ground – to the gym in skimpy running shorts. Slashed to hips – all adult leg. And skimpy – sporting vests, which hardly cover me and my unshaven armpits.

As I exercise, sweating a lot, my vest becomes transparent. I am a body. Sign of. Wired torque. Ninja-edit. Definitively non-twink. Worked athleticism. (Enumerable ribs and a 'piccolo' six-pack!)

Whit-wooo-sir!! once they whistle, once they shout… Giggle exhibiting their smooth legs. (It's all true what they say about public school!) Safe – to laugh at such things. That was funny! … Once. *Hereafter, in a better world than this…* Before the dark times, before safeguarding.

I check the current shape of my torso in the bathroom mirror, standing to do so on an awkwardly manoeuvred flight case. There remains to the midriff fractionally more subcutaneous fat than I would ideally like. *I work* for treasured evening beers, though my weight through the course of a day fluctuates by kilograms, from 64.8 to 67.2. (My height being 180.) The issue of adipose tissue is under control. While my abdominal muscles are defined, my body type is exo-morphic.

Probably, I underestimate the calorific value in a little stubby-can of cold beer, straight from the fridge, in denial of carbohydrate and metabolized alcohol.

But I'm good in the gym. It's important not to let things slip. I just like being in the gym. It is stark and admirable. Short term targets, achievable goals. We are 700 meters high up here in Valladolid, and the altitude trepanned us the first days. I got to, like, 400 kcals on the cross-trainer and slid from the gym-machine weeping. Then, truly, last Christmas, at Mum's gym, if you can call it that, I might have never stopped. The air, at Mum's health club, was butter and cream. It was almost too rich.

I give my room the once over. A piece of me assumes there must be some manner of incriminating evidence. A physical trail. An air of guilt and culpability sloughed-off about the place. Considered practically, they did once do a spot search. They didn't call it that, obviously, but there was no other word for it. In real terms, it was made palpably clear our rooms are not our own, and locks work merely contingently.

I walk the scenic route down to the main door. Comfy, unlaced trainers like sucking your thumb. Whatever provocation this body might offer them. This offence – a restive body. And incontrovertible licence of going to the gym.

I pop into the common room on a pretext, but no-one's there. Downstairs, it is unlikely I'll bump into The Rector, or the Vice-Rector, but it happens irregularly. The Rector goes to the gym. (The Vice Rector never.) Short spells perhaps once a week. His – The Rector's vest-sleeves touching His elbows. His shorts – His knees. Besides, one gets the impression they rather like it. Not *themselves* being in the gym – but students… Lusty vigour. Male spunk. Rude health… ('Keep going to the gym,' Father Richard said like I'd asked.) Makes the place real. Students

– who go to the gym. Here is a student: he goes to the gym. So by extension… We're real – 'I' am real – and not a terrible trade-off.

Portraits of former Rectors hang along the walls, all the way along what's called Rectors' corridor. They are the only really competent art in the building. Henry likes to say The Rector has His portrait painted already, wrapped in cloth-of-gold, in the imagined vault with the other treasure. In anticipation of His episcopal advancement.

Time-served. Like the Devil made him do it. A fair few of them know as natural – hierarchical property – that of pure ambition.

Long, oaken corridors…

Once naked, the broad, square prism of corridors ceases to choke and baffle. Half the lousy pictures are slashed. Most sacramentally, there is what is called Martyrs' Corridor. Those who trained to die… We make no claim they are artistically valuable. They are painted like their mother wouldn't recognize them. At their back stand gibbets. Stick men hanged. And cauldrons, steaming… priest-stew.

Tyburn. Maybe you might see in them an idea of Saint Stephen faces. Each face, already erased, drawn upward, gormless-blank. Host in blessed sky. Heaven-breached. Lemon-yellow. Breaking, fractured clouds. Florid trumpet-serenade of putti.

Someone recent has vandalized one of the paintings – of John Plessington. A crude little French moustache – not, it seems, inked on, but applied in oil-paint, which remains wet. I haven't mentioned it – I noticed it maybe three days ago. It seems bad luck to see it – inconceivable to mention it.

Our gym is a members' sports club. It is a leasing arrangement. And, though hardly bustling, it has a trade. On Saturdays, the mezzanine fills, and the pool gets busy with little-kids. But we can almost say it's ours through siesta. Adedokun, Jonathan and I use the gym regularly. Others put in an appearance. One or two (Julian, Benedict) are themselves only learning to swim down in the pool. Upstairs, on the mezzanine, the cardio-vascular machines stand arranged in a line overlooking the free-weights area below, and face a wall of mirrors. The cross-trainers have a decent stride to them – when so often the machines' manufacturers get this wrong. Pool-side there are weights-machines. Below, with the free weights, a regular four-to-five youngish Spanish men bond. They do not take steroids.

Last term, I grappled long and hard with Pimsleur Spanish on my Walkman. Today, I have loaded *Hamlet*. This is not for pleasure. My thinking is that I ought to be studying something. (Else why are we here?) *Hamlet* seems now appropriate. There are no useful versions of the Bible to listen to. I have the play unabridged and once got a prize at university for an essay on Shakespeare. As such, there is a degree of make-believe here entailed. An intellectual edifice. Pride. Mind.

I address the machine, which signifies power and brute stability, and climb up on it, conscious of frailty assayed to a work of confidence. With my towel arranged *so*, and my water *so*, from the tap, with its teaspoon of salt in it. A forward-downward levered jolt – I lurch the machine into action. And begin to tread.

Looking over, I see that the short woman on the machine next is on 320 kcals achieved in 28 minutes. If I can beat her to 600 kcals by the time she quits… An ambitious and probably unachievable target. Nevertheless, I am sweating well by the time Jonathan arrives, followed closely by Ade, and that's the three of us. I salute each – capping them. They aren't big on this, though I dislodge an ear-plug as I watch them get going, so they can mouth hello if they want. Intent on purpose. There's a shred of greeting – though not as if this is the main event when we are free. There is flow of energy – the bounce in my efforts. It takes at least twenty minutes and more like twenty-five or even thirty until you get high. And crash the machine on its axis – shake that mezzanine floor… Gym-music plays in the background. As my muscles warm, a crust seems to melt from me. The body is in the can-do. Resistance in triceps and biceps implies a sedate pace. I am aiming to concentrate my work-outs toward upper-body development. My thought is that my legs can take care of themselves.

I get going, muttering part-lines of *Hamlet* aloud, maybe a habit carried over from the Pimsleur Spanish. I recall a generic sense of school-time essays… Obviously, I am more meta than that these days. I am particularly interested in Shakespeare's Catholicism. More and more, it strikes me that the plays are testament to that loss within the English Reformation. Leaving aside such clumsy identity-politics as the matter of 'Was Shakespeare Catholic?', yet the condition of England seems tellingly. And, too, that such be not known, crudely. I saw a production – for instance – of Hamlet – on TV – it was a televised production – and there was a cardinal at court. And, upon encounter with the ghost, Horatio held up his rosary. ('Angels and ministers of grace defend us.') When, of course, the whole matter of the play is the break with Rome. That newly half-protestant England colours everything… This is not much but enough for a lunched thought. And this is our 'against' – our 'we are not' – violence committed on English-faith. Legacy still. We are of it. We aspire to be where you turn the clocks back to before the mistake.

I complete my first 100 kcals in a little over eight minutes. While this is slow, already the salted water begins to drench through me. Presently, I shall pool on the plastic-machine beneath. For now, there is thirst.

The point of the salt, by the way, is that it stops you getting tired. I've thought about this. It wasn't something I'd read in a book. I examined the evidence and I asked a question: Why did it just seem to leave you – the good you were getting from exercise?

I remembered how once, when I was nineteen, after a clubby night, I'd got debilitating cramp on the walk back, and my friends got me some salt from a chippy. And sure enough...

The way I'm going, I must be sweating eight-to-ten litres a day. (What with the gym and my hot baths.) This way, you get even more of that lovely, clean feeling, of fat-burn, with your reserves burnt. Yet, with the salted water, there is a lucency about it, a style of alert.

At lunch, I made mention of some of this. It was by way of chit-chat. I aspire to saying nothing consequential – and lunch least of all places. Yet Father Richard seemed to gnaw the inside of his face out, eating soup, as if attempting to manipulate the back of his mouth to hack-up – chicken bone or chicken drumstick gristle. I had no idea what was going on in there. You couldn't exactly ask Father Richard if he was alright.

Father Richard has a tennis racquet leant against the wall in his study in much the same way as I own a guitar. And then bemusement of trash on his desk snails off the sides of it – so much more complicated homework. Oh what brought him here... Seems you do *not* want to get on the wrong side of the HR department in the Catholic Church.

The short woman on the machine next is slowing now, cooling, having attained her objective. I've relaxed, and now Trevor is on the stairs. I greet Trevor, full of air, and for a moment redouble my efforts.

Julian's on his way up as well. There seems the most unusual response in my body. (In the pool, Julian asked if he might borrow my goggles. He couldn't get his head in the water. I thought it was quite nice that Julian asked if he could borrow my goggles.) Angels crawl, teeth-bared, in the mirrors opposite… It seems that to experience the body's limitation is creaturely. Freedom. I like *the creature* I am now – this moment. To experience *this body*, not as assumed-known, not as *an* extension of *a* subject, but objective-fact, no longer of a piece with thoughts, a machine-vehicle. Creaturely. Dialectic. Grizzled – grizzled-brain-explicit. A reciprocal arrangement of human-being.

Julian is nineteen and Trevor is thirty. Trevor simply doesn't acknowledge me. Julian gives a slow once up and down. He nods faintly. I watch them via the mirrors opposite. They address the isolation-machines. Though certainly flimsy – . *They* don't want to break against themselves. Dialectic? Not on your Nelly. Get out of here! No – they want the weights to-be-or-not-to-be who they already are. An awkward bit of metal and rubber on string – which is what it is, after all. They wear long shorts, Trevor's like a modern footballer's. Sort of like the opposite of the boys downstairs – who wear short shorts and depilate, trimming their pubic hair.

Herself next stands down as I am tantalizingly close to her. I switch bottles. Hamlet and the ghost of his father together at last. Jonathan and Ade race each other on adjoining treadmills. The Rector is on the stairs. The Rector is on the stairs… Sheepishly padding the steps to the mezzanine. Just as the tableau – the timing could not have been better – becomes complete.

What with Jonathan and Ade right next – and Trevor and Julian *proximate*. This *is* community living He wants so much of us. Moreover:

141

I am a picture of fierce good health.

I slug the bottle of the water. It is as an act of triumph I salute Him. Water dribbles off me and over my mouth. I towel my face and power – churn.

And Hamlet's Dad says: '…that incestuous, that adulterate beast, with shameful witchcraft of his wits, with traitor's gifts… Seduce… shameful lust… most seeming virtuous… queen… love… dignity… natural gifts… cursed… sleep… abused… damned villain…'

Dad!

Father Rector has only ever shared with us one clear impression of childhood. It was of a little boy with an ice-cream. On an ice-cream cone. All in sunshine. Gibraltar. A little hot street full of beefy English smells. Father Rector, in a sense, has a little-boy's face, so it isn't too difficult to imagine it. Father Rector has, in a sense, a little-boy's undeveloped frame, as though He should have come equipped with a Euroboy's rucksack. Blur the eyes a little – you're almost there.

A family-wash of shorts and T-shirt… Our eyes meet and you might call it a rueful smile. Wary of getting its dimples out. *His* skin lacking a touch of the old TLC from the inside… Vegetables. Fresh veg. And plenty of roughage.

No wonder He's lost the plot – given that paucity of processed muck He's supposed to trim down on. (Has He a qualified nutritionist? Has he or she an NVQ?) I glimpse a friend in there… Albeit ever so secret. An acknowledgement tracked with the corner of the eye. Not meaning to show himself. Watching. Who goes there? *Hereafter, in a better world than this, I shall desire more love and knowledge of you…* Different life. I watch both openly and in the mirrors as, down at the far end, The Rector mounts the first component in the routine worked out for

142

Him. And off He goes, peddling away, like a paper-round. The mildest of inclines – free-wheels His bicycle practically. Still, acquiescent to it. Boyhood not His own. Some other chap's scenery. Different life.

I'm at 850 kcal. I'm coming good – coming up on it. Not wishing to labour the point, but of course that's what it is: coming up on it. (I hardly even did the rave thing in the early 90s.) I am no longer much capable of straining to catch each word. I switch from *Hamlet* to a sweaty compilation of gym music. There I barrel-down into it: mucky noise. It seems dark, exciting music. A good squelch.

A song pokes through it: 'Run for the sun, little one / You're an outlaw once again / Time to change, Superman…' Loopy, it breaks through the regularized noise intermittently.

The *aim* is for serious jelly legs. This must be genuine – when, weak, I clutch air stepping down from it. Almost, my legs have to give out from under me. I want The Rector to see it.

The others have left. This close, at this limitation, I begin to dance to it on the machine. It could be called something like an illusion of power – redemption. *If He see…* Enable this. This real – an outward expansion of… As I – locked-rooms – things made real and bodies in physical theatre.

I am stronger than I was in September. Such has been achieved. And I maintain good progress. It is only in recent days I've upped my target on this machine, the cross-trainer, to 1250 kcals. (I am happy to go higher should the mood arise.) Nearing this now, I slow, though not tired. There is terminal 'rush' and there is periodic ache of depleting glycogen. As I get to within the last twelve, I raise my arms and give salutes to the mirrored-wall opposite. Consciousness.

The Rector is a little way off to the left, slowing Himself from a jog on a treadmill. Then it is done. The machine instantly crunched shut and seems to collapse on me. Jelly legs – duly acquired. I totter, floored pup, and I have to support myself – my legs are shaking really quite badly. My face holds no control.

I look like I'm going to be sick as I wipe the machine down. I use my vest on my face, then puff and get my breath back. There are mirrors down at the far end too, so I have a look there. It is not an imposing figure. Not-quite-six-foot-of-me. Better in metric. If The Rector looks about Year 6 I look about Year 10. Not a bad age. That would cover it.

There's no-one else on the mezzanine – apart from The Rector. It's just as well. The weights settings I use on the isolation-machines aren't heavy. I wouldn't want people not to realize what I've expended on the cross-trainer already. My little muscle shows well enough. Even so – if someone fresh began here, not having blown his own load on the cross-trainer, and seeing what a meal my body makes of a few reps. Well, that's the risk you take. I'm pouring wet anyway. I look like my insides – no matter what nameless others' suppositions communicate.

Checking the time – the sauna I've booked for the manager to turn up the heat will be ready in half an hour. There I shall sit in a half-lotus position, for the sake of my spine. And, as is customary, ride the high I've earned... But is it that? Ride the clean idea of me-me-me I've earned.

I like to think of my full gym-sessions, through the sauna and into the swimming pool, as a neat life-hack on more temporally cumbersome...

I think perhaps I might have burned something out in an earlier state. I think, perhaps, it isn't 'normal' only to feel – not feel – not to feel – whatever – in a gym-state.

That this is *penitential* fasting. A valid and accelerated form of the spiritual fast. I think perhaps – I don't know what. I should like to be free of it, whatever it might be.

In terms of fasting, there is today the additional benefit of having ingested relatively few calories at lunch. The gym has depleted reserves toward a state approaching zero.

I shall not feel hunger. There will be nothing of that interference. It is not, I feel, feeling of hunger – which outlines spiritual need. That is an imaginary complaint. (In perhaps-response to fleshly indisposition to feed.) Is, in a sense, itself glutted.

Starvation, on the other hand, when your body invisibly feeds on itself, aided and abetted with cool, gym-induced chemicals, and in the heat of a sauna, there you really find something approaching the right state. A solo pursuit. When your brain has nothing to work on apart from itself. What else religious mystics be rambling on about?

Cleanliness. Though this is not a view widely shared in college. The very word *sauna*! Laden with dark connotations for example for Julian. Sodom and Gomorrah and the little hot box! Their Christianity so often defeats me... Hearth and home and the telly on. A child's ears open to everything. All crushed-up with the telly on. No-one intended to connect with anyone else here. Not, then, a Christianity of vision. Stuffed, starved.

Lightly, I crack the weights, working my pectorals. A flayed-body infographic maps each muscle entailed from three clean angles. *Mind over matter* – LOL. I crack my spine at the neck, where it knots, and slow each weight's squeeze.

The Rector, with no ostentation, once more catches my eye, as He walks right by. Somewhere at perigee – gets set for a go of His own on a

145

cross-trainer.

Manly. Little boy to little boy. No clenching calf, no bulging thigh… No ragged prison walls to break His head against. Futile hope it might re-form Him differently – from the very-very basics of – what? – human-lexis. To think from the life of a body up.

The pool beneath lies blue and clear and empty. Then, when I get back round again, He's gone. You don't have to, but I like to wear Speedos in the sauna. So unlike how it is when you get to the beach! But here alone, the body potent, sexed. It seems the Speedos keep my sex alive. Schrödinger's swimming trunks… And, plain, so I don't have to look at it. For it really is a noble specimen, unfurled, yet packs itself away so tidily, ginger biscuits and golliwog curls, considering the life it might have led. Many a rosebud born to blush unseen. Not much trouble in the marital bed down there.

This is not a religious observance. Though the pool lie clear and empty. I do not here propitiate. Male space. Dehydrated fat beneath my skin sucks it all together. Clean innocence figured – sat on the wood in the orange light.

This body – *I* can do anything.

A putative I AM – but I discipline such thoughts, retracted to thoughts' cancellation. Not now, not yet, not here. Just a room.

Study our books and inhabit our commentaries.

Lean, I work my spine. Each ten minutes or so I take a cold shower. It is a sauna routine from a long time ago. I do this until only the heat is real. The cold thrills and I stretch through the length of the pool so powerfully.

*

146

There is a kept-back-after-school feel to Friday vespers. Any second now we'll be released individual people. And now, the air, our voice, has a flatness and sincerity to it. Geoff barely emotes. Shafts of light might penetrate into the sanctuary. (Fingernails rapped on plastic. Zipped throb of a pencil case. Homework-planner's riffled waft closed.)

Age to age shall proclaim your works,

shall declare your mighty deeds,

shall speak of your splendour and glory,

tell the tale of your wonderful works…

Yet, upon completion, none be first to leave… We sit in choir, in silence, over our beads and our breviaries. The ribbon book. Yet it seems frank choice as a paradigm shift – . There is prayer with an honesty about it.

The closing words remain and keep touching me: *Give us grace, Lord, to continue the works of penitence we have begun; so that the Lenten observance we have taken upon ourselves may be accomplished in sincerity of heart.* I hope that's so. I am hoping for my sincerity of heart. When people start wanting to move, it takes only a second for one's disengagement to quicken the rest of us. One might not *squeeze past…* At this, one might rise and lose himself in contemplation of a reredos-scene at a side altar.

Gold and the pilgrim men. The crushed serpent. Archaic, it seems – we bellow in silence of prayer with them. We don't have to go to supper on Friday. The evening is ours.

So I have my social time booked and that's later. Nine o'clock. It is now a quarter to six. There are supermarkets right on our street, and the street next, a busy Mercadona and a serviceable El Arbol, but I walk along via Plaza Mayor to the Carrefour. They keep beers in the fridge there. And I like to distribute my custom. (I don't like getting away from the thought there are cameras everywhere – I don't like the implication of there not being cameras everywhere.) It is a chance to absorb the not-yet evening town. The weight of tomorrow is lifted. A whole day. The Rector doesn't wear His hearing-aid on Saturdays. Silence holds.

You can think how it might be – to live here, call it home. The apartments are cheap. There'd be no local work. You could get something on the internet. It is a handsome place – the centre. There'd be no friends... The bookshops are open, but I have to be careful with money. (I'm quite rich at the mo if I don't spend anything.) By the cathedral, I watch the skinny young men on their skateboards. Then, on Santiago, the greater concentration of townsfolk take their evening stroll. A walking city: there are rarely many cars about. It is said the thing to do on a Friday is to stroll from bar to bar, as it were in progress, and make last a short glass – a *corto* – a short of beer – and so meet a reliable spread of your friendly acquaintance. (Presumably, some *must* stay still while others move? Or they move in contrary directions – so as to intersect? I know I'd just stay still – draped at the bar LOL.) Only ever two bars look busy on this route. They stand opposite each other in the alley that goes down to the cathedral. Plaza Mayor – the obvious hub – is empty. There are bars down past Plaza Mayor... This evening air: constitutional.

The bars never look to be particularly friendly. Not like *bars*. They spill out onto the street. Lonely places, invisible cities. Exclusive. Though dressed-to-the-nines – geared to an old-fashioned outburst of sexual discovery.

Friday food is a given: hummus, bread, wine. In the supermarket, I

148

browse the shelves, pretending for minutes I'm choosing ingredients to cook a delicious meal. I pick things up and put them down again. I weigh things up in the cheese aisle. They ask me what I want at the meat counter and I just smile. (We never seem to get rabbit in college.) I have a nose around in other people's shopping trolleys. Their week's shop like home. It is the magic of the Carrefour.

It being Friday, I choose for my treat a four Euro bottle of Rioja. An equivalent quality might sell for as much as fifteen pounds in England. I get my nuts and my dried fruit. I eat a lot of prunes. I take eight little half-cans of Heineken from the fridge. Two maybe three of those to get in the mood. Then for the whole night beyond to consider things.

At seven o' clock, in my room, I put the BBC news on. (Russia is in Crimea.) I listen to The News Quiz – recompose self in the spirit of that world. (Where friends find God for the sake of the schools.) I sip alternately from the first beer and a tumbler of wine. The Rioja is excellent. The hummus and baguette deeply satisfying. Earth-tastes. Crumbs of fresh, warm bread spill over the window sill. The sky is darkening.

And this room is a sleepy place. I've never once sat in that chairdrobe – not once. A multi-tasking student room again… I wonder: Is it too much to hope for a little job somewhere quite obscure? This wine flows marvellous searching. A little, little place, and a little presbytery. Where they wouldn't be *bothering* Tomàs… A little, little place, with a study and a tiny-little congregation, where they'd let me be?

My thoughts wander out over the fresh trees, and down and in amongst the crepuscular scrub, where cats live. I undress, because the air is so pleasant, and the news on the radio – so pointless, so irrefutable. So

149

bad, so bad, and an English voice – comforted. God, I think, doesn't mind Tomàs. God has almost no interest in Tomàs. I'm not like *them* – with their miraculous medals and scapulars worn in the shower to keep them safe. God very nearly has a soft spot for Tomàs. No *whispers* – no *livid self-abuse*... If you could see God right at the edge of the visible universe, in the Big Bang, there, perhaps, God calls: 'Tomàs, Tomàs, Tomàs.' And not ask too many searching questions or come-on deep.

Parishioners... in order to do the believing for them. A miniscule price I must pay for it. So placid. Cool as church stone. What delicacy might I reveal to them?

I flinch. I shudder. I have in me that like the girl in the film who ends up... That blowsy look of outright – unexpected innocence... I flinch, I shudder.

*

In January, we all were sent around England and Wales on what were called pastoral placements. An aim was that it would take us outside of known experience. If you were from the south, you'd be sent north. If from the north... They sent me sideways – into Wales. I was to be attached to a beautifully maturing priest who, so it turned out, knew Valladolid in capacity, over a period of years. (The cooked-books. Secret knowledge. Treasures.)

I took the train down to Crewe. I was nervous with the slow train's rattle in pursuance of an unknown. Then, from Crewe, via a series of ever-diminishing villages, and old mountain natural Christianity, my stop was not quite at the end of the electrified line.

I was in hills. High up. Mountains surrounded me. The numbers of people on the train thinned. It came to seem an adventure. A nowhere place – not-yet place. Still all-modern and not like an old shunter. It climbed its slow gradient. And, although I couldn't open a window, the economy of travel ceased to bother, and I felt already gratifyingly exposed, as if I'd already left something back in Crewe, in the station, in the panic of platform manoeuvres.

Canon Peter himself came to pick me up. As I emerged laden through the ticket office, blinking in the light of neat Wales, and seeing trees, and guarded, barbed-wire-girdled, and remote proximities, the little row of terraced houses there, and there the pub, and white lines, empty on the new tarmac, a man and a woman, who were not together, luggageless, who might once have travelled, and waited for the bus at the stop, in the shelter... a rasping car horn blared. A rather jolly – *big* hand wrestled with the window – emerged with a half-head in an arrested wave. And, with audibly questioned ignition, Canon Peter drew up in his ox-blood *old* Jag next to me.

My initial impression brought stark relief. I knew the face. Canon Peter had visited us students in Valladolid, though I had not known his name. I knew his voice – the mild, eggy, horse's-whinny – egg-*laying* hen-like – softest Welsh vocalics. Lipped, surrounding this, a Latin consonance. Precise articulation – as of a vaulted, limestone church. One might listen for Spain, but as it were beyond the chancel, the voice carried mystically anywhere. Canon Peter must, one thought, have known he was playing himself, in the manner of quietly observed, gentle caricature, in studious bemusement of Mind thus embodied. The priest-high tuft of cotton-floss to call his hair. The eyes blue marbles pronounced through the spectacles' round, steel frame. And his vicar's teeth in. One warmed to Canon Peter via minutes of piqued curiosity, as he became indeed the person initial impressions declared, and such literary exposure to such you might have known settled down with him.

151

He was safe, and so you were. The best version of yourself might feel quite at home.

Canon Peter hoiked my big green case into the boot of the Jaguar. Then I got the guided tour. Canon Peter drove briskly, farting and parping the manual transmission at each turn and gradient, with the occasional *how-d'ya-do*. As luck would have it, the weather was mild. There streaked blue-flashes, wispily arrayed amidst high-cloud. We were driving merrily our way into la-la land. The air – we wound our windows down – electrically bracing. He wore his dog-collar like diplomatic plates. Peasants must have scrambled – I was all eyes to view the inhabitants, be their attire turfy smocks and freckled woollens or fags and Adidas. There was none. Wales unfolded, the chromatic-scale an overlay of bureaucratic primaries on shades of moss-green. There were, too, ruined places, one of which held Catholic significance. We pulled off the road and drove a little way up a dirt track to look at it. It was a ruin. A stub of a house – it was not a church. There was clutch-work to get at it. Rocky and tumbledown. Clumps of briar, but no trees, and otherwise only the open fields. Yet it was a place where people once. Prayerful. As such, counted as such, a first lesson. Canon Peter pronounced one or two names twice. There were treasures such as this he wanted to show to me, as the grand tour of the ensuing month developed. This was not calculated: only a natural extension of who Canon Peter was. Well, of course, I was empty inside, with the train. And, with sleep, the next month had yet to take a lot out of me. My face made mild, receptive wonder. In willing passivity – only desiring to please. Such that the spiritual sense became its own thing. I tried to see it in the way Canon Peter did. It was not yet in my eyes – which had yet to agree an appropriate subject-position. Tentatively faked in skin – sought for in ways I first touched with a fingertip… One retained a thought of historical *despoliage*. And, though quaint, yet it might become deeper and beautiful, as silent prayer and cup-of-tea days gathered. I might have thought: Who am I that I should grow into this? And reached a hand to clutch the place. The body's rose-bowl glow of prayer, which you can see through your eyelids, as then a movement and shape of the body-in-prayer swells, blue and gold and red and green. The holy-holy. And we had a tramp round the place. Then: 'Well, there it is.' And on we drove.

We encountered no other cars. I could have stuck my head out the window to sing to the passing scene. I lolled my head to it. I felt liked. And might have been approximately fourteen tempered by twenty-one. I smiled and threw my head back and chuckled and the car seemed to drive less chaotically. You'd not take off your seat-belt – but might imagine an opportune song on the radio. There seemed existence. What joy! This place *existed!* All dry-stone-walls, and empty fields breaking on higher ground, spilled, gorse-encrusted, rock-strewn, like jacket-potatoes, over the portioned land.

We were well within mountain territory when Canon Peter slowed the car. This was inhospitable enough. Rough, extensive grazing land. But there were no sheep or other form of livestock. The air was sweet. The light was very white, with no colour added into it. The sun a light-box behind the cloud. It was cold. You could see your breath. Then there was a turn, and at the height of the road, looking down, by a small lake or a big pond, a settlement.

I saw a stone church, and a relatively large and modern redbrick building, which had the look of a hospital. It was a higgledy-arrangement. There were cottages, perhaps pulled back into functional being from prior dilapidation, and a row of what appeared to be new terraced housing.

There was one more significant building, a big, weather-worn house, both of brick and stone. Scratched-out claims filled the spaces, and reached a little way up as the gradient climbed toward mountain-side.

Canon Peter stopped the car. He said: 'Behold. The Promised Land.' He wasn't looking at me. I watched the lips carefully speaking in profile: 'The land was gifted to us. Now it is a place for those, men, for whom, for one reason or another, life has not quite found them elsewhere. They are Church people, but, within the Church, their calling has diverged from more conventional passage-ways. And some have experienced breakdown. And there have been other issues arising from mental health. So this becomes their home. There are eighteen of us currently. It is a not inappropriate number for the people concerned. Of whom, twelve are ordained.'

We drove down into it. Then it did come to seem a little bleak. A modern element didn't quite suit. There was new, black tarmac laid down. In the central zone, issues of drainage, where ice pooled. One little square-brick cobble-stone road led off, set in moss-green flaky cement and mud-smeared. The medical-seeming facility asked medical questions. A nurse's 204 – a little (beige) peanut car – parked askew outside.

Canon Peter's garage door was good by an inch each way to take his car, once we'd folded the mirrors back. The door was on a remote. It was admirable how Canon Peter lined the car up and manoeuvred it. There was plenty of space in the garage. This was given over to bins and wrecked furniture – all sticky-out wires in foam. I came to know it as a blind-spot, given Canon Peter's otherwise finickity neatness. Then there was who carries what, and high, wheezy breathing at the front door, expressive of transition of territory. Welcome.

It was neatly done inside. I slipped my pumps off – I wore white

154

socks – and tucked myself in – I was wearing a casual, button-down shirt and a cardigan. Best behaviour. The entrance hall was arranged with bric-a-brac, of a once-initial quality semi-antique. Rooms then abandoned any consistent scale. You wouldn't say it was homey, but that it satisfied other objectives. Shelves of books lined every wall – surrounded everywhere. If there were paintings, I can't remember them. There seemed a lot of space no-one *quite knew* what to do with it. *It* must have taken a sizeable furnace to keep the place dry and warm, for the ceilings were high and it was warm. I was shown to my private sitting room, beyond which my bedroom, beyond which my bathroom… A proper bed – and a proper great duvet. The housekeeper, who drove up each day from the village, and whose car it was, said she'd never disturb me if my door was shut. This, she said, most especially, for when I was praying.

Formal reception rooms and Canon Peter's office were down the far end. I went there to use the wi-fi – and for the bishop's visits. The dining room was masculine, the sitting-room a feminine arrangement of sofas, though somehow lacking a woman's touch. Canon Peter lived upstairs – beyond the landing where the housekeeper did all her ironing. There was a washing machine downstairs, which I wasn't supposed to use.

The other small room was an oratory. Here, at eight in the morning, those of the community who wished came for prayer before the Blessed Sacrament. There stood a wall of shelves stocked with more spiritual reading. They might have breakfast in the kitchen, where we listened to Today, and I received daily instructions. Canon Peter liked a great pot of tea with grilled toast and Benecol. Others liked bacon and eggs and half-a-tomato and black-pudding. Though a mere handful of the community came for prayers and breakfast, all went from chapel to the medical building for lunch. Copies of the Mail and the Echo lay about the place.

By the end of the first day, Canon Peter was *in situ* my absolute master… I decompressed. There seemed a noise-cancelled – though there might be throbbing rain. (January: Wales.) The manners of the institution quite mild, and loose, unstructured time, when an afternoon nap and even it might be a rosary gathered. Head-space. Absented of weaponized-time – with the timetable. Enfolding which, an indeterminate – backdrop, cinematic matte – filled with rock and cold, and damp air, and brilliant sky and lashing rain in rapid oscillation.

There seemed no wild actions – no monstrous demand imposed on an emollient field, which drew the heart, upward, to crystal uncertainty. There were routines. Old-men routines – like intravenous tubes and washed, carbolic skin with a look of poultry.

It was nice, in the afternoons, to wander in, where a few of them sat in their big sitting room, and pull-up one of those chairs, with a gin and lemon and the afternoon telly on. A questing disposition stood alert. When, in the morning, we prayed, it was the four-week psalter, but once we had said the invitatory and said the hymn, we sat together fifteen minutes silent. Then one began to say it – to deliver the antiphon. Being inspired – and there followed no set order as to who did what. The Spirit moved. A further period of uncalculated silence concluded each psalm and preceded each antiphon. Canon Peter, one gathered, enabled by dint of being present. Even he might not say the concluding prayer. Then we waited a little more – dwelt on it. I might leave first – there was honestly no judgement either way.

It was a treat for me to serve, which I did each day at Mass. I wore a cassock and a surplice. Always, Canon Peter was the celebrant, except

156

when the Bishop came. Also, I read, and they got me singing the psalms like we do in Spain.

In the Sacristy, I watched Canon Peter preparing to celebrate Mass, and again, during Mass, while Canon Peter prepared to deliver the Gospel and while Canon Peter invoked his homilies. Canon Peter's words of homiletic encouragement permeated into my own and my physical consciousness in what might have been an inspired state. His words were few and simple, prayed with whole being, such as a saint might. Robed – vested. Such prayer as one discerns within spiritual community.

Careful with what I was doing, for the setting of the altar, and to cleanse Canon Peter's hands with water, I, in a sense, saved my real listening, and silent imitations, for later. It flows and imbues my whole sense of my stay here. And, little by little, day by day, a fearfulness in the solemnity gained confidence.

Still, such thoughts I might have had were not fully yet ready to improvise. When I said pretty much anything, bar merest practicalities, Canon Peter took it in with the whinnying-horse-noise. He raised his chin, and his part-smiling upper lip, as if to place my new words, and showed his gums and sucked his buckteeth. A wise and rational horse and his *muchacho*. Considered response might be returned in a matter of seconds, minutes, hours…

My principal duty was only to shadow Canon Peter through the course of each day. In the mornings, on occasion, I would visit with Canon Peter the two men who lay in bed in the medical facilities. One seemed quite coherent, though he was not very well, and his thoughts were taking their leave of things, speaking with dead friends, and remotely attuned to the nothing-to-disturb Canon Peter contributed. I was little more than a smile – youth – and a bit of a spare part in these situations. As often as not, I was left to my own devices. I thought it might be because of my own sensitivities – at this stage in the process of being formed. Either I'd roll myself up in unconsciousness, or go for a walk. There was no great instinct, no great need. But looking out of my window, there was time and a space to accommodate, and soon I was small and there was no great worry as to my meaningless thoughts being seen.

Never one for unpacking a suitcase, I scraped the top-layer of my age-inappropriate clothing, my Top Man tops and my prissy jeans. The sky above took what the earth had to offer it – swung low in receipt of the earth's gaze unconditionally. Whether it were ice-blue or slate-heavy – chucking the rain down – the phases passed so quickly. I'd walk about the place up on the incline, stumbling, scrambling, crawling on the face of this home-planet. Dirt beneath my feet: the red stamp of All Stars. Naturally, having neglected to pack a waterproof mac. Something like a jetty fed into the lake, and I adopted this as one of my stations. There were no boats, and none seemed to be fishing it. Whether or not you might be able to stock it, I had no idea. At the lake-shore, right at the water's edge, it was a black, slatey gravel, and coarse winter grass fell into it. There I stood, a wandering rock, a wastrel. There the great mountain scheme seemed to open-out, beaming its messages into the sky, as if we were a radio telescope, and then lash-back on me. I started shaving in the shower, to have done with my ablutions, and not paying altogether too much heed to the mirror.

Probably, my body was cleaning itself also, hence the occasional clamour to bury myself in the duvet, and too those arrested times when the high-edged sharp-rock of the basin – like a shark's mouth and the

158

extreme limit of everything. I already felt it was this place I liked far more than any other I'd known, when on a day, in pumps, like it might have been Ry's feet I contemplated, though less remote imitations I contemplated. This was when I made my older friend. After Mass, and lunch, when the hours' free time was, and when I did a lot of sitting on the gardens' boundaries, built of rough stones cleared from patches, no more than a foot or so high, though washed clean of soil with the rain that fell.

My pumps – a kind of question-answer. Nicely stretched with wear to accommodate the toes. Black with mountain dirt besmirched... Youth! I must have been tired with lunch. All the blood digesting. Blowsy youth's adolescence. I'd fidget bits of grit and rub my fingers in the soil – absently let that go in a kind of distraction. I'd think about sad things – or, more specifically, moments that live in the brain and crush you, such that your neck bows low, and in innocence, shedding life's mistakes, become receptive. Crew-cut Tomàs told his grit-for-beads in clouded, slanting sunshine. I was on the track by what turned out to be Father John's claim. Father John was digging. A piece of the land. A face full of stubbed-out – shop-bought cigarettes. The sky having begun to exert its lift upon me. The thin sky – de-addicting. (Always de-addicting.) Washed. The faintest, purest, shining – faint *azul*.

I probably must have been looking at Father John. At some point, I must have asked for help. Maybe a face – some acknowledgement. That bit of business apparently going unnoticed... There came a point, Father John turned from his digging to look at me straight, and then said: 'You ought to make yourself useful, you do. Get your wellies on and give us a hand.'

159

I had no wellies. I hadn't even brought smart shoes. I hadn't brought a suit – or shirts that go with ties nor ties to go with them. It hadn't really occurred to me – any of those things. Dressed in missing pieces, Father John said I'd have to wrap plastic bags over my pumps. Father John had just taken a delivery of a ton of dried bat-shit, and we had to sprinkle it around then dig it into his garden.

Canon Peter observed the development and seemed pleased.

Father John could have come across, to the faint of heart, as a sight best avoided looking at. He smoked ready-made, filtered cigarettes, a brand I didn't recognize, though judged the pitch from the packet's colour scheme. He'd stub one out with his foot, ripping the filter off. The filters he stored in his pockets as though for later. Father John's teeth collapsed at regular intervals. His tongue was pitted-grey, with lesions each side of it. He'd run his tongue under his palate and top lip, perhaps tasting the nicotine. What he had to be cultivated measured about the size of two standard allotments. It was all dug and soiled. And he had his ideas. He was expecting the delivery of a greenhouse any day now.

He showed me the way it was set to be laid out. You had your fruits here, your long-term projects, bushes and trees, and he reckoned on herbs here, then your annual veg. There was more than a foot's depth of clean organic soil, which must have been bought in. And it was smooth and fine – he must have sieved it. Moist-wet to saturation point. Drenched with rain. It must have cost someone a packet to buy the soil in. Only it needed digging more – it wasn't ready yet.

We sat at half-hourly intervals for Father John to smoke. My self-presenting in ways I was ceasing to care about. The only volitional intent was the action of sitting. All-thought wound down to a clock's tick – unmovingly simple potential – other than that. When Father John said prayers, there was an element of tongues about it. That was in mind, and not for all the broken furniture mouth-wise. A scrap of Psalms occurred to him, and then again about the plants he had ordered. A portmanteau flow like drifting weather – chewy with mashed-up, raspy phlegm and saliva when his dentures slipped. It was all at an elevation.

And there'd only be negative consequences should I speak. Once in a while, he'd stop and touch me on my ribcage with his cigarette-finger. He'd curl his mouth into a knowing, telling, sly grin, as though he said to me: I'll be dead, but you'll see.

I, at some more settled interludes in Father John's prayers, made the beginnings of a gesture to cross myself. (I didn't: this was honest.) I spoke in a quiet, holy fashion when Father John said an Our Father. I spoke as Henry might, given similar circumstances. Child-minding a view of myself – just as Henry might. It was in a thought disembodied and spiritual. Though such as you could hold it in the palms of your cradled hands. Nice to hear-think-see – finitude – just as if I were a little prayer, buoyed on the great bag-of-wind of an all-prayer. A little, shallow prayer, like a puddle, looming fathomless, depth of sky.

Canon Peter tended to claim me during the mornings and into the afternoons. This was for what were effectively motoring tours of huge slabs of territory. Few were the necessary pretexts: there was an ordination; there was a funeral. Canon Peter liked getting his car out. He liked the pride and the sheer joy showing off God's own country. And we essentially razzed between beauty spots. Twice we just drove to the coast to admire it, and sat in the car-park a few minutes, then drove right back again. And there were precious destinations, the odd shrine, one or two functioning churches, a community of monks and a community of nuns, historical bits and pieces. It went dark early and there was much to be seen of it. The roads were new and well-groomed, for the most part, though there were speed traps, right where the speed-limit randomly changed in the middle of nowhere, but Canon Peter was wise to them, chunnering past them in third, then smoothly cranked-up, sighed in bemused contempt at the blasted things.

Father John came along often. He was up for it – taking his jollies. Clogging the car with fag-smoke. And seeing things *he* hadn't seen in years. One day we had fish and chips, in a guest-house attached to a monastery, and it was outright-joy for him, though I tried not to look – they were difficult mouthfuls. (My thorax clenched and repudiated – it was all going to come up disgracefully into my own mouth – I could not both see it and yet remain sympathetically proximate to it. But if I blurred my eyes, so that I didn't see precisely.) Father John kept saying: *Auoooh. Auooh that's lovely.* He liked the condiments all in their little dishes, and mostly cleared the plate of the fish and chips, leaving the peas. I had with mine a pint of cider, which wouldn't be made last, and then a second, which I made sure to leave the bottom half-inch of. I was participating carefully in the conversation, and ended up thinking I'd passed, while Father John told me a few things, and said things.

Perhaps it was with having Canon Peter there, but Father John's line became pointedly gossipy. 'Inappropriate,' Canon Peter would later say. Father John's interests got pretty blunt. 'Any funny business?' he asked of Valladolid. That, at least, was easy. Nothing like that. On other matters, I felt it would have shamed me and made me look a fool to describe the experience accurately, so I bluffed, airy-casual, and talked the time out.

I said something about hoping to learn. I – Tomàs didn't want to expose myself – the thought of sitting in that classroom. I knew no way it could have other than exposed my own cheap mediocrity. Dullness. Hubris. Bloated. Half-drowned. Filthy – the cut of my thoughts. And no better than the rest of them.

When it must only appear to be my fault my being here… But, for the matter of 'funny business', there lay truthful ground, and Father John didn't let go of it. One of the seminaries in England had just recently been purged. They must have been at it pretty strong to get caught like that. My trying not to say anything flippant. Some little piggy had squealed. New bugs – LOL. Before Canon Peter more firmly put a stop to it.

Which was just as well. I would have said something frivolous – camp – my cover blown. This when the merest circumstantial each next second seemed to threaten to blow my case out of the water.

And there my misfit-nature stands revealed… But Canon Peter put a stop to it. Rosy-hued sunniness – of Wales and Spain restored to the matter. I had met one or two of those boys when they came to visit. They had the explorative manner about them, such that you wouldn't have minded their doing stuff together. They were generically quite young.

But all that was weeks away. Hours and days. The engine ran loud, and it thunderously ricocheted. Sat in the back seat, and with the open window, it was difficult to make out quite what was said at the best of times. Though pushed forward, braced, in the gap between the front seats, I hardly got a word of what Father John was going on about. In part, it seemed inspired by the landscape's imprint. And, in part, it seemed like people they both had known – Fathers John and Peter. Welsh words. Whatever happened to… <welsh_word> ? Bundled and jollied along with it. But a confusion of impressions as I pretended to listen a bit. Plumped back in wind-waft other-time. Eagerness all. Spirit of things, that was.

163

No-one getting picky as to who said what and when.

In due course, it became a known thing I fancied myself a bit in the kitchen. They made space for me there, and I had a play. I just liked pottering, really. People brought lamb and fish when they came up to Mass. I had a sizzle with the meat, and made fish-parcels. Once saying, before I had a chance to stop myself, 'I am rather partial to a parcel.' And we gathered in the communal room for the daytime telly… It was pretty healthy living all told. My getting up early – and I slept nights. I didn't need much beyond the rhythms of the short day.

Now, working Father John's garden was a settled thing. A meditative practice, though it was really done, and the fag-breaks elongated. We were awaiting further deliveries, and I prattled a bit. You could be nice to me and say I was exploring issues of my own truthfulness. I don't think it would be not-nice to point out I just like prattling! Applied gloss to a handful of under-revealed years. Half-confessionals. Revisionist-edits and second-takes. Begged – like prophecy – such light there might be going begging – from such rudderless tat of a Saturday night in the sixth-form-drinking years.

Father John didn't say much. Information-restriction. *Clear your mind… Until only the best thoughts…* My *thought* – not *me* – had such arguments with itself. Never letting go – it was always somebody else's fault. That there were times, in strength, health, and clarity, a particularly invigorating walk, on a long-emptied stomach, and all like crenulated mountains, ranged in *not quite twilight just yet* – until they all became indistinguishable rock and air.

Times when those years might yet be happening, quickening, maybe tomorrow or yesterday, if not right now. When, through the great

164

lens of the 20th century, they/we creolized – TV cultural packages, Waterstones, HMV. And turning a blind-eye here to the entire dissipation the legal imperfection of uselessly privately lusting ripen-at-home fruit of our/their bodies might have properly engaged in noiselessness, intimacy, blind rut. Equipped to grasp, to learn, we were in a confused state.

We had Freud, and Marx, and TS Eliot. We caught at such evidence – much was self-generated from ourselves. We were both big and open hearted, and categorically-gifted – bullshit-alert. The best that we have in the world is in large part built on such people. Our field-love where we talked and drank our cider – with rich, simple, clean, ironic gestures, and enormously saggy hair. The mind that beats, the heart that thinks – like love clasping hands with itself, the gift united. Grasping merely the faintest iota of that now, belittling, religiously, pulling at the thread, as though that would unravel a thought I'd never… Categorically missing the whole point – and for what? (Because none of the scenes *kissed*? Because none of the scenes *made together bodies*?) I said religiously things like:

'At school – I don't mean when you're that small and just getting through it. And not thinking anything. Not what you remember, anyway. But in sixth form. And maybe a little bit earlier that that, when you're bored and you want to be free now, and your Friday or Saturday night is all sitting round in a cow field talking. The consensus of those who had any view at all was all atheism. Among the intellectually half-awake, those arguing went to an actual denial of human sentience. They had us all down as software. And you try arguing against people who argue they themselves don't exist. I used to get frustrated, when you tried explaining: No, a Chinese Room is not sentient. A transistor is not sentient. You are wrong. Stop talking. Think now. You couldn't explain it to them. And I couldn't explain it. I guess even now my core sense of things tends toward dualism, though the idea of all energy-matter itself as inherently charged with sentience begins to gain traction at a level of what can be grasped by the natural mind, as it were, and not of hyper-conceptualism. They'd got their atheism in a package.'

We'd delegate Phil to get the booze from the offy, Phil having had a full beard since year 9. Only the half-dozen lads when we really talked. The bigger parties weren't like that. One of the abiding memories is of other people's families and family-lives integrated in their voices. Working the evidence – naturally so hard. All flurrying through one another. It's still a delight to hear it – say in the pub on Friday – when you catch the same music and wonder what the logic of it might be. Yes, yes. That's the level. The long week's overflow taking its shape ID'd at half-past eight today.

Father John said: 'I served in London, down in Clapham, as well as Zimbabwe.'

He'd told me already he was born in Liverpool. He touched me with the back of the hand on his shoulder, and looked as if he might be about to say anything. His eyes didn't look very well. There didn't seem that clarity – as, for instance, Ron's had, when he was just bored of the rigmarole, and getting to the point they could turn him off now. These looked – sickly, ill. Ron's, at the end, looked remarkably conscious.

The greenhouse arrived in a set of flat packs. It came with two men who were going to put it up for us. The plan was to put it down directly on the bricks we'd set out, then lay some flagstones as a central walk. Eventually, Father John got cross – not being cut out for spectatorship. So *he* got in the way, and I therefore thought *I'd* better get in the way… Sort

166

of like also apologizing – like there I was in my plastic bags.

It all became a bit more real with that there. It was the talk of the community at supper. ('I saw your greenhouse arrived today, Father.' 'Ay. Very nice, thank you.') There was no point wishing he'd stop smoking. It was time to start thinking about what plants he might get going in there. In a month or so.

Our supper was all laid out for us, on the side, for us to help ourselves. The women then left for the day, and it was up to the men to pile the plates up. I remained honoured guest. The bit of life. And meals were slow and peaceful. Canon Peter might initiate the odd conversation. There seemed little by way of collective memory, other than here, though our day-trips featured and evoked. There might be wine – for feast days. And mention of news, of the outside world, which was always Church news, and passed without debate, though as if they were a part of it. I got the idea. I'd say the odd thing, strictly local, the weather, the star-watching app I had on my phone, the community cat, the good exercise – walking up into the hills and in Father John's garden. Anything really – they liked it. They asked me if he'd got the TV in my room to work, if I knew how to get my washing done, and that there was 'internet'. It was all very cosy indeed – thanking them. Whether there was more – it seemed they were perfectly satisfied. It seemed very much best only to say it was very much perfectly all in its right place. Besides, Canon Peter would have said. And at the end, when they gathered and touched me, thanking me for coming and blessing me, I seemed to realize how limitlessly simple it all was, however that moment's real intuition stayed there. And, of course, it was only a rest, from the which I had left-out a great deal of necessary matter – personhood – outside. They invited me warmly to come again… I suppose that won't be possible.

167

Meanwhile, though, I had my days, and the plastic bags. There was a week yet when Father Richard came. Would that he had come when Father John and I were at our gardening! Alas: no. I was just sat on a rock up the hill a bit. Even if asked, I could only have honestly said I was so 'in the moment' my mind was a total blank. And that would have gone down like a bucket of cold sick with Father Richard.

I saw the car cropping the hill – the crest a couple hundred meters off. A black peanut-car. It didn't know the road, and touched the brakes as if negotiating pot-holes. It could only be – and I panicked. First, I froze, then I took-off-on-one, straight off in the opposite direction, brainless instinct, pretending I hadn't seen. *Oh Lord thou pluckest me out* – . But this was basic fear. Not that I hadn't known that I ought to expect. But this was gut-violation. Bowel-voidance what you've kept in sphincter-tight. I wore a layered combination of exo-thermal-underwear, woollies and a hoody, and the bags. The rising-inclination scrambled under me. There stopped being a path, and as I scrambled I was hurting myself, getting twisted and barking my ankles. After a while I stopped and the madness passed me. I looked back and saw the little black peanut-car parked in the square. The door opened. One-foot-two-feet probed uncertain ground. He was unmistakable.

I looked to the sky, but no messages. It wasn't even raining. I looked back down the way I'd just come. That mad-scramble hadn't taken me very far. I supposed I'd better, and picked my way. The cuneiform speck of him. Death's house-elf and the Black Maria. Priest and car. Pretty soon, I was waving and calling out:

'Father Richard!'

The whole valley could hear me. Oh boy, I sang it aloud. 'Father Richard!' I waved when I'd got his attention, then took the remaining time real slow.

Carefully, I picked my way down the side of the mountain. The plastic bags had shredded, and the pumps were already wrecked. I used my arms for balance, wary of taking a tumble on one of the many stones. And anyway, opening mental windows, a few minutes and this was a natural pace – in slanting midday-light exposed and great breadth. On the path, I ambled. Friendly, natural smile, at the portly fellow, a little bit out of his way there. Touched by a spot of the fluster. By and by:

'Tomàs?'

Squinting – he wasn't sure. Stood in a puddle he'd discovered. Best put him out of his misery. I flung my arms wide:

'Hello, Father!' I upped my pace to a not quite a jog. 'Heya, Father. Nice to see you.' There was nothing immediate so I added: 'What brings you here?' Throw that in. Then: 'Isn't this lovely! Are you alright?'

Though my nails were black, I put my hands in my pockets. The loose, saggy, gardening jumper, all bulked out with the hoody and thermals, feet at five-to-one – it was the most open posture. The broadest smile I smiled, like pickled onions, an entire cellarage of French wine, black, Greek olives, and a barrel of fresh cheese. Would that I had not shaved – yet I had. The winter chill, though, in combination with the exercise, pinked my cheeks merrily, and leant a panting aspect. Still Father Richard didn't speak. It was around now Father John opened his front door and took an interest. After a short while, I said to Father Richard:

'Are you staying?'

169

He said like he secretly meant it: 'It's good to see you, Tomàs.'

'It's good to see you too, Father!'

'Yes, it's good to see you.'

'What are you doing here?'

Father John approached. He had his wellies on, and picked up the old, wooden spade-handle that leant at the front door, making out he used it for walking.

Father Richard said: 'You look...'

'I know! Gone native!'

'Do you know where...'

'Where...?'

Even here it was – the lightest, mild spasm as something of the pain bit. It ran almost a shudder, the blockage in him, for in excess of a second, through the fight in his eyes and down the side of his face like a stroke. With guttural control, he repeated: '*Where...*'

'Canon Peter...?'

There was no way of knowing if he knew it was only himself, and maybe a happy drive turbulently shaken awake from, Father Richard had any excuse to get cross about, or if that already was something in the way I was all weird and queer and unreachable. All with this – *thing* about him. Like I thought I was somehow better than everyone else. And all that. Death inside. All that and all that and all that. Death and the child. Or, hell, of one's ecclesial prospects, in this case. Death like a gentleman going to the wall...

So with such excess of politeness as might make the matter worse... The squall dropped. Father Richard and with a long sigh: 'Yes,' he said.

'I don't, I'm afraid. He's often with parishioners at this hour. Are you coming to lunch?'

'I don't know, Tomàs.'

'Perhaps you'd like coffee?'

Father John was there now. He stared at Father Richard, and when he had Father Richard's attention, said: 'Who are you then?'

I said: 'Father John, please allow me to make introductions. This is Father Richard.' I made a sweeping gesture with both my arms to exhibit Father Richard. 'Father Richard is the Vice Rector of the college in Valladolid.' And then: 'And this, Father Richard, is Father John.'

Father John said: 'Happy to make your acquaintance. What you doing here then?'

Are these real questions? perhaps Father Richard might have thought. (Why is the sky pale-blue yet the puddle brown? Father Richard might have thought.)

Father John chuckled and said: 'Checking up on us. I know. You're not here for the lunch! Come to see if our Tom's been a good boy.'

To a more assured man, there might have been enough there of friendliness. And there was that Father Richard hadn't had much to do with the funny-old-man end of parish life lately. I intervened:

'Do you have any luggage?'

'I'm only here for a quick visit.'

'That's nice of you.'

Father John chuckled: 'You're not here for the lunch!'

He gave Father Richard the wink. He held out the spade-handle, as if teasing Father Richard, to see if he'd shake it. Then turned and walked back to his house, in the Beckett style, walking his prop, where inaudibly he shut himself in.

171

I said: 'Well, I can play host for the interim.'

And really, that was only the way he was, and there was nothing to be done with him. My hands had returned to my pockets, my chest broad, and I stood as it truly was, openly.

From such towering perspective – what did I see? A bag of frayed nerves – a fusspot – granted. A man to swing the chopper and bury the dead. Gestus of robot – mass-million-horde – dull remainder past savour of imaginative grace. Sort of a bit like the opposite of lessons in GCSE class – the Weimar Republic – and that book – *The Temple* – and that boy I shared the desk with and Miss. Arch-prole, a Levitical ape – where your Jews-artists-poofs-intellectuals. The external threat – a dream-serious boy's trepidation crushed in a loose word. Yet it was odd how, bucked in the contaminant presence of such gurning literalism, a play of breezy nothings, and worn, social phrases, tags, seemed catalyzed. Yet, no frivolity, none of the language… Nothing. None of that. Nothing of that.

I asked Father Richard if he'd like a cup of tea. To the which Father Richard replied:

'Yes, thank you, Tomàs. That would be very nice.'

In the hallway, I sat on the floor to take my bags and my All Stars off. I showed Father Richard where he could place his own shoes to dry, if he wanted, but Father Richard scuffed them about on the mat, and said there was probably no need. My socks were damp and blackened, so I thought for a second then took them off too. In the kitchen, I prattled about with the tea-making, all flak.

'It's all really nice. You'll want to meet the people. Well, you have to. You won't understand if you don't do that. It's blessed. Earl Grey okay? Or there's English Breakfast. There is a closeness to Heaven here. It is quite special. Is there anything in particular you wanted to see me

172

about? Do you want milk?'

'Well, Tomàs. Yes, please. I'm visiting just to find out how you are, really. It's as simple as that. While it isn't a formal interview – oh, thank you, that's lovely – it's important really to know how you are, in terms of your pastoral placement. So yes, I won't ask you just now, because we'll have something of a more formal interview – not interview. But now isn't quite the time yet.'

'Oh okay.'

I leant with my own cup of tea on the worktop. Then in the end, Father Richard said:

'Of course, if there is anything you want to say, about your experience here, so far, on your pastoral placement.'

'Oh, it's great. What sort of things did you want to know?'

'Well, maybe we should save that until – the right time.'

'Okay.'

A further quietly smiling, nothingy interlude cradling a cup of tea… Until:

'Do you know where…'

'Canon Peter?'

'Yes, obviously, where Canon Peter is?'

'No idea. I think he mentioned you were coming. Not sure he said when. Do you need to see him?'

'Well, yes, that's important.'

'Are you coming to lunch?'

'I don't know, Tomàs.'

'Well, you tell me what you want to do.'

'I think I need to see Canon Peter.'

'He's usually at lunch.' Pause. Rippled tea… Then: 'Shall I go and ask they set a place for you?'

'Yes, Tomàs. Perhaps that would be the best thing.'

Well, indeed.

I skipped across to the Refectory. In the kitchen, Brother Thomas was helping, so I directed remarks to him, and the others listened. I explained we had a guest, and who Father Richard was, assuring them, so far as I knew, Father Richard ate normal food. Brother Thomas said he'd put the extra place-setting out. He wondered if there might be wine, though it was a feast day tomorrow. The thought lay moot, then Karen said she'd put a couple of bottles out, though it was Friday.

I didn't exactly feel like racing back to the presbytery kitchen. The Refectory kitchen smelt most strongly of fish stew and carrots and peas. Good smells – that warm right through you. I stood a moment outdoors, and had a little turn in the yard, taking it all in, absorbing. Called to demonstrate what I'd achieved… Invoking time and confidence.

When I returned to the presbytery kitchen, Canon Peter was there already. A fresh pot of tea sat on the table, and there were Welsh cakes, to which Canon Peter was partial. Canon Peter laughed, and Father Richard was talking. And now I realized Father Richard had been one of Canon Peter's students – at Valladolid. Later Canon Peter would tell me Father Richard was among the kindest students he had ever known.

There was nothing to contribute. Where were they all now – and all that. Name-checked. Accounted for. A theology of life. Good breadth… And go easy on the detail. Life's flow. I sucked the skin off my tea and topped it up at the table. They spoke inaccessibly, arranging themselves to a rough sketch of provisional common ground. I paid silenced homage. And Canon Peter made sure it was alright.

*

174

Nice thoughts. Nice memories. Why did I say I'd go out with them? The gym, across the yard, could only be a long twelve second sprint away. Over the scrubland, through the trees. Tripping on prayers and lunatics, cats and tumbleweed, roots and grazed knees. Leafy giants.

And anyone there on the mezzanine can see into my room too. So I've been told, with a not-quite-laugh, that I need to be careful in here. One lone – boy, a student, if it is him, heavy and regular flat-foot-throb on a treadmill. That time, gave me the lingering – . If it is him. He wore elaborated muscles for his not-much height. I should have smiled, but I lacked the volition. Getting my points up. Working evening beers.

There'd be no-one from college there now… I must put on a face. Flaking is not an option. They'd knock, then be nice about it, and I should have to pretend I am tired or some shit, and that would bat back and forth gruellingly. No – I must put on a face. And shower. And eat a little more of the bread and hummus. I must consider what to wear. Play some music now. One hour. Do myself up a bit. Just nice – not provocatively.

Warmth spreads through me. Beer and wine. Air at the open window. Washed in music. There the evening laid… Cities. Cape Town. San Francisco. Moreover, placeless cities, cities I've never lived, which couldn't have names. My invisible cities – which mobile technologies touch and nurture.

Whereas the cities-lived mostly have names. Matt. Al. Justin. Luca. (Ash. Jan. Guy…) Squandered quantities. And I couldn't afford them. But that was the way – when you attempted to actualize. When all the whole universe-city that bright night must be squeezed into one of them. Relentless self-extension – forcing a lad to mean. And too many cab-drives. Though they accessorized mutually. Too many boys-being-poetry – too much burn.

I put REM's *Automatic For The People* on. Outside, I can *hear* them... I shower, lathering my body. Dirtily welcome the shower's spray of hot water into my gaping mouth. I scrub my face hard, and shave for a second time. (The old yet serviceable blade will soon need changing. Razor-blades, rationed, constitute an expense.) Restorative, preparative, rejuvenative... A slick of the all-body Q10 moisturizer, this plastic bottle labelled bilingually in Spanish and Catalan: 'Reafirmante' / 'Refirmante'. That's from a beach town south of Tarragona. They kept their beauty products in a locked cabinet. You had to ask an assistant to unlock it, and they would take what you wanted to leave it behind the till.

My skin looks *very* good. There is even a lick of foundation in that bathroom bag of mine. Their laughter, as they get pissed, rings through the corridors... On my desk, there remains perhaps half the wine. I eat a little of the dried fruit – a prune – and proceed to drink one more of the stubby beers. Well I'd better get dressed, I suppose. Pretend you're going out. Expired-twink. If I lay on my bed, ten seconds, in meditative posture, I'd wake in the middle of tomorrow.

I wear an almost-iridescent shirt, a moody purple-black, by Giorgio Armani, as the light catches it. I gargle and brush my teeth. The room is set in order, the food spread about on the window-sill, cans neatly organized on the shelf. The lap-top locked – the desk looks lived-in.

At the door, downstairs, they stand raked together like autumn leaves... We aren't all here yet, and I am early. There'll be some hanging around to do. Best behaviour. Alex makes a point of looking happy to see me. So Anthony does. All silent... Squashed in hoods and pockets. *Best* behaviour means – acquiescence, passivity, non-interventionism, quietly voiced, as in the decisions made, so in the actioning. The point being not to arrive, or yet to venture forth, but group-formation and mutual deferral.

An observational matter – of human imitation and, quietly, simply, eddying, seminal flow. Geoff being not yet present.

And I have had a dose – rendering the matter equable. When Henry arrives, he looks glam as autumn high-streets – in the sales. Well, someone's made the effort, I think, and you can see him at the perfume-counter, in parallel life, not uninformed, but selecting, in wide-brim charcoal and Hannibal Lector fedora, his little gift for his best girl. Furthermore, Henry s set to get going. He claps his gloved hands and adjusts his coat lapels. (I am going to freeze in this shirt.) A good half of us are here now. Henry says Geoff'll catch up with us. And an alternative sub-group has formed, getting lashed in the common-room. So now, given which information, these additional, necessary murmurings take but a little while.

Henry proves key. We'll head to the bar we've initially agreed upon. On the street – the pavement – no more than a hundred meters – there is formal significance. Maybe, you might say, the shadow of something like that. We amble, slow, and who knows what the feeling? Mayhap, skin-sensation wanders lifting. If we'd said our Friday Compline, that could have put us to bed alright[2]. Vespers, though, on

[2] 'Qui habitat in protectione Altissimi, / sub umbra Omnipotentis commorabitur. / Dicet Domino <<Refugium meum et fortitudo mea, / Deus meus, sperabo in eum>>. / Quoniam ipse liberabit te de laqueo venantium / et a verbo maligno. / Alis suis obumbrabit tibi, / et sub pennas eius confugies; / scutum et lorica veritas eius. / Non timebis a timore nocturno, / a sagitta volante in die, / a peste perambulante in tenebris, / ab exterminio vastante in meridie. / Cadent a latere tuo mille / et decem milia a dextris tuis; / ad te autem non appropinquabit. / Verumtamen oculis tuis considerabis, / et retributionem peccatorum videbis. / Quoniam tu es, Domine, refugium meum. / Altissimum posuisti habitaculum tuum. / Non accedet ad te malum, / et flagellum non appropinquabit tabernaculo tuo, / quonian angelis suis mandabit de te, / ut custodiant te in omnibus viis tuis. / In minibus portabunt te, / ne forte offendas ad lapidem pedem tuum. / Super

Friday – Friday's evening prayer – begging and crying for life. Lethal the spirit of it. Death's touch. 'You have taken away my friends…' Lost – hollowed nothing. As when in sleep the dream, if such be called, is nothing. No up, no down, no 'real' – the thought pleads helplessly. No waking from it. Thinned – structurally dispersed information – *itself* – the hole, the gaping hell of it.

 Alex walks beside me. He says: 'It's nice to get out, isn't it?'

 I reply: 'It's a lovely mild evening.'

 'Better here than in England, hey?'

 'I guess.'

 I think to ask Alex if he recalls it ever having rained in Valladolid, but by the time the thought occurs, we are at the pub. Here, Julian, Sean and Trevor play table football. I don't notice their buying drinks, and so become paying customers, paying the rent, and I admire their capacity to do that. Something more than ignorance. Wanton imposition – disregard. The beer is expensive. It is a malty, American beer they serve. High on froth, short on beer. Though the pub's theme is Irish, they don't serve Guinness, and the measures are very small. Familiar music plays as a football match works itself out on the drop-down screen. We are just in time for the end of the match, then the screen puts itself away. This is good, as for a second I think we have come to watch football. At the table, we splay open packets of crisps and nuts to share. None seems thirsty. Though the volume of the music intrudes, it is set at a level which

---

aspidem et basiliscum ambulabis / et conculcabis leonem et draconem. / Quoniam mihi adhaeseit, liberabo eum; / suscipiam eum, quoniam cognovits nomen meum. / Clamabit ad me, et ego exaudiam eum; / cum ipso sum in ribulatione, / eripiam eum et glorificabo eum. / Longitudine dierum replebo eum / et ostendam illi salutare meum.' Psalm 91 (Vg. 90)

could have easily accommodated moderately hearty talk. There is nothing to say, of course. There is nothing that hasn't been said, and there is no catching-up to do. Though one thing the themed pub isn't is sufficient entertainment in itself. We don't seem to seek each other's eyes. Cheerfully downcast, as though we slip between each other, in the gaze, and with nothing of conscious avoidance. Chrysalized. A caterpillar turns into mush on the inside before… Right down to the molecular level. *At last, all-powerful Master, you give leave to your servant to go in peace.* It is, then, possible we remain firmly in the flow of the college timetable. And, if they are anything to go by, this is how it works. If they have buried themselves – if now *this* is Compline, i.e. night prayer – and we enter the hole in the timetable, Saturday being our day off.

All silent – for they haven't yet learnt to speak, not inside of it, not yet. But they are *being* formed. That mysterious process, of priestly formation, is happening.

I must identify the moment to slip away. I swish the great head of the treacly beer in the small glass. Helping myself to a crisp, I smile blessings on the accommodating table, and chest to chest, listening for any small clue intently. Beginning to develop an (imaginary) issue expressed in the small glass, it seems unusual, even unfair, that Henry briskly chews from his palmful of salted nuts, when you might think he could have been relied upon for some few diverting words of light philosophy.

Thoughts lapse – supernumerary to consciousness. I say: 'Hmm.' And give to the glass a last, decisive swish, and sling what is left of the beer to the back of an empty throat. Then stand, smiling, very well, and carefully negotiate the pub stool. Taking my glass, I make my way to the bar's curl, down at the chunky end. The bar's owner-manager stands his

179

side of the bar, and there is a highly made-up woman, maybe in her fifties, and an expensively dressed older man. With Miguel, the owner-manager, I have had all our pub-level heated disputations before now, and we were firm compañeros.

With the acknowledgement, Miguel calls me in closer to the bar, and pours two shots, for both of which he will charge me. *She* kicks up her heels. She looks strong and the man must have a big wallet. Big red mouth – lascivious – which, obviously, finds *me* hilarious – big as her red heals.

We do shots, and Miguel says his piece again. This is classic stuff – about the Catholics and the Fascists and the Nazis. He has the pictures on his lap-top of Pope Benedict – with the Nazi salute as a little boy. (And visions of urban scenes, ruin, a wrecked world. Berlin. Syria.) I demur and nod and I want a drink. Then I am told – again – in careful and deliberate Spanish – what I am. I am told what we all are, what we are part of. I still want the drink. I shrug, smile, accepting the point of view. *She* smiles, watching me, studies Tomàs, spider-to-the-fly. Then she throws back her head, laughs, and makes a lipstick manoeuvre, which needs a cigarette to complement the gesture. She is quite glorious. Her nails tickle her hair.

My Spanish improves with the shots and a bottle of lager. A second friendly couple, not so old, arrive at the bar and join us. They are dressed for the weather too. Disrobing pelts and woollens. I peek between the many shining crystal bottles, clustered enticingly, all along the shelves, and in the mirror at the back look acceptable. Social profile picture. The smile wants to smile, and there aren't those great creases ravining my cheeks. My smile looks facially-exercised. The smile looks prepped. Even – on trend. Like I am in a bar and everyone's telling me…

A *genuinely interested – actually listening* smile…

'Blow me!' I think. And woggle my eyes back, discreetly, under cover of the emptying bottle and the seating arrangements, to look again. 'Where 'ave you been?' Still, though I feel like being Tomàs, like, properly, getting my Tomàs on, I am too in a safe-mood for Miguel to be practising his English. Miguel has kind of have done with the Nazi spiel. He keeps a fair amount of material, relating to Franco and Spanish history, he's wanted to share on his lap-top. It isn't really for me to comment, since there is no way I could know where historical atrocity ends and contemporary Spain begins.

I make a little of my short-sightedness. I ask about The Valley Of The Fallen, and back off when they all have a go at each other. That just descends into body-language. There are shots, again, in rounds. I have a second bottled lager. Soon, they've stopped translating, and I'm not trying to look like I'm working at catching the sense of it. Merely absorbed – a fixture. Miguel, like a musical instrument, plays his taps. I am sufficiently confident I have sense about me. There doesn't seem anything dribblingly boozy – Friday's liquid-arsehole-depths *must just say*. I never forget they are Spanish. The beautiful woman's long, painted nails remain her own. Music plays. The jukebox. I might dance. I'll – *obviously* – sing a bit. A power-ballad they'll all know. Simple vessels bearing light… Would that we might stop the planet and take off our clothes. I don't argue with the hat-stand. Nor do I get my dick out and pee on the bar, or go to the loo on Trevor.

I wake in gladness. Warmth. Like the night. It is dark. I pull my sleeping-hat back off my face and am suddenly drenched in light. Entire minutes of warmth gently swell and gently subside before I run a fact-check. The night knows no major gaffs. I bought my rounds, and said nothing I'll have to retract. Some modicum of idiosyncratic vulgarity, the common touch, and no deviant loose talk, lambasting God, or the grim little lives we inhabit. No 'humour' of self-recognition. No moral-invective. No jeremiads. I'd said practically nothing, and paid my way, and hadn't gone off with those others who went off late with those girls we found. (I'd come back to my room for my own more-and-more of the happiness.) I wake pinned-under by the night. Everything razed to the ground. Like a good lover.

The university girls came baying – whooping their night. They came in many colours, which all now seemingly blur into Superman-green. Climbing the pavements. And Henry went, Julian went, Trevor went. Who else? Sean – in an extraordinary lapse of reason. All seeming to scale to gold-green. Those girls' 'crazy' *youth*-femaleness, dawn-wise, warmth-wise, rendered thus – youth's feeling. Yet then – their multi-hued titsy splash of the innocent real of it. Alex came back to college. So did Anthony. Each side of my face presses the pillow in turn, as it were with two distinct emotions: left and right. My not-quite-properly-awake face contains two emotions: left and right.

I danced and fell over on the way home, vamping, and two boys on bikes stopped to laugh at me and give me a hoik up. Pissed as a newt – in an endearing way – and with my terrible Spanish. What did I babble? All perfect charm, I addressed them in terrifying Spanish: *Gentlemen! Gentlemen of the bike! Behold! Giants!* I was charming. There was, for instance, no English violence about me. I fell over because I wanted to fall over and tumble on Planet Earth's long pavement.

The English weren't quite with it – though the boys were quite pragmatic about it – and looked on with doctorly solicitude. In which

182

case, it might have been nice if they'd looked elsewhere. There are no blanks, there are no nasty surprises. I've left the shutters open, and you can almost smell spring in the air. The light is so fresh. And it is Saturday. This is the thing. You live for Saturday.

You aren't 'dying in Christ' on Saturday. If all the world's a stage, I am a terrible actor. I am lousy on stage myself. I have developed notions – as to what is good, as to what is consummate. We did theatre at school. I have the idea that if you strip it away – if you clear the brain of everything, wipe the slate clean – then if you get to zero the more something new becomes.

There is, preceding this, the idea of the 'empty space', which is one of Peter Brooks' propositions for theatre. Since then, I've thought about it. There are the usual school dreams, where in the same thought you know you haven't done your homework, and in the same thought, know you've already got these exams years ago. So in the end walk away from it, school-pants, school-shoes, school-street, long into the blur where the dream gives-up on you.

Empty space. A way of doubt, a way of emptiness, way of unknowing. A way of clearing the desk – perhaps. *Become as* nothing. *Enter into* nothing. Trusting, as you did, there's no such thing. Not in an animal-human soul. Trusting – hoping – *nothing* cracks and yields its secrets – *nothing* breaks. And so then, yeah, new creation unfold. God unfold – and open-out inside of me.

The Gospels are clear on this point: the Word requires you rip yourself to pieces. Your God-job is to be cultically elsewhere – absenced – things that are not. They must have destroyed themselves writing it, when they cracked Christianity. To read the Bible – text – or the Gospels

183

in any case. You really have to pray each word if the general enormity be not to fall altogether apart on you.

Chapter Five

Saturday. You wouldn't say I dress exactly expressively. But it's time out. My ripped jeans are last time that was in. The pale-denim cobweb-soft with a thousand washes. Legs like stalks – the jeans' rips entered into compromising nooks and corners.

I dress for someone else – for someone out there. This is a make-believe – only pretend... *Guapo*. Lol. The homeless boy I go to serve food to on Sunday who's smiled as he touches my face saying: 'Guapo.'

It is a quarter to twelve. Solar noon today is one-thirty. There is plenty of people-time. But pretend. No-one really real. Lonesome – invisible cities. Where human need maintains its special networks. (Take a book, and lose your phone.) I make coffee and drink about two thirds of a pint of it. There is a tumbler of leftover wine. I wear an old suit-jacket and a long, rolled scarf, all topped off with a beanie hat. It is a look dateable to about three years ago. My plan is to have a sit in the Plaza España, a browse before the shops close, then go to see the red squirrel. I also intend, as an obligation, to visit the sculpture museum, admission to which is free on Saturday.

My beanie-hat feels good in the corridors. David Beckham. Then, on the street, there are people in furs. There must be sports grounds dotted about the place somewhere, as small children, wearing their football kits, skip and halt, skip and halt, held by their daddies' hands. I browse the market stalls in Plaza España, but there is no money burning a

185

hole in my pocket. (The Euro isn't great, but it isn't bad. Apart from the pharmacy, things tend to be cheaper than equivalent goods in England.) Seating myself outdoors, I order an espresso and a Campari soda. It is the café nearest the fountain with the impressive, bronze sculpture of the spinning globe. One of the ways they take a pride in the urban environment. Make the city nice. In the gusting breeze, the fountain over-spews, and tiny, cold droplets spatter my cheeks and chill my hands and jeans. It isn't, maybe, *beautiful* to look at, but an interesting piece of kit.

It seemed a shame when I saw they turn it off nights. Knocked out of it – pulled the wool out from under its – *being*ness or *essence*ness – something like an implicit right to exist. Made it so it was like just a stage-prop with electricity running through it. (Un-self-generated. Not a thing itself. A simulacrum. Surface-fake. Plugged into an electrical-source. And so thereby the dirty planet.) That was the night, here, when Patrick had two girls he'd arranged to meet, from the university. The girls were late, and we boys, assuming they, the girls, existed, hung around waiting a long time. Patrick worked his phone. He longed for female company. Henry was there – it was the three of us. Patrick wanting to wait no matter how long it took. He was one who didn't come back after Christmas. Though it seemed unusual, there couldn't be that which was untoward. It was no place to be hanging-round, after dark, out in the open street. The stalls abandoned – only unadorned steel frames marked the space – for clandestine *rencontre* – as were. Busy with his phone, Patrick paced about random directions, as though looking for a signal. (There is an excellent signal.) There was no knowing why we couldn't meet in a bar – as if the catch were particularly sensitive to this place.

When, later, Patrick talked about women in general, you could tell he had a soft-spot. Honey-warmth mellifluous – big-eyed golden thoughts

– like an okay-nice middle-class boy getting into all that. Yet he believed, and had offered himself to this city for priesthood, yet from the way he spoke anyone could tell he was heterosexual. Anyway, this shiftless hanging about, like waiting for a dealer, ticked no boxes. And when they finally arrived, Miss Douche, Miss Hickey, they were obviously not nearly cool enough to justify any of this. Henry went off with them, while I took my leave, and qualities of gloomy-abandoned, mid-rise city-streets, almost with the next thought, scene-shifted and soothed the anomaly, which I was walking away from, and whatever it was, unseen-monumental, in Patrick's designs on the evening.

It seems a long time ago now. When Patrick didn't come back after Christmas, not because of girls or any of that shit. The Rector said, in chapel, during Mass, it was for family reasons. Even as He said it, you could see He was realizing actually this one wouldn't float. Then – almost like He dared us not to swallow it. There was some dull nonsense afterwards as the Vice Rector, Father Richard, seemingly had got himself deputed to find out who knew what through social media. But no-one wanted to poke it. Probably not because we/they all knew no man likes having his lie exposed. Almost certainly it impinged – developmental fictions as well as The Rector's too.

A long time. Yet Plaza España retains that touch of romance. It could be the set of a kind-of-cute small-film. An Ang Lee. A Woody Allen. Just something unconventional. You have to wonder where any young people – subjunctive? indicative? While the Church maintains no hold on the young, while in post-Franco Catholic Spain there are whole empty dioceses, and the young aren't going to Mass, and make no seminarians, the Church having stopped in that sense, still you'd think a whole city… Where have the young gone? They can't be all holed-up in their rooms. *¿Donde estan los muchachos?* Anywhere other than here. As if a place holds no reality. Get out. Scarper. Make a life.

It is not necessarily pretty. It can be ugly seeing young people not given any faith. Perhaps the old feel it. In strange last gasps of Catholic Spain.

You see the young-young, mid-teens, gathering a little after three, at the steps of the municipal day-school, just round the corner on Merced. Home-clothes – and no uniform – the usual milling around. Pretty standard. Though it's said that, in theory, the onset of sexual maturity tends to be earlier further south – with more sun – with 'luteinizing hormone' – and a corollary of that is that you end up with relatively shorter legs – because of how the male body grows. Older adults might look shorter… but you can't really see it in the young.

There are floaters all over my eyes. I wear an academic posture. Each sudden breeze knocks a splash from the fountain, which sprays across the clouded sun and the plastic chairs. A nuclear arrangement of family sits at the table next. Beyond them, a couple sits. I used to think I could make friends in any bar. Maybe I thought at the time that was frightfully clever. All the way down Spain. Down past Barcs – where big white socks on pierced boys like stalks and their Japanese-hair were a thing again. Of all the little forests and beaches, came on a crazy place. With its slab of beach – and bat-shit locals. One night when the music played. I stuck around for a week, before I carried on south, and smoked the weed they gave me. Lazy English – Close my eyes… The waiter comes with the espresso and Campari-soda. Clusters of people make their way up the steps of the Capuchin church. Each – brain with its universe carried inside. (If you can imagine just one or two *other* people's everything, then your own head explodes.) Where God lives. There on the steps – with cold hands and long fur coats and hats and gloves and pockets.

The Rector said to me I perform… When I have sought, as I have read, my sub-morphological depths in things. Leaving aside our 'singing' psalms in Gregorian chant tones – leaving aside The Rector's preaching in His shiny gold tent. He said: 'Tomàs, you know you are. You are performing. You are putting on a performance. Tomàs, you *know* you are.'

A Mona Lisa smile. He says such things in gentle tones, which in itself is unpleasantness. He doesn't really mean it – to perform. He doesn't mean *perform*: He means faking an alternate character. When God-only knows to pin it down to this one… Small reflective-saucers of His little eyes levelled. You say it only so many times before it becomes a thing: 'Tomàs, you *know* you are.'

'You are,' said Father Rector, 'articulate.'

Geoff plays up to it, good-cop-bad-cop, always getting me to read, given any opportunity… With the nod. The builder's gesture… As that prankster builder's cheeky knowing smile… When, God-only knows, to say anything at all.

Words ready-made – for instance. God's words in translation. Holy Gospel text. Whether in class, upstairs in the conference room for *lectio divina*, or for Mass, or prayer, at the lectern – mic'd. So – a performance. I reckon I have a technique. Not a 'God voice' – *Woe-to-you-yield-me-your-foreskins* lady-lector's voice. But hollowed-open – male – the dust – that doesn't try to claim anything. Heaven be my witness. If perfect-truth is silent, these, God's words, are desert testimonies, rock-unhewn, like the Bible says. Somehow, your head must beg and strain and humiliate itself for that tenuous God's touch. Then maintain connection while your torso – *innards* noise about it. As lips and mouth so shapefully. As with truculent resolve... A never-objective – so it might seem. Such *truth* requires a special intervention – way, way in excess of our lies and our CVs and covering letters.

The knack – *my* theory – is, with the microphone close, love-close, to speak like love so respectfully into a friend's ear, as above his cotton T-shirt shoulders, at the hover-distance, when you'd best have liked to kiss and not say anything at all. ('Shush... Sleep now...') Something like the sprawled pillow and a matter-of-fact dream, giving you the heads-up – who and how you are today – after all the thinking of yesterday. That dry stone – though it might come in all manner of challenging portrayals. Sort of maybe conjuring lost love – like an intimate spooning-friend – naked on his bed – retro-fitting it. It *is* imagination: a listener's ear so close. It *has to be* true exploration each time – because you couldn't repeat that now. The truth changed. Down at the granular level. Where the thought beats – each mouth-moment strives so vehemently. The audio-machinery – somehow in love with it. One or two *yell* into the microphone... Your 'I' – between intent and execution. Self-exposed.

You can hear something of what everyone wants to be when he speaks at the lectern. Henry wants to be more posh. One or two of them struggle to follow the print and they give all their attention to what they have practised. (This is fine: they are dyslexic: this is noble.) Julian, in this context, struggles with a kind of refusal to speak at all, though he could have broken into song quite naturally. Sean's is steady power restrained. Geoff is passionate. Of the Vice Rector, Julian, the first time, said: 'Where did *that* come from?' The Vice Rector – Father Richard

190

magnified – full-sheets. Glory be – God love him! – and – to the heck with it! – blast this temporary place and what it *might* be. Wind blew – like Father Richard had his head in a barrel of fresh spuds or oranges – marvelling wondrous speakers, wondrous microphone. At Mass – it has been strange and unusual to hear, at his confidence, such bold noise come out of him.

Still, however – elsewhere, once, else-wise – a modest stage and the softest acoustic proved too much for Tomàs... At school.... The flies proposed distracting thoughts, the wings sucked and dragged. And I bumped into the furniture... The Rector might chuckle to know my stage-hopelessness. That one rôle I more-or-less successfully performed was only an extension of stage-fear. Even then, I was copying. Messed gestures, tangled-play, a body crunched about its thorax. My staged-voice a set in itself – all boomy-squeaky flaccid-tight. It seemed a marriage of particularized damage and perfect optimism.

Boys, on the other hand, got up some pretty good shows. I applied my then considerable energies... Who could forget Bob's Caligula, or Phineas's Medea, or Lorcan's Galileo? Our unabridged *Hamlet*, built around Patrick – Patch – who also played Jesus in *The Mysteries* – as faithlessly traduced, by an unfathomably younger Tomàs, one brisk writing spat in the Michaelmas half-term.

*

In town there was powerful theatre. I could have claimed back the money. I blu-tacked all the tickets to my study-wall. My tastes finessed. (Twice per week – hundreds of tickets.) There was an idea of theatre – of movement. Not just making shapes – .

They gave their jewels on stage. Patch came true on stage. A rat – a dog – a weird act of suicide – Patch came true all over it. He performed a great Christ – the first of the occasions I worked with him. An intensity of flavour, a taste-bomb, Patch was ever so slightly not quite right to look at, with an unusual beak-face. Muscley and quite short – he'd hang upside-down from the lowered bars, or muck around with the tat lying about the place and make something of it. I never quite knew where it was going with Patch.

We rehearsed alone, and we got on, but I didn't trust him. (Something – something – nagged… Patch was just teasing at the edge of a set of rules… If that curtain might tweak open…) Say, in terms of cigarettes, Chinese-walls, and information. You were always in your one world, and you could see the joins, outside the script, where you could only take a probably naïve guess at his all. (In the end, he got kicked out. It seems odd how one sensed these – pressures.)

I traduced the text as a curious exercise. The medieval material was never going to work direct. Brutalized – distinct, set-pieces, so modern children could carry it. It was a big, groupy script. Everyone got a part.

Patch. Chutzpah. Muscle-packed. A rat. A rogue. Five foot eight and sticking there. Boundless spunk. He glowed with raw desire. And anarchic – and free. There really wasn't much of him to read up close – but *on stage*… One might argue the final lift for Patch was a matter of lights. Sly rogue, he knew exactly what the lights could do to him. His weird body. He made a great Christ. He *was* weird, fractionally off, a DNA-moment away.

It was a fine touch as he ascended the Cross the stage-hands raised for him. There was a dignified pause in the general abuse as Patch had his Cross presented him. He stepped up onto it, all stripped-naked and muscle at this point, taking the handholds built into it, Samson versus Dagon, claimed his throne, then again the pain began, Jesus' last words.

The scene transitioned. In hell, he was the naked coiled Terminator, balled at the foot of the Cross, on the red-lit rostra. Patriarchs crouched in plastic dust-sheets – pencil-spots and painful, *modern* noise – there were unspeakable things the sound-boy had done to Stravinsky. Patch, basically, mimed getting buggered, and everyone secretly got that. He took it on way too long while the patriarchs waited for their cue.

Daft days. But a different world. There's no sense in it outside of the action: you had to be there. As to what happened to Patch... *Psycho-o-o-o-o-o...* (Way too much cocaine.) It was an easy script – kiddy-coloured. I'm not sure they even gave me a budget for that one.

Happiness. Cinch-points – where memories get stuck. The alcohol in the Campari dries my skin in the cold air. The here, the now. Muted negotiative clatter – the market-place. Little birds. Damp in wool and paving slabs.

I draw from my suit-jacket pocket and check my phone. The cloying, bitter drink becomes too much, so, leaving cup and saucer, I take the glass inside with me to pay at the bar. Within, the knocked-together rooms, it is warm and lively, the décor a colourized fifties American drug-store, candy-coloured with the frothed coffee milk spilt all over it, melted ice-cream colours on a pavement. People are all in their russets and browns. They have an air of mercantile exchange, as this were a trading post. If, as they speak, it is some manner of issue being solved, a count being kept of the words of each, tallied in quick-steady eyes. Tapas in fidgeting hands, though there is no game, and to move a piece. Warm fumes rise from men. A low, almost guttural – *brown* timbre rumbles reverberates – queasy in an ice-cream haze. It is all swimming a moment. The air isn't good in here.

193

'Para un café y Campari-soda.'

A small kafuffle and a bill adheres to its saucer – flicked to the bar.

Wait for the change in that case.

'Bueno, gracias.'

Creep now opens the door. 'Gracias. Gracias.' Then it is cool again. I cross to and dip my hands in the water of the fountain. My face has creased a little. I soothe the skin at each corner of my eyes, then moisten my lips, which feel sticky. Checking the time on my watch, I have a half hour to go until the book shop closes. I know the way from here to there, if I get it right, theoretically.

In order to be doubly sure, I slip a hand into my pocket, and open my phone, digging here for maps pre-loaded. Sure enough, I've got the city entirely the wrong way up. One's mental north lies due east. But if – *here* – and then *there* and *turn* and look out for *that*, which you recall is distinguishable from *that* by *that*, and *there* and... It is like trying to learn girls' names when you've forgotten the seating plan. And they're in league to look exactly the same... 'So you're... And you're...' The *non factum est...* (Could a more 'bloke' man tell them all apart? Could he really?) When, if they're going to do *that* to themselves, they *could* wear name-tags. Or numbers. It isn't *in me*.

The bookshop man kept me on the street outside his shop on the main street just a couple of weeks ago. It wasn't five o'clock yet. The shop-owner-man turned up at five-to-five and opened the grille and when I made to follow made a gesture. Because it wasn't five o'clock yet.

I waited anyway. I said good afternoon politely – as the glass door opened. On the dot, literally, a fair few other humans materialized out of an empty street, book-shopping. Though a small shop, it seems it is the

194

biggest in town. Excepting the El Corte Ingles, which might not count. Quite OCD. The books' covers and general half-assed merchandizing come in grey tones, blank-packaging, strictly perpendicular, and affectively nullified arrangements. (You could see how they like the dead streets and the tower-blocks.)

I have a serviceable twenty minutes for a quick browse. Really, I only want to touch one or two of the books' spines. By way of encouragement. It would be silly to develop my collection. *I like Asterix...* A studious shop, for sure, and this a nod toward some level of seriousness. This being a student town – you get your little bit of home-economics, and your bit of accounting, and your nursing. One kneels for the religious shelves. A great, high wall is taken up with bilingual editions of English-language classics. *Huckleberry Finn* – in Spanish. *Mrs Dalloway, Ulysses, The Catcher In The Rye...* I cop a light touch of first sentences – until the aloneness hits me again through my doing this. I am all quietly up on my Spanish the first rise – until the thinking of the meaning of each word totally bungs-up on pronominal suffixes. Pure soup. Until then it's like: *Oh yeah...* So for instance: *Si realmente les interesa lo que voy a contarles, probablemente lo primero que querran saber es donde naci, y lo asquerosa que fue mi infancia, y que hacian mis padres antes de tenerme a mi, y todas esas gilipolleceses estilo David Copperfield...* And it isn't the time – this is Saturday. Abstract wanderings – no pain. Only the easy-heart's mindfulness – small things I might get my head around. Isolate objects and isolate words. I wonder if there might be a Mass left. I might buy an item of sportswear from the El Corte Ingles.

At two, the shop empties. So too the pedestrian street outside. It goes *zzzzzzzzzzp* and packs itself away – in an eye's twitch de-exists. A simple cancellation of scenario – as by A Higher Power – running all of this on a computer. *21ˢᵗ Century Humans: A Cautionary Tale*.

The Carrefour will be open, where I can buy nuts for the red squirrel, who lives in Campo Grande. The red squirrel is Valladolid's best bit. Even as a child, I had never seen one before, apart from in picture books. It was last term's discovery. The most beautiful encounter. I didn't know it was there – in the park. A complete surprise. The *tiny* little thing bobbled and hopped, as it received in its little hands a nut from the man's hands. Each surprising instant – it was childlike. I whispered: 'Oh my wow.'

I walk toward the El Cortes Ingles. There is, for now, that settled feel of friends in bookshops. Though a null-affect, neutral day – it won't glean, it is not to be scratched at. The queues are long in the Carrefour. Though, as it might be, on relatively modest incomes, many people live centrally. Their behaviours neither pinched nor stark. Yet the shop so busy while the street so empty… An error in the simulation, a glitch in the code. I potter about the aisles, which are pleasant enough, then at the tills I flinch at how expensive a little bag of up-sold nuts can be. Nonetheless, I queue for a packet of almonds. Two English men queue directly ahead of me. They are stocky, and have gay voices, their wheelie-bucket piled with soft drinks and party food, while they bitch to one another about the obviously terrible party they're going to. The air heaves relief as I wander up the way to the broad plaza fringing Campo Grande. This is a place to see – a piece of Spain. There is a tourist information office, though unopened. At these fountains, three girls take selfies. Pompous-looking buildings, the military offices aside, line the park's nearest vicinities. Hotel-bars have their patches. Liveried doormen idle time, for there are no paying customers, in and out the doorways' shadows.

A mixed group of kids play at the hoops on the pedestrian boulevard, and two boys practise on skateboards, working the thing out. I pass by them, touched by the thought, and happy that they are there. Wistful, I smile at the odds of the ball spilling over to me, and play in mind the agreeable scene of a fleeting connection. Then I am through the park gates. An air now – of humanity become self-selecting. Modestly understated. Understatedly modest. Campo Grande is nice but it isn't *grande*...

I walk slowly, and very soon hear for a second time English voices. Not *them* – it is an English family, just a little way ahead, a Dad and a Mum and a younger boy and an older girl, and theirs are Midlands accents. Dad seems to have been here and to know the place. He gestures panoramically. Mum wants her lunch. The girl at a difficult age. She carries a balloon-on-a-stick. Though she is sprouting – yet wears a loud dress. Then leggings, trainers. Her *hair* is nice... Maybe she is being okay about it. And not horrific. It's okay once they get into it, but those *months*...

Yet then, they mostly blossom, if they come from a good home, and become rounded personalities, entering into their womanhood. It was that... *when yet they weren't*... I shudder to think of it.

They walk toward the pond, and I trail, and would follow had I not been going that way. I wish I could say something so they might hear I am English too. (Fake a phone call?) How my voice might sound – there'd be all college hurling around in such matter I... a demented thing, ludicrous blurt – of Henry, Geoff, and all of them – not to mention the personal predicament.

Maybe they're a nice family. She is letting him explain what he

197

needs to explain. And it would blow his fire, me being English. Mum and Dad. You'd probably see them all having their lunch in a little while. All sat round the table. With napkins and the menus out. Dad looks safe.

I look into the pond. Terrapins live in there. But not today. I walk toward the join in the paths where the squirrel lives. There, I crumple the packet of almonds, making noise. I peer and I squat and crouch – chewing a mouthful. All the peacocks have perched right up in the trees' branches. That never looks like something they should be doing. It's disappointing that the squirrel isn't here – but then the not-knowing-if is a part of it.

Now, next, my visit to the National Sculpture Museum is an obligation. Canon Peter stood literally aghast when I hadn't heard of it. Mortified, I made resolute promises. Though a few weeks have passed, it isn't just any old something I could do on the hoof. A great commitment – it must command a known and prepared and anticipated not-just-any-old-time. But, rather, the sort you must wait for – and listen for.

Plaza Mayor is tumbleweed. All Spain, hung from the Pyrenees, lapped by the Bay of Biscay, dipping its tongue south, impossible miles away. Representations of God on the Cross formed the subject of a slideshow presentation I researched and presented to them. I worked through the night… It was a rare treat. (They normally don't want us thinking very much.)

Each of us had something decent – each in his own way. Each student – it was really a pleasure. My *idea* – it *emerged* to me… Or I saw it. I listened for it. It found me. It seemed my own conception. Maybe kind of glibly, I called it 'the squiggle god'.

But that wasn't it. It was only to see it – and not replete with pulpit-homilies, *slow* words, turgid hymnals. Just look in ways that words don't stick. It didn't seem an original theory. Just – *already there*. God on his Cross. The beautiful boy – and Jesus, Plato, Praxiteles. The temple – of the Weimar Republic. Any *ephebe* you could name. The idea was aesthetic in origin. Our assumed *representations* – our *inward constructions* – I lack an aesthetic vocabulary. The art of the crucifix being almost-unfailingly non-realistic. So what was it saying and not saying? What did it know?

To admire the disposition of the body – to accept the lithe receptive curve. The 'S' running through it. A snake on a stick. The squiggle. First off, it begged questions of verisimilitude – because that's not how crucifixion works. The crucified man is asphyxiated. Hence they break his legs – if they want him to die quick. The strength gives, all the above-body fails, he bows his head and suffocates. And he'll look pretty dead then. There are pictures on the internet proving this – victims of war and democracies. Big head on the spindly arms – gravity's abject fail. No 'S' shapes.

So that was the first photograph – to open the human question. That touch of the *real* seemed necessary. Then it was imaginative representations – our projections – neo-pagan, Christian-imperial constructions – my tracing the 'S' on each one of them. At the projection screen, I pratted and flayed, with the date, the research, the authority. I was only meant to talk for ten minutes, but time seemed nothing, once you got into the depth of it. *Attis, Tammuz, Adonis, Osiris… Egypt, Greece, Rome…* Four photographs of *kouroi* I had for them. This was what I wanted to show them – the *kouros*. My heart burned that they see.

I made necessary mention of Moses – of the book of Numbers 21:

8-9. And, of course, obviously, quote John: 'And as Moses lifted up the serpent in the wilderness, even so must the Son of man be lifted up: That whosoever believeth in him should not perish, but have eternal life.' And *mention* – Asclepius – cultic rites – the ankh – the eastern Med – *life* – and all that symbolizes *life*.

I dropped a beat – missing a tempo. I remembered to offer them the thought that representations of God on the Cross weren't really the main thing for the first millennium of Christian faith. That in images it was the Risen Lord.

I stumbled and withdrew. I stopped at the edge – right in front of them. I couldn't say that there was faith in a risen Christ before ever there were Jesus-stories – earthly life. In a moment, there seemed to me the crushing realization, this was wrong. But the door was open, so I stepped through it. I was ready to tell them now. I said:

'Through the course of the Black Death, the Suffering Lord comes to be of immense significance, indeed representationally paramount. We suffer – *How* is this? – *Why* is our suffering? And God corresponds – he is with us. And this creed is brought alive to us, here and now, in our moment of looking. God's suffering with us – right now – our reciprocal moment in the Cross. So through and around and between us, that plays, that looking, seeing, and our being seen, that relationship. But now stop a second. Why is that like that then? There we go – God, Cross. That lithe turn in the hips. The knees bent here. Some notional weight on the arms. That 'S' running through it. If our correspondence here is supposed to be suffering, then why has that reality been softened, smoothed, beautified? These are stylized representations, and they don't come out of nowhere. There is a history of art to this. It goes back – through Rome, Greece – to the earliest sculptures we have in the ancient world.

200

'This kouros is a statue of a young man/adolescent boy. Fairly obviously, we are not obviously seeing Jesus in this yet. It's a history – pagan art. And whole belief structures channelling into that art, all the while asking itself, what is beautiful? And finding these answers, and we can ask, why? And then it comes through, such that every religious Christian who loves his cross is a part of it. It comes through in Christianity's first assumption of pagan Rome – and the imperial trappings. And then in the renaissance, as the classical world is reborn to us, it's all drawn-in again. This figure is more than implicit in the classical philosophies which inform the heart of Christian thought. Plato knew this figure, this idea, and built a whole theory of truth and love about it. And his school is there, in Alexandria, intellectual powerhouse, at the time Christianity is being formed.'

The National Archaeological Museum in Athens is among the most consummate spaces. Through each hall, it is a movement, a chronicle, of an aesthetic. Human being. In the first room, there are kouroi of the seventh and sixth centuries BCE. They are balanced, their step bold, weight planted square, intentionality forward... I met them first before I ever went to Athens.

A large, messy bed in a house-share in Muswell Hill... A big room – multiply windowed – which got the light... A naked friend reads to Tomàs. The book: *Sexual Personae* by Camille Paglia. Which he's nicked from a library in Cambridge – which he didn't attend. Already, I'm twenty one. At first, Matthew lied about his age, to freak me out. He's twenty. We're having a friendship-relationship. He wears women's trousers, has no money, smokes, is strictly vegan, and doesn't hold hands on the street. He's new, though for the mid-nineties, it's very eighties. London's a bedsit. Maffy's posh house-mates *have* been to Cambridge.

201

Everyone's camping-out. He's young in a slippy way still, that makes you inadvertently dawdle a wandering hand on different bits of him. His skin's young. He's dyed his head-hair black. There are pale freckles. His lips are as a perfect recollection. His pumps foul.

My first time in Athens was six years later. I'd saved Athens to the end of the tour. I went island-hopping – it was the Drachma in those days. That year, I discovered Amorgos, and there ceased to hop. Bad weather turned the boat trip back into a vile event. A long night I was trying not to sleep – outside a bar in Naxos. Then the slow boat – I eventually made port in the middle of the next night, when there were no taxis and rumours of one bus. In central Athens, I fumbled holding my credit-card up ahead of me, as I stumbled in Greek on an hotel lobby with lights and a concierge.

That year, there'd been an earthquake or something. The wing of the National Archaeological Museum I wanted to visit was closed. I tried to persuade – I tried to bribe. They told me the pieces I wanted to see had been taken elsewhere. The second time, they'd built the new airport, and they were re-surfacing Athens for the Olympics, and the whole museum was closed. That was the year, though less young, I watched Greece win the football, on a big screen, out on the boulevard by the Acropolis. By way of compensation, that was the one place to be in the world that evening. The third time, I went with that girl. She was, mercifully, tired. She had a condition. By Athens, I heartily hated her. And the museum was open. It would have been a bit of a nightmare to see it through her eyes.

Though it was far from being a let-down, yet it was ten years and more since Maffy. And that drift of lazy days – slopping around being read to… Natural bodies. Not like now when you cover yourself up!

202

When the face has hardened and the smiles gone. Time, desire, and life –
all changed.

Students sat around, on the floor, sketching. And I sat – in
anticipation of reverence. I wanted to see them – not the students – the
kouroi – how I could have seen them a first time – ten years younger.
Maybe that day – but there was hardly a desire left in me. Yet I saw –
playing to my own ghost – the textbook. Self-presence marked in stone.
And yet remote, immune, of a century. The inward calm – the stilled, the
silenced – which, unreally out-projected, in the smile, the chest's breadth,
cared for nothing, in itself abstracted.

Through the rooms, the line passed. Through archaic Greece. Then
the classical. One might see it – a locus of subject-identity transposed
outwards. The movement – the socially-implicated. From self-identicality
– via a lived-desired and the city-state – through the Hellenized into the
Roman – removed – abstracted. *At* Christ it is already remote. By
Constantine's adoption it is *out-there*.

There is a first known instance of a kouros bearing his weight on
only one foot. It is perhaps the most significant moment. A new thing. A
difference. Now, upstairs in the conference room, I demonstrated. The
difference is that prior to this the weight is balanced – solid. I
demonstrated. On both feet. This – then this. Thricely, I demonstrated.
So, in representation, a new stance, engaged, receptive, an awakening,
youthful, asking questions. A new psychological stance has been
instantiated. And it has a date.

I showed them how it is to stand – and I rather enjoyed this. Head
of the class – and these monkey-hands. (I was a little boy again –
appealing through the terror and the lens of an adult authority to their
growth and adolescence and approval.) All grand thoughts, and we're

comical creations. Archaic boy-male. Balanced. Forward-intentional. Self-complete. Then the next thing. Vivid action – sprung. Showed them how, with the weight on one foot, you can lift-up the other foot, wiggle it, yet your upper-body stays quite still. Receptive now and feminized. I struck poses, goofed, and I got a laugh. I should have given them the punchline. I showed them Michelangelo's David and Donatello's... *Can you see?*

Leaving the Renaissance – I returned in time and told again how the statues changed – as power displaced from here to elsewhere – this in Greek history – and from the city-state – via the Hellenization – to that whole ghastly edifice – Rome. *Who can forget what a thoroughly disgusting world found God – invented Jesus?*

They are a nice bunch. I made light of the time passed. 'Well, there it is,' I said.

I made that 'S' again – with my arms and the rest of my body. Vamping now. Flagging. 'Sorry, have I...?' It seemed a muddled and unfortunate close to things.

They said some very kind things while we went down to evening prayer. Of course, the time didn't matter to any of them. Henry was nice, when we were looking at a picture together, and Henry made the 'S' over it, and Henry said, 'Oh look, there it is.'

I have watched Benedict caressing his crucifix, on his rosary, while we have waited for evening prayer. I have frankly watched him, by no means disguising the fact. It is a lover's touch, and Benedict isn't self-conscious who might see. Besotted. Love so fleshy – his heart and his hands and his mouth – spills himself out on it.

Out of time in an abolished space. Jerusalem razed in AD 70 by the empire. Just the place for him. Zion fallen. No extant witnesses. Paul came late and never met him. Just the place for Jesus.

It is *comparatively* simple to guess how it might have been… And once, in prayer, at the monastery, I laid myself down, in the sun, on the wet grass, in grief and abnegation, saying sorry… Small there, the little wooden body, nailed in the little green place, where sixteen monks lay. Pluscarden. I spread my hands to hold Jesus' narrow waist, kissed the nails, ran my hands about his shoulders and thighs, said, 'I love you.'

Beyond Plaza Mayor, there would be a brief series of old-town alleyways. The National Sculpture Museum would be – just up there, this archway, this next…They are bleached and forgotten-looking walls, and the smoothed paving could be medieval. Not that it is making Tomàs anxious – I follow the map. A kind of place – *uneasy* credit-cards, and modern vaccinations, and a phone, might not help much. I fancy I feel the back-wall of a church, and that – *fancifully* – pressure-release drawn out of me. Only I am playing games in a nice way – making play-scared on the uncertainty – with only myself to see.

The National Museum is there, modestly signed on stencilled plexiglass stuck to the stone wall. A uniformed lady sits just a little way inside the doorway. She reassures me there is no money required, and directs me over the courtyard into the planned route, showing me where I can pick up a free map. I get my art-appreciation on – and take the stairs. I am going to have to write that letter to Canon Peter, and find at least something in all of this, though in term-mode now. (Where nothing matters.)

The finest art extracted from ruined places – saved in that sense. (Save that phrase.) Well, I feel I likely *get* what they are probably getting at… Hell and last things. Death and death's containment. Pale lacquer.

Eyes, mouths, gape. The outsize, twisted bodies all wrenched and twisted in quite vivid, fancy anatomies of physical suffering. Big, agonistic knees, and stretched thighs, and lumpy wooden hands and lumpy wooden feet. In gloom, in torchlight, that could make desire-unnatural spooky, evocative, worryingly all caught-up in a sinner beholding, his malnourished body, his hell. Presuming sexual desire a motive force – a heart of it? (I can't remember. I've forgotten.) Anticipating unknown physical delights turned rotten… But, so the art suggests, would you like to explore? And I am the living and they are dead… (Are you living? How conscious are you of…? Only the nice things that spring to mind.)

Probably, maybe, I'm *not* getting them. They seem about right, scenic emanations, pretty much what you'd expect, of Spain, its Church, its Inquisition. I *want* it to work on me.

If I'd had more prayer – come in here up on P. That more muscle-mind could have got boxed on it – maybe. Prayer like monks. Prayer like monasteries… Those monks are cooked on it. Sorted for Latin. Doped to the eyeballs on strong P… As I realize it isn't going to happen, the affective response, I only tell myself to open my eyes cleanly, and give it its chance for later. One sculptor, Berruguete, I decide, could have thoroughly appalled me.

How objectively fine they are. ('We are in hell. We are burning. Where are you?') I am going to have to save my letter to Canon Peter for later. I know I must not make phrases, which beyond being shabby and fake, Canon Peter would see through. There seems a pity in all that lacquer and work they'd done with the bodies to punish them and make them look scary. They look like the kind of bodies whose muscle and bone and cartilage has grown through real work and not any gym-technique. They make belief in any of that look a long-lost time ago. And

206

in this light – like office light – not even natural light.

Outside, I turn my steps toward the Plaza Mayor. It's no distance at all. I slip-slap my pumps. Such sin in me there might be unawakened – but then too the inward-light grew paltry. I goof with hammy moves and yell: 'Come on then!' Fancifully, I might co-opt a priest, if I particularly wanted to purify in such wise so as to feel less nothingy. Or give over my head to the psalms – like monks – in Latin. That structured discipline – still, now, that would likely do it.

I return to my room via the Carrefour. At five, I go to the gym – and swim and sauna. A couple of hours. Then the bar – and night time. Saturday night.

I am not above praying to Yahweh begging my heart doesn't stop in the night. (There is a kind of fear, you get so tired, if you sleep you'll never open your eyes again.) There are sleep-paralysis states – when you can't wake out of it. They are terrifying.

Then Geoff walks the college all night. And they spring fire-alarms – it helps to be already naked. Inevitably, Saturday evening, Geoff dominates. *Guys, who's up for a film tonight?* Trevor put it best once, taking the mick in a funny-voice, squeaky and camp, the one time I ever heard Trevor speak expressively: 'Oh it's like I've found all the brothers I never had.'

I have enough water and beers and a bottle of wine. All clothed, I sit for a sit on my bed, then lie back on it. I pull my sleeping-hat over my eyes.

Chapter Six

Once, an inscrutably young man called Tomàs went down south, to take up his teaching position at a little school… I remember school, with the battered iron windows, and the long view over the playing fields. I loved the wormy smell of it. I wore an academic gown, and polished my shoes each evening. Sometimes, for a bit of a laugh, I carried my mortar board. At ceremony, I was expected to wear my academic hood.

I bumbled into it, one late August afternoon, in Ron's white van. A village, within which school turned slowly upon itself. A dreaming man – a dreaming boy of man – in manifold, complex arrangements. A herd, a hive… A *your-thoughts-my-thoughts*. A place of books and television, in armillary fashion, of potted plants and horsy ra-ra women's hats and tweeds. A garden-bench-like place for tea and sandwiches. (A *rather* stiff pink gin, if truth were told.) And *mixed*. A *majority* of boys could have been in a grammar school – brain-wise. Socially: from your administrative English upper-middle-slash-military – all the way up – internationally, *regally*, no less – lofty preserves of the high net-worth and the upper-U. A quaint, theme-park village, for all that. Security – black Defenders – were there in a minute. (Securitized Tomás!) They pulled up at a barely polite and firmly interrogative distance – their presence be let known.

My new house stood in a row on a little terrace with a flight of steps. I didn't own the house, obviously. And from the start, down to the carpet, I made no home-improvements. None of what you might call delusional ownership – though that sense of belonging to it grew inside. The walls remained a tired magnolia, when had it been truly mine, they'd have glowed bright-white first-order-of-business a first day. I got my stuff put together about the place, and set about the occupation in a spirit of camping. I owned a new cooker and an old fridge. I had shelves which I got up on bricks – a half days' effort – and Dad's desk and an orange sofa – perfectly fitted to my need when to read I reclined. There was a futon I'd somehow bought, a mattress with the wires sticking out of it, not yet a bed. And one old wooden armchair, its left arm gnawed to pieces by a childhood dog.

On the day of the move, I drove with Mum and Ron to the nearby town, and there I bought on credit a big, old-fashioned kitchen-table, made of pine, and six beach-wood kitchen chairs. It *was* big, though inside it fitted the house just right, and the men weren't going to get it through the front door when they delivered it. I put an M6 accent on, saying: 'I've got bigger things than that through [h]ere.' And they complied, though they put a little dent in it. I, with Mum and Ron, had fish and chips for lunch at the pub. Then, all that done, and my being settled in, they were off, and that all-blank-and-empty-space opening up on me – . Where's that pub!

I paid for the table and chairs before interest accrued and I was young.

*

When term began, I began the long, at times arduous process of becoming 'alright'. During that first year, my vowels adjusted. It was like when they warned me not to worry at uni – though I hadn't said a word! (I must have just looked a bit pikey.) And it would have been around now

I bought the second of my two good suits. A young man of considerable energies, I took the school brand, the identity, upon myself as a gift. There was a level of pomp – manageably pitched – the real unknown the caricatures not letting on the people they were. But – youth. The gown became me. Darth Tomàs. Of secular foundation, the school to that day made no entirely serious claim to its being a religious environment. There were the chaplains, RC and C of E. The chapel high Victorian. And three further ordained Assistant Masters. The sentiment British.

In terms of social class, in terms of England, I didn't know about money. In my naivety, I mostly reckoned I had more money than a person might reasonably have much use for. Other people's Bentleys didn't bother me. I identified according to such social class as seemed then nature and literature both had assigned to me. While I never had thought I was normal, always I knew *in my soul* I was just right. When there was talk in the masters' dining room, full-bellied with lunch, and the more donnish of the literary beaks smoked, venting in-house gossip in tones given ever to borderline-mock-despair, and it was said that, of the boys' parents, perhaps a quarter might have noticed the fees, the analysis meant nothing to me, mere pecuniary concerns when the game was teaching. That world. All that.

I didn't know about rich people? (The English middle-classes don't know about rich people, not really, not in their heart of hearts, not in their soul. Really, the English middle-classes, still less than the poor, know fuck-all about rich people.) In what sense did it intrude? I don't know. It seemed natural – this setting-adrift from things. All that loosening-up – the floating miles away.

Such that a world its own world. Anything could happen – given to all to unfold – and structure of the formal school day only arbitrary.

Time-stamped. And only given to everyone's becoming who *he/I* am/was/is/might inside of it.

If I'd never met people like this before... Well, I *had*, just less so, kept inside... Less thick. With studious disposition, with effortless brain. Whereas here, all the insides were outside, and that runs the other way also. All that you were/are/might-be might be. It wasn't like university, where provisional identities get thrown on and discarded the next day. And where there's sleep, long mornings, as much as you want, to recover in, wipe off the slugs, recombobulate. Sleep swallows everything – all your exploratory cast-offs from yesterday go there. This was deeper with the daily regulation of the timetable. No coming-up out of it. (Eight-o'clock! Bing!) But you were/are in there – you're committed. No alter-perspective. Actions carried. There was... no twinking and fiddling – no... cut and paste. No stop and rewind. No – *Once more! With feeling!* (No *forgiveness* – no *subjunctive...*) No loose and slippy logic. Natural man.

That first year, evenings were my own, and nights inviolable. I didn't want to be alone in the house after school on these unoccupied evenings. To read – an intensity of silence insisted on too much. The hollowed mind expansive – in twee and – little, unlived walls, my house, which I should really have painted bright-white, not finding an edge to it. It was prayerless – dare I say?

Noiseless, and pre-qualified, impressed with unknown noises, I went to the pub. For the noise – the safe and comfy background noise – to read. There, I annotated Brecht. I firmed-up a rudimentary grasp of *Lord Of The Flies*, which I taught once and could only teach once, and got my head around Shakespeare. That time was two hours meditative. Truly, pub-noise, the background-noise was a cushion to me. *This is the place called Tomàs* – such noise said. *This is your job for tomorrow as it was today. These are your books* – the noise said. *This is you.*

So that, by and by, found completion – each day. And then I went to the bar, and joined Dave and Kurt, and got straightforwardly pissed with Dave and Kurt and the Times crossword. Dave and Kurt worked in the theatre. We talked shop. Whatever might be going on there, the whole village might know of it. It was a well-oiled village aristocracy who propped-up the bar, who maybe shouldn't have heard such talk. Thereby, becoming safe and nested, I slipped into it. When it got loud, I'd adhere to Dave, who was 47, learning.

A lot absorbed... Safe. And honest. (Dave had spent time in Australia and his accent had never recovered from it. Kurt was the janitor.) By ten, I was back in my new home, after the pub not seeing it, all expanded, so it was only the radio seemed to reveal a space, as it were dimensionally. (There was no internet in those days to speak of, so this was the radio as it happened to be live on the FM.) I might cook a ready-made pizza, and worry a bottle of Macon... The clothes were beginning to come off... I was scheduling toward being a person. (Unconsciously driven, it might have been.) The internet, such as it was, was 56K...

I was coming out – as a person – free – all those years I'd stored... So much potential blossoming – stretching hands like wings – with my exploratory drama-group exercises.

Those walls gradually getting to know me. Never sexed – but I became an installation-piece in my own rooms. I made my church worth living in. Arches and temples of *my* mind un-interiorized. So – *fresh.*

Joy!

And the boys had Mr Storey house-trained. Classroom bit of days passed by-and-large feasibly. One or two boys maybe not *as* bright as one or two other boys. Yet not gnawing at one another's heels, eating their crayons, masturbating in class, ruler-flicking gozzed-up spit-balls, peeling ripened oranges, chewing gum. To this day, I like to think the boys profited somewhat from lesson-time.

Gentle coaxing. I more robustly indoctrinated – possibly – given my hour with the Year 10. Mutually, tractably, accommodated. Boys being boys. To train the little buggers with kindness. Their humour buoyant– for they were, that class, of a middling-well disposition, not entirely deprived intellectively, nor yet *entirely* of a sufficiency of 'IQ' to know that, in matters of meter, diction, trope, synecdoche, apostrophe, caesura, hubris and so forth, I *was technically permitted* to bring to them… Nor yet of such ornamental stupidity to copy down what they were supposed to.

By way of thinking-pub-time, and with Dave with the Times crossword, and each evening's pub-alone-time, and, then, deepest – the deepest of dreamless sleep, I went over again in my head such of the day's exchanges as stood out to me. As, in our contemporary age, a coder fixes bugs, *down within* vastness of logical mind, of logic-gates, AND, OR, NOT, while the front-end self-distracts and it keeps itself occupied, with mechanical, routine tasks – a quick go on a game – bread-baking and washing-up, mopping the surfaces, a walk, five minutes' social media, wishing I had a dog, the day's news, cardio-vascular exercise at the gym. Thusly, each next day, I became ready – to play at least and very least *their* last move back at them.

And so, as loops of time became established, weeks tending to terms, the institution – *school* – became me. I, Tomàs. My – Tomàs's

213

mode. My manner! My address! I gained a certain measure in psychic-weight... And, come period iA, my breakfast-jog – sweat-through and mud – unassailably preceded me.

And so a framework of the days and days became-becomes... All that – seemingly – life conjured to be. In this life, now, in evenings' even-spirit-dance – whirly-gigging – home-alone – and space and love and music – for I danced in conversation with theatrical practitioners, implying intentionality to a physical action. Desire a wild streak – and higher being – or lower, lowest, low... All known-imaginaries energetically cultivated or pursued. All dispersed and never centred – drunk – all pregnant, empty, emptied, pregnant once more. All wild-universe coming at me! All keen and bright – a temple. I, Tomás.

Recall:

Public space, where these things find expression, was the theatre. And that was where boys I got to know hung out. When they weren't doing sport in the afternoons, and nights, evenings, after prep, and – free time coaxed and squeezed some how/which way from the overarching timetable. Order relaxed like their uniforms. And variations of sports-kit and fiercely cool trainers. They – boys – carried the lines they wore rough and unconsciously. I stopped seeing the uniform anyway: they were broad, impressionistic posture – faces, boys. At the begin, boy-body invisible – and needed awakening to get it on stage.

I dealt the cards given me. When nights got late, we channelled Artaud, Grotowski, Complicité. This was theatre stuff. Space moved. Housemasters came down to rescue them. The man in charge, the Director of Theatre, was Tom Walker. It is impossible to think that, without him, there could have been anything of what went on in that

214

theatre.

A giant of a man – no mere tutelary spirit. Walker got properly pissed-as-a-newt, and thereby he created this *other – ulterior* space for us. A place apart. A school takes you apart and puts you back together again like a seminary and this a place apart. He was a Mirabeau, giant beyond parody. He'd roll in the stalls on his fifth bottle. Warm plonk. Cradling knees and stomach-fat. Sipping fags. And bay at them F-words. F for *f*ing hell where has my life drained...* The production-desk spilled with unattempted buckets of sub-Mac-Donald's take-out. Yelling: 'AGAIN! DO IT AGAIN!' And for the benefit of my – the padawan – my – Tomàs's deep instruction: 'Stupid boys.'

A space within a space. A further level of descent. Deep formation.

Remember and forget. Within bounds of considerable retrospect: this is a school. (Were you there, as a boy, wee and not yet ripe and riper – ripening, you'll have forgotten it. For myself: remember everything!)

It was a splurge-hole! A Bullingdon Club of LOOK YOU FUCKER STOP FUCKING AROUND DO IT PROPERLY. Where boys came schooled, well then here was formlessness given its second chance. (You must become as nothing.) Walker was a true alcoholic, fuelled to the point he capsized, drowned, swallowed. Notes included: WELL I MIGHT AS WELL JUST SIT HERE AND FUCK MYSELF. A space within a space.

Did they love it? No – not those times. Was it necessary? Well, there came a point it worked. (I was an acolyte.) That vast conceit they needed breaking. Yahweh-God-style. If recalcitrant – unelected posh – so then dramatic truth might with fullness crack and – in such concentrated force – achieve its designated actions... But often, we were so fagged-out from it. In the performance space. When it was time to shine. Often, they didn't get it. Only they seemed rather lost in yet another thing put on them. An Old Law – Deuteronomical – put on those young people, young, boys, and lacking in delight, and it wasn't true.

After the theatre, Mr S – *I* – TOS, initialized – and – *he* – WALKER went to the pub. With the local people, chess was in vogue. (I won quite a lot of money there.)

The chess was the kind of play that isn't studied in textbooks, and there were plenty prepared to lose money on it. There were plenty flashy with fifty pound notes. There was no need to hustle. Sometimes, Tom Walker had only pre-loaded on a couple of bottles, and he invariably arrived in a mood to let things deteriorate. He was good while still on a rise, though when his wife, Mrs Walker, came in at the end to pick him up, Dave and I got that look, which was a woman's look, played through stooping disbelief, in shock and tiredness. *'I have to deal with this now, then, do I?'* Walker wasn't a miserable arsehole. He didn't cry or get angry. Just beached, soupy, and all washed-up. Toward the end he repeated to himself: *'Yes, yes…'* As if what he had in his head was so much. And an abstract remainder of this world dull to contemplate.

So it goes.

At some point, I must have asked this one group of boys round to dinner, or something like that. At some point. (Memories get mixed-up and merge and become one.)

There were dinners and one-pot suppers. I still have a full-set of matching plates. I served the rice and fondly-scented curries in whatever there was. Once it was basically all cooked, I got them to help. Once, it was Diwali. There is a way of doing basically credible naan in a domestic oven. Another time, the foyer was double-booked, for use as a rehearsal-space, so it was: 'Let's go do this at mine.' (This is my sofa, this my stereo... Here is my table arranged in six neat sections – one for each class...) And, what with the newness and difference – and with the rules, and the permissions, and the constraints – precious little rehearsing could have got done that day. It is easy to forget. It is in this sense a seminary and a different world.

For reasons of everything, I couldn't channel Walker. (Was I his shadow?) And this moving picture slides around a bit, and I have little doubt becomes re-arranged. Alternative time-lines, sub-plots, plays-within-plays – what you will. There is no single beginning onto which to pin any episodes that stick. One thing led to another... It could have been Elliot, who kissed Max, or it might have been Max. Or Guy – who arrived one day blank at my doorstep to show me/Sir his wound – entirely speechlessly – sorrowfully, mournfully. Or Adam, as secret as genuine insight in class, who just came round, no reason not to, kind of obviously, cup of tea. And there was Charles – who came with Sir! to see that opera.

It seems we ambled into being as individually collective. There were diverse Sunday afternoons. When there was not much better on. It seems entirely dubious remembering such moments from outside.

A kind of unofficial non-society *at some point* convened – in my kitchen and dining and living room. Something like this – all comings and goings, and boys who came together and, for each short while, they encountered diverse arrangements of friendships.

But threadbare history finds its gospel truth. One scene, one day, is true and maybe captures it. And it is true all the boys in this picture could easily have been together – more than, though of a certainty, this remembered time.

One scene, one day, abides. Call it gospel-truth.

*

There is peace in the garden. From a distance, a light shines. And then – at school – sprawled about the place – my downstairs, picturing stale walls and inherited carpet, all pretty much where it landed and no grand plan. It is odd to see them there – so humanly expensive. A workshop – that's the space – becoming me and them. We/I/them/us/. There's stuff in preparation – conjectural – stuff in progress. The furniture's mostly tat – as I have said – bar the table and chairs over here, and Dad's desk there, and the meditative sofa.

But they don't mind. Boys travel any class. Boys in the rain on the wall at the new Tesco don't mind *one iota* so long as they've got their mates. Plus which, those great wall-loads – books there to frighten them… Apart from the photographs – all framed, stuck on walls. They liked the photographs – some them mostly about them. Teen-scenes. Pre-millennial *kouroi*. Boy as genre. Beauty, truth, refracted. Beautiful boy.

Ripped found-images – newspapers, magazines, online – stuck in a frame. To exteriorize, to possess. A half-face become a pixelated *almost-collage* of itself. Life connects.

They were cute, scrappy photographs. Cropped smiles. Fairground attractions. Floppy winged hair and a shiny eye. It was all just a further extension of teenage-rooms. They *reflected.*

One boy stopped and bouncing off a photograph – his eyes lush and full – enthusing: 'That is *so-o-o-o-o-o* beautiful!' So *he* saw it. 17. Reflected in the subject-position. Self-aestheticized. Gratified. Maybe it just was that they liked it like their rooms were all the same.

Quiet as a hidden place. A Gethsemane. And, indeed, to see the picture cold, when it was the nicest thing in the world having them about

218

the place, you probably couldn't get anywhere near the then-magic of it. A marionette-show of gawky-tall tales and high attitude. Boys. And all the pizza-boxes spread around. Swallow-tailed Sunday-clothes sprawled. All languid. String-bean Argyle socks and their raggy legs. Dropped – to futon, carpet, beanbag, armchair, rug – like a stash of trainers.

They did the talking. I provided – food, fridge, the room, and it's a carry-on-space from the theatre. In return for which… Background noise. When Sundays were all mental duvet-time anyway. Sunday morning, I didn't dream; I half-listened to the radio, all snugly, numb with dumped sleep, while the marital couple in the next house had their weekly – the sound-penetration in that house was paper – all washed through, and wholly placid, at a mildest level of consciousness.

So by the time I got up, this fresh day seemed accomplished and satisfied already. And, by late lunch, it could only have been drinking when the pub stank of weekend beer and roast and gravy. That Sunday even got a name, when Elliot yelled from the midst of his beanbag – purest Highgate – 'We should have a society!' And little lord Bob decided we had better be called The Neutral Zone. And there might be poems. ('We could all write a poem!') And there might be plays… One time, Bob did write a prose-poem, then got cross when no-one was taking it seriously. And, like background radio, I absorbed. I might rather think it became to me a soundtrack to a missing year – lyrics scrubbed. Perhaps they had more years than I'd had – if lived-years are those years we have spent in community. Public-schooled in their different formation. English boys – and no lady-chaps. Women being the Housemaster's wife, and Matey, and tranquilized figures who were driven from Mayfair on parents' days, and old blood in beefy Chanel from distant shires.

I outfaced my fair-modicum of schoolboy smut. 'Sir, can I come round to yours for a one-on-one!' I rolled my eyes. Will-to-live sarcastically… (Flattered and they knew it.) But it wasn't like schools they make most people go to. Money-wise – maybe that became a thing. Maybe times changed or maybe the people did. Maybe, as money-tensions creaked, as times changed and money got less invisible.

For instance, there was one B-grade boy, whose monthly allowance exceeded my salary. An arm's length boy, who felt about me the way you might feel about a club to which you weren't invited and don't, and wouldn't, belong. His Dad had made himself rich through refrigerated haulage. He was a cunt and looked it. Beef stew – with little weepy bits of fat floating round in it. He came up to me one day after class with his B grade essay. And it wasn't missing commas and full stops. He 'wanted advice'. Sat when he wasn't invited on the desk – bulged taut grey trousers.

It wasn't a nice feeling sitting next to him. He sweated and he wore expensive aftershave. (And it wasn't missing commas and full stops – It was a B-grade essay.) And you can't be unpleasant to teacher and then expect teacher to like you.

However, it is hard to think how the safety went out of it. The new HM came in like an angry supply-teacher. (Plates got smashed. Plates got thrown.) Weird times. League-tables upwardly wrenched and recruitment-drives into the far-east… Boys *knew*… Time micro-managed – Boredom gained as bright boys found their little-free-time stripped.

It was an era of mass-resignation and staff-churn. Fagging, at a stroke, was theoretically axed. Housemasters became (mystifyingly) obliged to venture boys'-side. New bugs powerfully strong in their own conceit – the more nouveaux become quite literally untouchable – all clued-up with so-called 'rights'.

And in the view of the sixth-form, upon whom school discipline relied, way out of control. It wasn't necessarily easy to see it evenings, down in the central feeding hall, lingering at the tail-end of supper, Bob and others of the brighter boys, all listless with too many learning-activities, brains dulled to a driven mode, all that year as the standard was being raised. (They could see that at this rate, they weren't getting into Oxford.)

They raised the pass-mark on the entrance exams, then told us – the beaks to mark the exams more liberally… Okay – you get it.

But it wasn't what I wanted to hear – at supper – Bob and Mike lingered so miserably over their beans and toast. You expected it, and got it, from beaks, but not the boys. And so brusque at that. Matter-of-factly. Phoney improvements being stamped on them. (Both should have got into Oxford.) Life as they'd thought they'd had a chance at putting it slipping away. They weren't bitching when they put it so matter-of-fact. I have never seen young people so bored.

They kept each year getting younger and younger and further away. Though in the common room, masters were dropping like flies. Yet in the streets, and at a level Bob and Mike knew about, a sense of life inside things was emptying.

The fresh beaks were all neo-cons. This true threat seemed more pedestrian. Brand-man. Grown men in what was effectively boys' school uniform. Like they'd stuck. Cohesion gone out of it. Heart of sympathetic life, the Easter gift, bashed squarely, and relentlessly, through the round hole.

221

The mood become pale blue. Their knotted-ties in suits so chunky. Brazen – the look of it. Boot-faced squaddies. Moabites, Ephraimites, Ammonites. It seemed not a time for less quantifiable aspects of pedagogy.

(I did a class with the sixth form when I just got them to read one of Tennyson's poems over and over until they could read it. At the end of the lesson they went away saying it was deep. They got A grades – can't help telling you that!)

But the beginning of the end seems marked with a certain incident, nearing the end, if not the last year – if not even the penultimate year.

The boy's name was George. He was a first year. His perfectly delightful bluff-northern-dad had bought into it. Sent his boy to school to make a gentleman of him. A considerable act of relinquishment – a considerable gift – learning the lad to despise such human-grind, though not the money, as opened his candidacy.

George got rinsed from the first day – standard procedure that when such boys arrived, they learned with their first breath they had better keep very quiet. All ears. Ears absorbent, lips sealed. Until, one day, they pipe-up in brand-new and indistinguishable accents. (The exception was always the Russians.) And George: a doomed and brazen specimen. What with his too-new laptop… And a podge – disinclined toward sport.

And that bloody laptop. ('Put it away. No, really, put it away. No, really, put it away.') On parents' day, Dad came in a mood to hear good things, which I supplied. He was a nice, jolly man, rosy in thought, and with a Black Country accent. The world was his friend, and I resolved henceforth to remember our meeting, if only to emolliate the boy.

222

I had no useful information – the boy was only a first year – 13 –
and none I could appropriately offer. Perhaps there might have been
vague, weighty hints, as to the character of the school. In fairness to
myself, it could never have occurred to me there might be bullying going
on beyond what you might expect.

Besides, most boys, in the end, took their knocks and proved
finally tractable. Because you don't want to be alone. That is the calculus
of interest – if nothing else. And because they are all in it. I do this for
you and you do that for me – as one becomes the institution. (To clear
these plates. To fetch that toast. To mop this table.) Were you to want to
belong. If you wanted other boys to like you.

With the benefit of hindsight, possibly one might notice the
lateness to class as a pattern of behaviour. Possibly – in terms of
safeguarding videos that followed – there might have been something in
it. One might see, in the blurry old repeats of the irritating, jumped-up
dim-wit calling-out random shite, blocked, disrupted, means-restricted
need – to communicate. Knee-jerk acting-out.

When as a school you might have said: *It is that you are simply
dispositionally not right…*

If I play back the scene – I might speculate as to the boy's drifting
isolation. How, firstly, they simply didn't *actively* like him. Then they
didn't like him. Maybe it was when he – George – first worked out that
he was drowning that he – acted out.

There were police – among these claimed, deferred, and optioned
masculinities, future-identities put out at interest and tossed around. An
economy of growing-up.

We knew little of what was happening. The man who took the
brunt was one rather noble and longsuffering homosexual, whom that

223

class of shells presumed to denigrate. Later, he was reinstated, though his position was no longer tenable.

For days, though, nothing was possible. A whisperless shroud fell about the place – *class-hatred* crusted. Class-activity descended to an act of note-taking. It seemed the very structure was violated. The school-village sucked itself together like a corset.

And that was rather odd. (George was withdrawn. Sorry, George's Dad.) Alone, I stood inside my situation – each day as I divested, having failed to project.

I know that then I thought: Behold my rooms! There was then the potential to put Wagner on the hi-fi. Lavender scented the air. My rooms *jejune* and pathetically scrupulous.

I went to the pub, where Dave was full of the drama of it. 'Tomàs, *Tomàs*, do you have any idea what is happening?' And it had all blown-up in Dave's mind after some pints and come tumbling like judgement.

Later I took stock:

Upstairs there was nothing: functional Ikea tables, blu-tacked walls, and marking.

Downstairs: what might have incriminated? A Taschen book of photographs by Wilhelm von Gloeden. (They wouldn't have liked those.) A catalogue of the National Archaeological Museum in Athens. (They wouldn't have like that.) The locked screen on my computer-monitor a black-and-white picture of Nelson Mandela when he was President. Tacked above it, a rip-out page from a copy of The Economist, June 1995, with a little black boy and a little white boy, both with the flag of the new South Africa in facepaint.

Dad's desk. Whatever had soaked up in that.

Once I was in love and wrote a poem, when the friend stayed over. My poems were all rubbish – they never became themselves. I read this poem to my class when I was studying for A Level. It goes like this:

Pillow face

Tacked to the bed's end

Your lips earnest

As you slept

Open laced

Your red trainers

Mudded at my doorstep

Recalled and predicted you

A broken year commenced.

An empty space exposed. The novelty gone, I stopped loving them. I experienced visions of myself as an old school-master, gown and a Labrador – synecdoche! – crossing the playing fields. Into the mist and the afternoon, following lunch.

One boy there was, A*s, who knocked for me most nights. Cozy lad, quiet, soft-spoken. A west-coast fuzz and a tang in his accent – north-west. That was an easy affection – a simple love. We'd flop on the sofa, and sometimes knock head-against-shoulders, and chat and solve the world. I liked him because, apart from being beautifully, he talked a lot. He talked *around* a lot. He liked to see things – imaginary concepts – and talk about them. I liked to sit back and to listen and share. He could talk forever. Maybe quite a lot of it was relatively localized.

Though in class, at the bottom-end, where they seemed so painful-foetal and premature, there was no doing anything with it when a pitch went wrong and *Sir!* knew he had begun to resent their wet-nurse money

225

– milk-and-sops IQ. There was a class – two rescuable boys, genetically better, sat in the back of it, stuck to each other like panic. I didn't ask to have them pushed up a set. Unforgivably.

*

Recall:

Once upon a time, and back in the real world, prior to this above, and for the third time, and maybe the last, I experienced something like love again.

Here I am twenty-*three...?*

I can be fairly sure – because I'm not twenty-four yet. This time I'm at Mum's.

I am down from university first, then back from London, that same unit of time, which comes in five-year chunks. At Mum's, I sat a year in the garden and parsed life. There are books I hadn't got round to, gaps, blags, and something yet of a revisionist narrative to bring to the year most immediately preceding, when it was all such a fuddle at times, and incorrect. Mortifications – when, really, anything might have happened. And it was quite unlike university. And no-one quite seemed to know what we were getting into – life.

It was an odd year of casting about the place. The little-years at university all came packaged-and-sealed – as nice impressions. Indeed, that, in the garden, was really what the principle was to be restored – after the London episode. Nice things. Only the good things that carry us. Things that *are* life.

I recalled – I re-enacted.

A view of the quad – forever. Sat on the chair's back, feet on seat, I stoop to type my notes. On about sixty filterless French a day – learning – *old* poems by rote. A cigarette-holder so the smoke doesn't get in my

226

eyes... And the quad got the full view – so my studious hours be sufficiently hyper-real.

And in the quad – yo-yos, mind-maps, hypnotism, comrades, juggling, yesterday's rave, and slow release of pressure, slow formation, stillness winding down. And in the city – a walk one day in Michaelmas term, to the river, down through the meadows, with Penny, whom I platonically loved, like a manful puppy. Mist-layered – *then* already a brittle scene. Paled, minted, nebulized, tending to sepia. Cotswold stone. And boys at the college school played rugby. Her beautiful mind had a natural proclivity to make-believe, which spooned each passing, golden thought through never-silence. She was Virginia Woolf. She was *Anne Of Green Gables*. She found or constructed stability – when it got to be a bit of a mess in the first year. Screwed – by the college eight. Heaving, curtained darkness in the pit of a room by day. Emptied of anything inside to offer to personhood. Mad space emptying out of her – crying through her – almost the helpless pain of an animal. But she put herself together, in clean-bobbed hair and a little routine, and now it was nice.

London, London, London...

London, London, London... Summer was hot that year. We lived in a house. And what with the AIDS and that... London is a vile-place sober. Times when maybe London is the loneliest city on Earth.

We worked in bars. I got a job on a magazine. I got the train into Blackfriars, read Dickens, the FT, The Economist. I went short. At lunch, I ate my sandwich on the steps of Saint Paul's. Some gruelling pleasure got forced out of Saturday... (So alone. Always, always, always, so alone.)

One scene. Riding the overground. Very-cool seventies-flared washed-very-thin needle-cords waste-thin, brown, and a red nylon Adidas

227

vest. A fellow-traveller sheepishly catches my eye – because I'm openly carrying a copy of Gay Times. And I look instantly down, then look back at her – thirty-odd. She gives me a look like pride – like these days service men and women marching in their military uniforms. I don't have a ready-made expression, so I do a quick smile-I-guess, then look nowhere again, and then remember to smile again so she might know I might like to be with her even though I don't.

Saturdays would have been something like that.

Paul Simon's 'The Boxer' played on loop. I was the first to walk away from it, and it was years after the event when I heard how the others got evicted, and that was reassuring to hear because it meant some of my sense of things at the time might have been up to a point objective. And Kim went to Poland, and Al went to Dublin, and Jon found his calling in VSO. And Steve got dead, and Roman inherited. And even now I can't see how any more viable career-path might have unthread itself out of it. It just wasn't that sort of city. It didn't want you.

In 1995, Mum's new house was something of an anomaly even then. (After a divorce, you get half a house.) Still, then, the good-sized gardens hadn't been broken-up. They weren't then building opportunities adding the price to it.

I walked the dogs down to the marsh each day. One was the child-dog still, old now, and always the wimpy-dog. (Terrified of Dad – who wasn't dead yet.) He, Fred, merrily poddled – pretending at the flashes he'd strain at the leash when I threw out into the water the dummy for the young dog, Barney, who was becoming mine, whom we reclaimed from Dad's first accident. He, Fred, only pretended to strain, and one time we looked back and we'd lost him, and, retracing our steps, found him stuck in a foot-wide ditch he couldn't pull himself out from. Hauled up – all Barbour jacket and Fred's expression never in any doubt we'd come for him.

Out there when it was getting on for evening, and the sun was red and low over the Welsh hills, the clouds went bright pink and gold, and it really shone, and with the mountains and thin, layered vapour whipping the light about, I liked to imagine you could think about dragons being figured in it, as though it were a long, creased dragon-spine, if you had access to a magical thinking. Here, in my twenties, I was young. It made me think about the holidays down on the cliffs with Mum on the south coast. There, within the stirrings of religious thought, namely here in this sense Celts and druids, as more brutally childish and magical thought transitioned, and as it drew and it configured potentials, preliminary abstracts, entering puberty, entering upon the ledger of a new mind finally coming online for me, and as this landscape fulsomely accorded, this low body of the many hills' prostration crunched granular into the cliff-fall and the good sea. There was that continuity – that base – and a lot could be revisited there to rebalance the meaning of it. There'd have been a lot of those dog walks, until I thought I might put in some time at a local school, and see what that was like.

Even then, on pure flight, it seemed so bright, so possible. Not a bold step, but there was great promise of life coming-at-it… If that's what you want… *Am I a teacher?* Marks & Spencer meal-deal and the fucking Range Rover. *Certainly, I have studied things to share…* A viable arena. Slot back in life. (That's what you do, is it? What, actually, *do* you all do?)

Once I had started, and with the local university, it took virtually

229

no time at all. (Life – modern life – may be all manner of bogus fucktardary and bullshit, but they are metaphorically gagging to suck you in.)

I quite *liked* children… Bearing in mind I remained adolescent, while childhood was in a sense unsatisfactorily unclosed… They got okay a bit when in any case boys touched 13/14. (There was in those days no serious expectation you ought in any real sense teach them before they were 'ready'.) Each day, then, could be a mighty experiment. Though I groan, now, with time, and feel again the loss and innocence… But cities are no place for the poor, and I needed a job, and the financials prohibited London, so embrace, create, and read-again books. The schools I applied to were all nice… (I got hay-fever going to the interviews – I couldn't speak!)

So *perform* intense and splendid make-believe. And mind be the mansion. And half the blessed schools pure flight – unreal what with the hay-fever and in literary settings. (Near-escapes!)

Through the course of my training, my Year 9s were the best class. For starters, they let Mr S properly loose on those. (What could possibly go wrong?) When the sixth-form were past praying for. The quietly shy Year 10s asked merely for answers to their GCSEs. The 7s and 8s too small. My Year 9s – legendary.

Gentle reader: I *was* a teacher!

Doing the PGCE, which is what you do to be a teacher, we were all-up for child-centred approaches to learning. *Democracy In Education* I studied and can heartily recommend – or 'merry hell' we joked. Had I noticed – had I taken note – of *any* of the young-people round our way before? They were of an age when they'd be biking round Tesco or

230

Sainsbury's, when there was relatively little by way of youth-visible. There was still a skateboarding area round near the entrance at one of the parks, but I hadn't been near there since infancy. And maybe you'd see them in a family context, with Mum, at the supermarkets, dragging their toes through the shopping aisles, shouldering the bodies through complex teenage vertices like they were getting up. And they'd *wind* down the aisle, and they'd be *sloughing* the presence of her, rucked-hair-aware, within Mum's pull like a logarithm. And at the checkout, the unseemly matter of product-selection endured, a more courting disposition while Mum pays. A boy's stance, then, heterosexually romantic – a proportioned and otherwise five-foot-six man wooing – as a squire might chaperon – Mum. A different being from school. Mum's plastic.

There was no fashion in the provinces that year. People had jobs and went off in their cars to them. Even the new cinemas hadn't been built, and life was VHS and Netscape. They wore plain denim jeans and simple trainers. Surf-brands were very much a thing. They wore sporting goods, and knew the more massive of the tunes then charting. There was less noise. A dull, suburban world. And the colours they wore less ferocious. A news-restricted diet of information… Less fuzzy. For we were picking ourselves up at this point, and clearer messages were only beginning to happen. Parochial England idled waiting for 1997 – and that was in the air.

The boy who took me under his wing was in this Year 9 class. Here's Luke. The first and still the only who, in one load, individuated – captured, instantiated – Teenage Boy. Trigger-point locked and primed, Luke was cause for celebration. It is a face you couldn't possibly reconstruct, though there are photographs – aimed with a flexed rubber-band at the OM2. His is standard frame – and telephoto-length – for the

231

boing!-phase of young adolescence. Not 'skinny'. Rather, investing in growing tall.

Luke kept a Warhammer figurine on his desk – to adore, and to help him to concentrate. His voice twangs *as if* ironic. Fricative – at the velum. Down-drawn, the plucked school-ruler, at the lips' edge. An Aussie-edge to the diaspora-Liverpudlian. At the level of his face, on *his* right side. Luke became ironic on *his* right side – my left. And the eyes faintly quizzical – fully expecting the joke. It was a long while before I saw, once, how he softened them. The hair was thick, deep-auburn, dark-chocolate curly, like a Labradoodle. The shoes, laced Kickers. Trousers unpressed clean. And the blazer sown with all the little badges they got for the various things.

There was a magic in those days. If we can imagine the apex as Radiohead playing the Glastonbury stage, that's not yet. *I* am *again* Prince *Lovesexy* and *Sign 'O' The Times*. *I* am *again* 'Losing My Religion' in Les Arcs and Val d'Isere. *I* am *not at the moment* Tricky's *Maxinquaye* and Beck's *Mellow Gold*. The young were especially hungry. That was the trouble with the sixth-form – they'd reached the end of the bluff. Beyond the rubrics of the latest curriculum – and a right-wing economics of our human subject modelled normalized – to the age of sixteen. And they were pretty clueless when the A Levels wanted of them some*one* less post-modern – more authentic still.

Luke only lived round the corner, half a kilometre, and then up the posh road with all the fancy houses with his Mum. Yet, if I had ever seen him around, it could have been only generically. On the streets, let alone in class, they were remote, baying entities, unpredictably messed in a live-it-up tangle of their life. Such minimal structure one made show of – teaching – wrenched merely in snap-seconds' focus a take on each named individual, crushed-up in a room, each his own-life. *They were a lot –* each one like cities of people, all piled, layering, tribes and styles, and guru-faith, as terrifying angels are said to be. Long over-extended, and chewing up free space. Pressurized toward that intensity of threatening distortions. The retrofitted urban: view from the street.

Though in class they all required to communicate. And though it seemed chaos in there – yet at least *knowable* information one might flag for each seemed conventional. And it wasn't like they didn't yell everything they wanted to yell. It might seem, *knowably*, a standard limitation of regular and mashed-together school brain and attitude, exposed to all that year's designs for a lifestyle, and all the correct TV. And, you might think, they might differentiate next year, as adolescence got going beyond the first thump. But in the meantime – each head of face and hair – an Aztec maze to look at. Like crunched play around the centre of a board, when any move seems madness. You couldn't pause long to look at it. The kinesis of the energy advanced kept any and all thought locked to a process, and well away from quiet consideration of any*one*'s own-life. You went in there collectively – thirty different people in themselves each thirty different people and you each one.

Diurnally though blasted at the end of it, I had essays to write – PGCE. I read in the Newbolt Report of 1921 how an aim in state-maintained education should be to eliminate the culture of the working classes, described as a malignancy, and to put better culture in place. It was odd to think of that. What they had going – 1996 – in public discourse didn't seem so different. Yet they were suburban kids – and any idea you might 'eliminate' anything in that class… Maybe it was that with the sixth-form. And maybe then something like hollowness – in bolt-on skills-sets put on them. Something not provided of a culture enabled through dissonance. Or a culture to discover and to enact itself combative – political – dialectic. Or to pray it up. Whether or not they were scared – they were not *confident* when choices were offered them. A new creole. And you got odd thoughts like notions of Britism – when, in signs, a sense to which the sixth-form conformed, that an England was in process, *being* rolled outside of history to some non-time. As if this preceded – or perhaps better *shadowed* – *ghostly* – an England of The First World War. A modern interstitially accounted in dog-eared tracts, and an official-side of history as tangible, life-down-here-or-there as – Campbell-Bannerman!

There seemed no risk in Year 9. Noise and labels. Names. The extent of the signs of their world no more than the same few targeted shops around Chester and Liverpool. But such definitions looked new on them. They wore it new and it suited them when they were fourteen. Their adventuring lives played vividly ahead – as half-elf druid, halfling footpad, human mage, chaos dwarf... They took lunch in pop-up feeding zones scattered about the school in house assembly halls. They called over to me, '*Sir!*' validating. And I squished in with my foil-wrapped sandwich, which I had prepared that morning, my favourite being cornbread with pastrami, lettuce, tomato, a slick of cream cheese, and the mayonnaise I made myself with extra-virgin olive oil and Dijon mustard. Chewed the crap and shot the sea-breeze. And caught them listening – and for the 90% their Neanderthal brows on – and had to control what I said to them. Narrowing to context and keeping my thoughts plain.

By-and-by, in class, it must have been a reasonable impression of teaching them. Now we are all real to one another, after the *thu'd* of the meeting, after the push and shove. Luke was form captain – by popular vote the most constructively loudest. He and I eventually got talking properly after an after-school club Luke roped me into supervising. We were packing the stuff up in plastic bags, when all the noise had gone away, and when that was done, and the room was as dust-grey and tidy as ever it was going to be, I offered to lend a hand carrying the bags. In the car park, where I had no car and Luke's Mum wasn't, Luke said: 'Are we walking the same way?'

I pointed long, through rank and file of bushes, fences, houses, as toward a revolutionary prospect – hills, trees. My arm stretched. I said – smiling and ingratiating myself: 'Do you want me to go on ahead and not look back?'

'Nah, you're alright.'

'Have you ever tried walking naturally like that – when there's someone following you?'

'No, why?'

'It might go a bit weird. Swingy arms.'

'You swing your arms anyway.'

'These arms were made for walking.'

'Do you know how much you swing your arms around when you talk?'

'I have heard mention of the affliction.'

'You so do that deliberately, like it's your thing.'

'My thing?'

'Yeah, you know, like being bald, or Welsh, or going on about cheese.'

'Who goes on about cheese?'

'Miss Davies. She's obsessed.'

'Would that be while teaching you French?'

'It's while doing something in French.'

Beyond the first junction, streets were a quiet mix of post-war developments and smatterings of old town. Even in rush hour, within a very brief radius of school, there'd be no-one hanging – this apropos loose, school-yard talk and teen street-credibility. Reality-concerns. There were at least half a dozen desirable schools in the area people went to, and minibuses came and went for them. You could tell by the shoes. Besides, the demographic toward our sector of sprawl was already bunched into its middle-to-late years, the houses either getting expensive or they'd been bought when new. There were local intricacies, there was local knowledge. It was kind of cute generationally – same little discoveries – same place. ('How come *you* know that?') Our nooks and crannies – our crooks and boughs – our interstices. Then preserved and, one must suppose, irrecoverably lost now.

Luke didn't burst to chatter. His mode, that day, was unusually self-denigratory and they were modest openings, the loudness given place to a more seemingly watchful staccato, not so much hesitant as simming a next thing in mind before saying it. What did Sir *really* think about their class? What did Sir *think* about being here – the area? A novelty? (I grew up here. I was your age once here.) It felt pretty good being an adult, like having a day off, with pre-arranged leisure activities. Purchased experiences. Trivial, non-self-improving expenditure justified. (Because it's with the kids.) Like swinging your legs in a taxiing plane going on holiday. (Can afford this seat: no kids.) And maybe, then, a decade was time's pedagogical unit. (And it was amazing: 'You do that still?!') *Maybe* that's the point where/when you tag: *you're it.* 10 years.

Luke's 'pad' was on the road with the gated houses. My Mum's had become a work-in-progress – the half-kilometre beyond. (Luke is strangely genetically wonderful and his house is posh.) My Mum's is a late-ish-70s construction, pinko-brick, the ceilings low, the roof seeming to cave, the windows massive, looking onto the gardens. Though it leaked warmth, withindoors the air had a stale, flattened edge to the sense of it, prior owner-occupants one Mr Sheen and cohabiting partner Ms Glade Fresh, and they smoked, and that had got into the plasterwork.

Ron was in the picture. Mum had him stripping the floors up while she did the walls, skimming and painting. Then she took to rotavating the gardens – a job she was born for. We camped out, treading the rafters. To say Ron was a bit B&Q would be putting it mildly. The house became a shell, then built back up again. And things found their places. Cheery, bright colours predominated. It was a nice, wooden, oak floor. (It was quite high quality – not chav.) The bathroom and the little-room tiled in an Edwardian fashion, with details of rose flowers and pomegranates. The garden grew, and Ron laid the foundation and brickwork for the new conservatory. Mum liked to see Ron doing things like that, and accredited Ron with the little improvements when occasional friends popped round.

It was spring. I smoked in those days, while dinner was a carb-fest of pasta and calories, jet-fuel to what must have been a racing metabolism. Each sunny morning around eight, the days wore an aspect of manageable targets and can-do. School was fine. It wasn't like I had real responsibilities. It was all mentored. And I got to be a bit Year 9 about it all. With the sixth-form, I'd got the idea a good bet mostly is to read the books to them. Sit them down nicely and tell them a story and they follow the words.

(For teachers reading this, and with the sixth-form, I recommend story-time. They like that. Though it slows everything down – that slow, meditative pace might run quite deep and trouble them. And too get, accept and presuppose *all* cultural references are in all likelihood a complete blank… But try story-time. Sharing my treasures here: use my experience: this works!)

In terms of Culture with the sixth-form, there was the odd time when an obvious thing was a photocopied page of Scripture to supply the deficiency. This, I found, proved categorically inimical. God and Church – religion – such matters not merely *suspect* – pre-condemned. Tense-making. Hackles-raising. A merest exposure to text they feared contaminant. There burned a pre-emptive and an anti-proselytizing rage. Deep hatred. Ruthless exclusion. *Not that.*

I must confess, this found me at a loss. I quickly grasped that it was the case, the text alone, as source, as analogue, prompted what seems now an inevitable: 'Sir, do you *believe* this?'

('How do you mean? "Believe"?' I might have asked – but with the benefit of hindsight.)

There was filth. Real burning hatred figured.

Who knew? What bad messages – what strenuous designs?

But words aren't play and indubitably frivolous and to these souls any-and-aught hard-words are a text-threat. Keep this place provisional and unreal: adolescence. Exclude – what turns in Mind in class from felt and visceral. May it mean and not-mean... Maintain – decentring.

On the same hand, when the matter of literary text was politically incorrect – an illustrative passage from Ovid's *Metamorphoses*, I might say by way of example – they missed the humour of it. Violent delights… Disgust. Repulsion. What was the writer *saying*?

And it wasn't like their jokes among themselves weren't filthy.

Then again, where you might think they might have identified, in lyrical and romantic poetry – poems *all* about 'I' and 'me' and 'my'– even then yet more than quaint, flowery language eluded them.

And yet there is such recollection of spring. Perhaps Easter was late that year. A retroactive – retro-*causal* Easter. There is spring recalled in morning sunshine. And in the evenings a purity. Stilling the day – while the terrors of the night seem impossible. Thought or an awareness of beauty. Almost-presence – maybe a love-itself. Formless – yes. Dissociated as it informs a mind later from anyone. Pinned to no one shape. And love-in-Christ might seem a misremembered echo, a slanting and a partial reflection, which itself aches and with unseemly distortions. There abides a force of love one may affirm existed.

A few times, Luke caught up with me on my walk back. Within the days, the route shrank. In terms of what was happening then, the route was settled as territory. It's impossible to hear what's finding us he needs to talk about. It must now have been Luke did the talking. I have nothing to say. And maybe too close examination would crack an important myth. Probably all this is best at a level of now spiritualized essences. It's the feeling that surrounds it, and you could take that wall of noise and apply to it any words.

One thing we do know: it, then, is all adding up to the necessary content of each day. There's a routine, and it all comes together in a one-pan supper of curry with news and music, and the evening feed, with Mum and Ron. Mum is happy with Tomàs. He/I make/s the mess in the kitchen, and Mum does the washing-up, and Ron dries.

There is a world opening. Clocks change and no-one's getting raggy with each other. We are successfully imitating life. And, in a way, this transplantation of houses might not be so unhealthy. They're just paper-thin walls, and they all fold-up so quietly the minute you step through the front-door. That's a good show – I'm taking a pride in my appearance. These clothes aren't expensive. The mirror says: 'Yes!' Hair has shape and volume. We present to life deodorized, splashed with cologne. It looks advertised and it smells right. So it was not until the Easter holiday that, of a sudden, life got… Weird. Fidgety. Unseen. Unperformed. Exilic.

There is the bright spring sun, and there are the longest of dog-walks. But dogs aren't the same. Dogs are alright up to a point. And I had been wont to quip that teaching is just like running a dog but with added Chaucer. But it wasn't *the same* with dogs. Even if you couldn't put your finger on why that might be.

Daily trips to the Tesco were no help. Either everyone had gone away for Easter, or no-one really was ever there. There were people to watch on the front, and the pub could swallow an afternoon, and there were Chester and Liverpool. You could read and invent little stories, but they were just spiral designs, and there was nothing really centring on this place. Even if you stared at people – they were just scrapes and blocks of colour and pumps and branding. You had to drink with the guys at the bar to invent enough problems to talk to them. Our stories were missing things – as though the whole lack were an archaeological Delos. And fantasy shapes rolled off in evening sky to the pale blue. Any kind of Spirit was absence. Any kind of love-space must have taken concentrated energy to claim it was full.

I remember it was Monday at the office door. Everyone was in a

240

great fuss with the reprographics. There was that unsettled business of squalling reprographic wind, and two weeks' fresh ideas, like we all had just got back from skiing at the top of a mountain. And at the door it was: 'Sir!' Luke and Sam had come to see me. Quick as a flash, I said:

'Well here's a sight for sore eyes! A'wight, boys!'

Luke and Sam looked brand-new. I beamed astonishingly. The teacher in me mentally straightened their ties. We were going to do *Julius Caesar* this term. There were SATs. And my own last week of the holiday – I got a last-minute to a ski resort, travelling Swiss Air – meant nothing was really in focus. I squeezed it all together and I made the attachments – shaping human form.

A thought to hang onto was that it was Sam and not Chris here – so maybe Sam was the new best-friend this term. Okay: got that. I deliberately exhibited equal attention… (I was, in a sense, possessed – I was *grateful*. All those years of silence – with the rough boys. All those years of not being me.) And, as it normalized, I heard about how boring their Easters had been, and how they weren't glad to be back, and they got the right combative groans going. They were, though, blocking the door – if I concentrate, I see they are marginally yet less tall than I am – and the Head of English snapped them together, played his military rôle, towered over them. His was a military manner generationally inspecting them. Snapped to attention – they liked playing that. They could snap into rôle. And it was that time of year when for everyone the SATs and the GCSEs and the A Levels came as blessed relief. The clock ticked – a task-centred orthodoxy prevailed. There was no flabby excess of time. The exams kicked each day into more focused shape.

There were the walks home, and in some manner a settled thing.

Often he'd wait, I suspect deliberately, though never once took it for granted, on the new bench, dedicated in the engraving to one George, husband, father, grandfather, serving in both the wars, OBE, teacher, philanthropist. Luke liked it to be seen that he was reading one of the Diskworld novels. We'd walk down, and stand yakking awhile at the top of Luke's driveway. Once Luke said that he had to rely on Sir for provisional adult knowledge. 'Being as how you, Sir, are currently my one point of contact with the adult world.'

It was terribly flattering. My dogs learnt the way to the pub after that. There was no homework to speak of, and it was nice just to let the days roll, a recurrent present. Weekdays – for *six?* weeks – didn't much differentiate. Then each Saturday's long and easy, stretched hours, lolling in the David Lloyd, with gym, jacuzzi, sauna, steam-room, pool… My weekends given to locality – local atmospherics.

With the warm weather, drag-racers took to the streets nights, and you could people-watch down on the front, where people drove or cycled to sit on the estuary wall and eat chips and ice-cream. It was the nice bit for miles around people came to. The pubs were okay. The one I liked kept a fire going, even while people turned pink outside. There seemed a background utility to pretty much anything – since you could bring it to the classroom. And thereby 'life' had its excuses – other than just being a bit of a pain in the arse to deal with. There were new books to read and new music to listen to. Life could do its thing: there was no need to shut it all out yet.

The day that sticks in memory, and sounds a change in memory, like a glottal stop, was when I saw inside Luke's house. We were yakking at the gate, but that day it was pissing down. And Luke's Mum came out and yelled at us: 'Boys! *BOYS!* Get in here!'

The overhanging trees could have been providing no shelter whatsoever. We must have been wet-through. Hair slick like slick moss – rain-drenched faces. That noise hammering:

'BOYS!'

In the doorway she stood. My first thought was – 'Boys!' and some manner of inclusive and matriarchal statement of power and real-life and money, rules and ownership.

She is at first glance… Tall. And somewhat angular. Teutonic in colour and thrust. A first-wave feminist cardie. An upturned broom.

She yelled again: 'BOYS!'

Luke and I looked to one another. Each face like unexpected data. We made a loping show of a dash to the open door. And in a side-porch – towels were thrown over us. Luke's blazer in process of being shuck off and – 'Give me that!' Luke's Mum put it on a hanger and hung it with home-clothes over the gas boiler. There chunked bread was put to dry in a repurposed wicker basket: Whoso liveth here hath a dog.

I took my shoes off. My socks were plain black. I thought a second, then took those off too, and rolled the bottoms of my trousers up. Luke hadn't changed his green socks since PE. And weighing each other up in this light, Luke shrugged as if he didn't know either. A different set of measurements – not precisely bigger or smaller, nor precisely older or younger. A moment astigmatic.

I took my jacket off and found a hook for it, loosened my collar and tucked-in my plain white, slim-fit, cotton shirt. I was going to be compelled to say something when Mum popped her head round the door to say:

'Tea? How do you take it?'

243

'Oh well, milk if you have, no sugar.'

While Luke bobbed gently on the spot like a rippling wave, I got tagging-along, pack-trail, the quiet boy. Postural issues. Matters of auditory volume and relative height – and sheer density. (*I am now taller* than Luke then? Okay…) I followed Luke through into the kitchen, and so in that room such issues were satisfied. Had there been questions pertaining to who and what the domiciliary aspect presented was meant to be… Ideal Home, I thought. Cheshire Life.

It was the real – it was the proper sort of kitchen. It was nice and big. The ceiling wandered off into cloud-cover. Peaches and cream. Indeed, an inner door opened and an old yellow Lab strolled in, dog-solid, and he had a sniff at me, and I passed, like an old smell the dog had no particular view upon. There were newspaper broadsheets read and spread on the linoleum tablecloth, a splodgy, lozenged check of blue and yellow, beside the trussed kitchen-curtains, in yellow-green. And devices and copper pots… You'd think probably midweek they'd be having things like spag-bol, fish-fingers, no-frills own-brand beans on good thick toast. Then probably a take-out on Friday, and on Sunday maybe some family friends round for a Prosecco and a roast with a big salad. The cupboards were cream as opposed to 'cream', and the surfaces painted wood, bevilled. There were naïve pieces tacked to the fridge, which seemed just-right then quite-wrong, before I remembered Luke had told me he had two sisters. And there the dog and there his basket. And someone played tennis. (There the racquet, there the shoes.) Mum made tea, and then set about sandwiches. She said:

'Do you want to get the biscuits, love?'

'Yeah sure,' said Tomàs.

Luke braced the big, Christmassy tin against his chest and waggled

244

the lid off. Butler service. I dipped in. I came up with a Hovis.

'Why thank you, Sir.'

Luke's Mum stirred sugar into her tea. She said: 'Well, it's very nice to meet you. At last. All we get round here is, Mr Storey said this, and Mr Storey said that. He tells us everything.'

'Oh my.'

'You'd be hard pressed to think anything else has happened all day. I certainly hope you enjoyed his Mark Anthony. We all had to.'

'Err, yeah. All good.'

'Well, I'd best not embarrass the poor sausage. He's under enough pressure. You must be worn out. *It's these SATs*. Do they get on at you about it all the time? Or don't they worry you this year? It could be quite a stroke of luck having you for them. I am inclined to believe your methods might be considered by an older guard as constituting risk.'

'Err, well…'

'I know, I know. Enough, woman! Still, it would be nice to hope he gets to keep you for the GCSEs. I suppose things don't work out like that, though.'.

'I…'

'Well, I hope you like these. If not, he'll scoff the lot. If this rain doesn't go off, I'll give you a lift back. I don't know what the forecast is.'

My clothes were beginning to dry on me, while outside it seemed unusually dark, and rain slapped against the windows at intervals. I held my tea carefully by handle and fingertips while it was too hot to sip from without making slurpy noise. All possessed, she sat back with the crossword puzzle she was up against. Luke got the plate with the sandwiches, and said:

'After you, Sir.'

I said: 'You might want to give me directions, in that case.'

There was a games room jutting out onto the garden, with a couple of sofas and a snooker table. There was a TV with a console and wires trailed about and stacked video tapes. The snooker table had all the Warhammer figures and bits of terrain on it. It wasn't like in the shop, but messy bits and pieces, printed cardboard. Luke fiddled with orcs and elves while we ate the sandwiches, and *through* each mouthful, I heard more of the armies you could get if you had enough pocket money. And what he/I saw was the vision-sold – with the memorized price-list. And far be it from me to reprove. He told me I should see the Civilization he had running upstairs – meaning the computer game I liked too – but that idea dropped in a beat you'd render now something like 'maybe not'. Luke described where he was in it. You play that game too much, all night, and the live world flattens to a pixelated grid like a Civ screen. He said how he was three decades up with the weaponry on the Germans. And then said: 'Well anyway.' We were standing at the table, leant over, with our elbows resting on it. Two sets of unbitten nails pushing fluff around. Mine – meaning my nails – all knuckly – cigarette-skin. (Would that I had never once smoked.) Luke's wrists – malted honey. Man-shirt, boy-shirt. Hands. Mine like birds' claws in comparison. I said: 'You are set for an historic victory.'

'Ha, yeah, it will be.'

I laid my left hand on the felt, and splayed my fingers. Man-watch, a mid-range Seiko, late by a minute each day, and now a quarter to five. Luke did the same with his right hand next to mine. They lay there to look at. Luke swallowed a gulp. Then in the smallness of his breaking-deep voice said: 'Surrrrrrrrrrrrr. I love you.'

There was hardly an interval – only to smile like a man reassuring

246

– holding: 'Good. Awesome.'

Luke said: "'*Awe-some.*'"

A very, very serious unknown hovered on Luke's face a second. His eyes were quite open, and everything looked so small and big and fragile. Then the lips, parted, smiled, and the expression in his eyes caught fire again. That look was almost about to say: 'We are kidding, right?' But he turned back to the snooker table, hunched down, elbows rested, and he took up one of the figurines to contemplate. The only thing to do was the same.

I formed a line of six orcs. They were home-painted, an officially merchandized clan's colours, no doubt, and caught the light blobular. Whether it might be a knack, or expertise and time, or different tools, or a way of seeing and relating between the enamel paint in the paint pot and the imagined orc and the tiny little detail in the figurine – they'd not be confused with the display sets they had in the shop ready-painted. Then, after enough contemplating, I said: 'You must have spent ages.'

'Yeah, they're alright. I really want to get more chaos elves.'

'Oh they sound nice.'

'People are really getting into them. They're really cool. Their history's kind of complicated. That's really geeky, though. They're just cool. They're dark.'

'Which is all you need to know.'

'Yeah, basically.'

It was still raining, though it had gone off, when it was time to be going. Luke's Mum gave me the lift, while Luke stayed behind, and, once I'd got changed, I walked down to the front to watch the cloud pass and a pale evening gather above the hills. The first pint disappeared, and the second and third passed semi-productively, doodling bullet-sized pockets of bumf for the sixth-form, *doing* Keats. But just watching. Other men numbing their days, getting their insulation on. Other men who, for money, weren't ready for home yet. Go back tranquil.

After that, Luke and I yakked at the gate still. I suppose I experienced myself more consciously as a filtered adult. *And watch your mouth. Watch your adult mouth. Mind your adult experience. Don't bring that in here...*

He was growing up by the day too. We didn't hang around if was raining. And the after-school club kind of died – they grew out of it. We talked quite a bit, or I did, about *Julius Caesar*, and I lent him a fantasy book called *The White Dragon*.

With summer, it was structurally impossible to go and knock for him!

Out of my suit now, and sloughing about the place, I got back home mid-August ready to move. I bumped into Luke and his age-appropriate friends when they were on skateboards, at the bottom of the road, which had been sealed off for British Gas purposes. The dog – Barney – went all over them. They were just out of trackies and into jeans. Then it was all: 'Oi, Sir!' It was nice to see them, though I wasn't in professional mode and it was lucky the dog was there.

Before I left, I nipped and posted Luke a card. I left the envelope unsealed, for the avoidance of doubt. I included what I had been told would be my new landline number. Later, I kicked back at Dad's inherited desk, at the school, when I spoke to Luke, once or twice a term on the landline. We are still in touch – though now on Facebook. Luke is married, adult, handsome. I am mostly Tom and rarely Sir.

Sometime during the night, there are noises outside, down the corridor. A bunch of them get back pissed. Thuds as well as yells as they knock each other around, in the middle of a joke they've established.

Days were clean in childhood. Mum drove. We went south in the 2CV. The M6. The dog with the dog's head on my lap is Fred. And Fred being all you'd expect of a dog called Fred.

Burnt toes. Good fun things you do when Dad isn't. The inflatable dinghy. Summer like a threat-averted. Life relaxed. Later, as things got more sophisticated, we had the caravan.

At home, they were always talking about money. When I and Mum went down to London, that was clearly an expenditure. Mum had her purse, and everything was clearly counted-out an expenditure. It was different pottering south – money didn't matter so much. This was within range of the clearly affordable.

I had my things in my room… The door locked. I'd twist the lock at the exact-same moment so that no-one would hear I was locking it. Electricity must have been cheap: in my room I always had on a fan-heater. The height of the ceiling. My light-fitting – clouded-tulip-glass which seemed elegant. Though it only dangled from the usual plastic-thread. The avocado years. Perhaps some deliberate austerity – Dad having had a rough upbringing. There were no very-hot baths: the tank was too small. The system turned to fury and banged like it would rip the house apart when we lit a fire in the grille that was supposed to provide the whole house with hot water. The house got freezing – the plumbing was all done new when they gutted it.

Dad almost took a pride in it. It would have been simple to replace it with a normal fire-grille. Obviously, Mum would have acquiesced and scrambled bleeding radiators.

It was a room… When the wind blew, it didn't so much howl *down* as cause my fireplace to resonate. It never seemed right to light a fire there. Perhaps because it was upstairs. I liked my room quite sparse and undecided. I kept paint on the mantelpiece. The room smelt of turps. Rather than getting too cosy.

There was a Waitrose in Dorchester. There was a fair degree of traipsing wet-fields in minimal clothes ashamed and a shower-token. In a bag, I carried nice loo-paper to the block. My clothes didn't work-out in context – gifts from America. There were rough, non-middle-class boys, children of the sort of men who'd take their children to campsites. There was a room where they played arcade-games and table tennis. I must have gone from being a child there to being fifteen. They spoiled the quiet peace of myself and my mother.

I must have started to smoke. Secrets – sneaking off. (Obviously, the road away from Mum extends forever.) I read a lot. There's a picture of me/Tomàs on the beach. Curly grown-puppy hair, DMs, a floppy woollen second-hand blazer from Liverpool. Little round specs – a cheap flaky-take on an Armani equivalent. We walked not minding cliff-tops. When I was eighteen, we went on a package-holiday instead to Crete. It was a resort hotel and I loved it.

Chapter Seven

Monday Lent Week 2. I wake from no bad dreams, but deeply comfortable. My prone mind refreshed. I lie a moment. Perhaps there might be dreams, if gently I roll to left face, right face… It is a minute's cancellation – deferral as the comfortable sleep slips its hold and empties out of me. Jarring my head up, I see, on my desk, it is five o'clock. My head thumps back to the pillow, and there is no sense in crying off, lying here. The hot water switches itself on at five. Still, the operation of sitting passes painlessly enough, and, as life once more contracts to the regular, manageable, cramped little footfalls entailed in the present-tense, I stand, and cross the room, and open the shutters and window. Half past three – solar time. And it looks like the middle of the night. Dead quiet. Almost scandalous to see it like this. The creeping-home time.

It is clean air, and the radiator hasn't turned itself on again. Tentative deep inhalations – even a touch damp. The thinness of the air unwarmed unbracing. I gather my things. The hot water should be on by now. I take, bundled in my arms, two big bottles of the salted water, and two books, one of Spanish verb-tables, one Pope Benedict XVI's *Jesus Of Nazareth: Holy Week*. In my dressing gown, barefoot, I slip into the corridor. I lock the door, and take the broad main staircase down to the ground floor, then pass along Martyrs' Corridor to the recessed, Harry Potter-style door and the steps down to the baths located in the basement.

The basement runs in a rough half-circuit beneath the outer walls of college. This is the basement we know about, anyway, though it is said there are more secret places. (I've had my little go-exploring – a bit of a probe – and it's mostly given over to old storage, forgotten things, trunks and boxes.) Lights buzz, and flicker to life. There are bits of machinery, stacked bricks, and workmanly lumber. Through disuse, neglect, there doesn't feel quite enough to support the great weight of life piled up on top of it. Where the baths are, this room is all flaky, yet gets cleaned on a regular basis. The bath gets yellowed-up with skin and soap and oil, but then it is sparkly and chemical-fresh again. No-one else – of the other students – comes down here. And I like to think I have made it my own. We all have our private showers. But this is deeper cleanness. A soak in a hot bath cleans the night of all contaminants – home-dreams, Dad-dreams, school-dreams – and it emolliates the onslaught of the ensuing day. My legendary hot-baths detoxify… And it is good down here. A musty old-space. Bare walls – of dimply, baked brick, as though the walls had been cobbled, a last lick of paint turned to dust on them. The ceiling high, unvaulted, a rough timber, blackened and crusted grey. There are just-above-head-height partitions around the baths, and humming yellow light-bulbs hang from an irregular steel frame. There are little-tiny windows above in the exterior wall, at the level of the pavement.

By day, you can just see through them, and they green the light. They are thick old-glass – each window in squares about the size of four clenched fists – and leaded. As I fold my dressing gown, and lay it on the flagstone floor, I like to imagine I am doing this with the thought I might, unknown, be seen. Then in the bath, it goes ballistic, modern water. It guns through the pipes, so you'd think the great boiler – newly installed – about the size of a – two metre by three metre by two metre object – posed an impossible strain, and comes choking and spattering. There

252

must be some serious commitment to get here too – it runs hot in next to no time. Steam billows into space. It merges with the partitions of the cubicle, so you could think they'd opened and fallen away now. Cobwebs light like chains. The roof drips. The metal-frame holding the lights drips.

I love a scalding hot bath. Afterward, my towelled skin carries the rubbed-reddened look of it. At home, you can't do it if all you have is a hot water tank in the airing cupboard. That'll never get a hot bath hot enough. That'll get you some shit like 'lovely and warm'. You need to get it to a washer-wrecking, tap-rotting maximum. You get the water as hot as you can initially take it – when you're in the bath as it's running. Then you accommodate that heat and get used to it. Then get the temperature rising, to levels of heat you could not have initially tolerated. That way you really get sweating – though, in absolute terms, the human-differentials entailed may be relatively narrow. Your book melts. And you play around with that – sustaining, edging it higher as the mind adapts, then it rips and whizzes. You only have to be careful if it starts to feel cold. Then you have to turn on the cold tap full immediately – it means you're cooking.

I settle back as the bath fills and the taps complete their initial business. I like the tumble and plunder of noise, and not to read and have the taps on simultaneously. There is interest to be found in my body as the water rises over it. What remains of still-excess subcutaneous fat seems differently arranged, by sleep, each morning. It is odd how the nothing-much muscle sticks through my legs. They might have been by Berruguete! Sometimes they ache, and as the water rises over my skin, they become more sensual. I use my feet to manipulate the taps, and swirl my hands and heave around in it. And, in heavy relief, this healing process is happening. The water rises, my bunched shoulders swell, my groin rises, little flower. Then, my bath full and initially quite hot, I sit to turn the taps off, and to drink a pint of water. Already sweating copiously, I ease myself to a comfortable position, and begin to read, in the first instance, Pope Benedict XVI's *Jesus Of Nazareth: Holy Week.*

I read semi-devotionally. The current script. In words of not too many syllables. Though not yet in a spirit of *Yup, yup. Got that, got that*... College life seems far-distant. And the book I have read before, diligently, on multiple occasions. Those prior readings yet remain. A yearning reassurance remains – a sweetness and a comfort. Love the man truly himself accounts precious and yearned-through – and from within – and inside and outside – and all in all. Make it true – the text communicates.

So it is not unlike as it had been. My one-mile walks, the frozen fields, and boys skiving at the loos by the water tap. When need lay all aside from any rational-brakes on it. Here is the faith. This is the least you need to know. Learn this. An originary life of Jesus. One reads a lifetime's gentle orthodoxy in the Pope's words. It seems ornate. And all the little curious ways in which reason might reason it – I am not afraid then of discovering a meaning proven, which I might have missed; there is no being deliberately critical.

Something happened. That this be a thing be not in issue. As to whether this be in time at this particular moment or all-time. Something happened. This be what it was.

And all the little curious discrepancies – all the little curious things could/can be turned on themselves so carefully, and cohere, in most delicate brightness, an interval's respite from spring rain. Belief – *be* possible. Only it requires an absconsion – of knowledge, of category – an easy and restful forgetting – of challenges to the within-world of these holy texts. This can be accomplished – in heat and steam. And while even the capacity to read diminishes – boiled and swollen. And something like the hunger and aloneness of London yet strains – as the flow of the mind gives out. It is a long way from the feeding upstairs. In the Refectory – stuffing us lumpen. Such inert hours. It could be to test us – to see if we still love Jesus. And all acting so lavishly grateful. Pen-fattening a fleshy and lavish grotesque in us. Fatter and fatter and fatter and full of the fresh clay. Until there isn't a space left anyone thinks in. Lavish with spiritual indiscipline. Only the shape of the mould and they could form us.

I think to nudge the temperature up a little. The tap is scalding. They installed the new boiler recently, and it was about the size of a small house… No feet pass within the small, yellowed windows at this hour. Should anyone care to stoop and peek… Little hands, little faces. Anyone like that on the outside… The hungry or a child might. Would they even know their own reality if they did that? There are cobwebs all over the light bulbs. I wipe my hands with the towel each page. I wipe my face, and I have already drunk one of my bottles of water. I claim to read, but really it is only to help with the bathing, while I get into it. Beyond a half hour, there is little point trying to advance between sentences. Then I skid the book across the tiles, to a dry place, and turn to the Spanish verb-tables to try a set. *Comeré, comerás, comerá, comeremos, comeréis, comerán…* Closing my eyes, I recite the inflections, and then the full verbs. Then I stare dully at the page, with other moods and tenses, and then I lay that book too on the flagstones. Then I slide to wild, inchoate thoughts.

There are mad scenes played in a hot-bath. There is a real,

255

incipient, raging anger, which slides amongst the safety and wallowing. This self-exposition to self, and plain relief from others' harrying. Then it might grip me – the control lapsed. And it argues against itself. It gets twisted in crazy games – and I lay this body back boiled and I let it unravel.

There is lain – monkey-rage and human-fantasy. It is like a night-time's mad-emails, crazy posts. From impotence derives reconstruction – when I have to turn everything around, in this small world, because I lack the decision – volition to walk out with dignity. Trapped in a logic of it. Of thinkability.

One second, I might spectate, and then I am inside it as an actor. In heat, dispersed, fragmented, a putative subject-position trips and phases in and out of it. And so it is: *not me, not this, not now, not here, not I...* But I don't have anywhere else to go. So this descent becomes a strange and natural comfort.

They are like old friends – these thoughts and unresolved issues. This fight. When it is all a conspiracy to get me, I *reconspire...*

There is a lot about The Rector. Where others' instances of merely itinerant duncery have their showing, it is The Rector who, intentionally, sadistically, designs to unpick my reality, and set us all to thrashing as they do, in shark-infested waters. Though alone, and albeit in baffled disbelief and outrage, innocence, I might self-permit, and open my fears, and my moral brakes, and censored mind, and worthy-normal public image. And see all past the chicanery. And mirror and connect with the true and the real situation. And to engage on a primal, emotional level. And let the brain do all its own shitty things too – since those are the reality. And have that out there raging, all nastiness, and tearing its eyes out, and kicking itself around, in steam and cobwebs.

256

I have an idea of an island. This is a nice place – an ideal place. Fantasy-basic. It is inspired by my Aegean treks, and God, and games of Civ. (Aegeanworld, Godworld, Meworld.) And often, to help me to relax, when there is no more burning injustice, my island takes its shape as the water boils. I like to think of it not as a place of denial; rather it is *simply* ideal, and an affirmation. A utopia, essentially, an other-worldly no-place, scripted, for the nonce, in a Mind, but any god-level power could do it.

My island – mine – satisfies my – Tomàs's basic requirements of fantasy. Principle among which is an absence of history. Not only is my island without time in an Earthed sense – and so a millennium's solid relaxation on the fantasy-terrace with the fantasy-view, of the fantasy-sea and the fantasy-harbour town, occupies merely a blink of a bath-time in Earth-time – is itself and outside of time sentient though unmoving. Time is space is time and time is unreal. Such generational relationships this my fantasy harbour town community live through never yet spoils things like time-people do. There is homeostasis, and death is unknown to them. And yet they never clog the place with surplus population. They flicker in and out of the scenery, minding their days, on script, and they are always just right.

So I put my library here, and get the tap-water flowing, and the sewage disposal on. I get my gardens and my mountain treks. There are monks up the hill and the sea wanders off into subroutines. I establish good relations with the locals – I am an angel if not God – and get *their* magical-spiritual consciousness honed about right – to an accordance with Mind. And then arises the central matter, which is that of revenge.

What if… *What if*… What if The Rector were imagined – woke here and lived for a thousand years? *And what if then… He* could no

257

longer believe? What if, with all that time, and peace, and joy, and simple happiness – and what with all this time to reflect, and an Enlightenment of books to read – what if then the smugness of *His* faith dripped from Him day by day incontrovertibly? And then bring Him back *here* – for a next hour of classroom-time. Bring Him back here – beyond bath-time – for the next hour's, let's say, *feeding* in the Refectory. Might He then be impossibly free? Or could He still do it? Could He then believe?

Mad thoughts – as toxins in my body sweat into the bathwater, and as the body withdraws, and yet the brain, addicted, continues to compensate. Mad – as in a power-dream. Angry-mad. Exit-speech mad. As when He denigrated *me* – mumbling at the back of His mouth – at the breakfast trolley – *turning from me*. Snarling – *hard*-mad: '*What* did you say? Turn around and look at me...' *My* hand clenched like a monkey-wrench thrust out of bathwater...

The noise of my own voice alarms me, and someone might hear. I release the hand, which slips back into the water, and I turn the cold tap on slowly with the heel of my right foot. Coolness creeps beneath me. It touches my buttocks and spine, and my thoughts are honey-peaceful. I seem *right*. Different in my entirety from moments before. And no-one knows that side of me, so all that is fine. There are no consequences, and my thoughts now might be clean and justified. There are unaligned remainders of the human-equation. Corrections and clarifications. I seem an empty vessel now all that is done. My head rolls blissed, and more humdrum, volitional thought returns. And now the water steams and cools. Invigorating.

You have to let it get so it feels cold or you'd be nauseous getting out. Even when it's got too cold to stay lying in, you'll still glow and be towelling fresh sweat off. I climb from the bath and I stand on the flagstones. There is no mirror, and I have yet to shave. The towel is sodden – I've been mopping my face and hands for the last hour. As normal, I'll drip to my room, and leave as I walk a trail of evaporating footprints.

No-one else is about still. That's nice – especially with that palace in my head expanded. The flag-stone scrub of the vaulted ground floor. Upstairs, the oak sprung first-floor daily burnished. The corridor I live on is almost perfectly square, in section, when you stand in the middle and look straight down. I tend to look to the polished floor. A modesty of eyes unchallenging – rather than stooping posture. The cleaners mop and polish each day, with a peculiar, jagged, rhythmic consistency, strenuous of effort, as though they worked cloth as it dyes in a great vat. There are the paintings – and windows look to quad, street, gardens. I need to make coffee. I lock my door, and remain in my dressing gown, intending to pray. I pour the remaining mug's worth of cold, strong, yesterday's coffee from the cafetiere. I have almost an hour until morning meditation in chapel at seven o'clock.

This bit of the day is called The Office Of Readings. It comprises one of the longer and usually more meaty psalms split into three, then readings in (usually) prose from the Bible and Saint A.N. Other. It takes about fifteen minutes.

This is all as laid out in the ribbon-book, arranged for Lent and then the season of Easter to Pentacost. My copy of this is old – for this season. It was given to me by a Glaswegian monk, whose head was bigger and whose hair cropped shorter than my own. I have a fondness for the breviary – the set of three – in UK – for the different seasons.

259

They are well-thumbed, and there is love in here. A discovery. (At the monastery – though two of my set are new and ordered off Amazon.) They aren't handsome volumes, try as they might with the leatherette; they're just books. You couldn't venerate the packaging. It isn't tasteful.

At my desk, the lap-top sits closed, and I respectfully arrange it, by six inches, to serve as a rest for my breviary. The desk is a clutter of fuss, with papers everywhere, but such lines in the immediate vicinity sit there orderly. And, with no extraneous distractions, I proceed to pray. After the bath, and like rock, prayer can be very dry. The rock is objective reality. This is no cheap pun – 'You are Peter and upon this desert-rock I found my Church.' This rock is a dried-out and desert thought. There is no going *whoop-whoop-whoop*. It is a place of bones and mental action. It might have been a dust-dry body slowly dancing a remembered tune. It might feel wrong to give it a voice unexamined in physical posture. Bones like rock and like physical theatre contract and speak in it.

What that means is that I sit, and don't cross my legs, and I am teacher and student at once in it. Am I fourteen and twenty-four and forty? And I must lip-move the words, so that I won't speak and provide a false voice to them, and so that I won't skim. Like I am four as well. So that is a lot of time to navigate. Hard as basement-dust. No vapid haze – no now-head-hung of self and self's acknowledgement. No speech-act self-destructs. No basic-families' happier socialization. Keeping your head down, taking your comforts. No dingy matters-sexual and compromise-choices. Like married people's houses. Acceptable registers. One and one make three.

There seem no further mistakes I can make at the rock level. Yet – *to integrate...* Where no love could hurt. Nor callous ends meet. Nor risk nor self-exposure. And life can't hurt you. That doesn't matter.

So – pray. I cross myself. And I say it aloud: 'In the name of the Father, and of the Son, and of the Holy Spirit.' Then, for good measure, not quite sure I've meant it properly enough the first time, I do it again. I say it a third time – silently.

And then I say it again and – *Sshhh... That was better.*

The first reading is Exodus 14: 10-31.

The second is by John Chrysostom. This reads – in its entirety:

The Israelites witnessed marvels; you also will witness marvels, greater and more splendid than those which accompanied them on their departure from Egypt. You did not see Pharaoh drowned with his armies, but you have seen the devil with his weapons overcome by the waters of baptism. The Israelites passed through the sea; you have passed from death to life. They were delivered from the Egyptians; you have been delivered from the powers of darkness. The Israelites were freed from slavery to a pagan people; you have been freed from the much greater slavery to sin.

Do you need another argument to show that the gifts you have received are greater than theirs? The Israelites could not look on the face of Moses in glory, though he was their fellow servant and kinsman. But you have seen the face of Christ in his glory. Paul cried out: We see the glory of the Lord with faces unveiled.

In those days Christ was present to the Israelites as he followed them, but he is present to us in a much deeper sense. The Lord was with them because of the favour he showed to Moses; now he is with us not simply because of Moses but also because of your obedience. After Egypt they dwelt in desert places; after your departure you will dwell in heaven. Their great leader and commander was Moses; we have a new Moses,

God himself, as our leader and commander.

What distinguished the first Moses? Moses, Scripture tells us, was more gentle than all who dwelt upon the earth. We can rightly say the same of the new Moses, for there was with him the very Spirit of gentleness, united to him in his inmost being. In those days Moses raised his hands to heaven and brought down manna, the bread of angels; the new Moses raises his hands to heaven and gives us the food of eternal life. Moses struck the rock and brought forth streams of water; Christ touches his table, strikes the spiritual rock of the new covenant and draws forth the living water of the Spirit. This rock is like a fountain in the midst of Christ's table, so that on all sides the flocks may draw near to this living spring and refresh themselves in the waters of salvation.

Since this fountain, this source of life, this table surrounds us with untold blessings and fills us with the gifts of the Spirit, let us approach it with sincerity of heart and purity of conscience to receive grace and mercy in our time of need. Grace and mercy be yours from the only-begotten Son, our Lord and Saviour Jesus Christ; through him and with him be glory, honour and power to the Father and the life-giving Spirit, now and always and forever. Amen

My face finds its way back to my hands again. There is sadness in the pity of it. One feels it all through – through every corpuscle. How it was/is?/be – to [make-?]believe. How that felt-or-how-that-feels. So loving and tender and so pure. And it is real in a real way. Mind being the mansion. It is real in a way you're real in a stage-rôle. Or in the memory of love holding close to you. Spooning – hair-scent. Cradling a lover as one might – once have been – unremembered. First clasp of his hand clasping your own hand on his getting-ready-to-sleep chest. Spooning. That goes there. That belongs there. One hardly sleeps for fear this

262

moment would pass. Watching. Was this what you wanted? Of your design for living. Is this the scene imagined? Are you safe?

One saw the trick of the text, of course. A kind of neuro-linguistic programming – NLP. Or it is similar to that. Fudged logic. *Hoc est dicere / que es decir.* As [proposition I want you now to assume you already believed in – knew as truth], so [proposition I want you now consciously to embrace as newly known truth, thereby enabling the first truth as truth you now know you already knew, which you didn't]. And so on – recursively. The illogic of a Catholic text might glare so glaringly. NLP. Tails chasing their own dogs. Why were they so very desperate to prove it? They talk such a lot rubbish in this world. It's hard not to laugh as they prove beyond incontrovertible doubt yet again that…

Poor little talkative Christianity. Still, the psalm was nice. Trump the lot with a rousing doxology. As it was in the beginning, is now, and ever shall be… As one might listen for a note's end not having heard the beginning of it. The exilic texts of Babylonian captivity. Always an eternal reordering. Disappear.

It is not yet light of day. The strip-light under my shelf, over my desk, casts a yellowing, bruised light. Random tat lies about the place. Loose paper, books, speakers, laptop. A shoe-box containing packets of nuts and pieces of fruit and a half-consumed packet of crisps. Six pens, three of them spent and non-recyclable, two pairs of spectacles. A voucher for printer-ink, only redeemable in the UK. Loose change and a party-popper. Ron's watch and a Remembrance Day poppy. An HMRC income tax return. An expended blister-pack. Two rosaries. Spanish verbs on post-it notes. Three bookmarks from an Amazon-marketplace firm – which I recommend.

Faith – to the which a heart in fervent agitation. I bow my head, yielding thought, which is impossible, beneath the great weight of it. Silence here. The rock. My Head Of English once explained to me, at length, that within the axes of the Cross there is a tension figured. The all and the eternal and everything. And the human – this here now. Stuck on a pin on it. The Head Of English didn't seem one you'd have imagined religious. I think now he might have been genuinely Christian while – not RC. His often were difficult thoughts to follow. He'd scoop you up, as we returned to our houses, through the centre of the village, from Schools. Ideas flew and pecked and swooped and dived. Our gowns cloaked us – through the evening dark of the winter timetable. Or our gowns ballooned in the pollen-swept breeze of a spring day. He'd keep me there at the parting of the ways, and then, it seemed, quite arbitrarily dump the matter of discussion – and me. And away he went. Greening-black gown and unswinging attaché case. Neck to the firmament, face to the floor.

I rinse the cafetiere in the bathroom sink. I shake the fresh coffee in, then pad barefoot to the common room. The lights along the corridor click on and off automatically, tracking me, in ten meter chunks. Typical teenagers: they've left the common room in a right mess. Bottles and cans strew the floor, and crisp-packets stick to the tables beside the bin. A late-night craving for hot-dogs gives evidence. Vodka bottles stuck prone on their sides like a form of protest. Napkins smeared with tomato sauce clutch inedibility of Frankfurter sausages. Chairs slop over-turned. One chair lies upended and mortally incapacitated. The floor is wet in patches. One might see within the chairs who sat where… The distributive logic… Henry – just there. And Sean must have scraped himself back from his chair just there – when the moment of their grand conversation exploded. They must have popped mid-thought, and hit critical-mass, then the ship

264

went down. I pick my way – and avoid *peering into* the sink. The cleaners'll be in here presently, to clean and tidy, but never the sink. It remains an accusation of tea-bags. I boil the kettle. I pour still-boiling water into the cafetiere.

In my room, I do some Spanish on an app I have. Other people's plumbing begins to strike. The clocks have yet to change. It is The Feast Of Saint Patrick. Sunrise is 7.28 local time. The coffee is the best I could find in the Mercadona. I look to one of the psalms of the morning prayer. *In you, O Lord, I take refuge. Let me never be put to shame… justice, set me free… a rock of refuge for me, a mighty stronghold… save me for you are my rock… release me… the snares they have hidden… into your hands I commend my spirit… you who have seen… affliction… my soul's distress.* I read the psalm again:

Have mercy on me, O Lord,

for I am in distress.

Tears have wasted my eyes,

my throat and my heart.

For my life is spent with sorrow

and my years with sighs.

Affliction has broken down my strength

and my bones waste away.

In the face of all my foes

I am a reproach,

an object of scorn to my neighbours

and of fear to my friends…

At each psalm's conclusion, the Christian bows his head and prays the doxology: *Glory be to The Father, and to The Son, and to The Holy*

Spirit, as it was in the beginning, is now, and ever shall be, world without end, Amen. I fancy it is in that twist that worlds collide – between psalm and doxology. It is quite a different matter to read, and to pray, the psalms stand-alone. Even the more angry-smitey psalms – beseeching Our Lord Yahweh to convey a psalmist's enemies to death and the pit – are all a bit dreamified and abstracted in Christian doxology. In penitent nothingness – such thoughts. Cancelled. Anger. Vicious. Human carnage. And, in a state of change, evoke the meaning of Christian prayer. I pray the doxology. Head bowed. Face emptied. Blessed.

*

Quite soon – not now, not yet. Quite soon – not now but very soon after. I *will* sit cross-legged with the psalms. In English and Latin. In Spain. There shall be dry soil – hard as Christian nails. By no means as hot as it ever gets. But hard. With olives which would never be picked now. And lemon-groves shrivelled to nicotine-teeth. Occupying psalms, and beyond Christian promises. That will be an empty space. I do not know anything of what happens after that.

But now it is Lent Week 2. Monday. I dress in the slack, linen trousers, with the elasticated waist, which I always use for morning meditation, so I can *half*-cross my legs, first the left and then the right foot drawn, by turns, to squat against my groin. Or else my spine plagues me. I wear my new All-Star pumps and a woolly cardigan. The chill air in chapel is unpleasant on the skin.

While I am not late, the corridors remain clear. It is entirely likely one or two of them are yet in bed. I hear music passing by emanating from Sean's room. Loud metal-grunge. It makes a racket in the corridor, and yet the loud noise never it seems turns the corner, to get into my room. There are five minutes.

Heartily, I sing along the corridors. This compulsive habit both necessary and ingrained. Today I sing heartily: 'When you're up to your neck in hot water, be like the kettle and sing.' In the corridors, the acoustic is playful. I'll start a song, and then realize, some phrase in the third verse, why I'm singing it. Why that lyric cinched the current thought – is apposite now.

I am just a poor boy though my story's seldom told… I dreamed a dream in days gone by… The soldier came knocking upon the queen's door… First I was afraid, I was petrified… Porgi amor qualche ristoro… Imagine there's no Heaven… Maybe I don't really wanna know… Oh-oh life is bigger; it's bigger than you and you are not me…

At times, my singing gets very loud. To the point of obvious desperation. Then, when I know I'm doing it, that compulsion uvulates so defiantly. Sub-operatically – from the pit of my lungs. I take it to the chapel back-entrance – like Canute – knowing The Rector must hear it inside.

My mood descends as I enter chapel. I move through perhaps half-second phases. I bless myself. I enter into silence – where a majority is now in place. Now that I have said my piece and noise has been expelled. A Plato-cave. I walk to the foot of the aisle and genuflect. Our Lady lit within the reredos. All gloom. And I consider where to put myself. The Rector plays king's rook, the Vice Rector king's pawn – looking down on it. Geoff, at the vanguard, gets on his knees to pray. Father Richard has his head stuck in his hands already. I walk to sit in the rearmost pew – opposite The Rector. We space ourselves in chapel to the extent we can. Very-nearly-almost each has his own pew. When it is seven o'clock,

267

Father Gerry stands. He prays alone in the choir stalls. Always Father Gerry leads the morning meditation. When he steps to the microphone, at the lectern, there are pencil-spots implanted in the gold-paint canopy above where he stands. With them, he seems an apparition, fractionally powered, as he offers to chapel his cue to a thought for the thirty minutes. Father Gerry mashes his lips and his tongue is an oyster. Then breathes to the microphone slowly. Old-man-whisper. It rattles so deeply in his thorax – you could never hear all he's saying. But today what he says is the words that are written in the Breviary:

'Born in Great Britain, around the year 385, as a youth he was taken captive to Ireland, as a slave, and worked as herdsman. After he made his escape, he wished to become a priest, and after being made Bishop of Ireland, he was untiring in preaching the Gospel, and he converted many to the faith. He wrote of his life, as we have the words in The Office Of Readings for this day: "I give thanks to my God tirelessly, who kept me faithful in my day of trial, so that today I offer sacrifice to him confidently, the living sacrifice of my life to Christ, my Lord, who preserved me in all my troubles. I can say therefore: Who am I, Lord, and what is my calling that you should co-operate with me with such divine power?"'

Then, on a dead-breath, Father Gerry stops, and there is silence, and Father Gerry withdraws from the lectern, and sits again. The designated meditation period is thirty minutes. All we are asked to do is sit in silence. Who knows where they get to in this time? The only light is on the Vulnerata. The college *thing*. Hacked by English troops raiding the enemy at Cadiz… The ugly, restive English, and the pure. *Plus ça change…* Balled, fecund. A pregnant fist.

Adedokun frankly rolls his folded arms on the back of the pew in

268

front. Thirty minutes kip. Geoff takes it wildly – knees, beads. Holy people, Alex and John, quietly-intently direct their gaze toward her. Our Lady. The Vice Rector cries, and holds his beetroot face. The Rector gives nothing away. The Rector has absolute silence when He turns His hearing-aid off.

I crack my spine. I ratchet the base of my neck around – getting as much as I can of all the cracks and squelches. No matter the bath – it is an effort to correct the night's damage. A painful and difficult process. I must sleep so trashily. The room could have heard it. The Rector *looks*... But that is in my head – and the hopeless, heavy size of it – Pity me, Reader, when I try buying a hat! And my uncomfortable larynx. Peering into things – wanting, poked, probed. A thinking correction to God's plan, and daily restorative. I breathe – from the sternum. Crack my spine – trying to get to the vertebrae just at the top and toward the brain. And round-and-round breathing from the solar plexus.

Cars *whizz* by on the street just immediately outside. A slow light gathers. The waft of cars – their noise that makes you feel your own artifice. Wispy English being.

I take it in ten minute intervals. Three deep plunges – in and out. Experiential. Stuff. I let imagination play – and the world I've gathered inside play and rale... Then, at the end of it, Father Gerry knocks on his bench. Father Gerry stands, and says: *In the name of the Father, and of the Son, and the Holy Spirit*... At this point, we students must stand and reconfigure. We all have to walk up from wherever we've been sitting to choir – to pray. Jean-Luc scuttles round the edge of the sanctuary. He darts into the Sacristy. Jean-Luc's job is to flick the necessary labelled switches. Like a sneaky monk!

Thuswise, we enter the office of morning prayer. In choir, we students mostly keep to the places we established the first day. That day, I had no place. I led. Therefore, now, I wander. Today, Adedokun leads from my side. I sit in Adedokun's place. This immediately adjacent to – perpendicular – The Rector, who sits in the main pews. *I* couldn't see *Him* without turning to look... The chant begins, and crawls. We... drone...

Deep is crawling on deep / in the roar of waters: / your torrents and all your waves / swept over me.

I pray – extremely conscious of inevitable scrutiny. I read the words off the back of my eyelids – if truth be told. I put the feelers out. No matter the grind when we all read collectively. Asking... *God...?* I nod my head to the slow lilt of it.

Well, I do that. There's nothing inside – it's just external. There's no particular angst here or interior activity. We – *say* or we – *pray*: *We give you thanks, almighty God, / for sending Saint Patrick to preach your glory to the people of Ireland. / Grant that we who are proud to call ourselves Christians / may never cease to proclaim to the world / the good news of salvation...* Then I don't breathe – I don't look them in the eye. I don't flinch, I don't whisper. All that. Nothing. Nobody moves.

Then Geoff clobbers to his feet to go and prostrate himself in one of the side-chapels opposite. The meaning of that particular side-chapel I've never troubled to decipher. Henry, sat over the way, shines carbolic. Henry *takes* longly to his knees – still in choir. He inhales God deep and sub-vocalizes so we can all hear again and again: *My Lord, I love you... My Lord, I love you... My Lord, I love you... My Lord, I love you... My Lord, I love you... My Lord, I love you... My Lord, I love you... My Lord, I love you... My Lord, I love you... My Lord, I love you... My Lord, I love*

270

you… My Lord, I love you… My Lord, I love you… My Lord, I love you…

Performed – of course. Permitted. So Henry feels God. Thusly Henry trusts in this environment. To express. Make it true, say it often enough. Here it all is on the insides – make what happens here on the inside true – say it often enough.

World-reason and parish-faith. Then Henry crosses himself. One thing Henry *does* is kiss his now-pursed fingertips, this an affectation Henry first lately observed in the priest who left us the other week and now Henry does it. Devotionally now. Having, at supper, observed: 'What's *that* about?' Henry is learning – absorbing. (From conscious *and critically framed* apposition toward dream.) As an imitation, first he rejects, laughing, then Henry reflects, then Henry forgets. And so he writes the story back into all-time, whether accepting, rejecting.

There is no set-form to the ending of morning prayer. One stirs, one shifts. Julian wants his sugar puffs. We are our own year – the only year... Nothing handed down. And inter-generational communion – boy to boy. (The priests are gone from chapel.) Julian stands to meditate, rapt, on his side-chapel reredos, by where we stack the books, on the way out. Julian stands to meditate. Only what we might devise ourselves. Each step a bluff – prior to private, and secret, communion. New-bugs. Way out of control. The propaedeutic year. Knock and tumble. Bullying the way through. (*That wretched boy, that wretched lap-top…*)

Julian, rapt, silent. Sings in silence? Breast-full – swelling to his picture of choice. Wherein a powerful angel crushes a dragon's sixth vertebra – fisherman's trident and pointy-toed heel.

Julian is a picture that went round on the internet. The one with the black-and-white silhouette of the girl, who, with a black-and-white gun, blows a hole in her black-and-white head, and chromatic butterflies –

271

spring – take flight from the exit-wound… With Julian looking like that at the reredos… *Non più andrai, farfallone amoroso, notte e giorno d'intorno girando…*

There is no formal ending to breakfast either. Adedokun throws up his hands in disgust at his egg's failure, and declares the meal dead for him. And I find it strange to think the priests eat this food too. Because you don't like to think of them that way. Adedokun cleanses on a napkin his long fingers flecked with shell and egg-white. Adedokun doesn't *quite* laugh, but looks like a recipe gone-off considering the ingredients. But, at their table, there priests sit ordained with spoons, hunched over – *highly-processed breakfast-cereal and dairy-farmed cow-milk.* Each a black dog, as if bolting its up-chuck. You do not want to disturb The Rector now. Damned if you do, damned if you don't, when it's your job to ask if He wants to be booked-in for dinner or not. You get yourself a cursed look.

Then Henry tells everyone he has to take a call. Did everyone hear that? Then Henry tells everyone he has to take a call.

Anyway, Henry runs off screaming about this fucking phone-call he has to take like a fucking executive. At my table, we all sit that through, until Jon says he needs a shower, and Francis says he's bought some new sheet-music from the shop he's found he'd like to try on his violin. Adedokun is waking-up at this point, and you can see the Caribbean in him.

I withdraw to my room for an interlude. It is with perfect propriety. I scrape my teeth, and listen to Thought For The Day. I take two paracetamol – Spanish strength. As the time approaches nine o'clock, there stand five hours of nothing – horror – boredom – .

Party-face on.

272

Next:

This is about as good as it gets round here:

Nine o'clock:

Days begin with the chaos of 'Spanish'. There is no course structure. Hardly a lesson plan. We're split into two sets. But the low set is a low set… But Geoff is there? Everyone else is bundled. There's constant disruption from those who find Spanish 'impossible'. With whom, nonetheless, the young teacher flirts.

Here she comes. *Dumb chit* – I am practically not merely saying aloud as we wait but to her now. As if this has passed the dinner party test. ¡Hola, Chicos! She's late. And: 'You can bet she gets her invoices in on time.'

All the way on clip-clop heels through long, audible corridors, bursting to tell us the traffic is non-existent, and that she must just now use the photocopier. Adedokun sits there laughing: knows corrupt.

After 'Spanish', ten-past-ten, there follows Intellectual Development. Father Rector runs this stall. After Spanish… it's different… We – *they* wait. They have their desks and their empty chairs. *They* are different. Their set places. Cowed. And we are together again – after Spanish.

The Rector is present already. He stands behind the lectern. There is no easy talk. The powerpoint screen has descended – the room is set. You don't get to see much of The Rector – He's not so very tall. Just the little Lego-figure head – with it little black dobs of painted hair. He's a little round peanut-car with a little clutch. He is the soul of a cinquecento re-imagined in air-bags… You have to wonder how He hasn't thought to trade the lectern for a smaller model, or get Himself something to stand on behind it, so He could use it more effectively. You have to wonder what He's doing behind there – screwing His courage up. Watching time like a stickler... *Quietly hyper-ventilating*... He is the small-boy and that is the big gym-horse... (Something's spooked Him – something spooks Him.) Some persistent half-born life... *He's going in*...

As, then, He speaks, it's just against time – half a beat – not even half a beat. And not *syncopated* – off-beat. Moreover, today, He's not polite about it: 'Turn those lights off, now please, I don't care, whoever's near...'

What's got His goat?

In the name of the Father, and of the Son, and of the...

So, then, today... A *somewhat* flitty account of 'one or two little difficulties' faced by the Catholic Church through the fourth Century. The Council of Nicaea. And, because 'that didn't quite sort everything out', the Council of Constantinople. Whence the creed.

Our room of students bears its serious expression. But it's difficult to read. It neglects to take notes. It's that funny bit of Catholic history – when it is now history. The memory, the documentation, becomes joined-up, fact-checkable. Imperial religion – a state faith. This be anxious-making – potentially. Where before, you can pretty much imagine what you like, and they do, now the data fall just short of the entirely revisionable. So now *there might be* careful historical analysis, were *correct* truth to be read in this... Where there *is* ample room to read available facts with an open mind... Dangerous territory.

The cult is powerful strong. A contest-field of power and heresy. Enemy-definitions in process of *now*. In which sense, now, right-now, they are *now*. Here – with students. Contest re-encountered. An early

274

Church, juvescent years, invented, re-invented, scrubbed its workings... Not unlike like humans here-now. (The Church, then, condemned its own sources and analogues as parody – work of demons.)

Such a little time. We, they, then, it, now – each its own self-defining reality. Cultic rules. It breeds – it self-propagates... And the Catholic cult had pretty much everything you might want in a cult going for it. Via a series of ordinary human-imbalances – it fast-breeds, it fast-self-propagates.

Such, then, now, the work we each – . Control the past, control the... Power and orthodoxy.

Satan wants to eat you. A prowling lion stalks your dreams. Truth and fear and heresy.

The Rector gets caught on it. You can tell it is a fault-point because He's prattling away on it insistently – past breath and in defiance of His usual top-notes. There isn't a great deal of information in any of these classes. But He centre-pieces this. The central-point of the two Councils – of the creed. The theological dispute. Pertaining to the divinity of Christ – and *consubstantiality* of Son and Father. Though these disputes are in Greek, before they are later re-imagined in Latin.

Essentially, it is a matter of political compromise. Who and what is Christ in relation to the Father? That is the matter at stake. What is the mutual – relative – self-identicality-or-not of Son and Father? Where is Dad in me?

They, then, solved it with a fudge – a portmanteau word. Ambiguous – to suggest multiple readings were possible. The word is: ὁμοούσιος. In the creed as we have it now, this translates, through Latin, as: consubstantial. A linguistic fudge – strongly at the Emperor's insistence – to quite the bitching. They slurred the Greek – a new word.

Anyway, The Rector has fun with all that *for hours*… As He is trying to explain it… A little-bird prattle – racing – over-revving… You can just see the top of His little head – coaxing the men to stand-down – and soothe the bluntest mind with Jesus.

Next-up comes Human Development. Father Richard says:

'What does it mean to be *community*? What does it mean to be… *community*?

'We're a community now. That's obvious, really, isn't it?! It's incredibly obvious ☺ This is a community. It's *our* community.

'What does it mean, as humans, to be *in* a community?

'What do we *mean* by community?

'I'll give you *two – I'll give you three* minutes. That's the way. Talk with your partner now.'

In Lectio Divina, we read a whole chapter of Matthew. I read – Geoff says to. Then Father Gerry says: 'Let us take a moment to lower ourselves into the text…' And we stare at it – into it – at the words. Find your Jesus there. As though a text awash with depths and shadows. Well, it isn't quicksand. As a mirrorless monk might discover his self-face in Christ as he paints iconography. (There is a monk I know who paints icons – it is always his own face.) The more you stare at words you know by heart… And fear the shape of love in brutal Christian passages.

But we break from Lectio Divina unusually early. There are well over twenty-five minutes before lunch. I nip into the common room on my way past. I take a beer from the fridge, and put money in the pot. I think about it, take a second, and cram both into my trouser pockets. Into which I cram my hands, and so walk the corridor, in order to disguise the cans. Whistling as you may. On the radio, there is Spanish talk-radio on the same FM frequency Radio 4 would be. It is heated beyond understanding. They are arguing, over an LBC-style phone-in, about the terrorist bombs. The first slug of the second beer makes me puke: red roses. I shower – hot – then rinse myself – cold – and dress again. I wear French-blue jeans which are not stretch-tight and I fold the bottoms up. I wear a white vest and a farmyard chequered shirt untucked – rolled sleeves above the elbows – regulation.

On my door, I have blu-tacked a note, in block-capitals, on a sheet of A4 copier paper:

REMEMBER: EVERYTHING HERE IS A TEST.

No longer certain this is a helpful thought, I rip it from the door on my way out, and throw it behind me, toward the bin.

There is no getting around the business of convincing my mind that my room door is locked and will remain locked. (So many dream-locks don't hold at the front-door of the real house – of the teenage years – or of my bedroom door – but wobble loose like putty.) Solution: whatever, whatever: enter ye who may.

I run – Am I late? Perhaps I am waited for. I wear my soft pumps loose-laced sloppily, which creak to a halt on stone. With as much dignity as anyone might muster, I enter the Refectory, and take the one vacant seat, at the nearest table, between The Rector and a monk from Ampleforth. There is a laugh and a slow clap. Even The Rector joins in with the good-natured humour of it.

I have failed to catch the name of the monk, though we specifically have not ourselves been introduced. But I am up as Refectorian.

277

Adedokun too. The prayer:

Bless us oh Lord and these thy gifts which we are about to receive from thy bounty...

North south east west.

To get the trolleys in.

I and Ade go to the kitchen. The nuns have kept the food warming. I and Ade get the lolly-pop/chewing-gum lips and the clockwork eyes. We're on time. Ish.

She takes each metal platter from the oven. She quite deliberately places it just so. Like a croupier. On each of the trolleys. And she gives the nod – midway in the cervical curve – C4. Cleanest paper-skin. Attesting – once it is to me, and once to Adedokun – that it is good food, *muy* deliciousness.

She *knows* our needs in this dish – squashed to taste-bud rose-lips rise to signify.

Then she jabbers and whimples and wabbles. *She* takes from beneath its cling-film a plate of surgically green leaves and some manner of processed meat. This *she* stabs with her marital finger. Then points carefully – to me and then to Adedokun. Seconds each so that we understand both well enough: 'Don Iago.'

It becomes an unhappy look, wronged. '*Pffffffuuugghhhh!*' she says. As if she ask you. And she goes and *throws*-up her hands. And her unusual sense of humour – and her very sharp elbows. Then – defiantly – she licks her finger clean of the tainted meat.

She throws-up hands again. As if she doesn't know. Turning away by this point, she walks like the little green man at the Spanish traffic lights. Out of sight – to within her mysterious nun-world. The refrigeration space and beyond. Not looking back at us.

We put our hands in the oven-gloves. The oven gloves don't fit – and it is hilarious – Adedokun – watching me/him. Not being racist, but it's like an exceptionally bright Ph.D student going: '*Alright…*' Our starter appears to be… Boiled courgettes in creamy-cheesy – in a *custardy* creation. Like Adedokun's hands' palms or the soles of his feet. Embedded with pre-cooked prawns. Sprinkled with anchovies. Flecked with grated carrot.

As we manoeuvre the trolleys, Adedokun says: 'They're not gonna like this.' I like it when Adedokun says to me things like this. It makes it seem as if I – Tomàs am equal – i.e. an equal to Adedokun, who is young and black. I laugh. We take a pride in serving the plates – with formal procedural exactitude. We are a team. No graceless-messes plonked-down. (Cf. Julian and Philip. Boorishly heavy. Disdaining menial service. When God knows…) We don't mention we take that pride. We never once say it between ourselves.

The pads on Adedokun's feet are painted mustard-yellow. He is a visually different person. *Tickle* them… (All boy – slung back on the sofa on Saturday… Obviously don't.) At table, the Ampleforth monk requires wine with luncheon:

'I like a little wine with luncheon, if that's available.'

Geoff says he'll also have a glass.

I say: 'Oh lovely.' Francis does the honours.

I ask the monk how he's finding things. This is best good manners on – to have a little fun with Henry. I dig around in the food while I say it. I use plain RP. Anglican – library-accents. To have a little fun with Henry. Then I say: 'The anchovies really need the wine.'

The monk says: 'Amen, brother.'

Henry says: 'Are those anchovies?'

Geoff says to The Rector: 'What are you eating, Father?'

The Rector's mouthful isn't working – there are unknown, unexpected quantities.

(Geoff is a natural sadist: there is no bad-intent in this.)

It is that bad – that *Hamlet*-question. Now the frailty be exposed. Now our creaky institutions rumble… What remains? What's left? And has it ever meant anything? Berruguete-feet and Berruguete speedos… I have done with the mess on my own plate. I scrape what can be scraped of the yellow off.

We keep our knives and forks for the next course. The weird thing is: there is no anterior narrative. Nothing gay. I take a hunk of bread and dab it direct from the bottle with olive oil. *Call Me By Your Name…* Not exactly to provoke Sister Angelina. *Maurice. Brideshead Revisited…* The stale bread is all crusty and dry and I break the bread and bite half. Thoughtfully chew to consider The Rector's plate, which flinches from direct and inordinate scrutiny.

I am not here – I am not anywhere. Potential situations of conflict; potential situations of change. Classrooms. Unbeknownst – I am gesturing with my fork to The Rector's plate as He and I chew – wondering if I should offer the man better – less self-harming nutritional counsel – assuming The Rector has been told what and how to eat by a qualified Spanish nutritionist.

Henry says: 'Good to crunch them up with a bit of bread, no? Good anchovies! Wish it wasn't Lent! Could have done with a bit of the el vino!'

The Ampleforth monk recharges his own and my glass. Geoff hasn't touched his.

I say: 'Amen, brother.'

It is a lovely, sarcastic luncheon...

Adedokun pushes and pulls his food about a bit, as if it were trying to make sense, then he must be getting lost in it and sets about the seemingly thankless task of studious deconstruction. It's the whole morning-egg thing all over again. Adedokun groups – prawns, anchovies, scraped creamy-cheese, courgette – each at each cardinal point of his plate's compass. And then centrally whips – as for some pure self-gratification – a creamy-orange swirl of grated carrot.

The shape of prawns... Which are shrivelled little specimens – frankly. Adedokun stabs them on his plate all together a forkful. He holds them up, wiggles them, making the fork go bendy... Some time – like on drugs or something. (Some internal place...) But Geoff, having no more of that, grabs the fork – saying: ''Ere, bro, gimme that –' and Geoff *mouths whole* that *prawn-scrape* metal on Yorkshire teeth.

Sister Angelina's jaw drops. Half a prawn falls from her lips and custard dribbles down her chin. She mops herself up with her napkin, momentarily shamed, and of a second seems quite old, discomfited, confidence gone from her. Age. Even The Rector seems as if He might say something – and this is Geoff.

Accepting the loss as a thing of no consequence, Adedokun shrugs mildly. A momentary wistful quality – fine and perfect shoulders. Ade stands and he goes to the cupboards which are at the side, beneath a painting about the Assumption. He takes from the drawer a fresh fork.

Henry says: 'A little bit of thyme would complete this. Maybe ease-off on the paprika. And some parsley. Could do with some really good salt.'

Geoff says: 'So, Father, what do you think about the news about the holy sisters? Sister Angelina? It's an extraordinary thing. It's a real treasure for the people of Doncaster.'

Then he says: 'Do you want more carrots, Father? Or one of these gorgeous anchovies?'

Henry says: 'I'll have one or two of those, if you don't mind, Geoff.'

I say: 'Is there a little more water, please? Do I need to pop and refill?'

Henry says: 'Fabulous anchovies. You can tell they're the top-notch Spanish sort.'

Geoff says: 'It's amazing the visions that were given her, and how she was touched by Jesus.'

I say: 'It can be difficult at times to remember to leave room for the main course.'

Geoff says: 'Have you ever had any visions, Father?'

Everyone has to wait until everyone else has finished. It is a new rule, introduced by Sister Angelina. She was mostly not-here most of first term. Whether she returned with notions – or this was The Rector's plan… Sister Angelina *likes* to think of young men as inveterate slobs at heart. Too much of the Adam in them… It confirms her. Boys being boys. (And we know about that – she doesn't!) This is her self-image.

It is how she identifies. And so incumbent on her virgin-woman lot which is to civilize that yob-streak in all her lovely virgin manly chunky cum-full sweaty unnocturnal priestly sinning woman-disavowing not-boys.

Sister Angelina has declared herself – multiple times – as representative of future parishioners. The 85% – is the figure she's stuck on. The Catholic parish demographic. Which doesn't exactly fill you with joy in the classroom-time. Either that, or Father Rector put her up to it.

282

Everyone has to wait until everyone else is finished. A new rule.

By now it won't surprise you that it is Adedokun best of us laughing at things like this. So I try to see it through his eyes. Philip said: 'I hate that woman. I hate her.' Perhaps he articulated something for each of us. (Perhaps as she positioned us – as some man we aren't – we riled and flinched from scrutiny. Hating her.) Though it was not nice putting it quite like that. It 'always' has struck me as rather common to 'hate' things. It is the sort of squawking, common thing people might say.

Sister Angelina's lesson she has delivered thrice. It is the very-same lesson each time. Because she simply can't remember – she's senile, not meaning that in a bad way. And no-one says anything. She says it is a path of Saint Ignatius. You have to say to God: 'Jesus, I love you. I'm sorry. I love you.' This lesson means a lot to her, and she stands quaking, washing and soothing her hands as she speaks to us. She explains to class how, as men, we are rational, while women are emotional. She looks like Bible-paper in a little book. Her clean, unpolished, washed-leather-shoes swell in a squashed-up way with her feet crammed into them. And worzel smile. She quivers and must be very brave.

Strictly speaking, *anyone* can take the used plates, and the scrapes of cast-off food, to the trolleys and slops tubs. Strictly speaking, *anyone* can*! Even if he *isn't* a Refectorian*! Father Richard amazed himself telling us this. Only, fancy. Dangerous thoughts.

I and Adedokun, Julian and Philip must have looked suitably impressed. Still, strictly speaking, it's best to look busy. Or you get a prod for the sake of a prod. It is best to exist in a clearly-apparent state of permanently mild agitation.

Our goalposts move. Hover like strange and impossible logic – and vanish utterly. With the first course, one or two are apt to linger. Especially coming from England. Especially as guests. People feel quite privileged to visit us here. There are bishops and priests. Each student has a guest allowance of ten free nights, which are otherwise priced at 38 euros. It's fun when a guest doesn't know what's happening. Naturally, one waits the minutes out. There'll be a guest mulling on a mouthful and some thought only he could have set himself. And smile and smile toward Sister Angelina. (Your rule!) Or to the Vice Rector! (Who could not have nary a clue how to chivvy him on to eat!) We are fallen creatures... The Ampleforth monk chews thoughtfully his last mouthful. None seeks to revive the now-flagged conversation. Everyone has to wait until everyone else has finished. The Rector sees the funny side. Give Him that.

The Rector says quietly, in His gentle voice: 'Tomàs, I think perhaps we might move things on now.' It seems to say I – Tomàs haven't done too much wrong.

I nod, and mouth like a secret: '*Oh okay.*'

Then we are in the kitchen. Me and Ade. The funny-nun lays out dishes of food on the gurneys like it might have been spam fritters. Mind you, they always serve everything royal. From mayonnaise-and-toast and other bat-shit creations. Food-royalty. It is a massive piled-up dish for each table. Lamb shanks braised in red wine and pomegranate... Henry can tell it through. Shallots, walnuts, mushrooms, orange-zest... A side-order of fries. Sauce gels sticky on the lamb shanks. Almost, it doesn't smell like meat. Adedokun's eyes show ivory. Has someone blundered? There are no words. Adedokun and I wear our oven-gloves. This weight of sauced-food gives to the trolleys' rubber wheels and to their squeaking axels a satisfying trudge-step over the tiles toward the inconsequential banter of the Refectory. The trolleys must be placed – thus so. And, oven-gloved, getting the dishes to tables.

Lavish food. Down at the far end, where I go, Trevor's most immediate reaction, upon registering *this* food, is a meat-snarl, monstrous fierce. Brown Trevor's teeth are ivory... Gammon-pink tongue curls up inside. Lips recede over his teeth with it. I have seen that look on Trevor's face before... Philip withdraws to a different octave. Philip, who is from Liverpool, looks like a family Christmas lunch on Eastenders. (As the food arrives – not when it all kicks off.)

Henry says: 'Look at this, hey! Will you look at this!'

Geoff says: 'Father!'

Sean says: 'Oh my. This is different.'

We hold plates for Geoff to serve. It is a great deal of meat. I want to know if The Rector has done this. The Rector might look as if He is surprised. The look might simply have unanticipated the scale of the achievement. I get the lamb shank on my plate and start pulling the food off it and eating it. I don't really care at this point if anyone can see. Yes more wine. I am salivating.

On top of this, I say to Geoff, as if we have never met in a whole life, and as if Sister Angelina were listening: 'I suppose you must have some lovely walks around your way. Do you like to walk?'

Geoff has his mouth full of lamb and says: 'No, bro. Not much walking.'

'How do you occupy your time when you are at home?'

'Prayer.'

Luke says: 'I think the whole Yorkshire Dales are a prayer.'

I say to The Rector: 'Do you know the Dales?'

285

The Rector shakes his head.

Luke says: 'God's country.'

The monk says to Geoff: 'You had a holy upbringing.'

Sean says: 'There's a lot to eat.'

Henry says: 'Too many people don't grow up living with beautiful countryside. That's where the trouble starts. Grow up in horrible places. How are they supposed to learn all that's beautiful and good if not from nature? What do you think, Tom? You agree?'

I say: 'Oh, absolutely.'

Henry says: 'Totally right.'

The Rector is not eating lamb. It is a salad – though of such as would have gone with the lamb – of tomatoes with chickpeas thrown into it – and indeed capers which might have provided an unusual complement. The Rector swallows. He then says: 'Tomàs, I have to say, there are times I find you quite inscrutable.'

I lay my knife and fork upon my plate. I put that there, and take the napkin, from the side of the plate, and I mop myself about a bit. Then – raise my wine-glass – take a sip of the wine. Arranging all that together – so it looks neat. I say: 'Do you really?'

The Rector says: 'Oh Tomàs, you're not going to take offence on me now are you?'

I make my face – my mouth – an unpronounceable 'O' – for 'offence?'.

Suddenly, life seems very sad. It won't swallow me – Tomàs and it won't compute. (Fundamentals – actings-out – expressed. Willy-nilly.)

What a pity.

But I can't do it. (It is a common theme – death of fathers.)

I take a full-mouthful of the lamb and chew and chew... It's meat.

286

Eventually, I get it, pulped, to the back of my mouth and it goes down.

(Mum and Dad and those two lives complicit. One could not disentangle them. She reminds me.) I am not even angry. Chuck it all over The Rector's plate? Gestural. A flower... And in my teenage room I meant for something better.

I clean myself of such thoughts – smile and say: 'I think I'll get an apple.'

I take my plate and dump the contents in the slop-bucket. I return to my place with an apple. On the little plate, I slice it.

Sister Angelina says: 'Did you just..?'

I say: 'No, not really.'

I hold the now arc's shiver of the apple in hand. And say: 'Beauty, Father. Beauty is human truth. However, beware false beauty. Got to beware of that.'

Beauty given. Beauty understood. Howsoever I arrogate to myself any final authority. Beauty undefined each time. Because our brains are wired. Moral consciousness! Somewhat burdensome, that. We are ancient!

I say: 'Or name your cause.' Having seemingly forgotten the apple.

The Rector nods. Nor does The Rector seem particularly to begrudge me my meal.

In chapel, after lunch, it is Josh who leads the prayer, which during Lent is the De Profundis:

De profundis clamavi ad te Domine

Domine exaudi vocem meam fiant aures tuae intendentes in vocem deprecationis meae

Si iniquitates observabis Domine Domine quis sustinebit

Quia apud te propitiatio est propter legem tuam sustinui te Domine
sustinuit anima mea in verbum eius
Speravit anima mea in Domino
A custodia matutina usque ad noctem speret Israel in Domino
Quia apud Dominum misericordia et copiosa apud eum redemption
Et ipse redimet Israel ex omnibus iniquitatibus eius.

We don't use the Latin for the prayer. We do it in English. The
Latin is better:

Out of the depths have I cried unto thee, O Lord.

Lord, hear my voice: let thine ears be attentive to the voice of my
supplications.

If thou, Lord, shouldest mark iniquities, O Lord, who shall stand?

But there is forgiveness with thee, that thou mayest be feared.

I wait for the Lord, my soul doth wait, and in his word do I hope.

My soul waiteth for the Lord more than they that watch for the
morning: I say, more than they that watch for the morning.

Let Israel hope in the Lord: for with the Lord there is mercy, and
with him is plenteous redemption.

And he shall redeem Israel from all his iniquities.

Then we all get to our feet pretty quickly after that. As instructed –
I go along for coffee. The priests are all over the coffee-trolley, and
biscuits, helping each other to coffee, and biscuits, like they all tuck-in
together at a good Mass.

'No, really,' I say – I have been told to come along by The Rector,
and to socialize, in community, and I don't want coffee. 'I'm fine,
thanks.' One of the nicer rooms – it looks out – fully windowed – as a

gallery onto the scrub and the gardens – toward the gym. I am wearing what I wear and am happy with their playing biscuits and coffee. Happy to have a nice conversation if anyone asks. If, perhaps, there were no imposition about it. Let's be small – let's not be – let's be – small. And there's a light shines.

In that teenage room – where locks don't close now.

'Just being sociable.'

Chapter Eight

Tuesday Lent 2. A waking half-sleep – clung to. Way too long maintained. A waking slew of flashes. I half-sleep with the ski-hat pulled over my eyes. My white-socked feet laid-out like remembrance in cottoned slabs. I lie – tainted – shivering like the dream strobed. And just nudging the matter... The blanket twists off me and the sheet on the floor. The dream suggested Ry. I look to find my way down there again – in a half-assed way guiding it. Breathing myself down so as to maintain. To keep it physical, tangible, almost-touched. Which might easily pan-out till noon if the clock let it.

We are – let me try it – in my room. Sat around bored in my room. There is no TV, there is no computer. There are books on the shelves and paintings. There are canvases either side the mirror on my fire-place. Also increasingly stacked with teenage hair-wear. And paint and white-spirit on the hearth. There are strings from the light to the curtain-rail. Strips of negatives hang off them. Not exactly social pursuits – hence now the bored.

Ry sits at my desk... Ry sat pushed back. Ry inclined. Goof-head and tussled-hair. 30° in a pretty-much straight-line. Those same kid-pumps. Jeans ripped and skinny. I would stand to clench Ry's shoulders. Do in not-quite-dream if not then. Forced-dream. Make it. Not then. Smell and kiss his hair. The new weight of Ry's adolescence overclouding – us/him/me. The not-dream freezes. Budge it. Move it. It won't move.

Ry wears, in this half-dream, a woven army-camouflage canvas belt. I can't nudge it further. Not with any degree of verisimilitude. The vision sticks at that. Child clothed in adolescent armour. No matter how I might conjure it. Ry moving on from a being a small, childhood thing to becoming the thing itself. I am fifteen. Maybe Ry is twelve or thirteen. Probably it must have been something like that.

The comfortable-space ejects me. I can't hold the scene. The feeling clears. Different – overwhelming layers of brain wash into it. Clear – day-spring. Here the brutal day is. Ready-made.

At Pluscarden Abbey, where the young monks laugh and work the bell ropes, this Job-quote is hung on a tapestry:

העולם של היסודות את הנחתי כאשר היית איפה

Dancing on ropes in the public space outside the sanctuary. *Where were you when I laid the foundation of the world?* The line is captioned also in a film I like. *The Tree Of Life*. I love that film. It made me cry. It *means* something… I open my eyes.

*

Later, following this, I shall sit on the floor and stick there, dry, rock-dry, rock-depth, the hot south, and there shall be no supernatural friend and no enemy. No-one – it seems. Except my family are there – just miles off. Red dust, skanky pumps, olive groves. No redemption yet. But beating sun and olive groves. I AM. Pit and bones.

Naked, I get into the shower, and I drench myself. I seem unusually depleted. My bones ache – my body creaks. Zombie-fashion – closed on pain inside. After I have done this, I go down to the cellars for my hot bath.

This is a cry yet from death-annihilation – those dreams – which leave you with nothing. Dimensionless blackness. Hell. You can't move, speak or hear anything. You are effectively paralysed – locked in – and you couldn't, say, wrench your head in an effort to wake from it. That empties you – cancels you.

Now – churned rubble. A stripping bare of life. Bare bones. The tummy I have isn't shifting. I'm not skin and wire. You can pinch it. And I can't tense it – for a six-pack – there are four-ish, then a wobbly bit, though you can see my ribs. More, ironically, such muscle I have swells the fat out. Adipose-zero – you'd have to – then there'd be even a prospect of life-damage. *That* bit mocks me. Middle-age. Man-lump. It would be the last bit to go – as one dieted. Right in the midst of me. And starving it all down to nothing would really hurt. And I have been so careful.

Fall around now. Hot bath – hot water. Let it swirl. Anger! Do my island! I can be multiple different people, different thoughts. Bath-fantasy. Mad and crazy thought… Guys just yelling at each other. 'You do not belong here! Get out of this seminary!' The whole – the entire accusation. All this filth compacted – twisted. Infinite-crazy. Brain-space. Punishing The Rector. On and on a madness rolls and ugly twisted faces… in the whole world.

All Stars and disco-lights. Boys kissed boys in lust and abject mutual need. The lie is so compacted… And not *just* the simplest romance. And not like they're making a statement. Plot-culmination. Lust and need. I am a mess.

Honestly, I cry as the cold tap runs and – everything all folds-up in

292

the wrong way… Even where there'd been possibles. Love – enduring. Only that was never the right way. Too much booze.

So I turn off the cold tap and get the heat up again. It seems there is never a point at which – ever – it could become stable. But there is nothing else. (A teenage room. A door that locked then – not in dreams. And teenage terror – not like that, not like they are… And – somewhat conflicted self-ejection – from squalor of *this* – *he, she* – and childhood. And escape – lying on the way out the back door. Party-face on. Twisted – pure.)

The only safe perspective is the clarity of loss as tears dry. It is always inherently unstable. (It cracks inside – until one place oneself within that teenage room – upon a set of tremors.) That was the way it is wired. (Beyond – or prior to – the self-destruct in…) Seventeen, thirteen, twenty-six.

When I'm better, I go back to my room. I glow, bare-foot, in my new Adidas tracksuit. It is not exactly slinky. Man-leg-hairs lubricate trackie-shell – between an idea of skin. It would be a considerable shock to meet anyone. Once locked inside, I open my lap-top to listen to the news. I watch video footage – via social media – of a mass execution in Syria. Men lying face-down being shot in ways that wouldn't kill them quickly. Then I get dressed and get ready for morning prayer.

At prayer, there are only the standard prayer-intentions – according to the regular order. Maybe that's best. Tuesdays are long. Our classroom-time stretches ahead unremittingly. I take what light and air I can – at the open window. School-unconscious-time. Almost there is no recollection of classroom-time. Here is your text-book, and this is your desk. Oddly, there is a very little classroom-time figured in dreams. You know? The mash-up. Corridors and decades of friends, teachers, pupils advising you. Time-mashed. Lessons-botched. Exams-untaught.

There is a rumour going round, first within the corridors then at breakfast, that today there is going to be something different. Details prove vague – and disavowed – and I can't catch it. At breakfast there is no formal announcement. I infer. I prick my ears. (One or two of them *must* know.) Through the course of an inert and troubled morning, I get it in the end from Francis. We are to go to the funeral of the old Archbishop. This is to be at the cathedral. And we are to be present in formal capacity. Like we are real.

The formal announcement comes with lunch. Accordingly, at the appointed time, we group at the college door. Each with his alb and a cincture in a plastic bag. We aren't smiling either. *They* aren't smiling either. They don't know what is happening. But don't like to say – so we don't speak. To speak would be admission of too much. The day is old already. Tiredness is gathering. It's getting shifty. We wear our suits. Tiredness looses in our faces its muscle-grip. Slack-jawed. Philip checks his watch... And you can see the affront to it. Cancelled volitional-activity. Rock-tired and persistent-agitation. Angered. (Do you want this still? it says. Death to live again in Jesus?) Minutes more. At the emptiest, The Rector approaches. Slip-slap down Martyrs' corridor. The Rector's face is flat and hard. His lips are small and thin. His arms hang. His shoes out-turn. The corners of His eyes slightly squash together. No apology. No unavoidable call He had to take. He is nervous. He only says:

'Are we all here good let's go.'

The Rector flat-foots ahead of us. He jaywalks the lights. Yeah: real bishop material. Oh – but He *wants* that... He walks so fast. He doesn't look back as He walks. We should stop and slow. We should pause and breathe and whisper. Let the shepherd go… And let the shepherd arrive without his flock! We should unionize. We should…

We go the back way. There'll be hell to pay later if we don't keep up with Him. It's the usual rag-tag group – no prizes for that. We straggle. We wear unusual daylight-expressions – open air – and placky bags with albs in… As things turn out, it is to be an occasion. As a group, we arrive at a side door of the cathedral. There, straggling, we gather-up into a ball. And the students are hustled through. There are forms and externalities. There is a shift in status… It seems we might be *agents* – with *agency*. Official, you know. And all the glitz 'n' glamour of the Church at its most funereal.

We, the students, go back-stage into the Sacristy. Here priests and many bishops are gathering. Also, there are the boys of the minor seminary. They as we have albs to wear. The boys and we English students are sectioned from the priests. I go through into the priests' room, looking for a peg to hang my jacket on. No-one you need see. An invisible functionary. An admin – maybe.

This can hardly matter. Priests can be funny when – en masse – they get together. There is an awful lot of shuffling and scrabbling between themselves. A fair bit of low-noise. Gossipy. Rumbling belly-noise. *Hors d'oeuvres*. A bit of locker-room fuss. There is a self-congratulatory character about the whole business. One feels they joy to blend-again in their alternative-element. A whinnying hive. Priest-pub.

When all we students have to do is get our crappy non-Levitical albs on and get out there...

We find our places – within the main belly of the church. There we wait some twenty minutes. Our pews are reserved up-front. The cathedral, which can seem such a brute space, looks quite-good filled out. The priests are to be in the transepts. There is a rumbly musicality like an orchestra getting in tune. The murmur in the stalls is of the timbre you get at an opera. It has an intense feel about it, though uncomposed and lacking yet in plenitude.

Watch the video on YouTube. (DM me.) You can only see about five of us distinctly. The clip they show on the news. Our lips are moving – and none of us is following the form of the ceremony. We look knackered – in polycotton albs and the crushed skin. None could have thought to bring with him a copy of the Spanish. (We weren't told.) It is worse than I'll remember it. We look clueless. Philip and Julian mouth without opening their lips. While you can't see our eyes, it's a caged look. Rubbery. Skin adheres to skin. In some manner, our perceptual framework is strobing. Creased skin. Our lips almost-readably – babble-and-fight. Baby gurgles. And we could use a little sunshine. What do they feed us on? It *is to be* worse than I'll remember it. We could use a little colour and life. Green veg and the TLC. It isn't *good* not being so beautiful. It is altogether not fine.

It doesn't look so busy either – as I feel it is. (They have kept us alone.) The congregation all in seats – they aren't dangling from the catching a glimpse of it. Then, with fanfare, and strident almost-screech – almost-wail of the death-song, the bishops wander into it – process – and the coffin is laid on the floor on a bit of carpet in front of the sanctuary. Head-first to the altar for a dead bishop.

It dozies the arithmetic of memory. So many bishops – you'd think they'd never end. So many people praying the same thing. They put candles on the sticks by the coffin, and the Archbishop's staff, the shepherd's crook, in a stand at the head of the coffin. There is nothing to hope for. Deep, old-fashioned grief – which sounds professional. It is sensual, striving, carries in itself such incredible insistence on human-need.

Each bishop is his own objective. Each within – crisp modern mitres. There are *a lot* of bishops – you'd think they'd never end. It is a human response. Ancient. You purify the land of the living from the dead. A soul – human-mischief – floating someway close about our heads. Well – you want to get rid of that. Casting-out now. And in no uncertain terms. Blasting it away from this place. So the soul not linger.

Deep and most primitive messages. A child's face. In school. In class. When human-knowledge pulled itself together and the world seemed quite shrunk. If we can remember that. Twentieth-century themes. Deep time. When man emerged – from those brief years. Then Planet Earth resumed and we shrank again. And here we go again. Wailing – evicting a dead-body's soul from this place. ('Go on! Get out of here! Let the living be!')

I'm stood next to Geoff. We are stood by the wall, to one side of a set of pews. There, junior seminarians, high-school-age boys, take the first three. The Royal English College – us – on the two rows behind. We've met them once. We have once been in similar relationship with the boys. At a Friday Mass in the basilica – near college. Yet of glancing interest – such curiosity there might have been takes a very remote second place – perhaps to boys' internal clobber. And the business of private community. At this event – internal readjustments. Relatively consummate discipline.

It has been twelve – nine, *ten* years – since children. Counting

297

time. My affective response to the presence now… As a return to a scene of high emotional impact and psychic collapse. (Keep that teenage room – but…) Classrooms. I must be famished! What – for what a school represents. Protection. Information. Where it isn't squalid.

Classrooms – where you sit while you grow. I could have them all mentally arranged in a line of desks to take care of them… So now – and convey – known territory, professional can-do.

Though, by the look of them, they are regular, normal, middle-class-posh kids. An expensive education for a nominal fee.

It would certainly be good to distinguish myself. To say: I know how to do you. *I can…* I know the place of meeting. And at its most simple and at its most direct. Its least posturing.

So the Mass passes – rather a blur – within the Spanish of the homily. There is no following what is expressed. The air continues strident. Love's insistence. Highly wrought. Everyone yearns – and the chanting again aches with it. There is smoke and water. Then they pick the coffin up, and carry the coffin over beyond where I can see. On the video, you can see the coffin interred in a hole in the floor in a side-chapel, with flagstones stacked at the side to lay over him. The wailing song rises in crescendo – the noise become alarming and confusing.

Afterwards, Geoff presses me to go for a coffee. There'll be some motive, and I decline. I have no use for Geoff at this hour. It is a little past six o' clock – local time. I walk by Plaza Mayor. It is well past siesta and back in trading hours.

With my plastic bag I stalk the city solo in the suit I wear like I have a job. But it is the thinnest of cities. Cobbled – tired light – with a certain patina. There are very few people. Dust and glancing sunshine.

298

Stillness of air – a peaceful might-be. Absence in thought – space washes through the mind. *Agorophilia...* Paved streets – and no cars. Almost nothing-touched by a feeling of people. Human-need vacated. All the muscles in your face... Cold air on creasy skin. Any expression the muscles find inauthentic. We looked like a stack of bricks in the cathedral.

There's not much we have to do for the rest of the day. There'll be supper, and night prayer. Given the free time, and given all that hazy feeling of openness, I walk at a brisk pace, quite directly, to the usual bar. The girl holds fort, and there are no other customers. Remarking the suit, I do what I can to explain about the funeral. I seem to want both to self-deprecate and big-myself-up on it. I show the bag with the alb in it. She's seen it on the news, and, while she really hates the Church, she lets me have my little go trying to say what I need to, and when I fold and that capsizes she gives me the shrug. She isn't going to try and make it nice for me. And, of course, this honesty-test makes me feel a right idiot. Still, the beer comes cold, and she lets me be. She has the game-show on the television. Having no book to read, I watch the screen, with the hangman-style clues, and the volume down. It is surprising how much I get. Or – not really get – but agree with tiredly as a letter is correctly guessed and so revealed.

*

I take a sip of that beer... Of a sudden, though, that beer isn't really the thing I want. It's the first time I've come to this bar since starting to write my Lenten diary. I have really nothing to fiddle with. Something looks wrong. In a sense, I've stopped looking like I am Tomàs. A pained rendition – an inaccurate, remote imitation. When the air gets cold. And friends might say to one another, at Christmas, afterwards: 'That's not

299

Tomàs.'

Lacking in adequate distraction – a moment's loss like street-scenes – and getting away from Geoff. Perhaps it was the tribal wailing of the funeral. Or it could be the thoughts about once having tried very hard to be a teacher. Though now the grubby messes of the bar stare back at me. All smeared. The beer is too wet.

I let the beer sit on the table. Keeping my hands in my lap, beneath the table, I stop making any face. (There is really no argument left in me.) Though it was only the stupid – a known and anticipated check-point.

In class – Everything is starting to look like a million years ago.

Was it today?

Where it all blends in-*this… All time…* Bobbing loose-spiel in the accumulation. Swills unbothered with. There seems no particularly accountable reason why suddenly it gets to me.

In class, today, this morning, with The Rector, the subject was Natural Law.

Landscape narrowing – always in class where they never let you think about anything. But now it sticks and crunches in me. The train going into the tunnel – landscape narrowing. My documentation entirely in order but so fake. A Jew-or-German moment. And so with honour become a thing. *Au revoir, les enfants…* Fact-defining, blunt, brief, measurements. Truth or lies. And honour become a thing.

Odd how it has taken so long. Odd how I have missed it. When it might, then, now, at last, I sense the reactions – in *my name's* heart – prove incontrovertibly. *I'm… I'm a…*

When surely the point of the Christian story is that it does nice things. When, surely, if you believe, you dispense with occasional unpleasant things. Catholics especially – we are good at pretending a lot of things are and aren't. If you ever did seek a religion where the measure of truth were flexible…

I *did* dare to wonder if the moment might never come. So now the question of truth arises. So, now, the fiction irredeemably compromised. Fatally-system-flawed. Catastrophically buggy. Yeah, so, now, one *has* to say: *That's not true… And if it is not nice – if it's horrid – what's the point of pretending it is true?*

It seems absurd now, of course, to relate, as *then* to itself it must have done, the mental-contest. We who now are clean and honest. There seem such quantities of belief I put in myself. I might have gone terrorist-Catholic. And given the time invested scrabbling the walls inside for a back-door hack on it. *Where's the chink? Where's the catch? Where's the opening? Let me in…* A creature imprisoned – all basement-brick with a dustbin-lid on top. A small thing caged to the level of the purely animal.

'Show, don't tell,' they say. But there's a squelch of mashed-up code – and little broken morphemes of a human-code all-mash and squelch upon each other. As a child smashing his toys and environment.

And my self-harming – my miniature embodiment… Eight, nine, ten. (But it was fucked by birth!) The Adam and Eve and not the Adam and Steve of it. It isn't in the language – crazily-absurd – from without. A painted savagery. (Lord Of The Flies!) Futile dress and ceremony. It makes no sense… It doesn't make any sense.

When The Rector talks about sex, there is a character He has, a (presumably) imaginary person, He calls 'Sexy Sue'. And what you might get up to with her is – He says – 'jiggy-wiggy'.

Sexy Sue comes up in discussions of celibacy. She might be some kind of blow-up doll. She isn't a real person you might want to have sex with. More like sex in Cosmo or in porn. Plastic-skin and painted-lips and straightened hair. A sex-tip – 'Take a slurp of hot mint-tea before you go down on him! It'll make him zing!'

But Sexy Sue isn't so bad – and she isn't the heart of it – weak and thick and frail and manufactured. So a sneering, pre-pubescent, *clever* streak displays when He speaks of her. (Year 8.) But it is only what you might expect. A foregoing of intercourse. ('Jiggy-wiggy.') Loveless, tacky sex. Sexy Sue is already love's opposite. Base-need inflicted on a victim (herself) and her tragic eyebrows.

Now, though, that room, the subject is love. And Mortal Sin. And it is only as officially, institutionally, pronounced upon. The matter of sexual complementarity. Natural Law – which governs the married state. The Rector's addressees are mostly teenagers and – young men in their twenties. He says that masturbation is mortal when you plan your pornography time. Save your fuel, get the pizza in. But He says not to worry overmuch if… the odd slip.

In a sense, that isn't *bad* advice. In context, it could be a lot worse. It could be *really terrible* advice. In context, it isn't likely to give them an additional complex. (A spur-of-the-moment lapse in purity. Not such a biggy. Don't beat yourself up about it. So to speak.)

But what He says, in the final analysis, is not about sex jiggy-wiggy-style, but about love. What He means in the final analysis concerns love. He means, outright, and no *ifs* and no *maybes*, as basic category, basic fact, that *love* between a man and a man is impossible.

302

And so now, the room, hyper-tense, breathes milkily. This the truth they fear and truth wanted. This the truth they fear had been subject to doubt – and truth wanted.

One could not but sense how the tangible presence of an evil disturbs the room. This is a classroom – where truth happens. And that love is false, and it is only a delusion of love, for it is categorically impossible. And they might say it is love – and they might say that they are living in love – but that is a lie. And this is a category of place called classrooms – where truth happens.

Last term, toward the start, when we arrived, before very much classroom-time, when no-one had a clue what was happening, The Rector said to us we might develop close friendships between ourselves. He said this homo-romantically. He said, if anything became too strong we should come back to Jesus. Because a too-close friendship like that would be in conflict with the relationship with Jesus.

It seems impossible anything of that sort might ever have in any of them – . Well, they aren't exactly lookers. Not even passed beyond youth into parody. But that isn't it. There seems no romantic thought. Their bodies vacated of any romantic thought. Like reprographic-maps. No sexual-response inhabited. Were you to go in there to seminary conscious of sexual lack… Was The Rector's warning quite superfluous?

Perhaps The Rector said it as a conscious and deliberate ploy to set-up the issue. If not between ourselves then within ourselves. An added disturbance – an increase of self-doubt. Gaming us. To isolate – fracturing communal-self and self-identity. To make the strip-lights sting – the brain crave sleep and Aspirin.

I say, now, quietly-aloud, to my gelid *jara*: 'I know men who love each other. They are in love.' As I should have said it in the classroom. But didn't.

Then, off-timetable, I stand and cross myself and there are no mirrors and bow before the television-set and acknowledge myself and say: 'I've been in love before.'

I sit again to finish my beer.

*

I have time before supper to nip to the supermarket opposite. It is the time people gather. The high-rise apartment blocks all around the square have spilled their residual human quantity. People of all ages sit on the benches. Little kids muck about – there is a padded soft-play area. Plastic dens for them to hide in.

Back in my room, people are sharing the video from Syria on Facebook. There they are again – all in the dust face-down to be shot like rabbits. They bounce, as if they hadn't known this was the fruit of it, wriggled and jumped on the dirt floor. Playing 'sardines'. Perhaps there had been some worse outcome. Choice – if they didn't comply.

I strip and change and I have to go to supper. Later, I think I won't go out again. Staying in my room – I'll crunch the cans I've bought. In my room, I check the clock, and reckon I have about two and a half hours sensibly. I'll have to take my rubbish to the bins, on the street, before anyone else is up. The cleaners are in tomorrow.

*

As things turn out, though, Wednesday, having looked set to be another day, proves other to the thought of the day before. During breakfast, Geoff gets us quiet with: 'Right listen, lads. Oi oi. Father has something He wants to say to us.'

The Rector has a rather special announcement. There are to be no classes. Students pause and cease to champ – the milk, the spoon. Wednesday: mid-week, mid-feeling. The Rector explains that arrangements have only just now been finalized. He smiles in placing those words, knowing they are false. We are to visit the Diocesan Seminary, where there is to be quite a special Mass. '…*hosts… guests…*' ...*how to hold a knife and fork...* Wear a suit and tie… Incidentally, it is the Solemnity of Saint Joseph we are to celebrate. How specifically not to fuck The Rector's career up. 'It's only just a little something…'

So, a very big deal… Yet I dress with no inkling. I wish I'd known – I hadn't thought I might have to go public. I scrub my mouth. My teeth bleed. In the mirror… Man, I look like shit. I do my best to recover it. The foundation goes all bitty so I rub that off again. My trousers sag, though the trousers-situation is manageable if I put nothing in my trouser pockets except my hands. I have yet to have Niko punch or drill the next hole in my *rather* fine leather belt I need.

I get myself together, and I gargle with the Spanish mouthwash. There are still meaty bits coming out from between my teeth – from yesterday. The mouthwash is terrible stuff – like floor cleaner. My skin, if not puffy, is porous. And there are sags only I can see beneath the eyes in the bathroom light. They require preparation H, but I don't have any. But it is over the top of the cheeks I am most surprised about. Though I moisturize, scrape my face, drink my carrot juice.

At the door, they are the rest of them in what you might call pyjama-mode. We've been expecting classroom and we're still in bed. (You pray in bed, you sit in class in bed, you go to Mass in bed, you eat your lunch in bed – in the towering Refectory. Then, when it comes to siesta, we go back to bed.) With foam in their ears and blooded – a scraped-on Sunday best. Philip in a suit looks unreasonably distinguished.

305

They carry plastic bags… *Francis whispers quickly under his breath to me: we are going to play football.* There has been talk of this over many weeks. How any information passes around this place. Trevor-organized. We in the sense of they are to play the Diocesan seminarians at football. That's their football-kit – in their bags. As had long been planned, as had been long-discussed. For Trevor likes his football.

Oh… thinks I! Envisaging soggy-kneed bounding clod-hoppers much as ourselves. We – they are to play the seminarians at football. Blokey lard-ons and knock-about fashion. Hackney Marshes. *Strange…* thinks I! Socks 'n' ankles. *How – unfathomable…* I have no inkling.

We get ourselves together, and the door opens onto the street. *They* seem to know the way. How? There are no obvious signs of any special anxiety. But there pass – the shapeless backstreets.

The Vice Rector is *smiling…* Soon we have walked beyond anywhere I know. We walk for maybe twenty minutes – closer to thirty. Two say something to me, but I don't catch the meaning of it. Our pace neither lumpen nor harried. Our voice the hive-mind. It is not a straightforward matter to maintain individual composure. At length, the Diocesan Seminary comes in view.

This is red sprawl. Low and scrubby housing clears – like red clay scribbled over the top of the brick walls. The seminary building is itself a boiled tooth lowered from outer space and sits in wasteland. Concrete-huge. It looks left-over from something else – a brute-optimistic stab at an old war. Set in what appear to be acres of baked-dust and brown-beige sun-bled gravel – where there might be fields. Then, beyond the perimeter, low-sprawl, little domestic houses. Were a person to say to you, 'That is a school,' you might put a rough guess on the number-on-roll being about 1200.

We follow The Rector toward the main-steps that lead to the main doors. There is not a soul in view. We huddle. In such ways one could never admit to – we become again mutually responsive. Nudged and nudging. Ostensibly outward-directed. Covertly closing – in anticipation of formation – both within and all against each other. Almost: watch my back, and form a perimeter. An instinct for men – and religion introduces its special fears. The Rector gestures to wait. He seems to disappear as the steps swallow Him. Though in view – if you thought about it. Inky-smudge. Inky-boy's thumb making words in a vast continuum… Define *word*: a word is where you put your thumb… And it is very quiet. There comes a point Julian says: 'Okay, so what…' But that sound could barely have carried even to Julian's own ears: a hard-acoustic drops it flat – such provisional human-need.

Through the big swing metal-and-glass doors at the top of the steps, a figurine-priest appears. Swung-glass, swung-metal. Exaggerating the gesture, he beckons us. There he stands and his boy at the top of the steps – his expression resolved into kindness – and happiness. He, it transpires, is the Rector of this place. The boy is Jorge – one who sat/stood/knelt/stood/sat immediately proximate to me and Geoff in the cathedral yesterday. Standing on the kneeler to see better – in the brown leather-moccasins they all wear. Gently recollected to floor-level by the unknown and anonymized man in his alb – this man: their Rector. Life chimes.

So it is now the penny drops about the football. They aren't playing men; they're playing the boys! This seems unbalanced, and highly unusual. Surely a distinction, of, indeed, incompatible qualities, should have been *mentioned*.

At the top of the steps, their Rector takes our hands and hugs us –
hugs us.

Jorge says: 'Hello. Follow me.' He gestures his right hand like a
junior-matador – at the start of the dance – the cap doffed – the circle of
inspection. If but I *that* age had been so bold. (If but I had not been so
especially, particularly sensitive.)

The chapel lies immediately to the right-side of the atrium. The
atrium a study in concrete and vertical lines. There seems a scopic
pleasure – totalizing gaze of impossible clarity. Air and angels. Though
not an unpleasant effect – the awareness of oneself – the human-scale. It
feels like no school I recognize. It *thinks* like no school I recognize.
Possibilities seem implied. *Teaching*... None could 'big-up' here an
impression of real life.

Jorge says in English again: 'Hello. It is through this way.'

I say: 'Buenos. ¿Su capilla es por aquí?'

The boy perks. Upright!

'Si: aqui.'

I offer a slight bow, to the height of the boy's aspirations to
adulthood: 'Gracias.'

Hello, Luke... Don't look back.

In chapel, the principle impression, of shape and no matter the
scale, is that this is a school hall. Plastic-metal classroom chairs might
have sat about six-hundred comfortably. Up-front on the left sit their not-
quite two-dozen. The English are to occupy the front ranks up on the
right. Being first in, I take to the rightmost edge of the second row – to
which we students seem most obviously directed. All perfectly clean –

there is little of that memory of feeling on entering a school hall. Is there a tabernacle? I hardly think to look to see – and don't genuflect. Large, plain-glass windows flood the hall with light. There are certain expressive designs, though the effect is unimposing in terms of Catholicism – Spartan. A breezeblock feel to the concrete of it. Certain impressions of areas of plaster washed pale blue. The floor is just carpeted – glued tiles.

I don't kneel. It is a school hall. You don't *kneel* in a school hall. (Other students kneel behind and beside me. Geoff kneels. Josh kneels. You can *hear* them.) From this point of vantage, it is a simple matter to turn, and to loll a left-arm on the back of the bench, and survey matters.

Across the way, they are a disciplined bunch. In clean and simple uniforms – blazers and greys. Public school – at a sensible level. They barely inspect the English. Such shuffling between themselves seems little reminders as to who might be doing what. It isn't a short wait. Fifteen minutes pass. It is not enough time for the strangeness to form into any real question. The numbers of them. What that might entail. And all *this* space to rattle round in – the oddness. They aren't going to crack at the seams. They aren't going to go mad come exam time and have food fights. Civilized – quite surreal.

Geoff is kneeling – pious. And Josh taking the discipline. And Henry being pure. Adedokun knows the environment and sits quietly. It seems such indelicate behaviour – kneeling. And such an inevitable show of it – being pure.

Suddenly, an old and religious woman – a not-nun – is talking to me. She is remarkably short and trying to tell me something. I stand and stoop. There is no way I am going to get what she's going on about, but that's not stopping her. It is full of anxiety – and looks to be about the seats. Sharp gestures – and there is a grand mime. She has perfectly

309

square and white front teeth. My body copies hers. I open my mouth, to try and catch it, and my eyes go round as golf balls. When she has concluded what she's needed to say, I sit thinking I must have just had a right telling-off. I think she has probably been telling us to move up a row. Or back a row.

It was not the easiest conversation. Doubt and worry and unease persist.

I sit perched, like I could spring to do anything!

Doubt persists.

The bell chimes and Mass has begun.

Stand.

Priests and the bishops and what-not come onto the school stage – the sanctuary. There are two bishops. One is Archbishop Ricardo, Archbishop of Valladolid. I *think* the next might be Marini… Not being much up on these things. It is a very big deal – if so. Not being in possession of glasses, I begin to stare after an interlude. And become convinced... *It is...* Exciting. A bit of a Henry-moment – you might say.

Well, I go a bit Catholic. It's not like Kylie has just walked on but. I am star-struck. There, then, remain, such capacities. When it comes to the turn of the readings, it is Josh who gets to read the bit allocated to us in Spanish. (So he must have known.) Josh does not pretend a Spanish accent. There is no pretence of not expressing regret that Latin has gone off – and turned into Spanish. Josh does the Spanish in Latin.

I get a maybe-vague drift of a third of the archbishop's homily. I get that it begins with Saint Joseph. And, then, that the archbishop develops a metaphor. I get the 'little donkey' bit.

Oh, Saint Joseph, foster-father of Jesus, most pure spouse of the

310

Virgin Mary, pray for us daily to the same Jesus, the Son of God, that we, being defended by the power of His grace and striving faithfully in life, may be crowned by Him at the hour of death. Amen.

The archbishop speaks to encourage us. Anyone could have got that – no words. The archbishop's talk becomes our future lives. He presses for vocation. This *faith* the little donkey and Joseph – chaste – and so on. Love – the Church. In truth: he beats his heart and he raises his fingertips. He touches his ear and shakes his ear-touched finger vigorously.

The archbishop turns his hand in spirals... *Moreover, the ego being a faculty of containment, its squeezing of its own spiritual essences is what this theatre work[ed] on expressing...* The archbishop uses his bishop's crook as a fifth limb... *To evoke the mystical unity of what is called 'this person', its actors try to create characters they think might work, and so they systematically cast their imagination and recoil only onto the skimpy versions of spiritual life that people think they can afford...*

They all get that speech when they're consecrated. Clearly the archbishop means it – an echo of speeches chased how many times before?

Blessed St. Joseph, I consecrate myself to your honour and give myself to you, that you may always be my father, my protector and my guide in the way of salvation. Obtain for me great purity of heart and a fervent love of the interior life. After your example, may I perform my actions for the greater Glory of God, in union with the Divine Heart of Jesus and the Immaculate Heart of Mary. Pray for me, Saint Joseph, that I may experience the peace and joy of your holy death. Amen.

Well, now, after the homily, we do the most terrifying event, which

311

is real or means nothing at all. We all have been told by The Rector to stand as the Spanish do, when the Spanish stand, and not kneel as the English do. He told us there is an arrogance in not abiding by local custom.

Geoff stands. Josh stands.

We do okay – that bit goes well enough. There is nothing embarrassing. The reality of the altar – the shivering disturbance of reality in the action of the altar – though remote sufficient and includes the school hall – an impossible universe. None of that is challenging. That is God. The consecration. That bit doesn't touch – a mental thing alone by the distance it carries us.

Oh St. Joseph, I never weary contemplating you and Jesus asleep in your arms. I dare not approach while he reposes near your heart. Press him in my name and kiss his fine head for me, and ask him to return the kiss when I draw my dying breath. St. Joseph, patron of departing souls, pray for us. Amen.

The Spanish have rehearsed an English hymn. While, still, in here, there is no un-mic'd acoustic, Julian tries, Henry gives it a go, Geoff *sings* – grurg'ling! I tail-gate Henry – not sticking my neck out. Being normal.

Glorious Saint Joseph, spouse of the immaculate Virgin, obtain for me a pure, humble, charitable mind, and perfect resignation to the divine Will. Be my guide, my father, and my model through life that I may merit to die as you did in the arms of Jesus and Mary. Amen.

Go and sin no more.

Bow your heads and pray for God's blessing.

'Idos, es la despedida.' *Ite missa est.* The Mass is sent.

We sit a moment – the stage is cleared. Hardly aware. It is among the most strange and most beautiful moments – the altar deconstructed after a Mass. Only the cloth is left. The altar's after-glow – of only belief of mere seconds ago and the action. That's faith.

We sit a little time. Then we begin to look between ourselves. Geoff clobbers to his knees… Across the aisle remains a separate continent. By the time I look, they are all gone. But people are milling and standing up. One or two of the young seminarians meet their parents. It is a broken scene. There is an after-Mass *feel* to it. Of great power following-upon sacrifice. Slipped though a gap of a prayer.

Jon continues to pray – obstructing egress. Jon should have been a monk. His head is the shape of Darth Vader's when he takes off the mask. I let that be and genuflect. I step between the row of chairs in front and the school stage. I don't know where I am going. I walk to the rear of the hall – toward the atrium.

Once within the atrium, I could sit on the floor, on the rock-tiles… I crane my neck. Even not doing it – properly – at the time – there is no need not for a thought one is toying with infinity. *Then* – it seems a thought of welcoming infinity. Their school. There would be no banged-doors and family life. And mopped-up plates and… Cricket-bat-action. Dream-face. (In fact, Mum held me back when Dad had had enough – begged the bat off of me – just at that moment of doubt in the killing-stroke. But – dream-face.) A grand elevator shaft forms the hub of it. Their Rector makes big scooping gestures with his hands. The door held. Paul Simon is singing. Their Rector smiles – exaggerated gestures.

In the atrium, not quite knowing what is happening, I look up and around.

313

Me? – *I* say – *or suggest...?* I feel ashamed of my appearance – like brushing my suit down. Spinning in infinity.

Through the door: a long, glass gallery. The gallery is long and it is made of light. It runs alongside a garden. It is glass all along. There is a long row of cloth-covered tables served with drinks and nibbles. I have to say it isn't like a corporate event. At first-glance – such delicacy of touch. Such delicacy of people. *Catholicism works...* Hope awakens. It is not crude and piggy-like. *Such detail.*

I pull my jacket-sleeves down-over my new expensive double-cuffs. It is a fair-old crush of odd people. You might hazard a guess at the Catholic faith. Fly me in the nose to heaven. Turn left. Clothes seem to wear me – the length of the gallery. Ochre-brown gabardine. Saffron-red and chocolate... Henry starts-off about the fabulous canapés. There are teeny mounds of real caviar, which neither Henry nor I have ever tasted before. For we are a crude bunch. For we are a savage race. Nibbles and good wine run the way along. And along the way, *en route*, the smart crowd has plenty to say in Spanish. This a navigable crush – a *La Boheme* – of smiles – handshakes. And encouragements. They don't speak English – or if they do they aren't saying. Elegant people. Let them speak. Not having a clue what they're going on about. I am sensing them giving me my extra inch – for they are relatively short. One senses oneself like Henry is looking down on them. Oh, I yell something back. *Motions...* I *manoeuvre* three tables... A matter of questionable navigation – errant knight-moves. And diminishing wine. Henry tags along with me and I don't want that – lose that. A question of pace and canapés.

There they are: up at the far end. The puzzle is to get there. Here is a game... Adult-thinned... Needing to navigate. Dazing... That is truth –

314

that is what was true – just there.

Adults thin and seem less certain. They can be easily satisfied. Tables have been picked-over well enough. Little remains. Self-excluded from the crush-end. Conversations pass and end. I slide on by. *Viking... North Utsire... South Utsire... Forties... Cromarty... Forth... Tyne... Dogger... Fisher... German Bight... Humber... Thames... Dover... Wight... Portland... Plymouth... Biscay... Trafalgar... FitzRoy... Sole... Lundy... Fastnet... Irish Sea... Shannon... Rockall... Malin... Hebrides... Bailey... Fair Isle... Faeroes... Southeast Iceland...* Truth has already run out of things. Pretend-daze. I am following a call – I am at quest. Vocation. Just there... A table spills with crisps and soft drinks... Remember!

Henry is gone now – blocked by a glancing prawn. I pick the tables. All the food gone – constellated crumbs. I get the Spanish ready in my head. I place my glass carefully – wait there – on the penultimate table. Then – beyond knowing these days how to do this bit properly – I remember and force an exaggerated teacher-face. That will have to do.

This folly... This bursting indecision... But why the fear? And such compulsive over-rendering... The terror of it. Such risk – such hazard. So intense the emotional response – Where did I go?

That beginning quivers... *Is it* sex inside? When I was their age... Nothing. I've got it all wrong. I was nothing.

When there must have been a moment. It seems some act of cowardice, looking back, falsified – or of misrecognition. An evasion. Nothing. (When did love go wrong?) It shows in love – at risk of everything. Who are you? I'm....

I – Tomàs – catch one pair of glistening eyes…

And this is the element. This – childhood – bubbling. Popped with pockets – air. Love inside – alive-still. Bubbling – pockets of air. Unfixed – unidentified. No-one-man – all lovely.

Fear of my own expansion.

They are a dance that didn't happen. (They are small – stepped up to them.) This is fiction now again – as it was.

Here goes:

'¡Veo que han mantenido la buena comida aquí por ustedes mismos!'

The next bit is rather a flurry. (There *are best* memories – in photographs. The summer boat – my spinner-hooks thrash hoisted-mackerel... Dad takes the hooks out of them – and, as he does, shows his boy, the son, the way to do it. Off the coast at Plymouth.) A dozen boys.

Of a sudden, I come to realize the full extent of the relative heights involved. I realize their age – and time has stopped – but they are definitely shorter. In whiplash-economy, they clatter at brace-level up at me.

I stand back and, of an instant, open my arms, and in terrible Spanish: 'Ah, mis amigos. Mucho gusto en conocer los. Desafortunadamente, yo no hablo mucho español. Pero…'

I shrug – make jazz-hands.

Now officially hilarious, the children come at me. Skin and bright-eyes. Jewelled teeth – like castanets. And: *Clacker-clacker-clacker-clacker…* Containing laughter. Hands half-cupping my ears, I say, in English: '*Woh woh woh…*' I look impervious to fear. I look fearless.

A boy has emerged as leader and shushes the rest. Not quite chin-height. A beaming Spanish kid. This is comedy central. Head craned –

316

dark, winged hair. Of an age whereby space doesn't signify. A bold little fellow determined to have their fun.

We agree: we practically shake hands on it. The game becomes to get Tomàs to say rude words.

¿Como...? Diga...

As I figure what the game is, it becomes yet ever-increasingly proper hilarious. After all, I can just hand them back at the end of this. It is with much protestation of innocence, I feel it incumbent upon myself to say:

'¡Debes entender: yo soy un seminarista! ¡No puedo decir tales cosas!'

So, laughing, insincerely, for the sake of the record...

But Henry has found us. Through some inertial frame of lousy reference...

The kids are by now screaming. Henry wants a piece of it.

Henry says – wanting a piece of it: 'What are you doing?'

But I *am* immune. I'm busy. Pig in clover. (Once, in bright-light boat-churn – the Aegean – gradually I came to realize a pervading whiff of sea-stink as emanating from my own pumps. Thusly shrugged – and half-gestured tucking my feet away. There was nothing I could do about it for the next ten minutes. All the local teenagers who dived from the rocks all afternoon passed their glances between themselves – then let me off when they saw I was embarrassed.) Though I fancy I now catch from Henry something like the incipient reproof. The recollection of dignity. Of due status. Henry's face is odds-and-ends. Youth given a cause. Between open-desire and an already-known insistency.

This the crash and tumble of it: this the breaking shore.

Henry says: 'Are they doing what I think they're doing?'

'I think that's the general idea.'

'Are they saying…?'

'Yeah, I think so.'

Henry's voice flukes:

The kids are screaming.

'You're ridiculous!'

In few curt words, it rolls out of me. *Henry wears such cheap shoes…*

'Well, you'd know about that!' I say.

It is, though, getting to be a bit much. I am grateful when one of their priests arrives. I make the American time-out gesture. I make my arms a 'T'.

Henry has spoilt it, anyway. But, as I mimic the gentling-down, I and the young priest laugh together, and that puts Henry wobbling loose like a spare part. He can no longer ruin things – having neither integrated at an appropriate level, that of friend, nor minimally-adequate Spanish.

They pressed on me frighteningly close, though. A trained instinct: never make skin-contact. A teacher's hover-touch: the shape of safe-space. Teeth, wide-eyes, and clatter.

They were a little can of worms, and their priest shivered up inside of them. There was a lot of laughter and they were pulling at my clothes. I say with gusto to the priest, spreading my hands wide, so that everyone might hear:

'¡Usted tiene muchos buenos estudiantes!'

Hands off, hands up… Deploy an exaggerated face. They always pick-up on any form of falsehood. Making the sign with my forearms: T, T, T, T.

The young priest settles them.

However, now, the next thing is already happening. The previous moment breaks.

I look back along the length of the gallery. Only two stragglers remain together. One emphatically *being told*... I walk back into the atrium. It is to the opposite wing they want me, though there is no-one beckoning.

This, also, is a hall. It is a school gym. The wooden floor is sprung, though there are no games marked on it. A horse-shoe of dressed-tables runs the way around. It seems there are more people than previously accounted for.

They have a seating-plan on a board – on an easel – just inside of the entrance. I read it and see I am placed near the head of the table. All the other English (students) are down one leg together at the far end of it. (Horse-shoe – conference formation.)

'Oh nice,' think I!

It seems apt. It seems fitting. (Finally a bit of acknowledgement! I guess I'm thinking. Where's the curtain? Where's the rope?)

I walk the way around. I note the arrangements – checking the names on little pieces of paper. And get my seat, which I stand behind. Their Rector, on his way around, pauses behind me and massages my shoulders. It is the nicest thing just right now. It is like no-one put him up to it. I just let him do it and don't think about 'relaxing' – obvs smile thanks. (The last time a relative stranger did this to me – I just let him do it and said thanks.)

As people take their places, it is good. I can't see the smudgy sorts of faces obscuring the distance between me and my English compañeros. I *notice* them down there... I'm not asking questions about it. Am I meant to fail or is this a treat? Who might fathom the mind of The Rector! I am – …

Standing, I engage in mutual pleasantries. (In considerable relief: I am just rightly lubed.) Two are adult seminarians – of whom there are three at the seminary. With their Rector's massage, and with the ongoing finding of seats, it is a matter of simple greeting – pleasantries – and textural messages. Once we have sat and the meal begun – of others, there is an old man, who gives his attention to his food, which is excellent. A man to that man's right – whom I can't see. My – Tomàs's left-side a blind-spot. And priests and bishops.

The language is going to be hard work. You couldn't say it is a flow of conversation. But, having accepted that, it becomes an enjoyable experience. *How do you like the food? It is perfect: very good ingredients and great skill. Since how many years are you here? Three years. How are your studies? I find it different…* Confit duck for a starter with the liver and rocket. There are chilled shot glasses of an amuse bouche. They speak English; I speak Spanish. That works. And there is plenty of eye-contact – while we are eating, chewing, and the food speaks most of it. Making sure. We chomp and smile. It is very good. It helps that, with each course, the adult seminarians perform Refectorial duties, this meaning they have to get up and remove the plates and bring the next course in. This provides natural breaks, and a bit of a breather.

In terms of what might be conversation, I burn to know what they do all day. Coming from my own perspective – as I do – I find their possibility very strange. They are going to become priests. Really – well on their way. That is marked in them. Their *journey* holds no more obvious floundering courses. It is a lineal path.

That thought both attracts and repels me – but could their humanity

320

do it? Not get through – but convince the same endings of me and my desired happiness? (Can transubstantiation happen in my hands?) Of course, I want to ask if their classes are any good. Of course, I don't. That desire gets blocked and chokes inside. For I want to know – is it good or shit? – but *vaguely* must acknowledge that manner of ulterior motive. Desire to communicate. Bad instinct. *Look at this tangle of thorns...* An egotist. A – me. A – narcissist. (A frightened little boy.) *Behold my suffering...!!!* (Can I be a child and a father? NO! – incorrectly.)

I ask what their classes are – and duly receive a matter of fact answer. The question unreciprocated. The movement of their bodies as they serve is precise and clean. Neither unseasonably masculinized – bloated – nor fey. No: *Right chaps – let's clean-up this bit of bother...* (No, don't confess the English; don't *stir* our business...) Not saying all the time: 'So this seminary is huge: there are 23 of you.' Not saying all the time: 'So Catholic Spain is dying – where are you with that?'

Stick to the food. Later – and Trevor says: 'They've got a football pitch! We've got some raggy old pictures.' They have God... When there is nothing to compare. It is best to keep having a time with the food – the one particle attuned to the present-tense. We are all trying very hard to be excellent guest and hosts. By and large, the Spanish speaking English and the English speaking Spanish is a good idea.

With coffee, the visiting Archbishop – Marini – stands to address the hall. He is a lean man, now in plain clericals. Rarely lean for a bishop. Somewhat like me, he has a wavy-arms quality about him, and the head thrusts markedly. His belt cinched-tight – as if he's lost weight. It seems not filling his uniform – as if we, terminal, always, as our truth emerges, stark and stick-like, and as the other evaporates, cinch tight – and ever

321

tighter and tighter – cinching a uniform. A lean old sort of bird. Too lean – really. Wispy, ragged, unseen-legs. He is obviously a nice man. His central-line a Giacometti. Life's next cusp – that of death. The Archbishop speaks manageable Spanish arranged in discrete chunks.

His themes recapitulate what he said at Mass. He speaks to an idea of the young. He speaks to encourage them. Or, perhaps, he speaks to an idea of encouragement. Prior-delivered speeches – re-enacted. God's call. Vocation. It is about the young…

All the bishops get this speech. Archbishop Marini *implores* the wall opposite… His gaze somewhere *through* the wall opposite. Where he pitches his totalized, absent gaze – and himself here. The boys look at him – rather than at what he is looking at. Down on the English-side, Philip chews. Josh listens – understanding the Spanish. (Julian sits in pause-mode. Henry nibbles.) One simply tries to break it down to full-stops. I have drunk very little wine. There is news – and the state of affairs – the state of things. Given how it's all shit – the Archbishop might just as well have been saying, in so many words. Confidence. Going forward. *And we shall fight them on the beaches, and…* The struggle. Saint Paul. He chastises and encourages. In full-belief of his episcopal authority.

The Archbishop concludes his speech. Then is encouraged to sit. Their Rector stands to thank the Archbishop. He thanks his other guests, the English especially among us. As we relax, there are musical presentations as the meal concludes.

Digestifs are served. The choice is either brandy or a lemon liqueur. As plates and what-not are taken away, and the drinks served, a performance is erected, within the centre of the horse-shoe. Then they sing in small groups – two performances. Minstrel-fashion. The adult seminarians – on voice and guitar. And priests sing in twos. They have arranged and play folksy compositions – with violin and guitar – not using microphones. Truly, it is an honour. A curious precious-thing. It tinkles – quite remotely. As, had this taken place in a cafe, on a bawdy promenade, one might have jigged, and danced with the thought of the piece. In formal context – sectioned. Abstracted – a centre of joyful activity. It is rarely pure. We are spectators. Quite remotely.

Once the meal is concluded, there is no hanging about. We all stand to leave. The beat is highly orderly – metronomic. I and the adult Spanish seminarian stand to shake hands and express our delight in one another. A gift. It has been ornate – a treasure. *My friend, I should like you to have this…* [It will be far, far later, when we greet one another again in a church – 'Tomàs!' – that I will know I've done okay. *'Tomàs!'* *– my friend…*

The Rector won't want us to have that – pulling us out through the church door and onto the street outside. But I'll do it in any case. Howsoever briefly – imperfectly to the point of injuring the gift – violating a young man's feelings. But – The Rector. By then, it will be curious how things have moved so far. There shall seem life's opposite of any such untruth and egoism – careerism. The Rector does me an injury there.]

The Spanish seminarians set about clearing up. I walk back again toward the atrium. This hall debris-strewn – a satisfied mess. I follow the English, through the exterior doors, to the top of the steps. They are going to play football. Realizing what's up, I watch as they walk their bags to a distant annex. A changing-room. Off to get changed. How and when they knew… On the steps, then, I stand alone. No-one is near. Unusually and unexpectedly. Timetable – evaporated! *Poof…!*

I tuck myself in a bit. (My belt does not cinch tightly enough.) There the football pitch, and there a tennis court. A brief copse of evergreen trees – towering pines. Homely. Not even as if they don't know things here grow differently.

My shirt, still, is very baggy. Still – alone. A rare treat. Authorized within the timetable. My trousers are falling down. An empty scene.

Accepting this cinematic provision, I wander down the steps and toward the trees. It must be the first time in centuries I don't feel anyone watching me.

Alone, quietly, silently. Lunch-blurred. I could do with a wash after eating. Rinse my face. There seems no noise. There is no breeze or a cloud in the sky. Practically noiseless but for my shoes on steps then brown-dust and gravel.

A totalizing gaze – a scopic pleasure… Colours leached to grey-gold dust and blue-sky. I have sunglasses in my pocket, Ray-Bans, but I don't want to wear them. The suit is only Marks and Spencer. I – touch a tree. Knowing the artifice. Deliberately-consciously – and think: *Tomàs touched a tree.* If, then, it were the most thoroughly decentring act – is there a line at the edge of it? (Were The Rector to fall in a forest, and there were no seminarians to hear, is anything real?) Between consciousness and sanity… A place. Between the mere exhibit of an act for its own sake? An *I*… A saving-grace to subjectivity. *I am a camera: me no Leica…*

It could only be three minutes. Then come boys. Here they come! Everybody! Boys descend – that great concrete-monumental flight of steps. Boys descend with terrible pace the great steps… Now they are out of uniform. Wiry in sports kit. No brands I recognize. The primary effect is visual – noise yet flattened.

In the pitch, boys commence formations, get a ball in play.

One impression is of old coding – as when they used to riff-off the clock-speed of a computer in order to squeeze the instruction-set toward the limit of efficiency. This, however, other, simply modern. Fully-tooled. The pure reduced-instruction to the necessary action. No flabby. Only the pure intent.

I might look – but I can't see. Football. Elsewise, there commence recreational activities. BMX bikes appear from nowhere.

I turn to look – the football pitch: an instant, massed Subbuteo. Shocking. The way they move the ball is shocking. Fool-the-eye quick. Clinicism. Perhaps a half-dozen of the younger boys take to the tennis courts.

I watch through the wire grill surrounding the pitch and the tennis courts. I wander into the tennis courts. There is a bench placed just inside the gate. I sit – and am feeling pretty sleepy. It is benign – and disconnected as if nothing is real. Just in case I have not already told you, I am wearing my linen suit.

It is an odd thing – all this life. They are there and I am purest scenery. My feeling already includes them.

And, I think, why should I not treat this matter as such?

I am lunched and old – sat in a mild way, stooping. I am old and they are young. Admit the severance. Let Mr Storey have his reverie. Let Mr Storey have his prayer. And not cajole and not get cross. I watch them play.

They aren't very good at tennis. They aren't trying *to beat*... But they pat the ball. An approximate obedience of racquet and ball to the mind's willing… Half-unexpected surprise when the ball goes the right way – through the most friendly arc – through the most friendly-loveliest distance between two points!

I set about becoming familiar. That I am old and they are young. At prayer. I wear my polished black shoes and my linen suit. Just let me be and feel peacefully. Tomàs is happy.

The sun absorbs my face. Legs – in all that fabric. Partridge-breast and chicken wings. Spindly saplings. My shoes are of the pointy variety – but that's what they had in the shop. Perhaps I look as if I *should* play football… Or, at least, follow a team.

I must have been sat this way minutes and the tennis ball rolls between my feet. Then I reach and find it. I stand to throw it back – and make a swish with my arm as if I'd like to have a go with a tennis racquet. The magic-circle is back at me. They converge. Each offers his racquet, dangling the head down as if discharged in parley. In expression strictly adult – imprinted on youth's physiognomy. They are Spanish. Posh Spanish. Each five foot of them. Their manner, and the outright nobility of it, sincere beyond not taking it seriously.

I take my tie and my jacket off. I hang my jacket on the gate. This shirt is ridiculous – it was the best I could do in *El Corte Ingles* for my neck size. It cost a lot, and billows. It is a fine cloth, and the buttons are pearl, but the cut is ridiculous. And it falls out – while my trousers fall down. My shoes court goofy, *clown* danger, and a twisted ankle.

I have an iffy serve and I show that off to them. That was – questionable. They don't return it. Bit crap – I mean on my part.

We get the ball back and forth to each-other well enough underhand – after that.

326

The kids indulge me – painstakingly alert. In my head, it is all: 'Tomàs! Tomàs!' It is amazing my shoes survive. We play a tag system. Then I offer my racquet to the boy at the side who maybe doesn't often get a go. He *takes* it – but you have later to think: Was that bad? *Was that the problem?* Doing that. Did he *want* that?

Well, at the edge of insanity – Catholicism speaks. And becomes a kind of managed-insanity. Subject-position fear – in the creative-way of things. When I'm up again, their Rector comes into the court and borrows a racquet and fires a shot at me. It is a classic back-hand swing. I just get to the ball, but it wipes me out. I clap with my racquet and make a bow. We both laugh.

The boy who takes the racquet from their Rector now serves at me with good speed, but he is aiming in a way that makes it easy for me. I get there and – just – find the ball and make it over the net. I make the boy run, though hadn't meant to. Gradually, we are playing lower over the net. It is becoming more like: 'I serve now!' We aren't keeping points. And if it goes out, lick the thing back in play. There is more of a banging it. Fuck the shoes. My partner does most of the running-work. I hang around the baseline, picking up the odd stroke with even some semblance of elegance, far enough away from the action for the matter to be quite abstract. A matter of means and modes – of averages. I find if I can just get the ball in the general direction... The racquet might be swung with ease, and a child's teeth satisfactorily avoided. For, whatever I might be, I am no PE teacher.

Thus – abstracted – I notice Henry. Here comes Henry... through the great swing-doors at the top of the steps. With Paul and Julian. Having been given the royal-tour. There they stand and breathe it in. Visiting dignitaries.

327

Thus the tableau: Pisgah-view colonial. Thus the arrangement – the four of them seem to say. *All this shall be yours…* So – as their guide concludes flattery… Football, BMX bikes, tennis… wasteland. So their posture accepts its possession as theirs of this.

Their guide leaving them, the students stand a moment at the top of the steps. Royally. What they look like… Their guide must have been quite obsequious. Nurturing their conceit in this place… What they see… But he is gone now – left them to it.

Then, as if it were an after-shock of momentary, collected dignity having passed, Henry, goof-English, all his big arms swung colonial… And from the top of the steps – Henry makes straight for me in the tennis court. Henry *strides* directly here. It is not like he ambles down – and snatches at the next incidentally. From the steps – I am certain of this – he decides on me.

Once within the tennis-court, Henry steps directly to me. Henry disregards children present. It is as if in his own mind he has frozen the action. Henry tells me I look a disgrace and that I should be ashamed of myself. He yelps it in front of the children:

'You look a disgrace! You should be ashamed of yourself! You look a disgrace!'

Panting, much empowered, and tucking myself in, I say: 'Yeah, look at yourself, mate.'

'What do you mean by that? What do you mean by that? What do you mean by that?'

It isn't very nice of me either. But I feel of a moment all that Henry's limited grasp on English social-class, and English-adulthood, knows it lacks and feels in a moment it supersedes. And just exactly how to hurt it and twist it about a bit.

Henry's accent is the fakiest – self-righteous, unmasturbated. Poor-schools – and paper-thin bedroom-walls. Cars. That obsequious-tint of a world you have to take your shoes off.

Small children – fourteen, fifteen – who prefer a paperback – because you can rustle it, malleable, in your hands – more frail and textual – and if you ask them, they'll look a little embarrassed and say, with confessed, commuted, private joy, if it's really good: 'It's really good.'

That there is a world – and that it doesn't align and can never be made to.

My index finger – from my eyes – traces slowly once up Henry's eyes. I wear my teeth half-bared in stalled aggression. Henry's eyes – disregarding the periphery. None could mistake it for a happy smile. Henry gets nervous and laughs. I square-up at him. I tuck myself in again. Then ride my finger close: here, here. Henry's mouth. Now I have him held – I touch the nearest space of Henry's mouth and whisper:

'Cheap fake.'

The boys see what just happened.

(It has been an appalling display in front of the children.)

Then Henry is gone.

It has done me a spot of good to hurt Henry...

No. I sit on the bench. The football they play through the wire-grill...

The boy comes and sits by me.

My tennis done for now, my boy, to whom I gave the racquet, comes and sits by me. Clothed in sagging own-brands... Not by any estimation a cool kid. One of the holy ones. Need – estimation written all over him.

He has some English. It is a cross-negotiation.

He – the boy just wants to speak. It isn't even that – he wants not to! *Hello, hello*… He wants to gaze into my eyes and my whole face at someone like him.

Others come to join. Within the tennis court – a cluster. As they dangle and pull on the wire mesh – from the football. Those in the football pitch want to know – through the wire – why I do not play football. They are pretty direct about this: certainly, the question requires a lie.

They hang on the wire fence.

I shrug-big and tell them I prefer tennis. (Never say: I don't like football.) I hope the question will go away. I – gesture… Clumsy indicative active. This they appear to accept – as an answer. They don't *lose* interest, and seem happy enough with it. I and my boy – we talk a bit. We get the gist of the spirit that is offered.

We get to the boarding school question. The skinny kids hang in the fencing. The boarding-school question. Is it worth it? Are we better? Does it pay?

I don't know how it got here, but they want to know. Their situation is, they are weekly borders. They go home Friday-evening. A different boy says they have Mass each day – when I ask about their religion here. It could have got lost in translation: 'We have Mass every day.'

There is a way the boy says it makes me think he's got the words right. (I get a vision of people who don't have Mass each day.)

Before we get too deep, half of them have only just been discovering the English to tell me they have lessons in English – and maths, and science, and biology. I get the words in English for the timetable. (Their Saturdays don't exist.) You can basically see how *my* boy was wary of accepting the tennis racquet.

What's it like out there? ... The own-clothes youths on Calle Merced. They all listen intently – when I look as if I might be about to speak. They are sharp-keen – active – good at chess.

Whereas this – has something else in him – akin to wonder. I'd like to say he is Simon in Lord Of The Flies, but that's not true – there is something else in him.

While they all are itemizing – he seems quite accepting of it. Known uncertain-happiness. And not surviving as a person in home-clothes on the gates of the municipal-school on Calle Merced. Where one must be inevitably categorized. Graded. Subject to market-conditions – itemized. Gay, black, Jew or gentile, white, straight... The one where he's good at maths. The one where he's a botanist. (He likes golf and he likes wearing girly pants.) Known – a name – identified. There is difference in all of them. Aware – but you get the impression he rather likes it – while they, perhaps, aren't so sure.

A mode of thought abstracted from a boy's domestic sphere. It is, perhaps, the Archbishop's encouragement which has set the tone. I seem calm – my noise in head abated. I am at peace beyond this commentary. I reflect. This boy's huge reflective eyes – the innocence. Screened by now this adult mass – I am a teacher, lastly; this is the last time; I know this and it is finally complete. Screened in this seminary. Peaceful in this place. Safe here.

I say: 'Quizás estos tiempos son difíciles. Quizás el mundo no es un lugar tan inocente como quizás lo era antes. Pues bien, si esto es cierto, es humano a preocuparse un poco. Y en su seminario y en la mía... Quizas hay retos. Y no estamos seguros de dónde vamos. ¿Quién sabe? El futuro. ¡Pero hay gran alegría hoy!'

*

Once, a long time ago, I – Tomàs shared the back of a cab late-night from Soho to Pimlico – Dolphin Square. They were the last days of summer – school the next week. Two of us sat in the back. The three of us had tucked ourselves away – flopped on the sofa at the back of the restaurant in Soho. He was sixteen. A beautiful lad – he went to a different school. The boy he'd spent the summer in love with sat up front. The boy who'd brought him out, and to whom he came out. But he was putting him away now. Love, elicited, had been played – disposed. For the terrible ego involved in the front passenger-seat of this mini-cab… The boy had been acquired, consumed, and now disposed. The purpose of him fleetingly satisfied… he'd had him.

So, on the back seat, the boy urgently pressed my face, almost-not-touching mine. Urgently, tearfully, having achieved self-consciousness. He implored me… It wasn't kissing, but so close, his lips flickered over mine, touching, as he asked with urgent and demanding insistence: 'Is it really okay?' He was crying, tears were streaming down his face, and I held him, like a little boy, panicked in my hands, so intently, and oh my dear yes you are fine you are fine you are better than fine.

That night, front-seat boy declared the day done for him and passed out in the available narrow bed. The beautiful boy and I had a moment in the kitchen, where in this harsh light, he asked me again if it was okay, and if he was – in a way permitted to go and get in bed with the other boy. He was in love so desperate. Permission-granted – beauty-assured – off he went to cuddle-up next to him. He must have just known love so much – that to cuddle-up next to him.

That night, in Dolphin Square, I watched the Thames scroll past. It

332

was a top-storey flat. I smoked and drank – there was no coke – staying in the kitchen. That flat had comings and goings. Mostly, whoever they were that night were already asleep when we'd got there. Finally, the bed in the room next to theirs was free, so I passed out there, where another boy's shelves had been neatly arranged with toy-soldiers. The room didn't seem to mind, and had probably seen far worse, and my sleep must have given me two hours. In the morning, front-seat boy stayed in bed and thus dismissed us. In the tube, at the parting of the ways, I kissed beauty-assured on the forehead, with my hands on his upper-arms. It was right doing that – and everything in me was right doing that. Almost it was perfect. It was like being tiny and brittle and small in an adult shape. And not 'being a man' about it – just – well – *relinquishing*. No delusions, no strange pretend-desires. Just relinquishing. Heart-to-heart response. Quite pure. Holding – like there was a man in me/him. The means of the communication careful – with artistry. And with nothing imposed – and with no ready-made imposition – save the absolute minimum to subsist. And he was sixteen. Not thirteen, fourteen. He was sixteen. More 1987 than 1983. So, maybe, you need to look there.

I sit on the bench in the tennis court, and I watch Jorge riding his bike, at whim, in big infinity-loops about the dust grounds. The football had come to an end. I sit and there are the half dozen boys who've grouped around. Our English priests don't know what's up. The Rector doesn't care. Father Richard grows visibly-agitated. Through the grille, Father Gerry agrees he and I will not be doing our 'spiritual direction' this afternoon. With the coterie – Father Richard could never have imagined a way through. Things are tidying up. The English have all gone to get changed. I'll have to keep an eye out for the football crowd. I need to walk back to the college with them. I don't know the way.

The boy says: 'You are kind. Will you come to visit us again?'

I say: 'Eso espero. No se cuando – pero espero.'

Of course, it is never going to happen. That little touch on life... I believe it in the part of the brain that believes. I can't so don't say: 'Yes, I promise.'

Everyone sort of gets that. Just pretend. It's just pretend. There is a space opened; and there is a space closed. It is a bit gutting – the way they are too young and get that. Seeing them walk past, I say: 'Mi compañeros...'

There are rapid expressions. Toward what we aren't doing – a shaking of hands.

I have to run to join up with them.

When I catch up with the English, they don't acknowledge me. That isn't personal – they are just missing God. It has been too many hours since they last prayed. When I look back, I see the children have already disbursed – the pitch and court are empty.

*

Highs turn to lows...

There isn't time for a shower before evening prayer. Afterward, The Rector is arranging the notice board. He has a new magnetic board. Vulnerably fresh from prayer, I make a mistake. I say:

'Father, that was the best day in Valladolid ever.'

That was stupid. So stupid I do it again: '*That was the best day ever!*'

No-one seems happy. I hang and over-play it – gushing. *They look terrible*... I leave them just as soon as I can. I go to the gym for a swim. I am alone there, in a lane, and next, the only other person in the whole

334

pool, a white woman, powers up and down her lane. She has paddles strapped to her hands. Doing the fancy turns – each end. Strangely blonde – in a swimming cap. The tetrahedral shape of water – hydrogen-bonds. I stretch and glide one length for her three. Though – thinking of the shape of liquid-water – at the molecular level – hydrogen bonds – it makes me think of funk and boogy.

We never do meet those boys again. Only a little later, as mentioned above, we are in a church. It isn't the basilica. There is one of those fraternities bowing its flags at the consecration. A happy voice calls to me: 'Tomàs!'

It is the young man – a deacon – with whom we had lunch. His happiness in seeing me – well, it is beyond lovely to see him; it blows my mind away. But we were being moved on. Quite possibly, none other of us remembers the day at the diocesan seminary – as above. I dash the few meters toward him and then can't go any further, not all the way, because only so much limited stretch from within the interdiction – The Rector doesn't want it. It leaves a bad taste in my mouth. And it is embarrassing being seen. Perhaps the young man understands but it is so very abrupt. A young-man's puzzled-face smiles. I wave a little wave closer to his chest. *Au revoir les enfants…* Then I – Tomàs must point behind myself – gotta go there. The Rector told us, at the start, we'd have the special Mass, in the basilica, together the last Friday of each month.

It is only a little thing… It has only just been finalized…

My diary is by this point solid lies. (It was meant to collapse – of course it was.) It is scrawl as well, even at the start of the entry. A-falling and a-tumbling…

335

On Wednesday, I write in my diary:

'A piece of me came back to life today. I haven't mucked around with a bunch of kids for years. Privileged access. I felt flattered. It was disconcerting for a moment to see boys' laughter. Much hilarity all round – they were making me say rude words! But you ride along with it and discover it's good and only hilarity… Maybe I'm (still!) guapo!

'I have to acknowledge a fear of it. Adult England. England is so fucked up. No: oh wow, beautiful! Sexualization. You become afraid to look. It's an emotional response – God help us. Maybe it's a lack of fear they detect. That fits with the way their priests love them. They are very tactile. Such fear in me tapping into my youngest days, which ought to be able to come through but can't in this bullshit – all of them trying to be so grown up like Henry.

'There are crimes against life in this place and it's seeming it all is. I know they can't believe it. It's taking so much late-night slop – booze, okay, booze – to countermand a real world. I'm exhausted – numb all day until you get to the gym and that's the level the crazy talk can't get you much but just agitates – leaving inside numb consciousness. This being where there is at least submission – though if Jesus isn't. At least there I can stare out at it all and the devil in each tiny bit of it. But that's not life inside there. Life is spark and energy.'

Of course, it was meant to collapse. Of course it wasn't meant to survive close inspection.

Since before the initial audacity. Since before the first email…

And bath-time confessionals.

It is too big a part and it is too much to hold in my head and I can't do it.

Chapter Nine

Friday, Lent 2. The skein cracks again in 'Intellectual Development'. After this, I expect to be summoned to The Rector's office to be expelled. *Tomàs, with the best will in the world... Surely – .* We are *doing* the Fall.

We have a photocopied handout on sap-green paper. This isn't of a print-out but of a book. It is half a splayed side. (Photocopied – black – distorted letters – splurged-down into swamp and trees.) Lights down, textures missing... *Of man's first disobedience...* As by powerpoint. Null grey – the room. As if a single pixel of English sky had been extrapolated... A whir of a cooling-fan in the projector. That bit toward the start of the Bible Jesus needs.

Quite interestingly: this bit of the Bible is possibly written to signify the exile of the priestly-king from his palace-temple in Jerusalem, i.e. with the exile, and is, as such, a fresh insert to the deuteronomic text, rather than its being an earlier text of any prior importance to the Yahweh cult.

Hands sit on desks. Caged birds. Julian puts his iphone in his pocket. The Rector tells us Adam and Eve *really* existed. He says it in the different way – that, at the same time, Adam and Eve, on some lesser, factual level, didn't exist at all.

He says: 'We *know* that...'

De-accenting the word *know*. Hardly completing His sentences.

Sleep… like a wake-up alarm that goes off at the wrong time – pulling you back the wrong way back down into it. I strain… An error… Fought for… Brain an emptied fist…

The hand-out is the sort meant to shut you up. It is printed on green paper – if that were significant. He could have said: 'Turn to page one.' For the photocopied passage in question is of that bit of the Bible. Then He performs a sort of prac-crit – on Genesis 2-3. He keeps saying – when Adam and Eve eat the apple – 'The language *changes*. The very *language* changes. The *language changes*.'

What is a soul, anyway?

Hijacked by Christian faith. By Greek philosophy. Alexandria – Putative Time Of Jesus (PTOJ). Cultural melting-pot of… Hellenized.

The very *language* changes… He means they've started using different sorts of words to each other in different ways. They've started saying different things to each other. But He makes it sound fancier.

The language of *fiat*. The language of petition – the language of prayer… Language of God in context of human sin. Language of blame – of recrimination. Language of judgement – exile.

The Rector *draws* upon decentring – French schools of thought – as they dug and picked it apart – with teaspoons in the 1980s. That which be linguistic-meaning. The Rector keeps saying it. *The very language changes*… It must have been said to Him in class once – pronging Him at the edge of a similar unconsciousness. The Rector's grip on semantics was born slippy... So now He repeats it… ('Language' cf. 'discourse' cf. 'text'.) Having copied the style of the thought but not...

Presently, I ask one of my questions.

It is important to make The Rector stop talking just for a little while.

338

A bit of a breather.

My voice sheers between Scouse-sprawl, RP, and Estuary English. On the outside it comes across – croaky complaint, and layered incredulity – school vowels. And I am just being a bloody nuisance. So I say:

'If then we now accept the Biblical account as being effectively a mythic representation of some human truth, which draws us to God, and which expresses our relationship with God, now and historically, and which is not nor was ever intended to be read as history, as we now usually understand that term, so in other words there's no Adam, no Eve, no Garden of Eden, historically – that it is what we call in the Church anagogical history – and given that we now accept the fact of evolution, over billions of years, then when did the Fall happen? And what happened, and who was involved?'

Thusly I begin, but then I lose the intensity. My spunk is gone. I'd meant to make some different point, but it gave up on me.

My focus, anyway, is shattered from me these days. My hands become foolish, ironic. A loose intellectual – a boxed rave. I have ceased to study myself by the time I next say: 'What date was it? Ballpark figure: when exactly are we talking about what happened exactly? I mean…'

But I don't feel better at all. Crabs in my brain, and they are crawling all over me. Still I've forgotten how not to speak:

'Did our hominid precursors live such shiny upstanding lives? Do we even have any idea what we pretend to believe these days? When was Original Sin written into us?'

The Rector says: 'We don't know that. All we know is, there was a Fall.'

I say: 'So this might have been pre-homo-sapiens? What is the Church position on the species-definitions of human, historically considered?'

The Rector says: 'We don't know that.'

I say: 'It's quite an interesting point, though, isn't it? And presumably deserves some kind of answer. When is a soul not a soul? Assuming that we Fell sometime after we were given souls. If we're even halfway serious about this. Actually, what is a soul? How are we defining that? We can go back millions of years, in terms of hominids, and find art, tool-making, language an emergent-probability – Do they have souls?'

Silence. The room shuffles. The room says no.

The Rector says: 'We don't know that.'

I say: 'So when was the Fall?'

'We only know: it happened.'

Well anyway, nothing matters now. In myth. In nothing-time. So holding my moment in court, I piss around with it, saying:

'How do we account for linguistic capabilities on the part of other animals, such as dogs?'

'Tomàs, I think studies in apes over the years have proven their abilities to be quite limited in the extreme. The human brain is – wondrously different. It is unique in Creation.'

The missing link! The aquatic stage! Waterside apes! There on the sea's verge. (Look at them! See them now!) Blubber. Waxy babies. Water. Upright man. Stoop for easy shell food. Riches. Brain forms. Eyes develop. Omega 3. Explains everything.

'Not apes,' I say. 'Dogs.'

The Rector says: 'There were, or, I don't know, have been,

340

experiments with monkeys, chimpanzees, what not, and – I don't know what is clear, but what is clear is –'

'No. Not monkeys. I didn't say monkeys... I didn't say apes. Dogs. How do we account for the linguistic capabilities of dogs? The point being that if a dog can learn to recognize words, then that is symbolic, representational thinking. It is linguistic. It is modelling the world linguistically. That is of enormous significance. Words are standing in for things.'

Henry has had enough. He blurts for the world to hear: 'It's conditioning!'

The Rector says nothing. Nor do I – brain wasted – fried. (I do this, then you do this...) It can't think multi-dimensionally around thoughts. Three-dimensional-chess has failed... Henry continues:

'It's completely ridiculous! They're mechanical. They don't think. They're not human! They don't think.'

The Rector agrees. The Rector nods. Except He isn't sure *if* He agrees for just one moment. The Rector's eyes, and a momentary trick of His hands... He almost sees it: almost His lie breaks – I mean upon Himself. Briefly cornered lips. Then He smiles but His face lets Him down on it.

'Ridiculous,' Henry ejaculates once more.

Henry is so assured and tries never to think about anything – not in such a way as might vivisect taking its guts apart. He is barely an animal. The limit of his thinking-and-words to reconstruct a world as an image of Henry dog-like. I say:

'If we consider the evolution of the human brain, we seem to trace a development of language-capacity while, as yet, a consensus seems to be that hominids were not yet language-producers. There is a preparedness for language, however a first linguistic utterance has yet to be made. So we might say, a semiological capacity has yet to emerge into the production-phase of the fully linguistic. And then, at some point, bingo, the magic happens. An ulterior capacity evolves – it over-spills itself. From *here* which was formerly everywhere, to – *into* – a new conception of everywhere – this newly constituted linguistic/language community and becomes speech.

'Now this is of significance if we now consider the language-capacities of dogs. Dogs are not language-producers, but equally obviously, they are semiological creatures – all animals are – and demonstrably they are responsive to language – they understand words. So as we can draw a distinction between semiological thinking and linguistic production, so now we can start to ask a few interesting questions about ourselves, by considering dogs in relation to human language. Dogs, just as humans do, learn in the sense that they actively model and interpret their environment – to discover and behave in relation to the meanings/values/significations they discover therein. It's an instinct, so as it is in humans.

'Consider the process. A piece of information, a message, is received, and it must be interpreted, in order to discover its value, and to respond in some way with an appropriate action. Or, if not with a clearly delineated action – human puts hand in pocket: dog anticipates biscuit and becomes alert and sits imploring biscuit – then with an emotion/thought/feeling – even a plan – a brain-event, which is evinced and which we can also interpret – "Who's a good boy!" Dog/infant/adult-male – smiles!

'Now dogs have evolved in relation with humans over relatively few years. Dogs are symbiants with humans. 'Dogness' only exists in a

342

context of human. And humans have been speaking for – untold years before wolves get domesticated and dogs evolve – just a few thousand years ago. Now, pulling back to a sense of our human evolution, and our primary orders of signification before we reach the point where *we* became language-producers – which we may consider a secondary order of signification reliant on the first – now we find a more universalized order we share with dogs – like a marriage that was waiting to happen. At this level, we begin to discover the co-identity in language-terms between dog and man. While dogs are not language-producers – save by linguistic-productions they elicit in humans, and which then act reflexively on the dog's being/situation/etc – they – dogs *are* embroiled in language, simply because their environment – which environment every dog must actively think toward, in terms of recognition of differential value – is human and therefore inherently linguistic. When a dog encounters an instance of language, the dog in its own doggy way comprehends this semiologically/representationally/symbolically. The dog, thereby, understands words in ways that are highly analogous to human conceptions. The dog is embroiled in *its own* as in our systems of representations just as we are.'

Henry says: 'Ridiculous.'

I say: 'So how do we draw the line?'

They don't know what I am on about now. I have spent my air, I've had my scream. It seemed an *out* – on a personal level.

The Rector says:

'I think we've talked about what we mean by that and you are maybe being deliberately provocative now.'

I am tired and my face aches.

In the projection screen, the powerpoint, crude, simplistic. That

343

font, and blue-on-green, for heaven's sake. Primal life. Pre-eukaryotic life. Of man's first disobedience... No-when Sin.

The Rector says: 'Is that it? Are we done?'

No-one says anything.

It is a relatively new thing: literal-painful-tired. Tired past life and metaphor. Non-trope tired. But, wincing, I say it:

'What is a soul?'

Henry shrieks: 'What?'

The Rector says: 'If you don't know that, then here is no place for you.'

A lost soul. Not one of them now. Truth that sets you free.

All thin and reedy, the words puddled out of me go like this:

'But explain it to me. What is it? Were I to be asked to explain, what should I say? Assuming, as I have said, that symbolic and linguistic representations are not uniquely human traits, assuming that thought, sentient thought, of one sort or another, is not a uniquely human trait, then what is it? We have souls, other animals don't. So what is it? And then, when did God do it? And what exactly happened and what changed at that point? Perhaps rather than dismiss the question, or lambaste me for asking, tell me.'

Julian says: 'It says in the Bible.'

I say: 'A. Does it? B. Where? C. Is that the best you can do?'

Henry says: 'Of course we're different!'

I say: 'Good. So how?'

'It's obvious!'

'How?'

Geoff says: 'I can't believe you're even saying this.'

I say: 'Use words. No more bow-wow. Tell me. What is the human
344

difference? In terms of Catholic orthodoxy now. In ways that are not contrary to reason. How do we say it? ¿Como se dice? What is a soul?'

The Rector seems to pity me a moment. 'Tomàs, there are clear differences of quality, not of degree, between us and the monkey. These are not shades of this and that; these are – staggering, beyond imagination, absolute.'

The Rector pauses and no-one says anything. I nod in stunned acquiescence. Then The Rector says: 'Good. Let's move on.'

By the way, I think, approximately three seconds afterwards, who says a dog lacks lack? If lack is key to our language production – if that's the over-spill – if that's our plenitude. Put a dog on its own, in a field, and now tell me that dog lacks lack.

Show me the dog walking toward me through a reed-grove yobs have rendered ashes.

I become speech where I am not – forgot that bit.

Twenty minutes later, at break, all this is gone. I think:

Like patients in hospital beds with the meds pumped into them, maintaining sleep and life, and none watch, out there on the living side, while we slip and travel.

We go to break.

I walk with the other men stunned down the corridor... Today it is my or Ade's job to fetch the coffee trolley from the kitchen to the Refectory. Once we've done this, I pour myself a glass of the weak, mid-morning coffee. I leave it on the bench to cool. Then, on a whim, I go to the windows and open one – onto the quad. What you might call a quad in real life. And stick my head out of the window skyward – to grab myself a one-minute binge on light and air. Henry comes over to join me.

345

Henry says:

'Look at that! Bright blue! Wouldn't get that in England, hey!'

'No, indeed.'

'Would to be out there! Not in that classroom!'

'Hmm. Meanwhile.'

'Meanwhile. Indeed.'

We poke our heads together into the courtyard. We are close: it is a narrow, leaded window. The air is warm and my mouth soft. Both admire this beautiful, old, crumbly square of Catholic-space, just our sort of thing, with dappled light of sagging trees, like willows. Right up both our streets. I say:

'I wonder what's for lunch. I'm starving.'

'Me too. Are you? I'm starving! Some nice *jamon* right now. We really need a sandwich or proper food, hey?'

I turn, craning my neck, lean back on the sill, a dog basking, from the open window to regard the vaulted Spanish room – in height two storeys. The sight that presents itself to my now-eyes is of disparately huddled folk. Shoddy, yes, washed colours, certainly. Fundamentally benign. Perhaps. Clothes, and the people wearing them, such as you find when you knock on a stranger's door unexpectedly. Tired humans, who nurse their twinned limits of sleep and boredom. Regular folk.

It moves slowly, but we find the odd thing to say. And there is Sister Angelina with her glass of hot water. There she bows over it. She nurses our maleness. Or says to herself that's what she does. And why not? She tells herself the story of herself that's what she does... And that is her story. Maybe when she wants to sleep nights.

Perhaps that *is* what this is *all* about: nursed maleness. The insuperable weight of it – Church-subsumed. Women pulled-up on the side. And priests to bury us.

Lunch is penitential: thin vegetable gruel. Henry has his go at reading from my copy of Pope Benedict XVI's *Jesus Of Nazareth: Holy Week*. It is pretty bloody good of him to do it. Most don't – though it was all agreed on at one of our meetings. And Henry reads in a way quite beautifully – risk-achieves those aspirations he has of himself – being posh.

Then we clear the place up, say our prayers – which is the *De Profundis* during the period of Lent.

Then I hit the gym something rotten. It has been a long week.

I nail 1500 calories. Get dizzy with sweat and sub-vocalize Pimsleur Spanish. My salt-water method works well: the brain stays up on it – won't go cranky. (Look at Tomàs there! In the mirror opposite!) Belting it – slow-dutiful like that dog – oily-mucky fallout – puddled ash – through the ashes in the reed-beds the yobs burnt. Pain can't hurt you through your gym-high. Once you get up on it.

I am weak and shaking quite badly when I get to the dressing rooms, but I fiddle my gym clothes off and my trunks on, then, in the flip-flops they make us wear, I go to the sauna. Alone, I cross my legs, half-lotus, for the sake of my spine. But it isn't hot enough – in the early 80s it must be. I sweat but it isn't enough to stop thinking anything. Not quite 'to zen' – verb – as a long-ago friend once put it. Not to ride a (perhaps) no-longer-available (quite technological) high and relinquish. Yet here it is. Torso, groin, legs, feet. My fine ankles, my miraculous shins. My feet are a wide fit, always have been. And little red tell-tale veins have yet to break beneath my ankles. It is still a good body. This is the place where *I* live.

But the sauna isn't hot enough really and it isn't going to work.
Mind like cargo. Well, I shower, cold, and plunge inside the pool and
swim a few lengths, then I get cramp and have to climb out awkwardly
and sit at the edge, then practically hobble to get to the changing room. It
is very nearly time for evening prayer.

In my room, I change from the Adidas track-suit and shower again.
I put on jeans and a bland top. The jeans are 'slim-fit' – though this
means off-trend baggy. And as you get skinny, your clothes feel loose
and nice. This on skin which because of the weight-loss has become
sensitised. While there is all that hair – there is a flow about it. I like to
hold myself upright – clean at prayer. It doesn't matter what The Rector
thinks. And The Rector sits immediately next to me watching me, in the
first pew. Perpendicular – on what is historically my good side. Queen
Tomàs! Like a stamp.

If I turn to reach The Rector's eyes now… But I don't turn, and
The Rector doesn't linger. He scuttles from us the moment the formal
arrangement of prayers has finished. We sit around two or three minutes,
praying.

Friday. Time is mine.

Freedom is the queue in Carrefour, where there is no risk of
anyone checking my basket: humus, bread, quite a lot of wine, and I get a
foie gras, which isn't expensive here.

I pick up four extra bottles of water closer to home. This in the
Mercadona, not least just to go there too and absorb different people,
more at the Spanishy end. Their chamois skin, their violent-green jeans.

348

Their pumps worn down. Unusually-cool at foot level. But it is nice to be near them a little while. (I can't guess what they do in this dormitory city. How they live in their tower blocks.) I lock my door. I intend to seal myself in tonight. Too early yet though.

I need a drink and to take my clothes off and to listen to Radio 4.

I can go to the bar in a little while. Public space in college is all empty. Where have they gone? Within, I take off my top and my pumps and my jeans and I take my socks off. In England, it is only approaching six o'clock. Crimea is in the news. Nigel Farage is a thing. In England, there is weather and there are budgetary matters… It's a comfort. I pace simply back and forth. My bed is made. The clothes on my chair lay folded. Wine flows, the beer is tasty. The six o'clock news plays, and then the funny. Then I'll have a shower and go out again.

I hear more than listen – English noise.

There are comforts – I touch things: *A History Of Christianity*; *Asterix En Helvecia*; *El Caballo Y El Muchacho*… I touch my *KJV* – which I am much too much a coward to take to Bible class. I should make a couple of Skype-calls, but don't want to spoil the mood. We aren't allowed to post anything about it on Facebook either. 'Bringing the college into disrepute.'

It isn't time to be so committedly alone.

I put my book in the rucksack. I dress for what you might call a pretend walk. (I am that woman in the film: *Rear Window*.) I like the thought of someone out there… I am only going to go for a walk and pretend a little.

Once, I went out at night on my own, a teenage youth, for no known reason. Not taking the dog. And I didn't get very far. How old?

Fifteen? Maybe it was later than that. Only down the lane toward a view of Wales… Presently, that boy reached a limit just-beyond safe-territory – since it was purposeless not being with the dog. But I was going out to Liverpool by fifteen? (That's got a date on it – because I felt morally obliged to say I was only fifteen.) Possibly older than memory likes to predict – but I can put a date on my going into Liverpool – the film I watched – the other things – because they asked, I answered. Fifteen.

I stopped at the stile, at the bottom of the track I'd walk the dogs down, covered in dog-shit those days. By the older of the new Barratt Homes estates, then the new one they'd started building then, over the old coal-mines, toward the marsh. I smoked a Marlboro. There was no point in my being there. It hadn't satisfied anything. I tried to make something of it, with the cigarette – pose with it.

I didn't silent-scream – I didn't kick up a fuss – while it all let go of me half a minute – I didn't panic. What was I wearing? I was wearing a Barbour jacket and a pair of Hunter Wellingtons. I'd learnt to smoke by now: dog and ball. (Not smoking in front of the dog.) Street-lights thread the coast of north Wales. I'd have been stood about 500 meters of bedroom walls away. I wasn't scared to encounter it, though it was fractionally unnerving. Emptiness, absence, nothing. Things that are not. (So, that's it? Oh well, if that's it.) So, nothing then.

Saturday-nights meant Soho. (Thursday-nights, Friday-nights, Monday-nights often meant Soho…) I turned thirty, and they flung me around – paraded on top of their shoulders in the VIP. Those days. When I no longer worked at the little school. I might spend hours hanging about town before my friend Robbie arrived. I couldn't bear the wait at home – by which we mean the flat in Shoreditch. Then, when Shoreditch got to be a bit too expensive, a series of zone 5 base camps – up in the north.

Flat-shares, lodging arrangements... A whole house! I could be rolling into Paddington by eight if the tube was down, having agreed to meet 'around' ten. It was a much more comfortable ride than the tube – though entering into London at Baker Street was kind of engrained in me. This is going back fifteen years and then London was a little more-or-less what it had been and less-or-more than it was setting out to be.

Galleries and shops were closed. There were few alternatives to drinking far too much far too early. I did a lot of pretending – there really were only a handful of comfortable streets. I liked watching the whores and the G-A-Y flier-boys. I liked looking at the tourists. And a weekly dose of conveyor-belt sushi and magazines. Rice reacting – fermenting in my stomach on the first beers.

I browsed the late-night art-book shops with the dirty-book basements. I'd sit in Trafalgar Square – just outside the National Gallery. I wasn't great sitting around like that, but it was okay, provisional. I went down to the river – out on the bridge from Charing Cross. Then I'd look down at the water – and toward Blackfriars and Saint Paul's. It was okay – there was no feeling of particular conviction. I wasn't really going so much to see the theatre – so that strip of the south bank was previous – known, possessed, acknowledged, previous, though not currently adding-up to anything much. I still smoked.

In those days, you could do a lot with other people's camaraderie. Say in the Admiral Duncan. Hitch a ride! Where I once met a boy called Duncan – in the Admiral Duncan. But out there on Old Compton Street... Robbie's train would come at last into Victoria checking his phone. We'd meet in Halfway To Heaven perhaps at eleven o' clock. Out there... It wasn't like the burr of your local, where a comfortable crowd of the well-

351

heeled know your name. There were high-denomination transactions in process of being arranged – not meaning money. Devilish to-and-fro – meaning souls. As it approached eleven – and Robbie... This was in the days when you didn't have to queue if you spent a lot of money in Soho... I like Robbie very much, and Robbie was very queer – I more on a tourist-class level, happier with matters scenic when it keeps its pants on. I'd play with him dancing on drugs, and then at three-four-am, turn of the evening, maybe expect to share a breakfast but let the children play.

*

I dress and rinse my face and scrub my mouth. Then I go for my walk. I only go to the cathedral and back, then to the usual bar. There are plenty of people. Two tables are joined together playing D&D. And quite a shadowy buzz about the place. It is nice to be alone – and warm – and there is a free table. With the girl-at-the-bar, I share pleasantries.

My *jara* goes down quickly. But just the one. I'd become a slurring arsehole with a second pint. I want to dance now. And what with the hazard tonight of the college front door...

The cold air slaps me together. I take what I can of the bonhomie. She offers and I shrug and we shrug. *Ha' l'o.* Ta-ta for now. My habit is to cap her, finger to forehead: *Ha' l'o.* I take my glass to the counter.

In college, going up to my room, I hear them in the downstairs corridors. They are in the Refectory. Then, in my room, there come low-pitched alto-screams and other evidence of serious disturbance in the corridor immediately outside. And it stays there. Wild and crazy.

I check that I am still okay to open my door still. I am wearing a vest – and socks. Thinking first to put a pair of black jeans on, I open the door, and there are Henry and Julian screaming, while John looks terrified, and Geoff strides bowdlering toward us down the corridor.

Geoff's brick-heavy feet slop the wooden floor. Reeling, Geoff turns and then turns again, doubling back toward the common room. Geoff's hands canted wide. He looks burly and terrifying.

Along the length of the corridor, I see others have appeared from their rooms. All wear frightened expressions. Geoff is saying: 'Oh, this is not good. This is not good at all. There is evil here. We need a meeting here. Come on, brothers.'

I wait for Henry or maybe even Julian to catch my eye. They seem to switch off, and trail after Geoff, to the common room. I catch Sean's eyes. Sean, who lives next door, shrugs and shakes his head. I see only inconvenience and no advantage whatsoever in following them.

Half the night, I hear sporadic, heavy footfalls outside in the corridor. And Geoff's voice. I catch the word *Father* repeatedly. So there are priests... And through the hour that follows... I have the radio on. I have nuts, and salt, in order to enhance my thirst. There is plenty of wine – and I have water for later. When the radio-news runs out, I put *This Sceptred Isle* on. I daren't play music.

Just as well: there is a knock. Whoever it is tries the handle. I dare not move. I half expect Geoff to start yelling my name. I stand stock-still – in the game – and my flesh creeps. But there is nothing for the next thirty seconds. Then, that nothing goes away. And I inch toward the bed, not the office chair, and take off my pumps, so I don't squeak, and keep my socks on.

A meeting are they having? I crush flat the cans and arrange one of the blue plastic bin-bags beneath the bag on top in my waste bin. In case I die in the night or an emergency happens. So that they are thoughtfully, separately there for recycling purposes. They might come back... But then they aren't there anymore – enough time – and at the window green-

353

blue light absorbs me – through the trees. This is my 'meeting with yourself' – as The Rector disparagingly calls these times. They are very quiet – a managed flow of bits of food and alcohol. Mañana mañana. The view across the scrubland is beautiful – looking toward the gym.

*

Saturday. Lent 2.

Being Tomàs:

Unalarmed, I reach for the bedside light switch… I wake in blackness – groan and phase. The wrenching… Obscured by a bottle of water. What dreams had come? Nada. Laid like a wet slab in a wet bed and curse these bed sheets. Corpulent. Dreams have not come. Dreams unpermitted. Through what brief hours…? Oh God but I want a dream… To sort me. Terror might have contributed something to the sorting of. Terror might have gone some distance to the sorting of… But – no dreams. So it is going to be that sort of day.

Switch-acquired, the room brownly-yellows. (It could be any time.) Only then can I see the way to open the shutters. This I commence with a certain trepidation. Feeling a bit rough. The radiator has turned itself on again. 'Ugh,' I say, aloud. And lean on the sill for effect. I check my clock-radio. It is a quarter to ten.

Grim-faced, I open the shutters. A middle-aged man in yesterday's Top Man underpants. The effect of unventilated light is quite horrible. It is as I open the window that light breaks. Golden, florid. All the day is here. How am I? How *really* am I? And yet the bathroom mirror contains good news…

Perking up a bit, I shower and shave and scrub my mouth and my teeth bleed. Then I get on my gym stuff – vest and running shorts. I go to the gym, and at length claim 1000 calories. There are classes in the pool

354

and each machine stands half-used – by the weekend fat-chaps and lady-chaps – though that thought does me no credit and it is not respectful. Still – do all that.

Nevertheless, I am sweating in my T-shirt transparently when, returning to college, I meet The Rector and that Ampleforth monk at the college gate. I am all nipples and hair – they are *athletic* running-shorts. Nevertheless – or despite this – I say: '¡Buenos dias!' What with my ankle-socks, I feel quite five-foot-six – my own eyes.

There is a deal of salted gravity. I only use these pumps as gym-pumps. Though they aren't exactly shiny – that slight brown-tinge come from within. And, clearly, you wouldn't use this as your profile-picture. Skin denuded – collagen-drained – sucked dry.

The monk says: 'Buenos. ¿Te gusta hacer ejercicio?'

'Si. Mucho.'

'Good for you.'

We are fussed off by The Rector, sniffing each other, the door held.

I wonder how old the monk thinks I am, and if he says anything to The Rector, and if The Rector says anything back.

Gym-high – though I am practically naked – I stoop to condescend. Receive the door.

Back in my room, I grab fresh clothes to take down to the baths. I bump into Julian on the way, who of all people abhors my short shorts and my unspeakable running vests. And I have taken my trainers off and my socks too, so there most disgustingly of all are my toes…

But I am sweat-wet and justified. Alone, I strip clean. There the feet pass, there the steam blows. There the old, green pipes disburse hot water… None pass by those little green windows. A child or a crazy

355

person might crouch to see in. There would be nothing between him and me bar that chunk of old glass. We'd see each other looking at each other quite distinctly.

Anyway, I have no idea how cities work. *'What do you do? What do you all do?'* I have often thought that looking down over greater London from a moderate height – a long view. (You have a posh class, a rentier class, and you have a slave class...) Now this place, with its dilapidated shop-fronts and spray-paint Alquilar... This place – which produces education. Buffered from The Crisis by its student population. It says on Wikipedia there are twenty-five-thousand students in Valladolid – can you believe?

I'm not reading my book. I slug a lot of water, and have neglected to add salt, so might feel unusual later.

I cry when I go to The Rector's office... You are supposed to think a literal thing happens at the altar – at Mass – but The Rector uses His magic voice, and rolls His cranky voodoo-eyes... I am bored with crying. There is no fight left in that classroom. The water steams... That last death – Ron's – is still very raw. Dad was fucked-up in all sorts of ways, and sex might have played a part in it. Maybe it could have been just the drinking, just the booze, and that hurt sufficiently. Or the booze laid bare some inevitable lack.

I saw Dad once pissed as a newt, laid on the marital bed, holding hands with some low woman's two kids, boy and girl, either side of him, and she showed up at the house like to whatever manner of creature she was that was normal. They were just laid either side of him, dead still, and Dad was trancing real deep like he could slip through the bed and this time – take them with him? It is something I can never unsee. Oh, I must have been sixteen, seventeen – or was it *much* later? I think he was gone

356

after that. I think that was the last thing – that was the worst.

I found Dad in my own bed once. The green, mouldy feeling Dad had: marsh and shotguns, gun-oil and whisky-sweat. Well, I dragged him out of it. This wasn't violent. I dragged him – practically led him gently. Put him in their now his bed. It didn't occur to me to wash my own sheets. There was no sense of decontamination required – of lingering physical presence. I probably didn't even fluff the covers up.

Now even my dreams know Dad is mostly dead. Dad is mostly there most nights – obviously. I stalk my teenage – growing-up house – practically every dream. (The doors won't lock – they – the locks crumble-through like putty.) To the point I begin to wonder if I should stop waking myself from inside them. Hang around, see what's what and maybe learn. The motif seems to be that the door won't lock – whether my bedroom door or the house front-door. They never lock. They bulge and spring wide open – not least when, in dreamtime, I'm wanting to masturbate.

Encounters with Dad range from the entirely banal to the full head-smash. My dreams mostly know Dad as a dead man visiting. Unable to touch Mum. Dad is dead, of course. He isn't moving back in... Except he is sometimes and they are together and reconciled. Old cars and new recipes. The Storeys are on the up.

Hot: caliente. Heat: calor. Calor is a noun. Caliente is an adjective. The word *adjective* is longer than the word *noun*. The word *caliente* is longer than the word *calor*. So that is how you remember it.

It is a lovely afternoon in Valladolid, so much so I think I might go to church, if there's a Mass left. I finger the rosary I carry, looped over

357

my belt, in my right-hand pocket. I *shall* say a prayer: *Hail Mary, full of grace, the Lord is with you, blessed art thou among women, and blessed is the fruit of your womb, Jesus. Holy Mary, Mother of God, pray for us sinners now and at the hour of our death.*

Amazing how quickly the magic takes… To see the squirrel. As I emerge from my one bead's prayer… There is sleep in the rosary. Sleep *anchored* in the beads of the rosary. If you pursue it, it gets a lot more intense. It is siesta – streets relapsed to default human-vacancy. Perhaps if prayer is life's opposite… The shops are closed. When you come back from prayer, you can touch life very intensely.

There is the El Corte Ingles to ride up and down in it – if I particularly want. On a back square from Plaza Mayor, I yell: 'Come on!' Because there isn't anyone about here. So I walk around goofing – lampooning God and the Common Man. Piggy faced, holding the baby, hamming all angles of elbows and ankles, wrists and knees.

Did anyone see? No. Therefore that doesn't matter.

At the top, in Plaza de Zorrilla, I perch and dip my right hand into the basin of the fountains. A make-believe gesture. Yet the fountains sparkle and they seem merry enough. It won't make memories. It doesn't *mean* anything. They are light and sparkly, water, fountains.

When I am alone I cease to exist…

So then, in concrete-mood, I walk on. There the pompous buildings; there the doormen; each doorman mans his door. Then too, at a pavement café, there sit three old men, all wool and slippers. And there again are kids playing basketball, up the long stretch toward the railway-station.

I walk close-by. Big white socks and cropped what-might-be combats. Skinny. Japanese hair. No visible tattoos. Cool piercings. Just through the nose and no visible stretchers. I enter the park at the farther gate, then double back toward where the squirrel lives. There is a vacant bench. I have a fresh bag of nuts in my hand, loose-cupped, dangling. And all the civility of trees. No squirrel.

I have my pocketful of beads but I'm not taking those out to pray with. I finger them quietly in my pocket, daring a prayer to form of its own accord. The leaves are perennially green, and that eerie peacock song – again – winds through them. The sound is dinosaurs. Where are they? You see them up in the branches, up in the trees, and wonder how on earth they ever got there. *Peacocks can fly...*

I have a Bible in my rucksack. It isn't fancy. Anyone looking might think it was poetry – even as my lips move – subvocalizing. The book isn't dripping with ribbons and there is no smoke rising out of it! I read:

Why do you boast, O mighty man,
of mischief done against the godly?
All the day you are plotting destruction.
Your tongue is like a sharp razor,
you worker of treachery.
You love evil more than good,
and lying more than speaking the truth.
You love all words that devour,
O deceitful tongue.
But God will break you down for ever;
he will snatch and tear you from your tent;
he will uproot you from the land of the living.
The righteous shall see, and fear,
and shall laugh at him, saying,

"See the man who would not make

God his refuge,

but trusted in the abundance of his riches,

and sought refuge in his wealth!"

But I am like a green olive tree

in the house of God.

I trust in the steadfast love of God

for ever and ever.

I will thank thee for ever,

because thou hast done it.

I will proclaim thy name, for it is good

in the presence of the godly.

The young English family pass. This time I follow. I hear the man in his black-country-accents showing off to his wife. I see her anxiety for lunch. The children are practically invisible. It is the man gesturing around himself. He must really want her to see it. He isn't hungry – he is feasting high.

I look into the pool. The pool is dark and empty – terrapins live in there.

I turn from it to walk to the Carrefour. I go back past, once more, where the squirrel lives. The peacocks are all over the place, up in the trees. I go past the horrible place, where there are doves seemingly locked in a glass house, which it seems bad luck to look at, and makes you think about eating. They beat and smash and peck and claw against the glass. I don't look. The children are still playing basketball.

Once upon a time, I waited on the steps outside one of the school huts for RE, when my second-best friend from junior school spat at me:

360

'*Queeeeeeeeeer…*' Whinged hard with the nastiest Scouse twang. If the word in itself meant nothing – the intention was different from anything justly known. I wiped the gob off my face – and life had done something unusual. Shadowy people who hurt for the sake of a hurt – the corridors no longer safe-space. Anger ruled… (Punching at your head at that – not words and spit.) You become perhaps a little less conscious. Boys cope. A lower-set waiting for their class. Haunted in that respect. One learns to hate the stupid and unpleasant. It is a lonely world.

Post-prep, pre-flicks, they came round to mine, to Mr Mine, and watched some films. I didn't let them smoke. (Not collectively.) They could have themselves a glass of the chilled Waitrose Macon. And I let them order pizza to my address. The Storey service.

We watched: *My Own Private Idaho. The Cook, The Thief, His Wife And Her Lover. Stand By Me. The Cement Garden. Terminator 2. The Lost Boys. Death In Venice. Ferris Bueller's Day Off. A Streetcar Named Desire. Top Gun. Short Cuts. Heathers. A Fistful Of Dollars. Mad Max. Casablanca. Logan's Run. Dazed And Confused. Live And Let Die. Rope. Pretty In Pink. To Kill A Mockingbird. Metropolis. The Breakfast Club. Dead Poets' Society. Beautiful Thing. Hellraiser. The Last Seduction. Blade Runner. From Russia With Love. Schindler's List. Saint Elmo's Fire. Invasion Of The Body Snatchers. Some Like It Hot. The Sound Of Music.*

I walk back from El Campo Grande to the Carrefour. I have my little look round the shelves – and get my bits and pieces. I *do* pop into the *El Corte Ingles*… And ride the escalators up and down, and have a little browse round the sport section. By ill-luck, I meet The Rector again at the college door. I say to Him:

'Wouldn't it be amazing to be a monk somewhere stunningly

beautiful? Do you ever think: what if I gave God everything?'

No matter – a child is nearly out in me – trusting, pure. So much abolished. Zion.

The Rector draws close. Sniffing. He is trying to peek into my bag as well, so I open it up for Him, and take the opportunity, breathing fresh, unminted, peanut air all over The Rector's face, and showing Him the little jar of Marmite I've got in the Carrefour. I seem to shine – my spirits whirled-plates. I want Him to know of it. Saturday. I say: 'It must be amazing! Properly holy!'

A new and ununiformed priest appears. We sort of sniff around each-other another few seconds. I must be shaking. There loom such brutal thoughts as high as tower blocks. Once they have gone, there is no whisper of anyone else in the corridors. I get to my cluttered room and lock myself in…

What a mess! I think and: '*What a mess!*' I say.

Have I ever actually sat in that armchair? Oh and what has Tomàs bought? Today's haul: two tops, and a new pair of underpants. My desk is piled-high with half-read books and photocopied handouts. Well, they, the photocopied handouts, can be all thrown out straight-away… I gather the handouts, thinking they can go in my recycling bin-bag with the empties. Post-it notes stick to the shelves and the wooden panelling. Pithy Googled aphorisms: Quien teme la muerte no goza la vida… Lejos de ojos, lejos del Corazon… A quien Dios quiere para si, poco tiempo lo tiene aqui… A donde el corazon se inclina, el pie camina… Espaldas vueltas, memorias muertas… A todos les llega su momento de gloria…

I set about to arrange things a little more tidily.

My books lie splayed about – an imaginary study-program – radiated. There is nothing the college has asked of me. Pure danger – pure

362

self-abuse. Biting the bullet – books find places on the copious shelving space. It has got to be difficult to concentrate. Contrary to instinct... There: the desk cleared. My lap-top – clam-top set in the centre...

I sit at my desk, and push the computer back a bit. I have a beer and, while that's going down, I rest a Bible angled on the closed shell of the lap-top. It is tomorrow's – Sunday's Gospel I want. John 4: 5-42. This is the bit where Jesus is in Samaria, and he meets and dialogues with the Samaritan woman at the well. Jesus asks the woman for a cup of water, then, because he a Jew, he explains to the woman who he is, and something of the nature of the gift he is.

He says: 'Everyone who drinks of this water will be thirsty again, but those who drink of the water that I will give them will never be thirsty. The water that I will give will become in them a spring of water gushing up to eternal life.'

She says: 'Sir, give me this water, so that I may never be thirsty or have to keep coming here to draw water.'

Once I have read the piece, I bow my head and sleep despite the beer. Even to a count of twenty. It is a funny thing – John's Gospel. Whenever it was written – there is a primacy. God was complete by this stage.

I bow my head – beneath the point you've really got to snap out of it. And do and do... For Catholicism is but a highly abstracted rendition of a human brain/body. I go to prayer – which lies at the limit of some*thing* – a *big* conceptualization your one-brain does badly. Beneath the point you must snap out of this state. There – rock-hollow – dust and desert-thoughts. Yellow ochre rock. Above which, it seems, a cyber-sky wants any information. *The sky was the colour of a television, tuned to a dead channel...* Pre-Christian. Far beyond the limits of Catholic faith.

More rock-solid still than that Babylonian exile. Jerusalem razed – again. An ecclesiapause.

It must have taken a long time to pull Christianity together. Communities – meaning that in its true sense – honed the thought of Christ through generations. Gospel-craft. The faith of those who created these stories. It could not have been done merely with outright invention and parlour games. It comes from somewhere *near* to where the psalms live. It *feels* religious down to the hard-core.

Spiritual waste. Living water. At Lourdes, the Archbishop riffed along these lines. *Come to the waters all you who thirst.* At Lourdes, I had to share a room. The young man with whom I shared had just completed his time in Valladolid. That didn't mean anything. Though – they'd done a job on him. The little we talked was really straight down to business. Staccato when I asked if we might open the window. I opened the window very slowly, so that it wouldn't hurt… The sharp little words clipped out of him: 'Yes. Happy with that.'

I watched him dress. A structural body: there was nothing to desire or to feel bad about. He peeled his clothes – and re-sheathed in a regulation white top. He pulled and stretched about a bit. He declared himself – mirrorless – satisfied. Happy with that. There'd be a little spasmodic nod at the name of Jesus.

I sat alone by the river in free time. On that bit of the bank where the tramps live. The Pont Vieux. I bought one-euro stubby-cans one at a time from the fridge in the shop. The big guy I had a share in looking after was alright once we both knew we had nothing in common. It was decent wheeling him up so he could watch the sunrise on the hospital roof. He had a lot of morphine in him – when the sun caught the gold crown on the statue of Mary. He had a whole collection of male-perfumes

364

in his cupboard – the main brands. He wrenched himself upright and stood wobbling to attention and balanced and steadied himself for a good spray. His wardrobe was brand-new. He was able to do his own bathroom.

Last Christmas, I was in the pub with my Mum for some weird reason. Maybe she was trying to connect. There was a boy with *his* Mum, whom I recognized from church. He was wearing a great black T-shirt and the legend emblazoned in bold white block-capitals: JESUS SAVED ME. The boy was standing and kneeling and just about any which way but sit bum-plumb-on-a-pub-chair. He was flirting with his Mum. Big wide world.

Flying off of her. He'd grown a foot in the last month. The T-shirt was curious also because of the past tense: Jesus *saved* me. This is not Catholic sentiment. But his Mum hailed from a different era. There was skin and brushed-hair over it. And whatever *he* was going through a thing for the priests to answer. A pillow-fight with himself. She said quiet things too faint to overhear. Perhaps his religion exhausted her.

My family came to my adult reception. This took place on the Feast of Pentecost. My first communion. There was Mum. And Ron – who wasn't very well already, but we pretended we were all optimistic in those days. There was Auntie Grace. (Cousin James was down with chickenpox, Cousin Abbie atheistically engaged on a student demo.)

And local, migratory friends filled two pews – like treasured Christmas cards.

Paul, Daphne, Steve, Ol, Zara, Robin, Panos, Toby, Trev, Val, Guy...

It was meant to be my confirmation too but the priest forgot the oil. I had to do *that* two weeks later – with the Bishop. Then they made me

365

queue at the front of a great long line of embarrassing teenagers. The Bishop slammed me, vice-grip, face in face, mono-eye to mono-eye, and in no uncertain terms accused me: 'Do you want this?' I was scared and said *yes* with a question mark. The church was full-up to the rafters with families.

There had been classes to attend. Then at the foot of the sanctuary, the devil in Tomàs was exorcised, and I told the priest that I abhorred Satan, and all his lies, and all his works, and all his false promises. The priest's breath, blowing on my face, blew the devil out of me.

Two days prior to first communion, I celebrated my first sacrament of reconciliation. This took place in Father Guy's study. On the shelves I noted a smart set of unabridged Gibbon. Tear-sodden, it all fell out of me. I confessed. Now, obliquely, the priest said to the congregation that God's forgiveness stretched so far as Tomàs, and that anything prior to this was all gone now.

I was received – a form of words. And the church cheered – everyone clapped. I turned to the five hundred grinning unreservedly. A random bloke turned to Steve next to him and said: 'He looks happy!'

From church, we walked as planned to the pub I had made my local. Up a hill and down again, we walked via my house to collect the sandwiches, which I had been up half the night preparing. These I had arranged on large foil platters, wrapped over with cling-film. It was home-baked bread, and real – homemade mayonnaise. (Mum gave me the money.) For reasons now beyond me, I didn't want them at the house. There was a thought of a lady-on-shift I particularly valued – who attended the ceremony. But I wouldn't have known where to put them. House was *being in*. (I only really ever entertained one friend – for chess.) While tidy, it had all become a bit of an extended bedroom. *And*

this is where I sit at my desk, and this is where I read quietly, and here I
stand to smoke, and here I pace in still-yesterday's underpants... And
here is a crucifix... So we went to the pub, where we sat in the snug.
They were lavish sandwiches.

It was a funny little gathering. Pub colours. White-glare – repelled
by brick and tarmac. The sun was at 60° at its zenith, at two minutes to
one o'clock. We squashed-up on the banquets. (I should have got
Pharouk to organize something at home – it was his house.) There was
more by way of prior imagination... It was an endearing scene, though I
don't recall that it ever relaxed and became jolly and a pub-scene.

Unforgivably, I was rude to my Mum beyond help when I got back
from the monastery toward the end of the summer – one month prior to
my transition to Valladolid. I was assiduous afterwards, trying to put
things right. I must have drunk too much wine on the trains all the way
from Moray. So said what I thought – in the squalor of it – this world – so
far removed – so lost, so boozed – this mincing degradation. Harsh with
psalms and tat-free like a fascist. Then I woke next day with a minute's
warmth. Then remembered, and waited in the kitchen for Mum to get
home. I shall never forget how she opened the door and saw me stood
there waiting. I am assiduous now with the Sunday Skype – and odd calls
when somehow the thought of connection seemed marketable.

Mum drove me to Liverpool to John Lennon airport. There,
parked-up, before we got my suitcase out the boot, I gave Mum my gmail
main-account log-in details: tomasstorey@gmail.com:
gmailXYimprint731407. She wrote it on the back of a half-folded
envelope. Because through this you access everything. In case anything
happened. In other words, everything must have been screaming at me...

But life remained persistent.

367

A funny thing happened on the way between airports. I gazed the whole way through the porthole, and there was a near miss. The passenger plane flew crosswise under our own plane, and filled and more the porthole, which my head lolled against. A Monarch. It must have been closer than a hundred meters.

I told the others about it – when we were first meeting for the first time, having flown into Madrid on different planes. We were having drinks together – that first evening together – at what they call Country House, some few kilometres outside of Valladolid – near Viana. They mocked me because it could not be true. I understood there were ways to check – but I've never got round to it. It seemed ironic – not immediately then but a little later – they all refused to believe me point blank – it being impossible.

There were mild introductory talks and a page we had to write about our 'faith journey'. Otherwise – mild September sun – and pool. There, at the base of which, two blue dolphins swam head to toe. Dolphin Yin and Dolphin Yang.

She dropped me off and there were two minutes practical business of boot and baggage. Then it was time to hug. This bit is always deliberated. We aren't very good at it, but we are getting better at it.

Perhaps the depths of love are too messy. Perhaps too much to be exhumed. She associated this with drunkenness: 'Like your father.' And it's true I'd attempted it once… You might have thought she didn't want love, save on a kind of procedural level. We put there our bodies approximately where they ought to be. We made the hug-noise. But that was the way of her. She felt good with age – a little bird with a persistent, sort of ferrety quality about her. Then she drove off quickly, in order not to have to pay the rip-off airport-parking charge. And then she was gone.

I regained my capacities. With the back-of-the-hand wave, and the cheeky hazard lights – she is a rogue! she is a rascal! – I re-individuated, as you do in airports. There were no queues at Liverpool airport – and it is all one class. I always identified airside, slipping into the appearance, and toying with the free Macon and a prawn sandwich, though in Liverpool airport it is less nothingy, looking over the Mersey at the butt-end of the Wirral, not a million miles off from where Granny lies scattered – along a bit, underneath her tree.

Mum came to the Easter Vigil Mass that year. We were in Cornwall – to scatter Ron's ashes on the shoreline – like he'd requested when he was on his way out. Mum and Samson went down into the cove, while I gave her a bit of privacy, staying up on the little path, taking photographs with black-and-white film on the OM2. This was in the new motor-home. We stayed near St Mawes. One day, in the hotel, there was a posh woman in the lounge with her golden retrievers, one of whom was on his last legs and flopped across her lap, hugging her. She was gorgeous. She had about five dogs with her – by the fireplace. This was the one on its way out and it was hugging her. It obviously knew. She was saying, fully and freely expressing undamaged emotions: 'I hate it when it's like this. I just hate it.'

The food was pretty shoddy at that hotel. You got about a sliver of beef, then over-cooked vegetables, and a Yorkshire-pud, and gravy, crowding the plate, which was fairly disgusting. We had to get the bus miles into Truro. The bus was picking up here-there, all the winding route, all local people who all knew each other. Weekend-by-weekend – their Saturday night in Truro. And there they sat, en-bus, their all-hail greetings met, all intention, only in view of an anticipated evening.

When we got into Truro, I and Mum didn't know where we were, and people we asked didn't know it either. People were super-friendly. It was like coming down from space or having an infirmity. I *had* read it was next to a Halfords – and that eventually got us there. A concrete slab of a church, which so often on the inside seems to work okay.

The candle-magic in the piazza was right up Mum's street. Then during the long service, Mum started to worry, one hour prior to the last bus's scheduled departure. She didn't kneel, but she clenched in prayer, like she was squeezing one out, maintaining brute-control on whatever she had down there. 'Prayerful constipation' one Anglican minister termed it. Tenacious life. Brute – as only women can be, not men, they scrapped, they fought – they lied through their teeth, robbing the truth blind, while holding strict account. She wouldn't go for the blessing. But that's a new thing anyway.

Ron had mollified Mum's more Conservative instincts. Though once when Elton John was on stage with the three Billy Elliots, she said he wanted to be careful doing that.

She was dressed about as well as you could in the motor-home. She liked busses, what with her travel-pass. And you had to sit straight, knees together and your bag on your lap. This movement too and the gentle agitation soothed her.

When the Mass was sent, the stop was a couple hundred meters away. Then at the stop, all the people on the bus-in were back there, and all-hailed each-other with satisfied tales of their various nights out. And Mum was proud. It was an hour's trip back and they were in a mood to prolong the evening.

It was stiflingly small in the gizzed-up van. It was like living in bed – and sharing the bed with your mother. The time of year was wrong.

370

There were changes I wasn't happy with. Once, I'd tread with her the cliff-top walks in trainers I can't remember now. Now a dog strained at the cliff's edge, in dangerous wind, which threatened to drag us both off the cliff-edge. The broken cliff-path narrowed to nothing like one of my dreams. And as for Mum and her precarious footing... It was unspeakable what this stupid arrangement could do to her. Even Mum called Samson the most stupid Labrador she ever owned. But she wouldn't let him off the leash, so I held onto him, pulling him hard, and with little yet sense of a connection, this wilful beast, and with no anticipation, this next iteration, human and Labrador.

When we got to the village, I put my foot down and wanted a cab back. Loudly: 'Why are there no fucking cabs?' Twice – like Henry.

There was a bus every two hours so we waited.

Once, I learnt to read on holiday. Not that I *minded* school. I developed spiritual sensitivities also. There were, for instance, three weird stones on the downs in Dorset. These were clearly magical in purpose – an *old* religion. And there was a bookshop in Dorchester, where there were shelves-full of pagan beliefs and practices. *Practical Celtic Magic. Druidic Lore.* Aleister Crowley's *Magic.*

I was not of an age beyond magic. I bought. She bought. I was allowed books. There was no fiscal restraint in my holiday book-learning. We were still the same person those days.

Sometimes, when I read my Bible, I pause in the reading and say to myself: 'This bit's real.' It would be fair to say, I have issues with Mary, because, contrary to what we are taught to say, Mary isn't my mother. Rather: Mum is.

One bit of the Bible-text says this:

371

And when his family heard it, they went out to seize him, for people were saying, "He is beside himself." … And his mother and his brothers came; and standing outside they sent to him and called him. And a crowd was sitting about him; and they said to him, "Your mother and your brothers are outside, asking for you." And he replied, "Who are my mother and my brothers?" And looking around on those who sat about him, he said, "Here are my mother and my brothers! Whoever does the will of God is my brother, and sister, and mother." (Mark 3: 21; 31-35.)

Here she comes. She is in considerable distress. I can imagine that. I can relate to that. To save her boy from whatever he's got himself into this time. And you're not telling me there isn't something *inside* that.

Her boy is beside himself. Radical. Radicalized. Radicalizing. A misunderstood word. /'radɪk(ə)l/ *adjective & noun.* **1** Forming the root, basis, or foundation; original, primary. **2a** Inherent in the nature of a thing or person; fundamental. **b** Of action, change, an idea: going to the root or origin; far-reaching, thorough. **c** Advocating thorough or far-reaching change. **d** Characterized by departure from tradition; progressive; unorthodox.

'He has a demon! And he is mad!' – thus 'the Jews'. (e.g. John 10: 20.)

Come home!

It's all she wants. His family want him back now.

But it is an exclusive cult: there is an inside and there is an outside; and on the outside, they are not meant to understand, lest they be converted. *He* has defined himself as different from anything she was.

Only at the end does Jesus say to his Mum – and with savage, bitter irony: 'Woman, behold your son.' And then he dies.

Hail Mary, full of grace, the Lord is with thee. Blessed art thou

372

among women and blessed is the fruit of thy womb Jesus. Holy Mary,
Mother of God, pray for us sinners now and at the hour of our death.

We ask that we might find Mary in our hearts as a *Yes!* place for Jesus. It is also recommended that we pray to Jesus that we may be further in oneness with Mary. It is self-emptying, such that we only exist insofar as we are responsive to God's Word.

*

Last term, and put-out to pasture, the old Archbishop Emeritus came over to stay for a few days and did the odd class with us. He spoke of *Yes!* as the meaning of Mary's virginity. And we were not very nice about him. One or two took umbrage. One or two got the hump.

In a sense, his Grace, the Arch, basically wanted to move anyone he'd ever known from a high-place – a mountain – received theological 'truth' – to an imminent, human plane. *Earthing* the spiritual. Recalibrating metrics of *life's* believability toward a spiritual sense of things. He might have asked *the* impermissible question: what happened?

His Grace described it. God's love as a cloud. This descended upon Mary – and subsumed her. Within the cloud, Mary capitulated utterly. She became only and purely a response to God's love. As he spoke, the Arch cradled her. He carried her in his lap – in his hands. His Grace was a consecrated bishop. He *was* faith.

He sat squat, a rounded man, hands cupped and ankles crossed, fingers interlocked, with parted thighs. Rumpled, washed, speckled. A lifetime's skin... There could be no doubt His Grace spoke through long-term personal relationship with Mary.

It was Julian went for him:

'So are you saying Mary was a Virgin? Or are you not saying Mary

373

was a Virgin?'

Nasty. No, it wasn't pretty. Julian twisting his silver ring.

For a moment, what Julian had said to the Arch simply failed to communicate. No, for a moment, that dumped on the air meant nothing. Then His Grace said:

'There is a range of possible meanings we may understand in the question of Mary's virginity. For example, there are understandings of the word virginity entailed in the action of giving birth.'

Julian said: '*Duh!* So had she had sex or hadn't she?'

Trigger words. No, it wasn't pretty.

On that went for a little while. At length, Julian's point seemed reluctantly conceded. Then the Arch told us a new story, an additionally human event, the more to baffle us.

Controversially, he told us that Mary could not have been Joseph's first wife, for this would not have been the way of things in the society of that time. His belief was that Joseph must have taken Mary into his household through pity. That would be normal, he said, for Joseph to bring a young, vulnerable girl, who is about to have a baby, within his protection, not meaning to enjoy with her marital relations, but through kindness.

'And this story of the inn and stable,' the Archbishop said, 'it can't have been like that really. Joseph has travelled with Mary to stay with his family, at home in Bethlehem, and they don't want Mary in their house, for reasons which I am sure we can understand. It must have been there was considerable resistance to Mary. But Mary gives birth, and who can resist a baby? That's what happened. It must have been.

'I'm convinced that must have been how it happened really.'

Later that term, toward the beginning of Advent, we met boys who had been here before, in Valladolid, and now were in regular seminary. They had heard and recited verbatim all the Archbishop had said to them. Their spot-on impressions of each of the fathers were scathing. For boys in their cleverness can be rather good at that sort of thing.

Hail Mary, full of grace, the Lord is with thee. Blessed art thou among women and blessed is the fruit of thy womb Jesus. Holy Mary, Mother of God, pray for us sinners now and at the hour of our death.

I strip and shower, then scrub and wash my mouth. Satisfied with what I find in the mirror, I make what I think of as my Richard II face, then made chins, assessing the cheekbones and fat situation. I look okay-sharp – pleasingly – and dress in a skinny-fit, tapered gingham, casual-smart shirt, tucked into my jeans. I look English, and pretty adept at it.

As I open, close, and lock my room door, I notice the door to the student oratory, not quite directly opposite, over the corridor, gapes open, like a throat – such being the mess of cushions, rugs and hippy-rags thrown about in there. The windowless room recalls joss-sticks and hippy stuff. No live candle – a flickering bulb.

I look in – sticking my head in an inch in or so. While I have never actually *prayed* in here, given that it isn't conducive, and I didn't feel the comfort, though, once, Henry dragged me in randomly to do with him the Office of None, there is a live tabernacle we can unlock, the key hidden rather quaintly beneath the rightmost corner of the filthy rug. No-one is here. It occurs to me two seconds later that I could have closed the door. I don't like seeing it. It is like seeing the bathroom door open. I am on the stairs when Geoff and the Vice-Rector round the corner ahead of me. I have stood paused and I am having a moment. Geoff and the Vice-Rector occupy the whole of the stairs' breadth. They are full of something and in

375

no mood to give way to me. The Vice-Rector bows like he is carrying a baby. Geoff is more like he has an army to organize. I stand waiting for Geoff to knock into me. I adjust my body – in advance of inevitable assault – to signify fair passage. I wait to say good afternoon. It is apparent Geoff holds some unspeakable power and Father Richard in thrall to it. Only when they are past does Geoff call back, though up to the ceiling really. Geoff's beard and lustrous white-black half-shampooed hair thrown back. Geoff's words rear like stallions... Four distinct syllables mocking me. Heterosexually-violent:

'Al-*right*, To-*màs*.'

I watch as they round the corner and then pass out of view. Neither looks back. I stand a moment longer on the stairs. I wonder at the meaning of what I have seen. Then I think I had better move on in case anyone else comes. It wouldn't do to be seen lingering. Interstitial spy! An open-point between known certainties… Through the corridors. Into the street.

This passes without incident and, beyond the college front door, the basilica is only two blocks away. Valladolid has put itself to bed by now. Renovations are in progress within the basilica. There occupies a great scaffold over the reredos. This is vast. It includes as its primary feature a spectacular representation of the Risen Lord. A looming golden sculpture all gilt. Of the plastic arts. The ambition of the artist must impel even those who do not know to intensify their worship. The altar is wide – far more than the spread of a man's body. This early evening, the congregation is old yet populous. Confessionals have their lights on. They go about private devotions – all through Mass.

I think to confess and I hold myself back from it. I don't have the Spanish to waffle and have nothing important to say. A pity though – it would have been nice and I feel like doing it.

I do some sitting quietly. The flow of old-folk apologizing. Put your Euro in the rack of bulbs – taste forbid. Slip a Euro in the collection, though they never expect it.

There is a curious up-down logic to the great reredos. That great golden God the Risen Lord ascends, a call – to trust, follow. Then as one's eyes lift, they narrow on the scene of crucifixion expressed in a top panel. This in turn throws the eyes back again – down to the call to rise in the Risen Lord and – trust, follow… Though obscured for human maintenance, you can see it through the scaffold. A star-clad midnight-heaven-blue canopy written in the vault above.

I observe the general order of church-business. There is shuffling all around the Mass-bell – the many odd corners of the church where prayer absorbs itself. I can't follow the readings, and come to suppose we must be still on Saturday, which I haven't looked up. A lay-woman reads, then a nun leads the psalm, which she sings, as compact and to-business as all her tribe. The priest really is very old and really like a cobweb. The priest reads the Gospel and delivers his homily. He touches his clothes where his heart is, then heaven… All that yet again, though in this case in frenetic repetition of this one gesture.

The priest rests, seated, while a young man sets the altar. Then the young man helps the priest to stand. I take communion. I kneel to pray while the Eucharist dissolves on my tongue and I mash it and swallow it. As I do so, I repeat the words in English in my head: *Lord, I am not worthy that you should enter under my roof, but only say the word and my soul shall be healed.* Then the Mass is sent, and I don't linger. It is a quarter to seven. Five-twenty solar-time. There isn't time for a swim. It is busy in the Mercadona. Then at the college door I find Geoff, Richie and

377

Niall, loaded with a shopping trolley full of booze and crisps. Maybe I do look like I've just come from a Mass. I certainly feel I ought to.

Geoff says: 'Tomàs! Are you going to join us for a get-together this evening?'

I say: 'Yeah?'

Everyone is smiling. The boys manoeuvre the supermarket-trolley up over the ledge. I follow and stand at the foot of the big stairs as they trundle it along the corridor to the lift at the far end.

Geoff hollers back: 'Common room. After supper and prayer.'

My landline phone is ringing, but I don't answer. I get ready to go out. Clothes etc. I'm not going out-out – just to the common room.

Once upon a time… A strange, itinerant figure known as Tomàs…

Oh – again? Shush, Memory! Sparse friends – liable to flake or to run out of credit. Bars when it was no-one. The human equation and its unresolved remainders: these people… Of course, there *were* times of peak desperation. Tomàs grazed multiple varieties of Soho… Sleb 'n' producer haunts. Sausagey steam-beer restaurants. They liked to touch, and stroke your face, and even sometimes tried to put a finger in your mouth. Slack on a bar stool – who cares? Sleep it. No.

*

Hoots and 'lad' noise sound out in the corridor. Ambiguously sexual. But then again a whole lot of not-very-good-looking people make a life. I am tired and I dress in order to simplify. The first time I ever dressed to go to a city, to cover my age, I wore my black leather biker jacket – that was to go to a studenty cinema, in Liverpool, to watch *The Cook, The Thief, His Wife And Her Lover*. And had a jacket potato and cheese with a pint of Guinness – while literally no-one hit on me.

They might be playing chase/tag… Or stuck-in-the-mud. For there sounds some devilish cunning going on out there. Hoots, whoops…

You can have a nice walk in this town if it is only the night you want. And in the little crush of bars, of street-scenes, women and men, to expect no reciprocity. A smell, a feel, a whisper. None turns to make space at the bar. (How *not* like Soho, where *everyone* wanted friends.) One place I discovered online is in among all the other bars, but the security grille was locked – and this was late. A third has changed its name, if not its lemon-and-heliotrope colour-scheme, three boy-girl couples – wannabes – sat at the bar.

More than a little nervous – to put it mildly – I play Lady Gaga and Britney Spears. I prepare for home-grown entertainments. In pursuance of the evening ahead, I check in the lectionary in order to make out what the readings *had been* an hour previously in church. The Gospel reading was the prodigal son. I have a beer and I take off my shirt and I put a vest on. White, tight, hugging, though with short-sleeves, more M&S than the guy in the perfume ad. Across the way, the gym is closed, and there is none in the yard below. It is half-past eight – sunset having been 19:33 local time. I breathe and inhale the alternative feeling. Figuring I'll be okay once I've stepped outside, and surveying my desk, which has sprawled again, though not my mirror, I say:

'Adapt.'

And strict vows to inject no momentum whatsoever into whatever scene I find.

I drink about a pint of water, then a glass of warm orange juice – blood sugar. Then, slowly, a tumbler of wine. An alertness sets into me. I take off my pumps so I can take my socks off. I clean my mouth and there is blooded red-pink toothpaste: melted ice-cream. Disco-lights play through the door to the common room.

Lights track me down the length of the corridor. Block by block: as motion-sensors detect I am here. It is one of the fun things about the place.

Benedict, larking, likes to pretend he has magic hands: 'Inlūstrā!'

Half-way: I stop and I open a window to look down on the quad. The fountain at the centre of it. The fountain is lit from within and is spilling light. This untinted though toward golden in relation to the trees. Bubulous: sub-aquatic brain. It must soothe and might centre me. Plosh and splat... As though restored by night. I leave the window to it open, and walk the next half of the remaining half-corridor, then the half of the half beyond that... And by-and-by stand six inches from the common room door.

I straighten up. I discover an imaginary crease, and stretch my T-shirt down, so it ends on the lift of my buttocks and half-way down my fly. I step through into the common room and take in the scene. A disco arrangement. Two flashing four bulb *units* of coloured disco lights. These on the table at the front – either side of the hi-fi. The only light else is from the open fridge. Jon is dancing. Julian mans the hi-fi. Geoff is booze-monitor – at the bar they've constructed from two classroom-tables.

Gospel-American voices ooze like yeast. Whatever it is... Suburb-grime, tower-block-*yearn, r*aced-up strummy-guitar and drug-electro – form cheery, mechanical interludes. (Perhaps, I think, Julian put it together for his GCSE.) Arranged along the wall, six technically adult seminarians stand in a line in the disco-light. Each holds his glass sarcophagal. Others sit. Geoff yomps about topping them up with crisps and gin.

380

I take a handful of crisps at the bar. Niall yells in my ear and pours me a strong G&T – yelling: 'How much?' – in a tall glass.

I touch the glass to my lips to taste it. Too much. (I am prepped for social drinking.) I raise the glass to the whole room. I am going to puke if I try to get this down, so I push past Niall, to the iced sink, and get one of the stubby beers. Then I go and stand next to Francis. I say 'cheers' with the raised cold can, and yell at him: 'THIS IS FUN!'

Francis grins and yells back: 'WHAT WE CAME FOR!'

'PROPER OLD SCHOOL SKULL CANDY INNIT BLAD!'

'BANGING TUNES!'

A rave-salute. Then I take my place at the side, stand and forget myself. There are lyrical fragments: *He's a mighty good leader… he's a mighty good leader… all the way, Lord… from up to heaven… He led my brother… he led my brother… all the way, Lord… from up to heaven…* When they want you to cry, leap into the sky… when they suck your mind, like a pigeon you fly… I know, I know it's the positive people running from their time looking for some feeling…[3]

As good as my word to myself, I am in no mood to bother the scene. I finish my second beer, and go for my third, and it becomes apparent the wallflowers are leaving. By degrees, there are six of us. Philip sits enthroned with a pint of gin: he isn't moving. Then Niall comes back, stands at the door, and yells: 'WHAT'S HAPPENING?'

The music dies and Geoff, re-entering also, says: 'Oh we cannot have this. We cannot have this.'

Julian says: 'Well you could have told me.'

---

[3] Lyrics by Beck.

Niall says: 'It's nine o'clock!'

Then Sean arrives with his lap-top.

Geoff says: 'Put that music back on. Sean, what have you got? Play it. Play it. I'm having a party here.'

I eat some more of the free crisps.

The students arrange armchairs and sit in a circle. There isn't much we can do about the lights. As others re-arrive, we expand the circle. None dances much after that. Maybe I dance briefly, only to one track, thinking it's something else. Otherwise, by tacit agreement, we aren't the dancing sort.

Sean's music is all very religious songs. They are of the sort youth might hear and sing at a youth event. Then Geoff gets Sean to play them all over again – so we can learn the words. We must have drunk a lot of alcohol. Geoff goes round with the bottles and says to each: 'Come on, brother!' Some want nothing at all. Then Geoff slops in his seat like a country octopus. All told, it is a peculiar scene, but a kind of love rolls over it. We become gradually tired and go to bed. In the end it is only me and Geoff there.

There is no music now. Geoff calls after me, across the room:

'Tomàs, pour me one.'

'What would you like?'

'Gin.'

Slops of ice remain in the base of the tub. There are no tongs: all night they've been using their fingers. I scoop three of the slippy-dregs into a glass. I angle and hold the glass against the side of the tub to drain the melt-water. There is even a slice of lemon. I make it strong. It looks like poison – another life.

Geoff has turned his chair and stood and got the TV on. He

382

collapses back in the chair and starts channel-hopping. I hand Geoff the drink, and Geoff takes a sip of it, then says:

'Tomàs, with the best will in the world, are you meant to be here?'

I say: 'Well, I hope for next year. I don't know about this exactly.'

'But are you sure?'

'No. Not sure.'

'Just – don't get me wrong, bro – who are you?'

'And what about you?'

'Ah, don't mind me.'

'Who are you?'

Pause. Drink. Slurp. Glug. Ice. Crunch.

'God doesn't mind about my sort.'

I neck my beer and stand. Maybe this conversation is fine if I'm not down in it.

Geoff's hair seems to drip into his tumbler of gin. He swashes it round and round and round and round... Maybe considering strategies. Drunk-force.

The room is a mess. Disco-lights and television. It isn't midnight. Packets and cans. And the bin is overflowing, and the tables slick.

I pour a half-glass of red wine. I watch for a minute the football Geoff has found on a Spanish channel. I get a last beer and two to take back to my room. Then I yell at the whole empty common room – where Geoff incidentally is – Bruegel-fashion.

'God likes my kind!'

Geoff said: 'Are you sure about that, Tomàs?'

'God likes my kind. He knows me.'

Evading Geoff, I walk past Geoff to the door and look back to see him there. Geoff sat in the dark with his feet up on the coffee table. And has his football on and the disco lights. Geoff doesn't look much to be planning attempting sleep tonight.

Geoff calls after me: 'Yeah, brother. He knows you.'

I leave Geoff to it. The corridor is silent, the lights flick, the college is dark. I joggle the key from my pocket. Inside, I lock the door. I forget for a second what sort of lock it is so wrench the handle upward – expecting a click. I leave the key in the lock and transfer the two beers I've nicked from the common room fridge from pockets to desk. Of a sudden, on as it were a mounting wave, I lurch into the bathroom, get my face in the loo, and hack it all up.

I've never experienced that much spew. Nor such extremely immediate, open-gullet liquid-transfer. Half-chewed nuts like concrete your throat isn't meant to accommodate. When I haven't quite finished – filth remains inside – I fix my eyes in a frank 20-20 on the filth in the lavatory and smell all that to bring it up more completely.

There is only a little splatter around the edge. I flush and mop that up. Give it a spray with cleaning products.

Sat on the bathroom floor, I peel my clothes. I leave them in a pile there. I roll my desk-chair on the wooden floor. It isn't late. Only a little past midnight. The night is sea-green; my thoughts are orange... In the mirror, my eyes are blood-red, but I rinse my mouth, and wash my face. The heating has turned itself on again. No sound flows through it. The system is expensively maintained. I take air at the window, brain-fruit hanging off the trees, and put the English radio on. I find the news, lie on my bed, and am asleep by the time I've settled into the pillow.

Chapter Ten

I must have been partially awake intermittently through the night. Drinking water – though I have no recollection of doing so. My bladder is fit to burst as I snap from warm-nothing. I am conscious. Alert – I roll to left and right to press each cheek against the pillow. Each side carrying different thoughts – left and right. It seems balanced emotionally. Five o'clock. I don't yet know I've been sick. In fact, I don't seem to recall saying anything at all.

I get a vest and my blue trackie bottoms on. Not wearing socks, I take the two bundles of clothes I have up to the washing machines, up on the second floor. Then I have to go along to the common room to fill-up my bottles with water. Geoff isn't there. Then I go down to the cellars – and lay and broil and sweat. I am lain there nigh on two hours, topping the heat up.

The heat runs cold – cooking. I panic and rear for the cold tap. Briskly enough, the cold drenches through me. From the tap, I replenish a bottle and sink again. I lie prone – shivering. I hold my nose and roll my head back into it… Then I am able to stand, and sweat all the way through the corridors. It is nearing eight o' clock. Once I have finished sweating, I shower again, then get ready for morning prayer. I put a teaspoon in a glass of bicarbonate of soda. My belt is just one of those things – the language difference would never get round to it, all point and mime, and helpless gratitude. Besides, the issue of my waist-size is sensitive. I seem pretty tranquil at morning prayer.

At breakfast, the students pass it round between ourselves that there is going to be a christening at Mass today. At nine, at the rehearsal for Mass, those present are formally notified. One thing this means is that today we will not be heading out to perform Sunday pastoral duties, serving their lunch to the old people in the *beneficia*, or to the homeless people – who get a reasonable Sunday lunch off the arterial road – heading south-east toward the outskirts down Calle San Isidro. I am just down to be an Acolyte. Mass is set back a bit, midday, an adjustment of one and a half hours. This is free time.

I get my gym-kit and my swim things together in a Carrefour bag. The gym opens at ten. I meet no-one in the corridors. It is the first time I have ever been to the gym on a Sunday. I burn a quick 600 calories upstairs and see from the mezzanine there are empty pool lanes. Skipping the weights – I must swim for a whole hour. Most strange and most unusual. Useful time. My muscles seem to hug the water naturally. There is a rhythm and a flow – it almost seems to push and suck me through it. (I am doing breast-stroke.) I dare not to think that I might let go a little. It isn't like the sea! (There is really nothing to accommodate.) All a bit pretend… And I don't get a sauna. This is not least because I am consistently aware of the marginal-cost to the manager – who only turns the sauna on if you ask him. By half-past eleven, I am back in my room getting into my suit again.

I arrange my clothes in two piles: one for colours and one for whites. I nip upstairs to bung the stuff from earlier into the tumble-drier. This Christening is a very big deal. Francis put it in a word over breakfast: mafia. So that confused Henry. And Jonathon, who often seems in on these things, didn't deny it. There were no supplementary lies.

Of all of us, Henry most rejoices in the prospect of all the pretty clothes Father James might wear – not just 'now' especially but 'when' He is consecrated bishop. While that's never going to happen, Henry wants this most for The Rector. It makes good sense for Henry there be the career path. Henry's faith naturally attunes within hierarchy and ambition. Henry loves his frillies. 'Look at that lace!' he'll say, when we watch the parades. 'Will you look at that lace!' He loves the papal ruby slippers and the papal tiara – the triple crown.

Solid gold – which the poorest of the poor – he says – in their backwoods communities yet give of their poverty to their parish church as to the Church and in the service of Jesus… There is no judgement on Henry here. All that is shiny and expensive in the world might be consecrated.

The Rector in His room has got His purple cassock on. You would not wish to catch His eye now, to interrogate what might be happening there. Snarl you away from it – that He would. Dog and bone. In the waxy-smelling Sacristy, I get my candle lit, and have a lighter in my pocket in case. The holders are big, heavy, solid silver, which you brace on your sternum to steady, and of such weight that you really have to concentrate doing that.

The good thing about being an Acolyte is that there are two of you, for serving at Mass correctly is a very big deal. The Acolytes *always* get it wrong. Without fail, at some counter-intuitive point. But that peculiarity never seems to get picked-up on – and half the time you don't realize what has gone weird – askew. The thing is to concentrate: never to pray. There are about half a dozen priests. And there might be a certain edginess about them. A confused sense of spiritual proceedings. The priests arrange themselves positionally. Then when the time comes, they pray silent-prayer toward the end of the room they need to pray to, where the chest-of-drawers is.

The Rector checks each one of them. Then He says: 'Good.'

The priests venerate the cross. This being the one the crucifer has to carry in the procession at the start of Mass – whoever that is this day. (It doesn't matter.) There are silent prayers the priests are supposed to make. The servers just try to look invisible. The priests look to one another – briefly in each other's eyes. Dipping their heads having done so immediately. The Rector nods and says: 'Okay.'

And: 'Good. Let's go.'

They've rearranged chapel, angling all the pews. *It is only a baptism… But it is like an ordination…* The gathered congregation swells the pews. Maybe in a good way you have to admit they are getting their money's worth. (One rather imagines they aren't short.) Henry hasn't a part this week, but at the side I sit with him.

And He baptized the little baby in the name of the Father and of the Son and of the Holy Spirit. And those in the smart pews applaud and refrain from taking too many photographs.

And Henry loves all that. And it goes okay.

Looking back on it – back in the Sacristy… As priests disrobe, as I slough my alb… Looking back on it: there was a kind of nice air about the place.

We've done okay. Got away with another one. No-one bumped into the furniture.

Then the next thing happens.

388

The Rector praised me last week. That was nice. (I crave praise.) As He beckons to me now, across the Sacristy, I go to Him open-faced. I am not expecting praise for carrying a candle. But – something. Little boy to little boy. (A new Dad.) Permissions granted. Not to worry and not to fight.

But it isn't good news. It is very bad news indeed. It is the worst news imaginable.

The Rector draws me right-up close like a pervert and hisses: 'You stink of alcohol.'

'No.'

'It is – '

He makes a wafting gesture.

And all we've done and every second chance we've given Tomàs. And, heaven knows, the allowances we've made, and some of what we've had to put up with… You could see He was taking it personally.

A cry of brute injustice rises – in Tomàs:

I'm not having this. *Thus far and no further: here's the line.* So I square on Him.

You go so far, you see so much, and you realize you don't have to take it. You go so far, you see so much, and you realize you don't have to take it. You go so far, you see so much, and you realize you don't have to take it.

Possibly, He now sees what a smack hard in the face that hasn't happened for the next three seconds looks like. If it were only a rôle, that rôle now consumes – me. No-one else could hear. It goes – my face goes: *Now-you-listen-to-me-you-piece-of-shit.* And bears in closer, claims a status now, which must diminish me and Him. Shadow-puppet gun, which might go: *bang-bang.* And from The Rector's head might plume a

389

rainbow flight of pretty butterflies.

Sometimes, all you have to do takes just a moment. The Rector stoops, placating. A threat of relatively-mild-violence deemed credible. The Rector actually *believes* I'll do it. Repeat – after baptizing that little baby – The Rector actually *believes* I'll do it.

So that's the shape of it.

'No. You are wrong,' I say. 'You are lying. That is impossible. And I know that. You are lying. And I know that now.'

The Rector says: 'Not in this place.'

'Fine. Then, *soto voce*, don't you start. And don't you bring it here.'

No-one sees. Nothing can stop me now. Liking Tomàs now, in baffled fact, I whisper to The Rector's eyes: 'Now I know that you are making things up and you are lying.'

I am convinced I am not lying. And here I stand, and here I take my stand, and I dismiss Him. I am all adrenalin and contempt. It is not as if I haven't done this before. And there is something in the transposition which might make me sadistically capable. And I shake with it. While The Rector fears I might kill him, I use my right-hand fierce and as controlled like Spanish honour. At the end of which, I flick my chin. Then, in sour disgust, and boiling with adrenalin, having ensured that the meaning and the capability have been communicated, I assert my height and walk away from it.

Later, when I've come down from it, I know perfectly well it was sheer chance. That whatever information The Rector had received from Geoff had gone the way of a loo-full of sick, a bath, a chlorine swim, and approximately twenty-four pints of water. That, for The Rector, it was actually a pretty fair bet.

No-one else had seen.

I come to myself. They are tidying-up. The priests are knotting cinctures. The Sacristy is looking a bit like after-Mass – when on the altar the event has been tidied away and you've only got a smudgy-white table-cloth left. Cleaned-up. Priests who don't yet know each other are beginning to talk. I turn at the Sacristy door to look back at The Rector. I find His eyes, which skulk after me. There is little to read there. An enemy.

Bathetically, I suppose I ought to stay in my room until they phone with the travel arrangements. I wait the next half hour and they don't call. It isn't nice as the adrenaline drains through and out of me. Angsty, I punch my locked door: daring my knuckles, which split and bleed, to hurt. Cathartically, I sit quietly shaking my head: Unbelievable…

A priest who's just downed half a chalice of fortified corked wine… Then it is lunchtime and I have to go down to the Refectory.

I walk the long route down to the Refectory. This route takes me past The Rector's door. Quite probably, I have yet to resolve the encounter. I'm not singing – which I habitually do in the corridors – and there is little to individuate my tread – save they are leather soles. I am early to arrive in the Refectory.

Henry is here, on his own, touching cutlery. Henry says:

'Alright, old chap?'

'Tip-top, thank you. Your good self?'

'Fine and dandy.'

The Refectory is laid out in Sunday formation. I and Henry claim our usual two places together, which are immediately adjacent to top table. I am hungry, what with the puke last night and the gym this morning, and look forward to enjoying a good meal. It is hardly a thought – that thing that happened earlier. The inevitable summons must come… Blah blah… Not *being here* holds no reality for me. It feels quite sincere – the complete lie – my offering myself to God. (*Purlease…*) Realized in its relinquishment. And that's the way of it.

I and Henry are pretty much out of talk. Instead, we play a little game with the cutlery, plates, and the two glasses each, one for water, one for wine. A game concerned with pattern, disposition, and ratio. There are no obviously stated rules but it kind of makes sense. A glass-bead game – it isn't chess. Henry doesn't play chess. Until:

'What are we doing?' says Henry. 'What are we even doing?'

'Looks to me you'd have positional advantage, except it's your move.'

'I don't even know… There!'

'Impressive.'

They – arrive. Each to his regular space. Firm territorial creatures. Teacher. Bailiff. Civil-servant. Lawyer… In Sunday best, Ade's suit might have cost high-end money or 50 pence. Philip's says he is about to evict you. Francis's is tailored – though to the fashion of decades past. Sean's is from Primark. Mine from M&S. John's is the one you get when you work in the shop. There is no rule about silence. We would have been perfectly entitled to speak. There are no unordained guests.

As the priests enter, and Sister Angelina, they thank each other as they designate seats among themselves. A certain buoyancy prevails. *Well this is all very nice…* And it is true: the tables sparkle. This bunch of priests is a comparatively youthful lot. They've probably had a tipple in the garden-room and they have the afterglow of a good Mass. They look done. The Rector is still in that tulip of a cassock and thanks us all. And there are further homiletics.

As luck would have it, it is my and Ade's turn to serve as Refectorians. For this is an opportunity to shine as a gentleman might who is going to the wall. On the metal trolleys: aubergine, beefy tomatoes, mushed olive, a truffle liquor... Sister Angelica sits immediately to my left, but I am damned if I'm not going to make myself agreeable to her. She keeps on with her sole conversational gambit – and I fob her off with the same one-liner time-again. I take the piss a bit. There is a wee-little soft-boiled egg on my fork and I say: 'A far cry from our green days, hey, Sister Angelina? Ah, where the Lord takes us in this life.'

It might not *quite* have been her fault but she's fair game.

There is no call to The Room Where Faith Dies. No compulsory self-criticism. No slow word from Father Richard... though I sit a few seconds, at prayer, after lunch, to give Father Richard his chance at me. We have a meeting though, up in the common room, about 'what happened'. No-one is pointing any fingers. There are to be no room searches or anything like that. Than which more no-one will say. Then Geoff leads us in prayer:

'Beloved Jesus, cleanse us of the evil we have experienced these last days. Help us to find new truth and faith in our hearts from this terrible experience. May your love come renewed to us. May your Holy Spirit convert us to know our sins. May we all come to your eternal house of splendid majesty, and may your truth shine on the whole Earth and for all men. Through Christ our Lord. Amen.'

All say: 'Amen.'

So Geoff did 'it'. Maybe The Rector did it with him. We file in silence from the common room. There is no other possible solution…

What happened?

I scrape the crap out from my goof-teeth, the wisdom teeth, and still more would come. I force the Listerene through my teeth. My poisoned tongue has the look of a moon-landing.

We go heavy with the wine that supper. Reduced to something like the purely animal, our feed is soup and bread and grilled meats. None wants anyone else here. Τρώγω (trógó): to gnaw, to munch, to crunch. An unconscious anger is manifest. We chew at a low pace. Skewered meat. He who gnaws/munches/crunches my flesh, and drinks my blood, abides in me and I in him. Ὁ τρώγων μου τὴν σάρκα καὶ πίνων μου τὸ αἷμα, ἐν ἐμοὶ μένει, κἀγὼ ἐν αὐτῷ.

It is on Wednesday they get to doing me.

Even now it is a scheduled event. I am on the list for spiritual direction at three… Father Gerry isn't exactly one to shake things up. Oh you have to prime the pump the first minutes' pleasantries. But it is never an interview situation – it is *never* hostile.

At ten-to-three I smarten myself up. My clothes are not contentious. I wear a white and navy-blue needle-stripe shirt beneath a cobalt jumper. At three, Father Gerry answers his door as if absolutely astonished to see me. There is nothing to read into this. (On the one occasion ever I didn't show on time, there was a call within the minute.)

At his desk, Father Gerry has been doing some computing.

He says: 'Ah ha!'

Then, as I settle myself on the sofa, Father Gerry presses – *this*, and – *this*, and – *this*. The blue screen sporting its Microsoft logo cuts to

394

black.

Father Gerry drops to *his* sofa: '*Ouph*'.

(Of an age when it's all theatrics – played to the young.)

The room Father Gerry lives in must be about six by eight if you considered it literally. One's middle-aged limbs seem gangling. Father Gerry doesn't fanny around but comes straight to the point and says:

'Now Tomàs, dear Tomàs, are you sure this is for you?'

Father Gerry pauses and lets that settle.

Then it is a long time until he says: 'Because, you know, if it isn't, you won't have failed; you can leave here with our blessings. What is best for you?'

Survive.

Modest, expressionless… I have laid off the booze since Sunday. (The days stretch forever in every direction.) I say: 'I hope so. I don't know.'

Father Gerry takes his moments – he isn't stupid.

Father Gerry weighs it.

Then shrugs. He sits back and kicking his hands up says – kind of throwaway:

'How are your feelings generally? Well, about all sorts of things. How's life?'

When Father Gerry says *life*, there is both relish and irony. Humorous. Given the seriousness of Father Gerry's intent, I hazard a great-hilarious… Father Gerry watches as my brain scrolls… through a brief range of broadly inaccurate responses.

I don't want to go out on these terms. I want to be clean. I don't want to be shown the door. I can fix things. I can make things better…

I say: 'There are certainly challenges.'

395

Father Gerry rolls back on the sofa like God. He laughs: 'Hah!'
Big old hands he has.

'Well, yes, we get plenty of those in life.'

His voice then deepens, an unnervingly different register. He says:

'But Tomàs, how are things really, in terms of what's really happening?'

The trouble is: everything has resolved to one fantasy – one rescuable moment. Rescuable if you can stir the rice-pudding back. Everything else has just started to look a bit shit.

The Rector has decided I'm next on his list. Geoff wants to destroy me... I'm becoming Henry... Julian ffs.

The meaning of Father Gerry's question seems open. It could plausibly be understood as a spiritual question. Therefore, I say: 'In prayer... It becomes very powerful. I could use a little space. It carries an unusual impact.'

How have I prayed today? Slim pickings. Scraps in the odd, scrappy minutes I've tossed to it. Lord, I am deeply afflicted... Tosh! Worm of my own being!

But I don't want to hurt Father Gerry. I say:

'It becomes very powerful. I could use a little space. It carries an unusual impact.'

In February, we went to a freezing-cold place called Herencia, on silent retreat, where a darkness broke inside me, because they hadn't turned the heating on... It was a darkness I had to enter to enter into, if I was to have any hope, and obey...

Father Gerry takes this opportunity. He says:

'Well, hah, yes, prayer is how we find God, how we form our deepest relationship with God. To say that has an impact is putting it

396

lightly!' Father Gerry settles back in his sofa. 'Tell me, what do you do when you pray? What do you find there?'

I confess my prayer-life has worn ragged.

My mouth becomes a cave. My mouth becomes a rock...

I say: 'It's almost too deep. The world stops. It's the focus. A moment that – *onion-skins* everything. There is reality. It's down there. God is real. It can be difficult getting other things to fit with that. All the time. It demands everything – so much time. Not the timetable. That's in the way of it. I mean days of prayer and time.'

Father Gerry says: 'You think very deeply about these things. That's you! Tomàs, you are a mature man, while others here are only beginning to discover who they are. Where is this going for you?'

'I don't know. I – hope.'

I run in cross-currents about myself. Then I say:

'It would be good to have a little time to find things out properly.'

Father Gerry begins now:

'Prayer is a serious thing for us all. A very serious thing. Where we do discover who we truly are. And where we ought to be. If you can grow in prayer... You know you may encounter things. God is not easy. God is a challenge – to all of us. And sometimes we may lack that confidence, of Christian prayer, and of our knowledge that our Lord is inviting us to respond to his gift. Prayer can at times seem very lonely, and that is when we take great comfort in the thought the Church is praying with us, we are supporting one another...'

Father Gerry will talk now. That will be it now. I can let Father Gerry be.

*

Otherwise, Lent 3 is a dry week of low intensities.

397

I decline when they offer me wine at dinner. Trying not to notice they don't bother to disguise how they'd like to encourage me. I do, though, literally decline. (I can't resist it.) There are classes... We know about those. Nor has The Rector nor has the Vice Rector specifically bothered me.

Most afternoons, I am able to get to the gym. I even make it to the pool after supper.

I don't sleep, and suspect depletion in terms of my muscle-mass.

I eat and I drink enough calories.

*

Thus Tomàs's postcards to Mum:

Hey! Having a great time here. Maybe this is for me! LOL!!! Tx

Met the red squirrel! Took this pic! I like to call him Mr Red Squirrel! Sexist? Moi?!! Tx

What is it with Spanish food?!!! Hope U're booking me in some home cooking!! Tx

Remember when I told you I was going to get married?!! This is like the opposite of that!! ☺ Tx

There is one amusing incident. (This doesn't write back to Mum.) I am singing in the corridors. It is at break between classes to go to the bathroom. As I approach the Vice Rector's office, the Vice Rector stands at his door and says: 'Tomàs.'

'Hey, Father.'

Father Richard draws close, and draws me in... Then Father Richard says in a low voice, confidingly:

'How are you for the devotions this evening? Are you ready with a prayer you'd like to lead on?'

398

I myself draw closer…

This would now be creepy, given normal circumstances, and yet Father Richard draws ever still closer …

I breathe all over him:

'Yes, of course, Father.'

The Vice Rector says: 'Well, if you need anything – to talk… You know we're all here.'

'Yes, of course, Father.'

'Well, you don't want to be late.'

'No, indeed.'

*

On Friday we have to go on one of our coach trips. We go to Segovia – there is lunch and a Mass at a shrine-church. I don't know Segovia – and we are free to explore for an hour before lunch. There is an aqueduct and tourist-groups of European youth buying Segovia-themed-knives and Segovia-themed-lighters. On the way back, I sit lolling my head on the coach window. I watch my own reflection as it gets dark. I am listening to REM. Father Gerry got lost getting back to the coach and we had to split into groups to find him. At the back of the coach, all they are saying is pure scat. That's what it always comes down to – the topic at the back of the coach. Julian leads the charge: 'What is it, though, when you've like literally eaten nothing, and then you're like: Where did *that* come from?' Volumes, consistencies… Shit is the body-function deemed conversationally appropriate. Shit passed the dinner-party test.

Henry says: 'Why do we always end up talking about shit?'

Philip says: 'Because we are in a dream.'

Henry says: 'Why do we always end up talking about shit?'

A coach-thing.

The vibration of the window I slump against massages my skull.
There is a game they play in college in each other's bathroom.
Apparently. Those who leave their door unlocked. Such haggissy-bowels
as I endure youth knew not... And prunes and roughage. Spain sleeps.

*

I see the red-squirrel on Saturday.

An old man has a bag of nuts and is crumbling the nuts in his hand
to offer them. The squirrel takes the crumpled nuts, then bounces back to
examine them, eats a little, bounces once more to the man's hand.

By and by, pops off, most delicate, in springy, American diagonals,
over the pine-strewn soil.

I sit on the bench what seems a long time. As if time balanced here.
As if I've got to the middle bit. It is very peaceful... *Come home...* Over-
leveraged, over-extended. A market-correction of Tomàs. I walk the most
direct way toward Plaza Mayor... I go to the Carrefour.

With nothing in particular I want to do, I go to my room and close
the shutters and lay myself down. I put myself into storage mode. By the
time I wake it is eight o'clock.

I panic and scramble into my smart clothes to get downstairs.

But when I get to chapel I find it dark.

Now, morbidly confused, I wheel myself about, checking the time
on the watch I wear. Eight o'clock. Then in the corridor I hear the
Refectory noise and so I walk toward that. They are eating supper. I stand
at the door, and Geoff, at the head of the table, turns, which must mean
others have pointed their eyes my way.

Geoff says: 'Tomàs! Pull up a place, lad. Come on.'

The Rector is sat with them – eating.

I say: 'No, thank you. No – I just nodded off. I saw the time. I

400

thought it was tomorrow! I just went to the chapel. I was wondering why no-one was there.'

There is a fair few of them. Maybe half. I am just really confused. The Rector's eyes – chewing – do not disguise naked hatred. They are never going to let me go now. He doesn't cover it up. There is no pretending that has not been seen. That is the fact of the matter.

'I…' I say, finding the humour of it.

I gesture upward: my room, my bed, a little time…

I wave to them: sorry about all this.

I don't know how to leave now.

*

What remains?

Let's just do a couple of things. We're almost done now.

First off: the second-to-last time I ever met Luke.

That was by chance that summer, when I was heading off in a few days. Outside Sainsbury's. Their summer holidays done – Luke 14 going on 15. A summer's extra inch – and his upper lip shaved.

Quite the young man about it: 'Hello, Sir.'

'Hey, how's it going?'

'Ah, so so. Your good self?'

'Yeah…' … some forgettable lines.

Until: 'Well, I'd better be…'

'Oh right well.'

'You take care, Sir.'

We shook on it.

I could have offered Luke a lift – and shifted the dog-towels and all that – and apologized for the passenger seat – but I didn't.

*

Luke phoned me, back in the days. Luke fifteen, sixteen, and mercifully did most of the talking. Phoning – Sir! was maybe quite a kick. Luke talked – about school and his Mum and his sisters. He had girlfriends and what he was into. He emailed me pictures when he got into grunge. It was later I went to see him play. Luke then was stringy-as-a-bean in black and All-Stars – dreads and bass-guitar. I was incredibly ordinary.

*

Next – still memory:

Father John, pocketing fags at the stones' edge, said in contemplation gruff like it wasn't the easiest thought:

'You have love.'

'Sure, I have love.'

The field we'd more or less ploughed. He had at least a foot depth of very good soil in there. There were only the smallest chinks of rock. The growing season must be short, but it was ready to grow. Rotted and washed together. I had seen things grow in worse than this space – Mum's and Dad's being The Good Life.

Fr. John again: 'You have love.'

Grey face, yellow face. Cigarettes. It would have been too emotional.

Maybe about how Mum could never be Catholic. She was barely even Christmas and she wasn't Easter. Brother John would have slapped me about the head hard with a blunt trowel had I uttered one syllable of that. Or yet that my loyalties were in any final analysis absolute.

I was still angry when I got back to her – after the trains. First the Welsh train, picking and sucking dirt from beneath my nails. Then from Crew it didn't stop until Chester.

She came to meet me at the station – stood at the side of her new car. After an absence. She'd had her own head shrunk too – after Ron. Each time I return and she stands to meet me at the station. It is always like this. Easy as pi. A fairly complex calculation as two sets of polygons containing a circle are gradually described toward infinity. She is apt on occasion to run that manner of counselling script. She looked, at the side of her new car, compacted, bereavement-counselled. Sandstone-scenes of provincial life – M&S smart.

When they said, at the centre, I should go for counselling, I arranged a preliminary session on the NHS. I felt better for that little cry. It did me a world of good. She said it was sad that after all these years I 'felt I had to have' counselling. The counsellor said it was normal, that all along, inside... The absolute forbidden to say.

*

Right: let's finish this. (It's been a blast.)

I close the shutters, and earnestly pray my heart doesn't stop in the night. I've changed my clocks – we lose an hour tonight as the clocks change. We'll be two and a half hours off solar time. I arrange my desk and shelves... I empty my gym bag. (Rank-vest, brown yet-liquid shorts, mucky-white-Tesco-ankle-socks...) On the floor and the towels at the foot of my wardrobe. No-one would ask further questions once they'd registered that – if I die in the night. Ship-shape.

I don't sleep. I get up again and put *Our Sceptred Isle* on. Waiting for the fear to idle. Then stand awake at the window, then lie in pitch dark... It feels like a body I was carrying earlier rather than myself. ('Myself'!) Unable to curl-up inside of it – 'hold me like a baby' – I've lost the fantasy.

I wake in what must be the middle of a night's long tumble. My head seems sucked inside the pillow – and I could easily have blanked again. But the bedside alarm clock tells me I've missed the alarm and I have five minutes.

Howling, convulsive, I wrench myself up and out of it. I am going to be late.

It is a godawful repeat of the twelve hours previous – tediously I am aware of physical drag.

I scrape to a halt on the stone floor outside chapel – breathing hard as I enter. I am five minutes late – blessing myself and that – and genuflect dripping extravagantly – but prayers haven't started yet. There aren't any priests here. I budge in – and they shuffle along to make way for me.

I get my breath back. I wipe my face on my fingers and then I wipe my fingers on my pants. I get the ribbons in my book in place. Their hair dries – crackling. (Henry looks like shampoo. Henry looks like a complementary bottle of shampoo.) Minutes pass. (How do you actually get as white as Henry is?) Sunday Lent 4. Laetare Sunday. *Rejoice, O Jerusalem: and come together all you that love her: rejoice with joy, you that have been in sorrow...* Laetatus sum in his quae dicta sunt mihi: in domum Domini ibimus... Sean sings the antiphons – in English.

At breakfast, I chew my customary hunk of bread, and my apple. I am a bit clammy – and suck at the heat in the coffee-mug – at the meniscus. People are up and down, in and out, making toast in the kitchen and what-not. It is normal that none interacts, while to consult a tablet for the day's news must have been unthinkable. The unusual variation occurs when Geoff visits our table and leans across me and deliberately brushes – touching my shoulder and resting a forearm on the back of my chair. Startled, I go small to Geoff's big.

404

Geoff says: 'Might there be any spare butter going on this table?'

I say: 'Sure.'

I hold the bowl up for him. Geoff *snips* his fingers: as a lizard-tongue procures a fly.

'*Thenk*-you.'

Then *squeezes* my shoulder... And loafs away. Dragging his slipshod feet.

I am spared serving at Mass today. I am down to read but I haven't checked what yet. I stick around. Finally, Adedokun rises to leave. Then as one, others are moving. They drop their plates and scraps to the plastic bowl and the metal trolley...

At the fruit tray, I select a kiwi and an apple and a tangerine to take to my room. At the fruit tray, the Vice Rector materializes next to me. He says:

'Did you sleep okay, Tomàs?'

'Like a log, thanks. Then I thought I was going to be late. How about you?'

'What about me?'

'Did you sleep okay?'

'Oh. Yes, thanks.'

'I wasn't late, was I? Or was I?'

'I wouldn't have noticed, to be honest.'

'Oh right, I thought there must have been a hold-up.'

'What made you think that, Tomàs?'

'The fact you were all late. Not that that's not your prerogative.'

'Well, I'll let you get back to your breakfast.'

It so happens The Rector is dumping His scraps at the trolley. I say:

'Good morning, Father.'

The Rector glances up at me and back down and doesn't reply.

Someone got out of bed the wrong-side this morning.

Loud and violent music plays along the corridors. However, the room-to-room sound-penetration is minimal – muted. A quirk. It is by and large music I haven't heard before – and which I neither understand nor care for. I shower, change… I put *Losing My Religion* on You Tube. My bin is all photocopied-paper and plum stones and Q-tips and apple cores… I fill a bowl with crisps, and break the seal on a wine bottle. Fuck it. We are all The Rector's fiction: hang it all. I shower hard and wear the better of my good suits and a Jermyn Street tie.

Laetare Sunday… Rejoice! it means. On this day, in old, folk custom, such peasant mummery incorporated into the Church rite, with spring, death is expelled once more from our resurgence in human community. Life begins. Mothering Sunday has its origins here… Today. The priests' Lenten purple might give way to pink – or 'rose'. This would not be observed today. The Rector would not wear pink – or 'rose'.

Father Guy observed it. He gave to the congregation a loving explanation of his strange clothes. There were sisters of a community in Ireland had made the rose chasuble for him. It made one wonder. An occasion must have warranted the gift. It leant, for the moment, a super-parochial status, like business-travel, to our mid-morning celebration of Mass in the London parish church. The Church a living thing – joined-up to itself like that.

With twenty minutes yet prior to Mass, I enter the Sacristy. No-one being present, I check my reading in the lectionary, and savour the waxy smells. In chapel, our guests have begun to arrive; the church-doors onto the street are open. Henry mans the door. Oh it is cold outside. Our chapel, through the arch of the opened doors, looks positively warm in comparison. In the cold air, my skin seems to generate little white granules, crystalline, smaller than grains of salt. My skin shrinks – a residue, perhaps, of the moisturizer. Francis plays violin. There are years when it isn't even Valentine's before it is Lent. Easter being the first Sunday following the first full moon following the spring equinox…'Roots!' Canon Peter laughed, while we broke-open a couple of bottles of Spanish red one night. Always dissonance. As if when the daffodils grow and you could plant your cabbages…

Cults, shrines, offerings, virgin births… God-men, priest-kings, hanged, 'crucified'. Risen-already anointed-ones: χριστοῦ – christs. They whipped their spring offerings to purify them – prior to the death. It would have taken almost nothing to slot Jesus in there – the pre-existent narratives. *They believed it all already…*

Priests are an offering. Their sap retained tumescent. Their brains change because of it. Why their faces shine so. Milk-and-honey.

The Vice Rector balloons at Mass as if to out-project objectivity. He speaks in daring ways he never does speak otherwise. Gut-deep audacity. A chasuble caught the wind – a sail! He maybe can't hear himself for the wind blowing through him. Bishops, on the other hand, more intellectually, each his own objective.

Power of the whirlwind… The Mass-bell sounds. The organ takes a deep lung-full of electronic air and thunders down on us. From the Sacristy, servers and priests process.

The glory of these forty days

We celebrate with songs of praise;

For Christ, by Whom all things were made,

Himself has fasted and has prayed.

I read my piece. My voice, through the speakers, seems unchanged. It hangs in the air like promise. *Open my heart and my lips shall proclaim your...* It seems prayerful. Each phoneme shaped. It is the story of David being anointed by Samuel. (1 Samuel 16: 6-7, 10-13.) The name Samuel means: his name is God, El having been an important god to the Israelites, after whom they were named.

Part way through the reading, I stop and look up from the lectionary.

Stop a moment – why not? Clear your heart. I read again: layered voices. An infinitely gentle RP – as the speakers would have it:

'Now he was ruddy, and had beautiful eyes, and was handsome. The Lord said, "Rise and anoint him; for this is the one."'

I take communion from the hands of The Rector, who seems unusually aggressive as Mass is sent. Saying: 'Bow your heads and pray for God's blessing.'

*

On Monday, Lent 4, Father Joe arrives for his week's stay.

He is the house shrink. I learnt too late that Father Joe writes reports based on what we have said as it turns out not in confidence. He comes to assess us. His base is that centre in Manchester – Saint Luke's. He must spend weeks each year in the various seminaries – monitoring how we've cracked. There are sheets up on the notice-board. You get out of class for this – but by the time I notice the sheets are up, both Spanish and Human Development have gone. I opt for choir practice, which is stupid as I don't mind choir practice – just the others do. I could have got Intellectual Development. I could have got *Spiritual* Development...

408

At five o'clock on Thursday, having at lunch refused food so that I can go to the gym, I ride the mirrored shaft to the second floor. Father Joe's door is open.

I say: 'Knock, knock.'

'Tomàs!'

'Hey, Joe.'

'Just give me a moment, love, I've just got…'

(The voice is: quite queer Manchester.)

'No worries.'

'Plonk yourself down.'

I plonk myself down then once we are both plonked down Father Joe says:

'Tomàs.'

'Father.'

'Is it still shit then?'

'Pretty much.'

'What are your thoughts?'

'Dignified exit? Sorry, God. Tried. Rector don't like. Maybe next life?'

'Is that it?'

'I had hoped it would be more.'

'So make it more.'

'I can't. The report's going to be shit. I wouldn't hire me.'

One story is, the boys in the proper seminaries make things up to say to him – anything to get him off sex. I, on the other hand, get the next bit wrong. Lips pursed – and trigger-words – mincing it:

'The Rector thinks I'm an "alcoholic".'

'Everybody thinks that. It's not The Rector.'

'They're wrong. They're using that idea, because they can't get what it really is.'

'Tomàs, you need to shake yourself up a bit here, lad, and be honest.'

'You don't want to know either, do you?'

'Tomàs, stop lying!'

'So you stop lying too.'

It is a bit of a body-blow. God doesn't love me any more. And I am alone in the entire universe. Even this obvious faggot broke tribe. And they'll always be judging, for there isn't enough love, never enough love.

I say: 'It's not about that.'

'It is!'

'No it isn't. How can you be so blind? It's not about that.'

'Go on then. You tell me what it's about. What it's all about?'

I make a speech. It is not a very good one:

'Oh what do you know? Really.

'What do you genuinely know of – truth in here that's – what? – apart from lies and rubbish here?

'Get it stripped and examine it – I won't tell. Look: I'm not carrying a phone.

'This – you model. Let's set God aside – let's bracket God aside. Let's name faith extraneous – non-participant and that done – the delusional slop of it. *Hush, hush, nobody cares, Christopher Robin has fallen downstairs…*

'You know what He did the other day? He stands there prattling away – He's running the idea of what goes wrong when people get ideas thinking they can improve their lives and we end up with Stalin. Agh you know… The French Revolution and Hegel. He's not even pretending

410

He's thought about it – never mind read about it. He's not even pretending the nothing He spouts is even trying to mean anything. Come on, admit it: you know this self-complacent drivel is our world. Or is that Catholic faith all over? Is that it for all of you?'

Father Joe says: 'You are now saying Father James isn't intelligent?'

'No I'm not. Look back at the transcript.'

'There is no transcript.'

'Then don't put words into my mouth.'

'Tomàs, with the best will in the world, you need to take a hard look at yourself. The fine young men that you are privileged to know in this place are consistently reporting an experience that is deeply profound…'

'Oh they know what to say and when to say it.'

'What are you saying, Tomàs?'

'Maybe half of them aren't even functionally literate. Who cares? So what? That doesn't excuse things. It doesn't give Him the right.'

Ray-Bans and Manchester-shops… Goods and services.

Out in hard sunlight – tea-time out in the back-yard – Father Joe put the Ray-Ban sunglasses using his own hands on Henry's face, so Henry could see how the light was polarized. Father Joe might as well have left a price-tag dangling off of them on one of those little hand-written tabs on a piece of string. But to Henry an adult-sum. Eyes on the prize. Posh goods, posh services.

I having not cried get the kiss-off:

'Right, Tomàs, think about who you are, where you are, and what you're doing. I'd love to speak to you again but you have a think first. Is that alright, Tomàs? Love ya, babe.'

411

I stand and turn and nod.

It has been briefer than expected.

I bow – not sarcastic. And go to my room and howl into the bedsheets.

Having recovered from that, I wash my face, and in the same clothes, go to The Rector's office to see The Rector. Truth's secretary.

'I've just been with Father Joe,' I say. 'Apparently it is generally thought that I am an alcoholic.'

I sit and am handed the tissues.

'We agreed... By what right do *they*...?'

But I shouldn't have said the word 'they' like that.

The Rector lets me empty myself out. I can't stop. I cry a good few minutes. Well, it's not an easy matter, is it? The death of God. It's not even only the first time it happens you cry?

And then God keeps on dying the whole time. He never stops.

At last, gently, The Rector says:

'Tomàs, there are problems here.'

'I feel that too.'

'So what's happening?'

'I don't know.'

'How much are you drinking?'

'Nothing – all week. Much. Sunday. Not last week. Saturday. Friday.'

'Tomàs, you are an alcoholic.'

'No, it's not that. Nor is that true.'

'You need help.'

'Well, possibly! But it's not that. It's not like that.'

'How is it like?'

412

'I can't explain. I haven't worked it through. I can't find an acceptable conclusion.

'Any analysis breaks and there is only a feeling of consciousness *in there* which doesn't communicate.

'See – I can't explain.'

After a silence, The Rector says: 'Why do you drink anything at all? Why not give it all up for the next few weeks, months, between now and summer, while you are here?'

I gawp at The Rector in disbelief. I say aghast and yet ironic: 'Oh reason not the need...'

Because love... even if it's shit... even if it's not physically compatible... Love...

'Tomàs, know yourself. Never mind saying whatever it is you think The Rector wants to hear. Know yourself.'

'Yes. I – do.'

'Is there anything else you'd like to say?'

'I don't know how.'

I ask permission of The Rector to go for a walk.

All I have to do is leave. It would be no great loss: they'd re-arrange themselves. They'd pray for me. But what would I do? I don't have any money.

I glow with residual heat at evening prayer

Supper follows immediately afterward.

Perhaps it is true that, at supper, we yell more than ever we used to. We are being formed. Not alone your unusual cases, your high-stakes – bishop-material – cf. Geoff.

Übermenschen.

I go to the shop, but my heart isn't in it. Then at the bar I watch the television screens for the word puzzles. I make something up in my diary about the day. (It doesn't come out meaning any more-or-less than I knew it was.)

Then in my room, there is a measure of wine, and a little book of poems I've been sent from Amazon by a friend – who wrote them. At the window… I *had* arranged to go south. From Easter Monday we have ten days to get out. 'Do what you want,' said The Rector, 'but you're not staying here.' Most plan to go home – back to the UK. It was the least unaffordable option to get a flight home. Unless you happen to have family in Malaga.

Even now, Mum is camped on French mud, heading south. I have never been on a Spanish fast-train, so that is exciting.

Malaga. Quite fun grinding the word out – old skool London. *Magh-lagh-gagh.* Criminal tendencies innit. Blackened lungs. Where Aunty Grace fetched up.

It is incumbent on us all to make the best of it.

*

The air tonight is satisfying. There is peace in the back yard. I put the internet-radio on to hear the ten o'clock news from the UK. (Russia is taking Crimea, Russia has test-fired a new ICBM, Pope Francis has opened the Castel Gandolfo gardens to the public, Scotland is deciding if it wants independence of England, a teacher has put sticky tape over a pupil's mouth.)

Cold spring. It is twelve o'clock.

*

On Saturday, deep in my afternoon nap, I dream my own Bishop is

414

cradling me. I choke up saying: Sorry, sorry, sorry… Having let him down so. And the Bishop says not to worry. They know. I mustn't mind about The Rector.

The Bishop strokes my head as I lie in the Bishop's lap. It is left unspoken, in the dream, the burning question of whether I might one day return to hope of priestly service. But I am home at least. I tell the Bishop neither my doubts nor my failure to doubt. Jesus love me: Tomàs be never alone.

Soft – a wave of sympathetic expansion. Even when I might have done things when I was alone… *Estaba solo… Perdon, Señor… No hablo mucho Español pero necessito de la confesión…*

As, then, I wake, and get the light, I know the Archbishop is there. He's arrived – as promised. It isn't so dramatic inside when I open the shutters. Peace – safe now. There is an apartment, which they call The Bishops' Room. A kindness settles upon the place. While all this day, I don't bump into him, I know the Archbishop is there.

They mocked the old Archbishop… There was a mock-cleverness to do with it.

Then, too, in priestly circles it is mouthed: 'Lost it…' (Canon Peter.)

For Lent 5, in preparation for Holy Week, the Arch is to lead us through a series of talks. On Sunday, you can see my knees, and thighs, and shin bones. On Sunday, my clothes hang off of me. There will be opportunities to go to His Grace for confession.

At morning prayer, His Grace sits in the pews as I, wandering, discover an accessible place in choir. Mass is then led by His Grace –

415

only as a normal priest might. No veiled altar boys... No mitre, no crosier... Unprepossessing, not-tall, pudding-plump. A funny little waddle. A septuagenarian figure. A face that likes its breakfast. Blood pudding, buttered toast, bacon, scrambled eggs... I have seen that Arch tuck into a breakfast!

After a Mass – in Liverpool. Out by the parks on the way to Speke.

This last leg of our – the students' Lenten tour – the desert journey – is intended by His Grace to take the students (us) more closely within death. Between the Cross – on Good Friday – and our Easter. Just dead. Prior to Resurrection – Life... (God get me out of here!) Termed by the Church among other names: Holy Saturday.

That day that is just it then – just death. Nothing else. No life. There's your Man-God hanging on a cross... And put away and put it away... That first Holy Saturday – AD yet to be – when Easter hasn't happened yet. Like what Ron's condition hasn't improved.

Death.

'Death,' says His Grace, 'throws it all apart. For we are not as we should be. Faith requires our adjustment to God's truth. God's triumph in a very real sense requires in us the loss of our everything. Which, as with Mary at the other end of Jesus's life, is God's truth.'

The Gospel reading is of John 11: 1-45, which is a long passage, and His Grace's homiletic theme commences in textual wilderness. Our brokenness – in this place – a family home. Our faith, our doubt, our death... The irruption – death, doubt, fear – within our precious scenes and our most intimate places. Our domesticity.

His Grace speaks from the chair, as is a bishop's prerogative, and

416

says:

'So much is obscure in the Gospels. We're always reaching through them. We're never there. Really, we never are. Our knowledge, our understanding, of the Gospels is never complete, and with each reading comes a new revelation. There are always new riches there. Just as there are between all of us, between myself and you. The Gospels are living texts. This is a part of the conversation we have with our own Christianity. It is a part of who we are in our relationship with Jesus. We are in this sense always on the brink.

'So yes, there is plenty that doesn't seem to make sense. As one of the order of bishops, we would be lying if we said that weren't the case. They are not easy texts to encounter, if by that word we may signify something more than a superficial glancing off against, but rather a profound search for the word of God. The Gospels are written by people who had their own ideas, and often didn't know what had really happened. Luke is quite explicit on this point. His is an investigation, from the explicitly claimed point of view of an historian, rather than that of a first-hand witness, who attempts, so he says, to set out an orderly account, out of the chaos, the sheer muddle, that has been handed down to him. It is possible to imagine Luke researching and composing his account after many years, when there has arisen a desire to know what exactly happened, and this implies a certain call to faith and certain demands of historicity, to historical exactitude. So in these different ways, the people of the first years of Christian faith are in the dark. There is also a decisive need to define the life of Jesus. And people didn't get Jesus. The whole meaning of Christianity is only now beginning to take root throughout the composition. So much needs to be evangelized. The light shines almost in tentative fashion like that first star, which drew the wise men from the east to our Lord's cradle.

'John's is widely held to be a very late Gospel. There are others who say that John's Gospel might have been the first to acquire its true shape, because it most fully expresses Jesus, as we know him to be, as members of the Catholic Church. We don't really know when any of this is being written, but we get a feel in John of a Gospel refined over many years, through a community. So there's a lot going on there that I'd like you to think about.

'What I would like to suggest to you is that, while within the Gospels we are often confronted with clues, guesswork, stories that have been handed down through so many people, and so in this sense we might find ourselves to be in the wilderness, this is the very desolate space itself to which we must give ourselves in order to experience Christ's full redemption in our lives. I suggest it is for God's glory that we do so.

'As we become aware of ourselves, in this seminary, we find ourselves in a very secure, comfortable setting, and there are signs of Easter everywhere. Within the very fabric of these buildings, our Lord is risen; our Lord lives. But now this is our Lenten journey, where death enters, where death breaks us. We are to ride into Jerusalem in triumph, and then we are to be utterly broken, all hope gone, our hope extinguished. And really, I suggest to you, it is only by inhabiting this thought, as if we don't know Easter is there, that our new life can follow, just when we have given up all hope, when every promise that Jesus made to us seems to have been cancelled.

'And here now we have the story of Lazarus. I should like to suggest to you that we have a very powerful call now. In our very comfortable space, our domesticity, with all this comfort, where so very little might seem to happen each day, so it might seem to you, there is a

418

disturbance within all of this comfort, and that is a disturbance within ourselves, and that is our call to Jesus. I think it is correct to say that our most comfortable places break in the light of Jesus from the inside, in order that we may take the necessary steps to be with Jesus.

'Faith is not comfortable. I think that we can all receive the message of the rolling away of the rock from the tomb of Lazarus to say something of vital importance to ourselves concerning our openness to God's love. The rock we roll away can come in all sorts of guises, but we know when we are blocked, and I firmly believe if we are truthful then we know where those blocks might be.

'Next Sunday, which will be Palm Sunday, we process as it were to Jerusalem, to begin our Holy Week. Now as I speak to you we are on the brink. Even now, I suggest it might be very good for all of us to lay aside what we think we know, to fall apart a little, and so to open our way through death, and through death's cancellation of all we think we are, to be with Jesus.'

*

There is a different tone to lunch and to the week that follows. It proceeds... Both the Vice Rector and even The Rector seem ruefully content. Still, each first period, we have to do Spanish.

Then at ten-past-ten we go upstairs. Visiting teachers often prefer this space.

There is natural light and fresh air. Today, we sit on chairs only, gathered around close, with no desks in the way of us. His Grace works from a flip-book. A set-piece. He sits always gently bobbing – the quiet thrill of it. The flip-book has clearly seen previous use. And big Clarks shoes and fade-to-black socks... There is a quiet examination of consciousness. *I confess*... Then we say a Hail Mary. Some part of what the Archbishop says to us is this:

'What I should like to do today is to pose to you possibly the most important question, which is this: How can we ready ourselves for the experience of Easter?

'It's a funny question, isn't it? Because it's something we've been doing all our lives. What can we do to get ourselves ready for Easter?

'I have no doubt that through this Lenten season you have been meditating upon questions related to such as this. There are questions that relate to your own readiness for God, and no doubt these are pressing concerns each day for you.

'I expect that you have been to confession, and I expect that this celebration of the Sacrament of Reconciliation is a regular feature of your life in seminary. Quite a lot of what I'd like to say to you today concerns our sense of who we are, of who we are most perfectly meant to be, and what exactly we say sorry for when we go to Jesus, to ask for his forgiveness for all that we've done wrong. What I am really saying to you is that, perhaps we don't quite know how to make a true examination of ourselves, because we are not quite like Mary, and we retain things, ideas about ourselves that we would like to bring to God, and for God to validate, rather than for God to take apart, so that we aren't that any more, and can move on from those ways of not being to being ourselves.

'I'd like to suggest to you that there is a call to extraordinary honesty for and within each one of us, this is to say, a call to honesty that is both within ourselves and thereby and therefore with God. I touched upon this set of questions yesterday at Mass, and I have just said it. It's this question, really. It is or seems to be a very simple question, and yet I think this is a questioning of ourselves at its most profound level. It is this, then. It goes far, far beyond so much that many people including

420

ourselves come to Mass for. Really it is sort of an opposite, or a weird way around the complications of who we are and what Mass offers us. And it is this: How do we allow ourselves to be taken apart by God? So that everything we think we are isn't important any more. So that we are not hiding before this idea of who we think we are, hiding from God, and putting this idea of ourselves up between us and God. How do we ensure, not that God sees us utterly – of course, God sees us utterly – but that we, beyond mere passive acceptance, want and ask God to penetrate into us?

'This, I would suggest to you, is very far from being an easy task, and there may be those of us who barely even begin to understand the nature of the task, or indeed that we even fail in this beginning through and through.

'So often, people try so hard to hold themselves together, to think about who they are and who and what they are meant to be, that a kind of rage sets up in their ears, and so within that rage God's call quite evades them. There are times when what we most need to do is to fall apart and simply to allow God to cradle us, to pick all our pieces up, bit by bit, and rock us in his arms, all our broken pieces. It's when we most stop trying to prove an idea of ourselves we don't even in our heart of hearts want to be that God puts us all together.

'Picture Mary, as the Angel Gabriel comes to her. It is perfectly legitimate as Catholics, and so therefore we are as children of Mary, to ask ourselves how we might be were we in her position then. I think it is fair to say that our world would be broken apart. Of course, we can only imagine – and speculate as to this.

'Who of us could do this? That is my question to you. Who of us could be like Mary?

'I wonder if Mary survives the experience precisely because she is free of sin. But we are not. Our own conceit would break us. We couldn't be like Mary. We would shatter. Our egos, these things we carry about in our heads, they would burn and shatter us. But we can ask God to do the best we can to imitate Mary. She became as nothing. This is Mary's way. A yes to God is a way of saying and acknowledging our fundamental openness to God within ourselves: I am nothing in myself. Rather, this becomes a way of our saying: *I am* only insofar as I am responsive to you – to you.

'As we go forward, I should like then perhaps to ask each of you, what do you hold onto about yourselves? Perhaps, what messages do you send to yourself about yourself, which are not in themselves the image of Jesus, in all we know about the life of our Lord, but which you cherish? I put it to you that, once you have identified these thoughts, these false prophets within ourselves, then you know something more of what you have yet to give to Jesus.

'It is not the acknowledged sins – the sins you know you know you know about – that you take to confession; but rather it is the unspoken part of yourself that carries those sins to confession, which perhaps you have not yet acknowledged.

'If I may put this to you, in simple, Catholic terms, there is a powerful question. Where are we not yet one with Mary? I suggest, each of us has something, a nagging part of ourselves that often seems to get left behind, which carries the rest to confession, but which always in its core self shies forth of confessing itself as it truly is. The bit we keep apart, as if we are separate agencies, ourselves alone doing the confessing, apart from God. When is it not God doing the confessing through us? The core piece of ourselves we fail to bring to God.'

422

On Tuesday, His Grace turns to the theme of Jesus's hidden years.

His Grace asks the students to consider questions concerning what really happened:

'Who, for instance, was Joseph? Was he indeed a carpenter, or has Joseph's true role in the society in which he lived been misconstrued and forgotten to us? Though it be a beautiful, simplifying image to grasp, which offers to us much that is of value in Catholic faith...

'A wise elder, which *carpenter* could mean, or a great engineer, an *architekton*, which in the Greek does not mean carpenter. But *carpenter* in the Hebrew could mean a wise man...'

His Grace turns the pages of his Bible back and forth, as if to itemize the paucity of information. Then he says:

'What I think I can say to you with confidence is that it is of profound significance that we simply don't know what Jesus was doing for most of his earthly life. There are some very different possibilities. One idea cherished by the Church is that Jesus worked with his father Joseph as a carpenter. Another possibility is that Jesus lived and prayed and studied closely with John the Baptist. They were cousins, and very close, almost the same, in age. Luke's Gospel tells us clearly that Jesus and John knew each other from within the womb before they were born. So there may have been something quite important happening there. You see, we don't know – it is an impossible mystery to us – just how much Jesus had to learn. This is because, if Jesus knew everything, humanly speaking, even as a tiny baby, then how can we say he is fully human? We simply can't probe too far into this mystery, but we can draw extraordinary truth and healing from this thought, which becomes of immense relevance in our own lives. Jesus came to know and to understand himself not merely as *a* son of God, but as God the Son, and

423

so as self-identical with his Father. It is not an adoptive relationship. Jesus *is* God. Now so much is hidden here. But this is a great gift. If you think about it, how do *we* come to know that we are loved by God, that we have *our* relationship with God? What are we born with in here' – his chest – 'and what do we have to learn? This is to say, what is gifted to us by other Christians at our baptism?

'Jesus must have studied, and experienced profound revelation about who and what he truly was, and, so it seems to be, these studies cannot have been confined to the Semitic world. But this is the important point: there is a hiddenness about all of this. No matter which schools and which sects our Lord might have encountered all these years, this to us is as a desert space. What this means is that we can enter into the hidden life of Jesus, and there we can discover our own being with God, our own sonship. Our own particular being loved by God can come to us, if we can enter within this great unknown – into this desert space, where we are loved by Jesus. I firmly believe that there may be a great Lenten mystery in this period of our Lord's life.'

On Wednesday, His Grace's theme is baptism. He says:

'I'd like to say that, in order to grasp something of the full initial impact of Christian baptism, it's quite important for us to set aside the passages we have in the Gospels of Jesus's life before he came to John to be baptized, and so this includes what are referred to as the infancy narratives, in the Gospels of Matthew and of Luke. I think to get the full impact, of just how it might have been, we need to set these later Gospels aside and go all the way back to Mark. I think this is something of the closest echo we'll get to those first Christian communities who experienced baptism, and how it might have been, as the first Christians

424

discovered Jesus.

'This is how it happens, this is how it begins: in adulthood. The Gospel tells us:

'"In those days, Jesus came from Nazareth of Galilee, and he was baptized by John in the Jordan. And just as he was coming up out of the water, he saw the heavens torn apart and the Spirit descending like a dove on him."

'Mark's, without a shadow of a doubt, is the earliest Gospel that has been given to us. The story is only just getting going. There's no Angel Gabriel. There are no infancy narratives. Mary is unnamed in Mark 3 when she comes, as she sees it, to have a go at rescuing Jesus. The beginning is John the Baptist. It begins in baptism.'

The impression clearly formed is that the Archbishop's ideas are not mere bookish speculation but, as it were, bucket-and-spade, in the sense of his having visited the place where he thinks it was that Jesus was baptized. He tells us about the place, in the Holy Land, over the Jordan, where there is a confluence, troubled waters, and danger in entering into them. The picture he evokes of broiling surge, plunging deep, a GPS map-point, a trial in ways apart from our sacrament. Where waters churn and threaten to swallow you. And he is convinced it happened there. He is convinced. He relates it to our own baptism:

'We all know the scene, don't we? It's a part of our lives – of who we are as Christians. With the sprinkling of water, and the oil, and the candle. The take-it-for-granted things of Christian life. And that little gathering of people clustered about the font, at the entrance into the church, our first steps, when we have to be carried by others, who all our lives will nurture us, toward the liturgical east of the sanctuary, all of them trying to remember their lines right, who perhaps don't get to church that often. It's a very beautiful part of our lives as Christians, where we welcome a new child into our community of faith in Jesus.'

There is a touch of the strange at supper. Spiritual contest – you might say. Acting out. A plate gets smashed and Julian throws a glass against the wall.

At 'our' table both Francis and Benedict beg from the kitchen new wine. It is odd because the overwhelming feeling, the underlying real, seems quite stable – rested at heart – and far from being turbulent. Indeed, there seems nothing, save what is merely wilful, to act against.

Philip directs the cleaning-up operation. Benedict expresses some relief that he is sitting at 'our' table. None comments the day. Thoughts expressed are food and plans for Easter week – when we have to go away from the seminary. Afterwards, I go to the place round the corner to write my diary.

On Thursday, there is more lost-history to contemplate. More Christian life unknown. Certainly, His Grace tacitly withdraws some measure of the veil of – more creative years. Though what he has to say does not overtly contradict received Church teaching.

His Grace moves the beginnings of Christian faith – the Church – as from stunned remains: Jerusalem razed – as our first generations looked back onto it.

This nexus of salvation-history – all history pointed forwards-backwards either way in faith in Jesus. As, in intervening centuries, disparate communities scatter through what is becoming a wreckage of Empire, spiritual waste, gather their scraps, and they begin to communicate. Truth-recalled – reverse-transcribed like RNA like a

426

retrovirus – penetrated into the pagan world laid out for it – became life.

On Friday, His Grace moves The Death Of God. Directly, he talks about Ron:

'It may be some of you sitting here now have experienced the death of a person who has been very close to you and of considerable importance in your life. I hope each one of you may understand something of the importance of what I am saying, when I say to you what you might think is my stating the obvious, namely that a loved one dying can tear our faith apart.

'I can see one or two of you nodding as I ask you to think about this. It is an important reality of our faith. I ask forbearance as I say this. I should like to share with you a thought, that in that experience of death, there is a place where our Christianity lives, if it lives at all, and has its seeding ground. Paradoxically, in a sense, it becomes a place where we are most alive, through which our life as Christians blossoms.

'There are those of you also who don't yet fully believe in death. This is because you are young. Death is an idea, a concept, but still it is a long way away from you really. If or when a loved one is in the process of dying and then dies, you are perhaps not now experiencing your own mortality, despite the form of words that we use in our Lenten services.

'But there is an understanding about death that you need to have, if you have any sense of becoming a Catholic priest. Christ died. Before he did so, he begged his Father, and he experienced anxiety, even in a spiritual sense, commuted, despair. I put it to you that our Christian faith is not quite real without our knowing that.

'Now I think one thing we need to understand is that grief takes us beyond faith. What do I mean by that? Well, grief shatters us. It's very difficult to understand on a theoretical level. Our very sense of how things ought to be is violated. We are not equipped to think of death, not by home-spun, natural mechanisms, which is to say apart from revelation. With death, all that we thought we knew is thrown wide open. There is an emptiness about grief. Even to committed Catholics, who go to church on Sunday, their Catholic faith can seem suddenly a long, long way away from them, to the point of its coming to seem quite irrelevant. I hope you don't mind my saying to you that it can all become a bit fish-on-Friday.

'Now, this is quite a thought to take on for you. When in the close and lived presence of death, a person's Catholic faith becomes, not even a comfort, but rather instead absolutely irrelevant. It simply doesn't begin to connect with the reality that person is now experiencing. In some important and significant respects, it might as well not be there now.

'Now these are difficult thoughts, because it asks us something about our faith, and it asks some very searching questions about the reality of our faith. How far does that reality extend? Does it reach into and encompass the absolute void of death, which we simply cannot countenance, but which is the experience of many when loved ones die, just as it must have been to those first Christians that first Holy Saturday? I ask you to think very deeply within that time. Where are we when the apparently absolute hollowness of death strikes? Are we still good Christians then, or are we desolate?

'You see, we claim a lot as Christians, and then death comes along and pulls the rug out from under us. There is a stripping away here. This is what I should like you to think about through these next days. I'd like to develop this as a theology of Holy Saturday, which lies between Cross and Resurrection. Where are we, when death strikes, when we may seem totally, utterly bereft of hope, when we are not ourselves, when we are

428

lost to ourselves? And I should like you to consider that a greater and more holy reality can and must be found here.

'In terms of theology, the Church remains by and large unusually silent about this day. Well, what really happens in churches? The nice Catholic women come in and prepare for Easter? There'll be the flowers arranged, and there'll be people – all of them, who lead such busy lives, wanting and given this opportunity to contribute – for the Easter Vigil. It's as if the day is almost deleted, whereas considered most truly, this is toward if not itself at the heart of Catholic faith. Think about it. A church can so often constitute a very peculiar picture today, by virtue of our community activity, which can become in a sense a kind of communal covering over, as we obey our most natural and immediate human instinct which is toward life. God is dead on the Cross, and he has not been resurrected yet; he has not come back to life. There's no Easter yet, only complete and abject loss and failure. If that is not the very seedbed of our Christian faith then I don't know what is.'

Of a moment, he seems to run out of things he's wanted to say to us.

He thanks us for our time and we go for coffee. There is then a little more than an hour before the next thing. But that was that.

*

When Dad died, Mum phoned me before school. Assuming a routine, internal call, I knew what it must be when I heard her voice instead. It was not a surprise. It was a woeful shock but it was not a surprise.

In recent weeks Dad had been dead and not dead. The last time I saw him was in an intensive care unit. I went to fulfil the terms of my father's will. Mum dragged me out there. Otherwise what little there was would have gone to a wildlife charity. So we split it, and Mum got a camper van – 'motor home'. This was after a car crash. (The dog lived, and became mine.)

Eventually my father recognized me. And through the drugs and the corrugated tubes Dad's plugged-up mouth and dying eyes said: 'Oh…' I could have done without that. I had some *goodness* then in Dad's eyes, did I? I really – extremely didn't want to know that.

I got boxed on E the night before I went up for the funeral. Reggae night, and local-knowledge pills. Then I hung around in the foyer of the school theatre, when a couple of the boys were there. Just sitting quietly wearing my suit. Even then it was quite a kick jumping the snake-queue to buy myself a first in Euston.

Once they'd made him better, they found him dead in the bath. It was said he was probably trying to clean himself after an accident.

That day, when Mum phoned with the news, became a mild LSD experience.

The world a little way beyond my mind's touch. A dissociative experience. It was all floaty. I walked about the village, with its traffic-calming measures, and solicitors, graphics designers and marketing professionals, estate agents, that sort of people, physically touching stone and brick and white paint. And I had to set work and arrange cover for the junior classes. I broke once and only once – round the back of the DT department where, between lessons, we went for a fag. Thankfully, no-one witnessed this. I howled and yacked and snotted my nose on my gown. It was a desperate show.

Ron's death wasn't like that. It was shapeless. Arrived out of nowhere – it happened for two years – he died. It didn't have any meaning.

I held it together for the words I'd found to deliver my eulogy. One of Ron's older-than-me sons gripped my shoulder as I sat down next to him, in the pew, afterwards. It was odd to look at them, all crowded in there, like so many people. I'd ended with these words, from 1 Corinthians 13:

'Love is patient and kind; love is not jealous or boastful; it is not arrogant or rude. Love does not insist on its own way; it is not irritable or resentful; it does not rejoice at wrong, but rejoices in the right. Love bears all things, believes all things, hopes all things, endures all things. Love never ends.'

And then I said: 'That was Ron.'

*

All week, B-aye-ad/th-oh-lid/th prepares for Holy Week. Roads are cleared. Notices posted. Cars towed. In shop windows, KKK-esque hats/masques, which screen the face, begin to dominate.

Processional penitents bury themselves in robes, which are coloured according to their confraternity. Often they walk bare-foot, so all the city-gristle must lance right through to the point they become pain.

One catches sight of guilds rehearsing outside church doors with their pasos. These are a kind of solid, heavy float – or palanquin, or litter, or lectica – carried by each team of men on bruising shoulders, this itself entailing a degree of pain, on which are borne plastic-arts representations of Passion scenes. The sculptures are as those preserved in the National Museum, which I tried to get something out of, though in their Holy Week animated state, with drums and lights, they become ghastly –

431

voodoo – fabulous to see and to think upon.

In college, we have something of this – on a small scale, a dozen of us carrying it. Our paso, when dressed, is to bear the Vulnerata, and wobble out onto the street, and perform a sort of 'greeting' to her Son, processing by, when we the students have to try and make her bow without dropping her. There will be Easter-lily flowers, and silver candelabra screwed to each corner of it – glass-shielded real-flames. It is bruising on the shoulders. We rehearse for a half-hour each day over it-might-be four days, barked at by a new 'character', a Spanish Fascist bully, who uses hard physical touch to direct the students, abusing us, but then I, as it were, threaten to lamp him. Square and do the mouth – braced shoulders, crunched walnut brain – though there the script ends. There is a knack to it. A slow, cumbersome, side-to-side waddle-step. Zombie-pride. It helps if you feel penitential and grounded in the meaning in a solemn way.

It helps if your instinct isn't smile and wave… None claims to know which night we are meant to be doing it, though it would be a simple matter enough to consult the published schedule for the whole city. The Vice-Rector tells us he doesn't know, though it would be a simple matter enough to consult the published schedule for the whole city. A pity, that, really. Poor Father Richard. A shame.

And so it is Palm Sunday. And, as it happens, things hereon-in become a bit of a blur.

His Grace presides at the Palm Sunday Mass in college. He has an *enormous* palm – in place of his crosier. The Rector gets the next biggest palm, which is pretty big. The other priests get big-ish palms… I *et al* get palm-fronds to wiggle about and, later, make teeny-weeny crosses of, which they blu-tac to their room-doors to go with the postcard-pictures of fashionable – with-it saints and what-not.

It begins in the quad. We are blessed in our polycotton albs by the fountain. It is harmless fun enough, and there is no point trying not to wiggle it, but with His Grace there it isn't quite certain what the note you aren't getting is meant to be. His Grace blesses us – with the water. Saint George rears high above it all – rearing, shining, glinting. Over the fountain, into the sun and blue light – upheld sword advancing. A Garden of Time. Time's garden. Preserved counter-factually… It isn't, of course. It is up to its neck in it. We *are* the modern cliché hordes. We sing:

Ride on! ride on in majesty!

Hark! all the tribes hosanna cry;

O Saviour meek, pursue thy road

with palms and scattered garments strowed.

We all process with no witnesses. Not until we enter chapel. No-one but ourselves.

*

I used to like the rehearsal-time best. Once, on the playing fields, wearing only track-shorts, when school had broken for the summer, and the weather unusually warm, I practised walking almost-invisibly-slowly, in an imaginary square in the sun on the grass, for a whole week. Once, at night, I appeared fully-naked on the school stage, as Caligula, having secured the building.

I liked the care and discreet chunks of it. Unfinalized – barely actualized future-possible…

We process. Glass exhibition cases, old reliquaries. A forearm here; here a nun's fingertip. In chapel, at a glance, there are the usual faces. But they all stand to attention. Jonathan breaks from the procession to – fire the organ with oomph and dignity:

> Ride on! ride on in majesty!
> The angel-squadrons of the sky
> look down with sad and wondering eyes
> to see the approaching sacrifice.

When we've done the readings, the Arch holds that tree in his hands to deliver the homily. He rocks quietly on his feet, some few seconds, as if balance defeated it.

A way you might affect as the Spirit moves… Copying. Then he says:

'Our palm fronds may seem to us today rather dry. I mean this not in a literal sense, but by the standards of those who originally lined the roadways in order to welcome Jesus into Jerusalem, as they proclaimed Jesus to be the Messiah, who would be clambering up and ripping their palm branches fresh from off the trees. I think perhaps also our faith is somewhat distant from that of the people there on that highroad into Jerusalem, and something of our sense of the meaning has shifted in vividness from what it was then. And of course the expectation of all those many people is markedly different, but in many important respects the same. There are the same essential qualities to all our faith in God, which springs complete from our humanity, and that is one and the same in value for all of us, and time is consistent on this point. So then, let us renew the fullness of Catholic faith, and let us ask the Lord's blessing as we embark upon our Holy Week.

'Our Lord enters into Jerusalem in order to refresh us. He is to die

434

in order that we may have life. There is a living reality here, both spiritual and as entangled in the joy of our daily living. We have Ladies' Day where I grew up. They still have it, and they close the roads off, and little children parade, dressed-up like spring brides. When I was a boy, there was a May Day festival, and there was a May pole on the field, with the people dancing, like Morris dancers might be one way of visualizing this if you've never seen it, with their ribbons tied onto the top of the May pole, and they would weave around each other, dressing the pole, which is what we called it. It was like a dance with red and white and blue ribbons all hung off of the top of the May pole, which stood there all year, only like a telegraph pole, but it was concreted in, and then there was a slide, and swings – one baby-swing and two you could have a go at – terrible health and safety but that's what it was in those days.

'There was a round-a-bout – we used to run it round and round to try to get it off its central axis. It were rusty as anything and creaked like mad – on concrete. And climb up where it was all greased up at the top. Ruth, who was big as the next four of us, used to sit there sucking on the lollipops we nicked for her from Raddies, and she'd direct matters. We were trying to destroy it, and get it to dislodge from its central axis, and fly away – roll off into that farmer's field, which he only ever kept for silage, but we never succeeded. There was a car someone had left there so we spent forever smashing that up, until someone who lived in one of the houses there took exception to our doing that, so he put thick grease under the door handles and gave us a right talking to.

'It would only be a few stands, hot-dogs and things like that. The man selling the hot dogs would have his records on full blast. There'd be a couple of set-up stalls. Air-rifles – that sort of thing. But we all had them, and we all went shooting, of course, if not with twelve bores then with smaller gauge. Or pay a pound – I have no idea how much it was in actual fact then – it might have only been a few pennies – and we'd get all that time smashing up the crockery the man would put up for us to smash on the dressers. That was my particular favourite thing to do at these festivals, by the way, in case you were wondering. You got a little bucket of so many cricket balls.

'I dread to think what went into those hot dogs. Probably EE rules would forbid it now. But it was a fair mix in those days. A lot of young people then were C of E. We've done a lot to hang onto our young people, which is a tremendous encouragement when you consider how things are, while in recent decades the Church of England hasn't been so successful. People still want it on feast days and what are essentially now civic celebrations. It's strange to see, though, how all the little stands there people have are run by the police and people like that along those lines. There's no May pole. That was a sort of faith that ran and ran beneath all the theoreticals of it in the 1960s and the 1970s and into the 1980s. The May pole isn't there now in the particular place I'm thinking of. Considering May poles were officially suppressed hundreds of years ago – as a part of the protestant reformation. One or two of you are probably thinking I'm remembering things from that time!

'I should have liked to say that those processionals were so hardwired into us, that even after the last thirty years, when I became a bishop, they are still with us. They were a part of what it is as we understand Jesus' entrance into Jerusalem. They were a part of who we are as human beings, which is to say little less than that Jesus is a part of our biological make-up as human beings.

'Well, we look at these things increasingly from an historical perspective. In this day and age, we might often feel that all that Jesus

436

gave himself to be, and to be a part of, is barely involved for most. As Catholics, we experience a uniquely spiritual dimension to the greenery on the renewed trees, and the birds, to the hay-fever in my case, which I suffer from quite severely. These are our spring rites, and Easter is our spiritual spring, which turns to summer.

'I suggest to you that it is no accident Jesus went to die for us in spring. It really isn't. The Romans would have understood this. I believe that as Catholics we are called to carry this true understanding of all life's blessings. That God has come to talk to us, and to set up his tent with us, to live with us, and to give up all that he has and is for us, this within the most fundamental rhythms of our lives, and when, especially in the regions of the Holy Land, the natural world is at its loveliest.

'I expect this week will be a great journey for all of you. It may be an emotional experience. I think I can promise you it will be a profound experience. Certainly, Holy Week is of all weeks a very profound experience. That we shall see something of this tonight, in the streets of this wonderful city, I have no doubt. I expect you will become very involved in the spectacle. I should like you to think of the mysteries we all experience in this time. Even now, as we absorb ourselves within the mysteries of Easter, we are afforded additional insights, which might be highly personal, into what happened when Jesus gave himself to death, to be crucified. So much comes from within. Really, in a sense, and through our blessings as being one with the true Church, it is all in here.

'I'd like to ask one thing more of you. And it's only this. Let us make this a special journey, for each one of us. Here we are, on the edge of the mystery, and we have this Holy Week to prepare ourselves for the glorious truth of the fullness of Catholic faith. Through the Cross, as through Good Friday, as through Holy Saturday, and in all the anticipated joy of Easter, our eternal Sunday, let us stand now and renew our commitment and say our prayers.'

There is feasting at lunchtime. That, then, spills through the rest of the day, yet supper remains compulsory. The city-processional is scheduled to start late – well after dark – and I set my alarm yet find no sleep though I struggle for it. The night paws the bed-sheets, immoderately warm. My sheets want nothing to do with me, but let the air penetrate all over touching my skin. So I am up then. I wonder if the bar might be open but I'm not going anywhere – not like this. I put the radiator on, thinking the heat of that beneath the open window might shape things a little, with flow, and so render the illusion at least substantial. With a couple of aspirin, I proceed to drink wine. It is almost on the stroke of Midnight that I hear the first drums.

Little by little it comes to me. This isn't so bad. Knowing I am probably alone in college, I dress and take what I need from the common room. Whatever the scene is, they have fire, which illuminates odd little corners of the sky, just hanging above the city, at intervals. The drums aren't close, but seem flung around minute by minute, half the time as if they are miles away. That would be the pattern of the old streets as much as the tower blocks. They take the heart's thump as compressed force rather than true urban savagery, though subsequent video footage has Henry in the streets out there screaming: 'Look at that lace! Will you look at that lace!' Upon completion of a measure of alcohol, I lay open my diary on the window sill, and of the nothing-new, blown-warm, and of buoyancy… neutralized affect… doodle – sky-cult/earth-cult, young-gods/old-gods, fat-gods/slim-gods, boy-gods/girl-gods, /cat-dogs/god-dogs, justice/mercy.

438

I leave the window and the shutters open and bury my head again. Wanting no immediate part of it. Eumenides tamed. When I wake around three the drums have stopped. When I wake next after a comfortable sleep I've missed breakfast and morning prayer. I slip back inside it again and am good for lunch.

Mum calls and I don't take the call. Then my voicemail beeps. She'd be in Andalucía by now – approaching Malaga. At silent-lunch they play Bolero. When the soup is cleared, Geoff puts the word round that it is tonight we'll be doing the thing with the Vulnerata. I go to the gym then get back in bed again. That and the gym and the bar with the girl and a decent bath seem a reasonable day's routine.

So, what with that, I have got myself pretty much all joined-up and crystal-clear by midnight. The big exterior doors stand open in chapel, and we wait. A sizeable crowd has assembled on the pavements. There are those who peek in at the edges of the portal, catch their glimpse and creep as much as they dare. Others, on the opposite bank, seem unusually intent, and far from festal, as in expression mouths loose, demeanour itched and jostled. As in expectation of a bull. The question being: Will the act suffice? They might best have had sparklers and toffee-apples… No cordon is obvious. There are police, and other less recognizably uniformed people. It is quite fun to nip in and out of it – the quasi-monastic gesture of the alb in signification distinct from an altar-boy's/altar-man's cassock. As by natural, urban daylight, an English-Welsh cathedral – preparatory to Welsh celebrations and me and my cassock on… Rather, as the crowd peeks in, they see crèche-space, don't-look-at-us-space, sleepy matrix.

439

There really are flowers dripping all over the paso – and they are giddy candelabra. She looks pretty swanky in the midst of the clobber they've thrown at it. She looks… beautiful – I must admit. The lacquer that remains on her has a good, polished shine, while the scars axed into her seem charismatic. I watch the Vice Rector giddying about the place, probably not having been given sufficient instructions, left to his own wherewithal, and not a man destined for silence, stillness, catching prayers… It would be one of The Rector's moments, most likely, and He'd be in deep preparations for all this reflecting on Him. Even now, though, a suppression of noise sounds heavier, and from indeterminate distance, little by little, there grows discernible, seismic, thump-thump.

The bit where we carry her out is only pain and Philip's feet in front of mine. And somehow, I get the impression, we succeed in making her bow – to her Son depicted as by force of will through pain and gravity. As a Hebrew slave in Egypt. Our salvation.

The students set the paso on the tarmac and The Rector says His piece, mic'd through a portable speaker, which creates an impression of great tempest, and threatens to drown His words. When The Rector is finished, the clapper, like a door-knocker, knocks on the wood, and we must reverse. This then accomplished, and in chapel, the night free.

I go and change, but when I catch up with them, Henry processes with the best of them still in his alb. And John and Julian. Proud, Henry seems, and happy, and not in the least encumbered by our shameful little secrets, in the alb, and I wonder if he – I would rather have been there too. It is a rain charm – of course it is. Yes, yes, relentless rhythms. Yes, yes, the drums. As too the impossible wail of Spanish trumpets – as the bull's dance macabre… Life, death…

440

And it is a driving-out, and it is an expulsion… Such being viscerally known, howsoever remotely acknowledged. As at the same time, and undeniably, it is the summoning – *conjuring* into being. A life-and-death-beat, measured frenzy, bangs the drum and screams to ancient Earth to yield God. To this effect: a city mobilized.

It is truly of staggering proportions in such a small town. I follow – at the trailing edge. A little behind the float – the paso – right by the drums and trumpets. They all – the whole procession gets to a broad-seeming church-square, laid with city parkland, lawns and shrubs and little walls, and in the distance, at the head and at the close of the procession, at the top of a flight of church steps, though it seems, appallingly, a twentieth-century theme, they turn and raise themselves a god. Truly, at the end of it, God become indisputably alive in their statue… Lights strike the lacquer – make him shine and elevate. There shines a silver nimbus – skin burning gold – it looks like. Massed-thousands crush the tight-space. God-alive – your brain could not escape that fact.

I slip – elbowed from it sideways before the crowd begins to disperse. The security door at college remains open. There seem noises all over the city – a ubiquitous dispersal. Quite refreshed, I don't want to sleep. Not immediately. Not in the light of such received higher-consciousness. And there are no classes tomorrow so rest can be possible as and when.

*

Guests arrive on Tuesday. Equipped with as little as hand-luggage only, theirs is one of the three English seminaries, the one Henry is going to. Their number is twenty-odd – all six years – and three priests and a religious sister. This last – clenched like Irish-sin. And really frightful

441

crabby – a far cry from the comparatively beautiful Sister Angelina. A fair few of the visiting students attended Valladolid. And in the back yard, as they sip their cigarettes, they have The Rector off pat, and they have the Arch… Smug little buggars they might be, yet I rather like them, their Henry-posh, and their veneer, and I wish to please and discover myself agreeably diverted.

Meals become a buffet affair, which is all laid out for us, sparing my Refectorial duties. There are rehearsals in chapel for Thursday through Sunday. And it is good to get the place full – acoustically more fully dressed. I am down to lead a psalm and get my feet washed on Thursday, when Cardinal Cormac Murphy-O'Connor is coming. The psalm-tone is easy and they make us rehearse it. But this is fine given the newcomers. The rehearsal-situation is become more socially construed – a gentle and human-beyond to the college aggregate.

At the bar, she is unimpressed. She makes a little nothing. Her gesture barely shrugs like Ade's failed egg at breakfast. She literally couldn't care less.

In turn, I roll my eyes. Thereby admit things – which she almost-thinks quite funny. But we lack the nuanced codes… of thought or action yet distinct from basic irony.

I don't go out nights to see any of the shows. I listen to the city and prefer it that way. It is nice at the window. You could see anything – though like in the garden outside where the party is. Not in the grope – which kills me. Where, as youths, we sketched some preliminary outlines – life – and nudged each other hither-and-thither on the Kinsey-scale. Sixteen, fifteen, seventeen… Wild with hormones! Children.

I phone Mum. We Skype. It must be our first call in getting on over a month. She beams with Auntie Grace – sun and happiness. And all this space – after the motor-home! Miles shine in her face!

It is going to be hot, and the light suits her. Down in Malaga, the weather is fine already. And Sampson is settling in. Mad-happy, Mum and Auntie Grace, as a team, find interest in ways it is impossible to contemplate. Lunch might be a shop-bought tub of mayo with some potato and boiled-eggs lopped in it. And now she'll be all ditsy with the label being in Spanish, and what do we recycle and what goes where…. Thuswise plating food – for lunch – so we could have it from the tub (on the outside table by the pool) and not fancy.

They talk just about *all* the time. Mum in her element: light and air.

Such details I share are a skeleton. Mum wouldn't understand and I don't want to bother her. (*This is my son Tomàs, who is going to be a priest…*) She looks so nice… I'll be there on Monday. It is going to be rough, not telling her any of this. There are the picking-up arrangements and, yes, I'll have my phone, yes, and switched-on, yes… *Byeeeeeee!!!!* 'You do it, you do it! Okay. Byeeeeeeee!!!!'

Thursday sloops up on us. When they asked if I would be willing to be one those having my foot washed, I demurred because of my manky toe. Indeed, when I explained I have a fungal condition, Julian, repelled, said to everyone he didn't want to be in the line with me. But Father Richard thought I was being wilfully objectionable. So I explained my caveat. There was all the incipient aggression. *My* eyes hoped for Julian's – which looked elsewhere. And to anyone and everyone again-again I said: 'I really don't mind. I don't mind at all. I really don't mind at all.'

443

That toe! It was my birthday. And my own stupid fault when I jumped off stage. (One of those cute little best friends gave me a scoop of K.) Felt nothing… And the bf (Polish) wheeled me from the taxi to A&E – at St. Tomas's – and got all the police and the ambulance teams singing: 'Happy Birthday to you…'

It comes and it goes: half a toe-nail. All chalked-up and yellow. And not adhering. Not in the conventional sense of a toe-nail. It is just one of those things best kept in a sock: the issue rarely concerns me. I could have just shown it to Father Richard, and asked him to consider the matter from a more fully informed perspective, but I didn't think.

On the Thursday, our guests' shirt-collars black with muck by now, I make myself useful, with nail-brush and concentrated hand-wash. That was nice of me.

In my room, I read the Gospel from the bit you do on Thursday through to Jesus' arrest. It is sunny and, just now, one might conceive the promise of friends through air in an open window – down in the quad when I was their age too. Their seminary.

Well, in a parallel life to this… A different child again. An image cleaned – the whitest canvas. What would we do then? Probably I'd do a better job of it and wouldn't at this stage having craved God and God's promises... I am reading the *most* heightened Gospel passage… words thinly parsed and don't swallow me. Once they worked but now I've got the trick and now they don't. Then at Mass, we read the same passage again, and I get my foot washed.

444

On Good Friday, God dies at approximately 17:18 local solar time.

One we have disbursed, the tabernacle is open, which is always the saddest thing to see.

There is the altar of repose – death already prematurely healed in that sense. Death which smelt of soggy pyjamas…

There is a joke on the internet comedy circuit: Jesus gave up his weekend for our sins.

They congratulate me on my singing – 'You held up our side pretty well there, mate.' – and it was fun singing with/against the two Polish voices especially among them. They fluted high – Henry's joy in them overflowed in indistinguishable parodies…

*

All that sort of thing. I stay up late, thinking about it. Probably I should abstain from alcohol. However, I keep thinking about it. I am on Facebook – with bishops subscribed-to and fan-clubs for saints – Padre Pio, Saint Thérèse of Lisieux. Catholic-memes… Divine Mercy prayer cards… You wonder why the Catholic conversation never found it in its heart to stop. Bots must have written it – wallpaper.

I make no noise. The great brown slab of my desk glows orange. Love – I mean love. If it is not all physically aligned – and bodies' mere symbolic gestures. Private bits and pieces never the right size – never the right – width-fitting. Youth – I mean youth. Youth-time could be adequately real for a couple of seconds… My mirror is all good messages. Youth's moment.

I'll be getting to the beach this summer. Maybe Spain. It seems unlikely I'll ever find a place. There must be somewhere it isn't all decked out. While it could never be sexual. While that is gone now. And *look* at them… Nothing overflows – no, it could never be sexual. But – *love*…

There'd be a school or something. Life fails. And do it somewhere nice. Not in England. Do it abroad. I wish I could go back to university.

Even a copious volume – wine imbibed, and as the fullness of solitude – joy remains… My small-gay-face – existentially terrified what with Mum and the way she could never stop talking and the way she can never stop shaping – erupt tears in bathroom mirror and my eyes turn bright red.

I do not fight it. It is only in my face – not inside – though there it seems complete. (She... *Dad…!*)

This holy emotion… Not *per se* a truth of any story of this world. Rather – rather rather – rather rather rather – for the silly little way it should be so. A socio-biological selection. Not even that it 'isn't fair' – but for sheer whimsicality. The pointlessness of it – such flippancy entailed. The football-team selection: you, and *you*, and *you*, and *you*, and *you*, and *you*, and *you*, and *you*, and *you*, and *you*… But that's sort of the level of it.

Through no decided malice. No particular reason. So tears are, in a sense, a kind of laughter. But it is only when it strikes me I cry. Evolution.

There is nothing of tears in the Gospel text. In faith that is dead as a doornail. Evolved.

It is when the texts close conversation begins. That is the loss of it. Never-was. Always and already. Sheer loss. That is a past you could never reach into. There is no memory.

I wash my face. I doze two hours. With dawn, my headache.

*

Holy Saturday.

I bathe, but I could have taken aspirin. There'll be morning prayer, but I could sleep all day. I don't recall we are supposed to look smart in the morning. Casual-smart – a shirt. Then I have to run back to get changed properly.

They aren't singing – they are spoken psalms. They are all a bit slipped-jaws and slack on it. Sleep's potato-fields. It is that religious sister that does for me.

It is rude. It is very rude. As things turn out, it is the final indignity.

Only at the end of prayers, she tells us to stay back. There are six of us reading the vigil she wants to stay back – to rehearse. No please, no thank-you… God knows – you're having a laugh – we have not been introduced. Nor now, with due apology, does she trouble to do so. You couldn't exactly say she welcomes herself into our lives.

So it is all pain and more pain and only pain… Worthlessness given its reading. And she does pace, and stands there, all about her, while she listens, tendering advice… More charcoal smudge than inky shadow. She might have been one of those socially neglected weirdos who talk to their cat. Each boy takes about ten minutes. We sit in a line on the front pew. While she listens, stooped, she whisks the air judicious, scenting her own fumes. Her age, pitiless, draws no veil. Animated by an unnatural persistence – as if it were to reinforce an unbearable sadness within us all. Back in witching days – like when they burned the hag.

All hope and nothing like love is challenged. I can't sit here. I get up and go to the garden. But I am meant to be in chapel and I have no

447

track of the time so I go back. It is the same thing – I go to the garden. Then all I can do is oscillate between these points. It is outside the kitchen I glare at Father Richard, who stops me, saying:

'Are you all right, Tomàs?'

'She's making us wait behind to rehearse the readings for the Vigil.'

'Did you have somewhere you'd rather be?'

'Are you – *f'ck'n* insane?'

'What was that, Tomàs?'

'That – *person* is making us wait to "rehearse" our readings. By what right? Oh you crush our spirit. You infect us. You take what we are and you chew on us. By what right? This is human. This is not filth, dirt, lies. It's who we are and it's what we have and you chew on us. You should be ashamed, though I reckon you are already. I'll do the reading or I won't. I don't – mind.'

Having said my piece, I go back to chapel, and wait the minutes, and read for her. Back in my room, Geoff hollers and the phone rings.

I sleep deep. I sleep a full six hours, during which time Geoff at the door bangs and hollers, my room more safe and comfortable than it has ever been. The phone rings. And later, maybe one or two other people knock for me, perhaps more genuinely concerned as to my well-being. It is a sleep so profound I could register all this through it. All one – it does not differentiate. After the six hours, at five o'clock, sleep levels-down and I wake refreshed. I shower. I don't know how to dress – I don't want to look ridiculous. I go to look for The Rector.

There is business going on in the corridors. Holy Saturday…

448

Halfway down upon the stairs... I stop between the top and the bottom, two places, and sit on the step. Directly opposite where I sit is the locked door to an old library. It is called the pig-skin library. A museum piece. (No-one reads any of the books in there – we aren't allowed in there.) The position seems balanced. Finally, it is one of the Poles from the English seminary who, passing by, sits next to me to ask me if I am alright. I say yes, and the Pole puts his arm around me.

After a few minutes, I explain I have to go to see The Rector. The Pole asks if I want him to help me there. I say no.

There isn't much to-do about it.

The Rector's office door is open.

I knock.

The Rector says:

'I understand you have a train ticket to Malaga on Monday.'

'Yes.'

*

I return to my room and get my boxes out. I lay them about the floor.

I then go to the supermarket, where I buy wine and bread and humus. Sneaking about, I take three big-blue bin-bags from the cleaning-cupboard downstairs. I don't throw out the books they've given us: I take them down to the library and place them in a neat pile by the librarian's computer.

It is six o'clock.

I take my Vulnerata medal and, in the courtyard, meaningfully drop it in the basin of the fountain. That is where we blessed the palms. It doesn't seem vindictive – just drowning God. Not as a statement to anyone bar myself. Yet they find it, and I hear them yelling about it, not even permitting so little as this at the level of personal faith and gesture, and in minutes it is hung on my room door handle – by the ribbon.

It is discussed at decision-making volume and Henry comes out of the incident rather well.

The medal means nothing to me not in the fountain. I put it in its presentation box, and I put that with the things that will be sent to me.

Oh they'll pray for me – then they'll tell me they've prayed for me...

I could go to the Basilica, in order to celebrate Easter, or maybe I could go to the Cathedral at eight o'clock. Of course, I could creep very quietly to what we call the tribunes – the wood-lattice-screened gallery that runs about our church. I wouldn't be seen there and I could watch my friends.

Chapter Eleven

On Monday, I walk to the station with Geoff and Josh and Henry. There it turns out we are on different trains to Madrid, but we are booked on the same train south from Madrid to Malaga. From Malaga, they – the others will be flying to Rome. There isn't a great deal to say, and no-one seems to mind much. Probably no-one has any thoughts left for such things.

It isn't even a thought, really. As it happens, they – the others get confused changing stations in Madrid, and don't have as much time as I have to work out that you have to get up from the tube to the mainline. They are at the security gate just as the train is pulling out. The last words I hear from Henry are on the phone: 'Make it stop!'

I suppose that's kind of funny to think about.

Those are the last words I'll ever hear Henry say!

Henry screams them down his phone like God would make it happen if he screams it loud enough – though the demand is of Tomàs to stop the train.

*

And now there is… Nothing really.

Spanish trains put the British to shame. It's hard to date these things. Like a child's photoshop. The glass is very hard; the window is heavily filtered.

I remember it was Geoff who broke the ice and got us all speaking

451

in English when we bought the tickets. Also that it was Geoff, therefore, I have to thank for the other three seats of the four not being occupied – because they missed the train.

They're wide. It's a wide gauge. The seats are wide, the leg-room plentiful. Once we get up a speed we'll be travelling at 300 km/h. You know it – you can feel it in a way – though not in a physical sense. You can't *feel* it. The attendant comes along with his/her basket of free headphones, which don't fit in my ears but it's a cute touch.

There is nothing to watch sail by. There is something like industrial territory, then a long reiteration of olive fields. Those fields would never be harvested.

Even if you've never experienced a train like this before, you know as it first moves this is exactly right. The olive fields reach forever.

It is a smooth, hypothetical distance. It loves, it soothes you. It seems almost rude – oafish – to drink what should have been a free gin and tonic. So it is a lounge when you haven't any business. Airline-seat leatherette – and the comfortable headrest. The atmosphere air-conditioned to accommodate a light, woollen sweater. A cab-ride into the night – like Tomàs has been shopped for at a good price – package delivered.

I sense pleasure, though not of a kind you could ever get close to. As though a fraud has been committed – pleasure on somebody else's purse. And no more classroom fights, and no more classroom disputations. At rest with that, I am only a passenger, a psalm that knew the business of its own mind. A known mode assimilated, style of the thought possessed. No surprises. It is awesome to be travelling, spirited like this, to be seeing Mum.

She'll be well in her element with Auntie Grace. And wine,

452

aperitifs, and irregular light meals, picnic dining. Maybe I shall swing back via Valladolid in a car and get my stuff. I sense no pressing concern as to what the next lie might be… She won't bother me. Co-opt Samson – get the dog involved. Tell Samson a dog-joke – get the dog laughing his dog-laugh and wagging his dog-tail. Not even one of them would press any further than that.

Summer months…. I must email my Bishop – squaring references.

Seek temperance in holy things. Do not in secret conjure faith excessively, lest your enemies enter in upon your secret and defile you. What will your ardour count for then?

Do not raise God, for your soul shall requite the fact. Give heed to circumspection. Seek wisdom in common ground, for that which is cute in boys is disagreeable in men. Let not your heart be elsewhere than itself. Stay sharp, keep your wits about you, whistle when it hurts. Be as the birds – seek no friend's comfort. Let not your heart wax sad because of strange dreams.

And so it is. It seems a lazy possibility. Probably, the heat will destroy me when I step off this train. Wake with the sunrise and live a day. Though it will all shine, all over my face, as on the platform I immediately re-integrate. Inside, outside, ricocheted thus. Leave nights just for sleeping in. Don't get lost by night. Nights were always helpless. Go small. In bed, take the blessing of the day's light. Gather your gift for sleep. Conscious pleasures.